ALSO BY REBECCA KENNEY

RUTHLESS DEVOTION

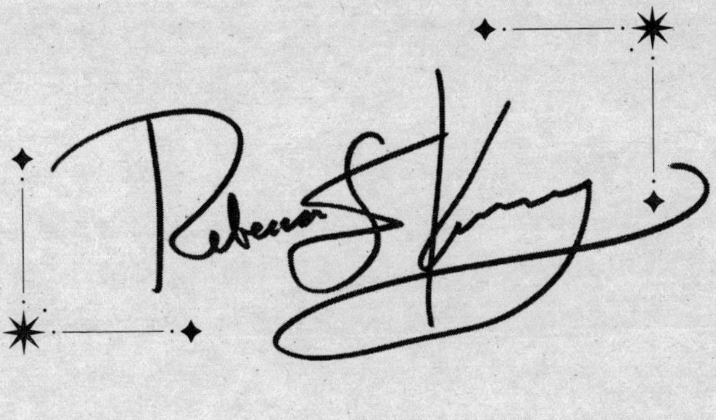

RUTHLESS DEVOTION

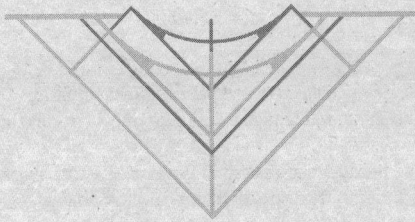

REBECCA KENNEY

sourcebooks casablanca

Published by Sourcebooks Casablanca, an imprint of Sourcebooks
1935 Brookdale RD, Naperville, IL 60563-2773
(630) 961-3900
sourcebooks.com

Cataloging-in-Publication Data is on file with the Library of Congress.

The authorized representative in the EEA is Dorling Kindersley
Verlag GmbH. Arnulfstr. 124, 80636 Munich, Germany

Printed and bound in the UK and distributed
by Dorling Kindersley Limited, London
001-351748-Jul/25
CPI 10 9 8 7 6 5 4 3 2 1

*To all the girls trapped in the pews of
weatherbeaten churches, sitting still and looking piously
perfect while a monster rages behind your ribs...
Set that beautiful monster free. She is your truth.*

Ruthless Devotion contains descriptions of verbally and physically abusive families, rituals, blood, murder, human sacrifice, religious rhetoric and trauma, and cultish overtones.

Whatever our souls are made out of, his and mine are the same.

—Emily Brontë, *Wuthering Heights*

1

HEATHCLIFF

IT'S FUCKING MISERABLE OUTSIDE. RAIN DASHES AGAINST the windows, like some god is tossing bucketfuls of the sea over the land—a storm off the coast, moving inland. We're only an hour's drive from Hunting Island, so we get the storms quick and hard, before they've had time to go gentle.

I'm nursing a beer. Running my thumb up the slick amber glass, watching condensation pool along my nail, then slide down in fat drops. The TV's off, and I'm just chilling, listening to the rain. I like the way it sounds, hammering against the windows, as if it wants to be let in.

A log on the fire pops and splits, its edges crumbling. I shake myself a little, tip the bottle against my lips for another swallow. Lockwood microbrew, dark and smooth and rich. Best in the county.

Then a door slams and I startle for real. Feet stomp through the big house, and Hindley storms into the living room. I'm a couple inches taller, but he's thickly built, his broad body stretching out the dirty white tank top he's wearing. He rakes a hand through his greasy, red hair.

"What you doin', boy?" he growls.

"Watching the rain."

"Fucking weirdo. Get up. We've got a job to do, a big one. Gonna need your mojo."

I gulp my beer again. "You gotta be more specific. You talking my rizz or the other thing?"

"The other thing. Get your ass off the chair and let's go. His tattoo's almost six months old, probably near faded by now, so it's gonna be a tough one."

"Faded?" I rise slowly. "What do you mean? Faded after six months?"

"This ain't no ordinary guy, okay? He's something different."

"What kind of different?"

"Didn't ask. Money was good. He's one of the customers who pay for the roof over your goddamn head, so get your jacket and let's go!"

"Fine, fine. Keep your panties on." I swallow the last of the beer and hurl the bottle into the fireplace. It smashes, and the flames leap for a second.

"You'll be cleaning that up," warns Hindley.

"Sure." I grab my jacket off a peg in the hall and follow him outside, hunching down under the pelting rain. The truck door creaks loudly as I pull it shut, and the engine coughs as Hindley tries to start it. I want to ask why Hindley doesn't buy a new truck, if our clients pay so well. But I know where the money goes—trips to Vegas, online gambling, whiskey poured down his throat, and coke sniffed up his nose. There's a whole bunch of ways to make yourself poor real quick, and Hindley's an expert at all of them.

"How far away is this guy we're supposed to raise?" I ask over the roar of the motor as the truck finally starts.

"Hour and a half. Then we go by boat." Hindley clears his throat. "He's on the island. At the old Lockwood mansion."

"Why is a client of yours at the Lockwood mansion? And why the fuck is he lying dead there?"

"He's a friend of the guy who bought the house off the family a while back. As for how he died, you know that's none of our business. We do the job. That's it. We ain't detectives."

He's getting too riled, so I switch to a safer question. "How long has he been dead?"

"Couple of hours, maybe? I was busy. Didn't feel my tattoo buzzing until now."

"Shit, Hindley. You were high, weren't you?"

"Shut up." His hand flies before I can stop it, cuffing the side of my face. "You may be drinkin' age now, but I can still whup you, got it?"

"Whatever you say," I mutter, glaring out my window. A dull pain blooms through my cheekbone. He knows I'm stronger than him. Always have been. He also knows I don't fight back. He thinks that's weakness, but I tell myself it's power. It's a mercy I don't cave his face in with a single punch.

I'm unnaturally strong. I've learned to manage it, but if I ever give in completely to my rage, I might kill him. And staining my soul with Hindley's toxic blood isn't something I want to do. So I've always let him use me as a punching bag, ever since we were kids. It's a habit now. Uncomfortable...but hell, I'm used to it.

"Any idea what state the body's in?" I ask.

"Could be bad." He sniffs, rubs a hand across his eyes,

and peers through the streaming windshield and the swishing wipers.

Hindley is one of the last of the Charleston Lockwoods—one branch of a sprawling family tree, gifted with the power to drag souls out of the grave and put them back in their bodies. The gift has deteriorated with each passing generation. Now it's so weak, he can barely manage to perform basic necromancy on his own. He can serve as a tether, carrying one half of the matching tattoo that links him to the person being raised, but he needs an external power source to complete the task. A generator, as it were, to give him extra juice.

The generator—that would be me.

I was never asked if I wanted to join the Lockwood family. Like most things in my life, shit just happened to me. Hindley's dad, Buckland, told me he was at some mountain gas stop in Tennessee when he saw me, a dirt-stained boy of five or six, crouching over a mangled dog that some truck had just smashed into pulp. I had my hands on the corpse, eyes closed, blood dripping from a bite on my hand, self-inflicted. A few minutes later, the mutt got up, good as new and perfectly healed, and started bounding around me.

"I didn't ask who you belonged to," Buckland used to say. "I knew whoever let you run loose on your own that young, so close to the road, was too damn careless and deserved to lose you. With a gift like yours, you belonged to us." Then he'd ruffle my hair and laugh as though he'd done me some great favor by kidnapping me.

I didn't understand that it was kidnapping until I was maybe eleven. At that point, I thought about telling the police, but the cops in this neck of the woods have got clay for brains and red brick for hearts, and I figured they wouldn't much care. Besides,

I had a roof over my head and work to do, which is more than some folks get. Plus, if I told someone about the kidnapping, the Lockwoods might tell the authorities about my abilities, and that could only lead me into way deeper shit. So I kept my mouth shut.

But as Hindley drives us toward the coast, I let myself wonder what my other life might have been like. Different family, different business. A mom, maybe. Siblings I might have actually liked. Christmases that didn't involve drunken brawls among Hindley, Buckland, and the cousins from Coosaw. Birthdays with actual presents and a cake, instead of me sitting in my closet, hiding from Hindley so he couldn't give me more bruises.

Imagining another life is a fool's pastime, though. Who's to know if it would have been any better? People suck no matter where you live.

When we get to the marina, we rent a boat and head for the island. The rain has slacked off, and there's a sickly yellow dawn leaking from under the bellies of the thick, gray clouds as we skim over the surface.

"Smell that?" Hindley sniffs the air.

"Smoke."

"Whoever killed him burned the place afterward. Probably thought it would get rid of the body."

"Wouldn't it?"

He shakes his head. "Normal bodies, sure. Not our guy. His tattoo links him to a Lockwood, and the house knows it. It'll keep him intact...mostly. Gonna be tough to bring him back in prime condition, though. You good for it?"

"Am I allowed to say no?"

Hindley cuts me a glance, keen as a hunting knife. "Nope."

"I didn't think so."

My help on these missions is never a question, always an expectation. And my well-being afterward—that's of little concern to Hindley as long as I recover quickly enough to be ready for the next resurrection, whenever that comes.

The Lockwood mansion rears up, solemn and eternal, from the crest of the island as we pull up to the dock. A couple small boats are already there, bobbing on the choppy waves. The bittersweet smoke of charred wood hangs in the air, but there's not a flake of ash on the sloping lawn or on the porch.

I try the door. Locked. But when Hindley touches the handle, it opens easily.

"Thought you said this place was sold," I comment as Hindley leads the way inside.

"You can't truly sell a house like this. Sure, we sold it on paper, but like I said—the place knows Lockwood blood. Shit...there he is."

The body lies near a sofa that looks like it's seen at least a century. In fact, all the furnishings in the place are super old.

"It resets to its original condition every time it gets destroyed," Hindley says. "Everything goes back exactly like it was on the day it was first spelled."

I've heard the Lockwood family discuss this place before, though they've never explained its origins. As much as I want to ask Hindley more questions about it, I know better. All I'll get for my trouble is another slap, and I'm gonna be in enough pain soon, judging by the state of the corpse.

Once, a couple years ago, I hit Hindley back. I thought I'd won the fight, too, until I woke up in the middle of the night with the muzzle of his favorite revolver jammed into the soft tissue under my jaw.

"We got a good thing going here, Heathcliff," he said hoarsely, his face hovering near mine in the darkness of my bedroom. "You and me—we're sym-by-tick, you might say."

"Symbiotic," I whispered.

"Shut up. You sass your mouth at me one more time, raise your hand to me *once* more, and you'll be out on your ass. You won't have a pot to piss in, and I'll send the cops one of them anonymous letters, telling them all about your powers. They'll catch you and lock you in a lab somewhere, if I don't kill you myself first."

I could have fought him then. But I knew an all-out fight with Hindley would end with one of us dead, and I wasn't ready to go that far. So I yielded, and I waited.

Since then I've been waiting, saving, drinking—dying.

Hindley snaps his fingers in front of my face. "What's wrong with you? Let's do this."

I shake myself a little. "Yeah. Where's his tattoo?"

"On his hip."

Hindley kneels beside the corpse. All the hair and most of the skin are burned off, and everything's crispy black and raw red, but I can see the bullet hole in his skull. Somebody shot him and then burned him. The house kept him mostly intact, like Hindley said, but it let the flames chew at him, making my job harder.

With the help of a relative, like one of the Coosaw Lockwoods, Hindley could probably manage to drag this guy's soul back out of the Vague. But the client would wake up in a disintegrating body. We're talking the worst kind of zombie-revenant shit— organs barely functional, skin sloughing off, a body so desperate for nutrients that its natural hunger morphs into something way worse.

That's where I come in. I don't just bring people back from the dead—I can restore the bodies to like-new condition. The Lockwoods used to have that gift too, way back, but it's faded over the generations. Which is why Buckland felt like he'd struck gold when he found me.

Hindley may hold the tattoos for all our clients, but I'm his meal ticket. Without me, he'd never get the juicy post-resurrection payout that's included in every contract. And I need the connections he has to the supernatural world, at least for now, until I figure out a way to get some of my own clients.

Much as I hate it, Hindley's right—he and I depend on each other to survive. The brewery does a half-decent business, considering we both suck at marketing, but the way Hindley spends money, there's no way we could live on that income alone.

Steeling myself, I kneel beside Hindley. He drags down the remnants of the guy's pants at the hip, and the fabric pretty much disintegrates into ash, exposing a swath of discolored skin and a tattoo of a cross-shaped Celtic knot, smudged-looking but still distinguishable.

Hindley yanks his hunting knife out of its sheath on his belt. He's a big hunter, Hindley. Hunts for the hell of it, and most of the meat goes to waste. Me, I'm damn good with a gun, better than he knows, but I don't hunt. I'm a meat eater, sure, but I can't stomach killing animals myself.

After carving a thin line in the top of his forearm, Heathcliff dampens his fingers with the blood, then lifts his shirt and claps one hand over a tattoo on his ribs. He places his other hand over the dead man's tattoo. The twin marks will serve as his guide, allowing him to locate this guy's soul in the Vague and pull it back into the body.

The dead guy's tattoo starts to glow red, the light leaking between Hindley's fingers.

"You ready?" he asks.

I nod, angling my body so I can place one hand over each of his.

This is gonna hurt. It always hurts worse when someone else is siphoning my power through themselves. When I'm performing a resurrection on my own, it's better. Not that I've had the chance to do it on my own very often. The Lockwoods don't usually trust me with the names or tattoos of their clients.

I don't remember when I first learned to perform a resurrection. But I must have known something before I came to the Lockwoods because I healed and resurrected that piece of roadkill. Of course, animals are easier to revive. They're part of nature, so there's no need for a tattoo or a link of any kind. I can just pull some energy from the nature around me, condense it, and put it into the animal while I'm reviving it. Simple. Sure, a few plants might die, maybe a tree or a bush, but the toll isn't too high.

People are not animals...not exactly. They have immortal, individual souls. As much as I wish that weren't true, there's no way around it. I don't like to think about what that means, afterlife-wise. All I know is, you gotta have a link of some kind to the person you're trying to resurrect—like an address to where the soul's located. Otherwise you'll never find them in the Vague.

I've been into the Vague a few times. It's confusing, but not as scary as some might think. The tattoo's like a line, leading me to the soul I need, and as long as I follow it, I'll find the right person. Then I just have to pull 'em in, like a fisherman reeling in his catch. Problem is, the longer you wait, the farther away the soul gets, until eventually the line dissolves and you can't find them at all.

This time, I won't be going into the Vague myself. My job is to give Hindley the fuel he needs to do this. It's his consciousness heading into that other place.

"Mors aperit ianuam," mutters Hindley, butchering the pronunciation as usual...and he closes his eyes.

A raw, choking, mind-numbing pain rushes through my body as Hindley sucks power out of me and into himself. It feels like having my heart vacuumed right out of my chest cavity, like having every vein and nerve ending zapped with electricity all at once. Worst thing I've ever endured.

"Shitbag's already way out there in the Vague," Hindley mutters. "These fuckers never make it easy. Once I grab him, you do your thing."

I clench my teeth and hiss through the pain. That's the only acknowledgment he's going to get.

The inside of my nose is burning unbearably, crinkling like it's being singed with flames, sending hot spikes of pain up into my sinuses. The sensation of my heart being compacted and suctioned through my ribs increases until I can't stay quiet. A groan grates through my clamped jaws.

"Shut up," snaps Hindley. "I've almost got him."

A white flash of pain blots out my vision, blazes in my brain like a searing supernova. "Oh fuck," I gasp. "Fuck, I can't..."

"Don't you dare let go!" Hindley barks. "I got him. I got him.

Once we reset this guy, that's a nice fat payout. You'll get your cut, too."

The agony I'm enduring isn't worth a measly ten percent. There's a slick metal taste coating my tongue, acidic bile inching up my throat, shudders wracking my body. *Wrong, wrong, something is wrong. This isn't normal, isn't right. This one shouldn't be allowed to come back...*

"He's back in the body," shouts Hindley. "Do it, Heathcliff."

I can feel the shape of the soul now. In my mind, it's an oily thing with needlelike claws and a hissing maw, clinging desperately to the inside of the body. There's something real messed up about this one.

"Not sure about him, Hindley," I protest. "Feels wrong this time."

"Set him right, or I swear I'll cut off your balls and serve 'em to you with sauce on a pile of fucking spaghetti!"

Don't do it. This is wrong, wrong, wrong...

But I have spent years telling that voice inside me to shut the hell up. Years working for the family that calls me theirs, doing what they want. When Hindley yells at me again, I silence my inner voice, and I obey.

I bend my will to the job. I heal the charred flesh, repair the organs, recreate the torn skin. The drain on my energy is enormous, a flood of power gushing from my body into the corpse of the client. A roar of sheer anguish bursts out of me as my own vitality feeds into the damaged body. Makes it whole.

When it's done, I can barely see. Blurred vision happens sometimes, especially with the worst cases. Should clear up in a bit. I peel my clammy, shaking hands away from Hindley's, and I collapse onto the floor.

It'll take hours for my energy to return to normal levels. But at least I'm conscious. Sometimes I pass out.

I lie there for a while, waiting for my vision to clear, listening to the ticking of the grandfather clock. Eventually Hindley starts pacing the room, muttering.

As the pain-fog lifts from my brain, I start to understand why he's worried. Our guy should be up and talking by now.

Stiffly, I manage to sit up. The moment I do, Hindley lunges over and smacks me.

"The fuck?" I exclaim.

"You did it wrong," he snaps. "The guy isn't waking up."

I blink at the body on the floor. The client looks good. There's even a tinge of healthy color in his cheeks. But he's still unconscious.

I run my tongue around inside my mouth, tasting the coppery essence of blood. "I did everything right."

"He's supposed to be awake, and he's *not*. You know what a sleeping guy can't do? He can't pay what he fucking owes us!" Hindley kicks the sofa furiously, then yelps and grabs his foot, swearing again.

"I got nothing left, okay?" I rub my forehead. "He'll wake up sometime. They all do. We just gotta be patient."

"And what are we gonna do while we're waiting on Sleeping Beauty to join us?" A vein in Hindley's forehead bulges with rage.

"We could bring him back home, put him in the spare room, wait for him to come around."

"And if he doesn't?"

"If he doesn't...once I've recovered, I'll take another look, see if I missed something. I can't do anything else right now, man. It'll kill me. I need food, then rest."

Another thing about resurrecting corpses—leaves me with a hell of an appetite.

Hindley seems as if he might argue, but then he stares at me long and hard. I must look like shit because he grumbles something and then nods. "Fine. We take him back with us. But the second you got your energy back, I want him awake and paid up, got it?"

Slowly I climb to my feet, gripping the back of the sofa to steady myself. "Sure, boss. Whatever you say."

2

CATHY

A FALL BREEZE WAFTS THROUGH THE OPEN-AIR SECTION OF Aunt Nellie's Fresh Farm Goods, ruffling the hair of suburban moms and their squalling toddlers. Some of the younger customers are just here for the vibes, snapping photos of rustic wooden posts and weathered bins full of colorful squash, but the mothers are more intentional, determined to jam pesticide-free nutrition down their kids' throats.

"Excuse me, miss?" The voice is strident, pointed, and the woman's eyes pierce mine, full of sharp discontent. "These tomatoes don't look great." She holds up a lumpy one—fully ripe, probably delicious, but malformed. Not your picture-perfect Pinterest tomato.

These are real, honest-to-god organic tomatoes, not plastic fruit from Ikea. That's what I want to say, but I've learned to bite my tongue.

"How about this one?" I pick up a more symmetrical tomato and offer it to her.

"There was a fly on that one." She winces.

Yeah, the flies land on everything. It's a fucking open-air market.

"You can always wash it before you use it," I counter in my sweetest customer-friendly tones.

Okay, maybe I spoke a little too sweetly. She looks at me through half-lidded eyes. "There's no need to have an *attitude* about it."

"Why don't I see if I can find some better-looking ones in the back?" I suggest. This conversation is heading to a bad place, and I don't have the patience to keep it civil. For the past few hours, I've been feeling…thin. My emotions, my spirit—hell, my fucking *soul*—feel threadbare. Soft and fragile, like jeans worn through at the knees, ready to pop a hole any second.

When I feel like this, I know an episode is coming on soon. I don't know exactly when it will hit me, so I have to keep living normally. Like some kind of secret agent, I mark the exits of every room I enter, chart paths and escape routes in case I need to run, take note of the nearest patch of forest where I can hide.

Right now I'm frayed to the point of breaking, and I can't deal with this woman anymore. I want to tell her to go to hell—or at least to a chain supermarket, where the produce section is curated for visual appeal instead of natural value.

Before I can say either of those things, I stalk away from her, through the creaky door, and into the air-conditioned interior of the store.

This part of Aunt Nellie's has the country-store vibe our customers are looking for: a circular table piled high with textured beeswax candles, tiny jars of golden honey with chunks of honeycomb drifting inside, sprays of dried grasses in glazed ceramic pitchers, brass honeybee magnets, hand-carved wooden bread boxes. There's a wall of jewel-toned jams, a rack of slim brown packets containing dried herbs, and barrels of old-fashioned candy.

I'm responsible for most of the displays, for the artistic flair and the *vibes*, because I know our target audience all too well. I actually don't despise *all* of them—just the ones who decide to be dicks. The ones who want the "organic" label but complain when those products end up being naturally imperfect.

I love things that are raw, wild, crooked, unfinished. They're so much more honest than things that are cultivated, symmetrical, punched out of identical molds.

I'm sure a therapist would have plenty to say about that.

Pausing by the register, I speak low by Aunt Nellie's ear. "There's a woman outside looking for the perfect tomato, one whose virgin skin has never been touched by an insect's filthy feet."

"Oh god." She rolls her eyes, brushes back a frizzy lock of brown hair. "Fine. I'll deal with her. Can you go out back? We've got a shipment coming in—that new microbrew Sarah ordered—and I need someone to sign for it and supervise the unloading. The guy called to say he'd be here in five minutes, and that was...well, five minutes ago."

"Sure, I got it."

Aunt Nellie calls Sarah over to handle the register while she goes out front. I head out the back, closing the door to the retail section carefully behind me. Then I move on through the dim, dusty maze of shelves in the large storage room to the double doors at the rear of the building. One of them stands half-open, admitting a swath of pale daylight. I push it farther back. When the sunlight hits my skin, I cringe.

Sun sensitivity is another sign of an impending episode. Death is coming for some poor denizen of this town—coming soon. My skin feels like it's crawling, crinkling. I want to wriggle out of it and run—run far away into some dark forest where I can scream and howl at the moon.

I drag my fingernails up my arms, even though I know scratching won't help. I've tried it before, countless times. There's only one thing that really helps when my pre-episode jitters get this bad—sex, hard and heavy. It takes the rhythmic impact of another body to help me forget the torture of being locked inside my own. Too bad that's not likely to happen anytime soon.

A truck door slams, and I jump a little. Boots crunch on the gravel, coming closer.

I see his shadow first. Tall and broad. Big shoulders with the casual tension of a man who knows what his body is capable of and is ready to exert that power at a moment's notice. Narrow waist, a slant to his gait, more saunter than stride. Against my will, my whole body tightens with taut awareness.

He's in the doorway now, a black silhouette against the daylight.

"Got a delivery here for Nellie Earnshaw." His drawling voice vibrates in sync with my nerves and ripples under my crawling skin. There's relief in the depth of that voice. A deep well I could quench myself in. Not that I'm desperate enough to try.

With one broad hand, he pushes the second door open, flooding me with bright sun. I wince, fighting the urge to shrink deeper into the shadows.

He huffs a low laugh. "What are you, some kind of vampire?"

I scoff in response, then grimace as the skin between my

shoulder blades tightens. It feels like centipedes are skittering up my spine. *Come on, Cathy, pull yourself together.*

Taking a deep breath, I stride past the delivery guy, toward the pickup. I can do this; I can focus long enough to see him gone. "I need to see the size and number of the crates."

"Sure thing." He follows me and pulls down the back door of the pickup so I can see the contents.

The crates are marked with a stamp in dark green ink. *Lockwood's Cypress Honey Lager.*

Aunt Nellie's doing business with the Lockwoods now? Dad's not going to be happy about this.

As I step back from the pickup, I glance at the delivery guy. I can't help it.

He looks to be a couple years older than me, probably midtwenties. His skin is rich brown, a birthright more than a tan, if I had to guess. Elaborate tattoos cover both his arms right up to the short sleeves hugging his biceps. More tattoos peek from the scooped collar of the T-shirt and crawl up his sinewy throat. He's got clifflike cheekbones, a sharp-cornered jaw, deep-set dark eyes, and black hair falling over his heavy brows, framing his face in shaggy waves. His pecs swell against his faded gray T-shirt as he reaches up to grip the edge of the truck bed. God, even his fingers are tattooed. And those long, denim-clad legs of his should be clamped around a motorcycle...or maybe a horse...or maybe...

I swallow, pulling my gaze back up to his face. His dark eyes glint with humor and heat, like he's reading my mind.

"I'll, um...I'll show you where you can put it. The delivery, I mean." *Fuck.*

I head back inside, hearing the scrape of wood as he hoists one of the crates out of the truck, the scuff of his steps as he follows me into the gloom of the storage space. I don't turn on the lights; there's enough light from the double doors.

"Here's good." I point to an empty pallet.

He moves past me, leans over to set down the crate, and sends a spicy rush of amber and sandalwood and male sweat flooding my senses.

My skin, my nerves, my whole body is *screaming*, aching.

Using sex to ease my tension and soothe some of my worst symptoms isn't new for me. I've fucked a lot of guys in my desperation to feel better. I usually pick the ones who are just passing through—guys I'm pretty sure I'll never see again. That way Dad won't find out and literally murder me.

It's not like I have a choice. Physical pleasure is necessary if I want to stay halfway sane in the hours leading up to an episode. Masturbating doesn't do the trick; I need the rush of someone else's body, the crush of their lips on mine, the rapid thump of their heart, their living soul printed onto my bones. That throb of life is what I need—the heat of blood under skin, a balm to soothe the scratching claws of Death. I need the flavor of cum on my tongue to erase the cloying, sick taste of decay.

The delivery guy straightens, looks me in the eyes. Licks his lips. "Is the little vampire strong enough to help me with unloading? I got another run after this one, so the quicker I finish, the better."

The quicker I finish…

God, I thought overseeing a delivery would be less dangerous than dealing with the tomato woman. Guess I was wrong.

I can't fuck some random delivery guy. Can I?

"I'm strong," I tell him.

His eyes crinkle a little at the corners. Not exactly a smile but close. "Of course you are."

I follow him back to the truck, trying to ignore the furnace roaring through my body, the softening heat between my legs.

He grabs another crate, holds it until I've got my arms under it. Our fingers brush momentarily—his are thick, callused, dirty.

"Got it?" he asks.

"Yeah."

It's heavy. I'm thinner than I'd like to be because of days spent mourning and wandering with no chance to eat, but I'm tough. I can do this.

I stagger to the pallet and set the crate on top of the first one. It's crooked, and as I grab the edges to straighten it, a splinter jabs into my flesh.

"Shit," I hiss.

"Splinter?" He sets down his box and grabs my wrist, peering at the sliver of wood. "Hold still."

I couldn't move if I wanted to. I'm galvanized to the spot, rendered motionless by the curl of those thick, warm fingers around my wrist, the press of roughened fingertips against my sensitive skin. He lifts my palm to his mouth, clamps white teeth around the splinter, and tugs. With a pinch of pain, the splinter pulls free, and he spits it aside. "There."

A bead of blood wells up on my skin. We both stare at it...and then, as if by agreement, we look at each other.

My skin is on fire, my nerves shriveling and screaming in the blaze. My heart pounds faster, faster, terrifyingly fast.

He's still holding my wrist. Large, dirt-stained fingers

wrapped around it, fingertips pressing the thin skin where my pulse flutters.

His eyes are dark brown, almost black, deep as a nighttime forest and rimmed with thick lashes—the kind any girl would be jealous of. He has a strong nose, not quite straight. Jaw like an anvil, sharp-edged, rock-hard.

My muscles tighten against my bones, and my nerves quiver. The person I'm supposed to mourn isn't dead, not yet, but it's going to happen soon, and I'll be damned if I endure this misery until then. I need, I *need*—

I leap for him, clasping my hands at the back of his neck, hauling his mouth down to mine. He tastes like hot sun and salted almonds and beer.

His hands immediately slide across the small of my back, urging my hips against him. He's hard because of course he is. I'm Cathy fucking Earnshaw. I'm a walking wet dream in a miniskirt and a cutoff tank top that hugs my tits. Long legs, full lips, big eyes, a cascade of curly dark brown hair, a huge smile. The quintessential Southern "hot girl." This is the persona I cultivate as carefully as the displays in Aunt Nellie's store. It's my Dr. Jekyll. No one ever gets to see Mr. Hyde.

With a low snarl in his throat, the delivery guy kisses me harder, moves a hand down to squeeze my ass. He's turning us around, backing me up against a stack of boxes—canned goods—and I pray they're heavy enough to withstand what's about to happen.

The kiss breaks, and in the frenzied haze between us, I reach under my short skirt, pull off my panties, and stuff them onto a nearby shelf. His zipper rips open. This is happening, for real— I'm going to let him fuck me bare, right here in the shadows of the storage room. I'm protected against pregnancy but not STDs, and this guy looks like he's been around.

"You good?" I whisper.

"I ain't got any diseases, if that's what you mean."

"Thank god." I hitch myself back onto the edge of a box and open my legs. Whether I believe him or not, I'm going for it.

He moves in between my thighs, and I get a glimpse of a big dick—attractive as dicks go, a shade darker than his skin and longer than average—right before he pushes inside me.

"Shit," he barks, surprise in the hoarse exclamation. "You're so wet."

"Shut up and fuck me." I claw him closer, my fingers digging into his muscled shoulders. He feels good. Solid, strong. Strong enough to hold me together while I come apart.

My breath is shredded with panic and frantic craving, jerking from my lungs as he starts to move, to pound my pussy. The thick heat inside me feels so good, I want to cry.

"Harder," I whisper.

He wraps a forearm behind me, gripping the back of my skull with one broad hand as he fucks me. He's keeping my head from hitting anything, but my spine is still being jammed hard against the boxes over and over. I don't care—I welcome the impact, the brutal force of his body dominating mine. It's what I need—to lose control on my terms, to not be so entirely at the mercy of the thing that lives in my head.

"Yes," I gasp brokenly, my legs locked around his waist and my nails driving into his broad shoulders. "Yes, yes..."

He grabs my face with his other hand, takes my mouth roughly. There's a honeyed heat in his kiss—I didn't notice it before. He's tongue-fucking me while his cock plunges between my legs. Then his hand drops, finds the place right above where we're joined. He locates my swollen clit and starts circling it with his thumb while he fucks me.

I'm writhing, lust-seared and desperate, straining for the climax. When I'm mere hours away from an episode, every sensation is already heightened, and it doesn't take much to push me over the edge. But there's a grating mutter at the back of my mind, a self-condemnation, a dark chant of *slut, slut, slut* even as I try to claim this bit of relief.

No. I will not slut-shame myself. I refuse to feel guilty about what I do to survive my life.

If I can orgasm, the endorphins will ease my torment for a while. I'll be able to function a little better, at least until the episode finally hits.

But that stupid judgmental voice in my head keeps pushing me back from the edge.

"Please," I breathe hoarsely. "Please, please…"

"I'm not coming until you do." His whisper explodes against my lips, a desperate promise, and my body tightens suddenly, as if his oath were a command. Oh thank god… I'm coming, sharp and hard, a knife to my clit, a blade of pure light shearing through my belly. I release choked little sounds as my pussy convulses around his dick.

"Shit," he groans, his arms going rigid and his hips ramming tight against my body. I feel his dick pulsing, deep and hard. He's coming inside me, this guy I just met. Didn't even meet him, really. I don't know his name.

We're heaving, still locked together—sweaty, filthy, shuddering. He surges into me one last time. Groans. Pulls his cock out of me, shining wet, and backs away. He stuffs it back into his underwear and zips up his jeans.

Instead of hard-muscled arms and a warm chest, I'm alone in the empty air again. The afterglow is good; it has temporarily muted the creeping unrest beneath my skin. I grab my panties and pull them over my shaking legs. When I stand up, I feel his cum sliding from between my pussy lips, soaking the panties.

He's staring, breathing hard, devouring me with his eyes like he's taking a photograph of the way I look in this moment. The flare of interest in his gaze, the visceral intensity of it, makes my heart race faster again. He seems about to ask me something, but then it's like a curtain drops over his eyes, concealing the raw emotion and replacing it with a casual grin.

"That's one load taken care of." He winks at me. "I'll finish up with the crates. You'll need to sign for them."

"Of course." I tug an elastic from my wrist and bundle my curly, brown hair into a messy knot, so it's up off my sweaty neck.

He watches me, and while my hands are still occupied with the knot, he reaches out and sinks his hand into my hair, sliding his fingers through it slowly, indulgently, almost tenderly. Like he has a right to enjoy the sensation.

A fresh surge of arousal rolls over me, along with a wave of panic.

This isn't happening. It's always one and done for me—I never want *more*.

My hand flies before my brain catches up, and I slap the side of his face.

"We're done," I say, breathless. "We got what we needed. I'm revoking consent."

"Are you now?" Hurt twinges in his eyes for a split second before a slow smirk curves his lips. "Whatever you say, sweetheart."

"Don't call me that."

Still smirking, he gives the crotch of his jeans a tug before stalking out of the storage room.

He comes back with a clipboard, and I sign for the delivery.

When he finishes stacking the last crate, he takes the clipboard and inspects my signature. Reads it aloud in his deep, drawling voice. "Cathy Earnshaw."

"That's right."

And then he shocks me by putting out his right hand. "Heathcliff Lockwood."

Oh shit. Did I just fuck a Lockwood? Dad's head would explode... "No way. You don't look like a Lockwood."

He hooks an eyebrow. "How would you know? Our families don't exactly run in the same circles."

"Well, I...I've heard you're all redheads. The freckled type. You look...um..."

"Like I came from a different gene pool?" His eyes narrow, and his voice grows more velvety, more dangerous. "You're not about to ask me where I'm from, are you, Earnshaw?"

"Of course not." I bristle at the idea.

He chuckles, letting me off the hook. "It's fine. I'm mostly Italian. Maybe a little Spanish, Romani—who the fuck knows? Never had the money to burn on one of those DNA ancestry tests." He slams the back of the pickup. "You take care, Earnshaw. It's been fun. I look forward to the next delivery in, say, three months, depending on how fast you sell out of our lager."

"We're not doing *that* again," I say tersely.

"Right. Because you revoked your consent." He takes a step toward me, and I shiver, not because of the chilly breeze raising goose bumps on my arms but because I can feel the heat of his body and I desperately want him to grab me, crush me, pound me until all conscious thought leaves my brain and I'm a melted mess in his hands.

He leans in slightly, not touching me but in my space, magnetizing the air, commanding it. He flips up one page of the clipboard, rips off the sheet beneath it, and hands the second page to me. There's a number scrawled along the bottom of the receipt. "Anytime you want to reinstate your consent, let me know. Happy to drop off another…load."

"You're an animal."

"Says the girl who jumped my bones like a bitch in heat." He backs away, hops into the truck, and grinds out of the back drive in a roar of exhaust and a cloud of gravel dust.

I watch him go, still feeling his fingers in my hair like the caress of a wishful ghost.

3

CATHY

I DETEST GOING TO CHURCH. BUT I DON'T HAVE A CHOICE, not while I'm stuck living with Dad.

My childhood home is my best bet until I can save up enough for my own place, which is going to take forever because it can't be just any place—it's got to be isolated or at least near enough to the woods that I can escape into them during one of my episodes. And I can't have roommates. It would be too hard to hide what I am from them.

So I have to attend church with Dad once a week, a chore I make more interesting by wearing outfits that are just short of scandalous. The middle-aged moms and righteous old ladies are going to gossip behind my back anyway. Might as well give them something to talk about.

Today I'm wearing a backless, halter-top sundress with a sweetheart neckline. I covered the bare skin with a sweater, but I let the sweater slip off one shoulder as I follow Dad up the steps of the church, my hand skimming the iron rail with its peeling white paint.

My father is a burly man, thick-necked and big-bearded. His

hair is still mostly brown, but streaks of gray wriggle through the curly beard. Above his bristly mustache, below bushy eyebrows, his pale eyes gleam with a hostile intensity he can't quite suppress, even when he's being friendly. He carries a worn leather Bible with the same hand that tried to feed me a knife last time he got drunk. I told him it tasted bad and I wouldn't take it, which surprised his beer-addled brain long enough for him to think better of his actions.

I don't know if he remembers doing that. We've never talked about it. We're trapped together, he and I, at least for now. Surviving our situation means pretending certain things never happened. Drenched in that pretense, we can smile and climb the church steps like a pair of innocent, God-fearing sheep ready for sacrifice.

There are two grinning greeters lying in wait to open the doors for us. They chirp, "Good morning," in falsely cheerful voices.

Okay, maybe it's not entirely fake. Maybe I'm projecting my trust issues onto them.

"So good to see you, Cathy." Mrs. O'Brien's voice drips with saccharine pity for my lost-lamb status. "I hope God speaks to you today."

Never mind. I was right about the fakeness and bitchiness. These people never pass up a chance to confirm my opinion of them.

"I hope God speaks to you, too, Mrs. O'Brien," I say sweetly. "And if he doesn't, I've got a few words—"

"Cathy." Dad's voice is heavy with warning. He grips my arm above the elbow, so tightly my eyes water, and he pulls me through the doors into the lobby.

Pastor Linton is conversing in low tones with a group of deacons. He catches sight of my dad and calls, "Bob! May I borrow you for a moment?"

Mark Linton is a ruddy-cheeked, bland-faced man with a smooth, blond comb-over rendered impenetrable by layers of hairspray. Today he's much paler than usual, and I can't help staring. There are dark hollows beneath his eyes, worry creasing his brow. The faces of the men around him are equally anxious.

Something bad has happened. My stomach quivers with terror—what if they've finally discovered my secret?

Dad must be thinking the same thing. He throws me a hard look, his *Cathy what have you done now* look. I raise my eyebrows, trying to seem innocent and confused. His lips tighten, but he doesn't reproach me aloud. That will come later, when we're alone. When he can unleash his full wrath without anyone else to witness it.

"Sure, Mark," he says to the pastor. "Save me a seat, Cathy."

"I'll be sitting near the back, though," I tell him.

He knows what that means...that I'm going to have an episode sometime soon, and I have to be able to get out when it happens. As a deacon, he prefers sitting up front.

"Fine," he says through a tight smile. "I'll see you after the service, then."

He heads over to the group of men. Despite the fact that I'll be a prisoner in this building for the next two hours, being released from my father's presence seems like freedom. Or it would if my skin didn't feel like it's about to crack and curl and flake off my body.

I inhale slowly, trying to find some measure of relief in the familiarity of this place. The stale-carpet smell, laced with a hint of spray cleaner and air freshener wafting from the restrooms. To the right is a door leading downstairs to the children's wing. I haven't been down there in ages, but I suspect it looks much the same as I remember: windowed doors along a white hallway plastered with coloring sheets and the occasional poster of a Bible verse.

In front of me, gleaming oak doors stand wide, leading from the lobby into the sanctuary. The pews are honeyed oak with dull rose-colored padding. Each pew has cloth pockets stapled to its back, hammocks for hymnals and extra copies of the Bible. The gray morning leaks a wan light through stained-glass windows lining both sides of the sanctuary.

At the front of the church, the oak pulpit is overshadowed by an enormous tapestry—perhaps the most significant element in the place. Because this church isn't exactly Catholic, Episcopal, Southern Baptist, or any of the myriad denominations so prevalent in the South. It's a strange amalgam of Protestant teaching, Catholic ritual, and...something else. Any stranger who walked in here would be confused by the contradicting elements of the place, like the confession booths in the back corners of the sanctuary and the small baptistry behind the pulpit.

But strangers never visit Wicklow Heritage Chapel...or if they do, they're gently turned away at the door. And the reason for that is hung up there for all of us to see.

The tapestry depicts a large cross with a faceless figure bound to it—not with nails but with vines in a Celtic knotwork pattern. Beneath the foot of the cross, below the ground, is a pocket of space, a tomb, where a larger figure lies, swathed in black cloth. Horns protrude from the recumbent figure's head. At least...most people might think they're horns. They might assume the figure in the tomb is the Devil, defeated.

But I've gone right up to the tapestry and examined it in detail. Those aren't horns. They're antlers.

Every member of this congregation knows the purpose of this church—its true mission—even if we don't discuss it more than once a year or so. Wicklow Heritage Chapel is located at the end of a half-hidden lane through the forest, a ten-minute drive or an hour's brisk walk from Old Sheldon Church.

According to our congregation's religious lore, beneath Old Sheldon Church lies the thing in the tapestry—one of the old pagan gods of Ireland. Dad says nobody knows for sure which god it is, although he and the other deacons have their theories.

Every year at Easter, our congregation joins with some others in the area, and we hold services at Old Sheldon Church. The true purpose of that annual Easter service is lost on everyone outside our congregation. For us, the service isn't just a pleasant springtime gathering but a reconsecration of the ground. We do it to saturate the earth with a faith and energy that is meant to be the polar opposite of the old pagan ways.

Besides Easter service, our congregation holds a midnight vigil at the ruins of Old Sheldon Church every month, and our deacons take turns patrolling the area, saying prayers, and anointing the ground with blessed water. According to Dad, those rituals keep the god quiet and unconscious...most of the time. Most of the congregation seem to believe in the practice, although it's hard to tell how many comply just because it's tradition, a habit that sets us apart from other churches.

I've stared at that tapestry during many long services, mulling over the concept of ancient gods and my connection to them—a link my father prefers to deny, one he has ordered me to keep secret from everyone in Wicklow. If anyone in town knew what I am—

"Cathy?" A light male voice at my elbow interrupts my thoughts.

I turn and look up at Edgar Linton, the pastor's son. With his artfully tousled, golden hair and eyes as blue as the sky, he's practically Cupid come to life—if Cupid wore a cheap gray suit with an aqua tie.

"You're back!" Immediately I hate myself for the obvious phrase. Of course he's back or he wouldn't be standing here, smelling like vanilla, looking as charming as ever. He has spent four years at Bible college and four summers on various mission trips and outreach endeavors. I've always thought he stayed away on purpose, and I sort of resented him for being able to leave Wicklow so easily when I had to get my bachelor's in marketing online. No chance of someone like me being able to have a normal college experience—not that Dad could have paid for it anyway. As a realtor in Wicklow, his income is unstable at best.

"It's good to see you." I reach out to shake Edgar's hand, and my sweater slips off the other shoulder.

Edgar flashes a brilliant smile, showing teeth that belong on a Ken doll. "I got back from Zambia a few days ago. It felt so great being able to help those poor folks. Truly amazing."

Yeah, he doesn't have a white savior complex at all. "Sounds rewarding. So what are you up to now?"

"I'm writing a devotional book, and I'll be helping Dad with the church—the young adults and college group, especially. In fact, I'm organizing a little get-together next weekend. A friend of mine has a private beach we can use. It'll be late afternoon and evening, a time for food, fun, and fellowship, where singles of our age can meet new people without having to resort to the bar scene. You should come."

Surprise momentarily relieves the sensation of claws scrabbling under my skin. Weirdly enough, I kind of want to go. I haven't been to the beach in ages. And if it's a private beach, there won't be too many people around, so it's less likely I'll be triggered.

"Next weekend?" My episode should be over by then. "Sure, I'm in. I've got this new bikini I've been dying to wear."

"Okay, or..." His eyes travel down to my bare shoulders, and his smile wavers. "Maybe, um...maybe wear a one-piece swimsuit... you know, if you have one."

"Oh, right." I press my fingers to my lips, letting my eyes widen with mock horror. "We wouldn't want my exposed navel to cause a riot."

He has the grace to look uncomfortable. "The dress code was Dad's idea."

"What do *you* want me to wear?" I slow-blink at him, a half smile curving my mouth.

Edgar flushes pink from his throat to the roots of his blond hair. "I...I, um... Wear whatever you want."

"How twenty-first century of you. I think I will."

He clears his throat. "Cool, I'll text you the details. Same number?"

"Yup." Same phone number, same email, same house, same job I've had for years. I'm stuck, a fish caught in a net, and I have no idea how to swim free.

Liberty takes money, which is in short supply in Wicklow.

Edgar's younger sister, Isabella, bustles up behind him, looking angelically pious in a long, ruffled dress and heels, not a hair out of place on her golden head. She barely glances at me before tugging his sleeve. "Eddie, Dad needs you."

"Duty calls." Edgar gives me an apologetic wave and hurries away with Isabella.

I sink onto the very end of the back pew, where I can easily access the door if I need to. I've had to leave a service twice before. I claimed nausea the first time, but that gave rise to speculation about a secret pregnancy, so I used a migraine as my excuse the second time.

I guess I'm lucky all this didn't start until I was around sixteen. After the first couple episodes, my parents figured out what I was and switched me to homeschooling. Mom stuck it out until I finished twelfth grade, and then she left. She's living in England now, with some lady professor. They travel a lot, and there never seems to be a good time for me to go visit them. Not to mention the fact that being in a crowded airport would likely trigger multiple episodes—and I don't want to think about what would happen if I had one of my fits while on a plane.

I'm happy for Mom. We FaceTime once a month, and I'm genuinely glad she got away and is living her best life. But I hate her for it too, the way I hate all people with *options*.

Aunt Nellie passes by, gives me a cheerful smile and a nod, but doesn't stop to say hi. As a favored member of the congregation, she's headed up front to chat with her friends. She'll probably sit with Dad. They'll talk about all the surface things of life, never once dipping into the matter of my oddness or his drunken rages. I'm not even sure how much she knows about his drinking. He's good at keeping secrets.

Mrs. Coffey seats herself at the organ and begins playing one of the hymns I've heard all my life. No modern service here—it's all the very oldest of old-school.

The words of the hymn are engraved into my brain, and they play in a doleful loop while I clutch the edge of the pew, my nails digging into the wood grain.

> *There is a fountain filled with blood*
> *Drawn from Immanuel's veins;*
> *And sinners plunged beneath that flood*
> *Lose all their guilty stains.*

Fucking creepy. And gross. My brain won't stop picturing a torrent of blood pouring out from between elevator doors like in *The Shining*, and I want to *scream*. The urge to shriek aloud is tightening my lungs, throbbing in my chest. The creature inside me is crawling up my throat, claws slitting tissue as she climbs my gullet, heaves herself onto my tongue, pries open my jaws—

"That seat taken?"

The gruff male voice startles me out of my trance. The blood in my mind recedes, and the monster in my throat sinks back down as I swallow.

I look up at the man who spoke.

Heathcliff Lockwood looms above me, looking like sin incarnate in a clean white shirt and dark jeans. The shirt's top three buttons are open, revealing the leaves and vines tattooed across his chest. There's part of a wing, too—a crow, maybe? The crisp shirtsleeves are rolled up to his elbows, baring his brown, tattooed forearms. He's got a few silver rings on his fingers—I didn't notice them yesterday.

He's pointing to the pew beyond me.

"You can't be here," I hiss.

His dark eyebrows lift. "Isn't everyone welcome at church?"

"That's what they say, but they never mean it."

He shrugs and wedges himself into the narrow gap between my knees and the back of the next pew. He's facing me, so the crotch of his jeans is pretty much level with my face. And he *pauses*, right there, looks down at me, and smirks.

The image flashes into my mind—me drawing down his zipper, taking his cock out, popping the head into my mouth, sliding my lips down the shaft. Heathcliff sinking his thick fingers into my hair, making me take him deeper. What would the congregation do? What would they say? Would my dad shoot me afterward for bringing shame to the Earnshaw family?

"For god's sake, move," I whisper. "You can't sit with me. You're a Lockwood. My father would kill me if he knew—if—" I glance around, distressed to see that nearly everyone in the sanctuary is looking our way. Conversations have stopped, and dozens of pairs of eyes are fixed on us. Blood rushes to my cheeks.

We don't get visitors here. I'm not sure what he said at the door to make them let him in, but he's drawing way too much attention.

Heathcliff squeezes past me and sits about three feet away, just enough distance to make it clear we're not together. He tries to maneuver his long legs into a comfortable position, then gives up and angles himself sideways, stretching them out. He's wearing the same work boots from yesterday. Crumbly bits of dried mud mark the carpet where he stepped.

The church's scanty choir files into the two rows of chairs on the platform, behind the pulpit, in front of the baptistry. The scattered groups of people throughout the sanctuary move to take their seats as well, many of them casting curious or suspicious glances at Heathcliff.

Luckily there's no one else in the back row on either side of the aisle, and no one in the pew in front of us. Moving my lips as little as possible, I mutter, "Why are you here?"

"Thought it was about time I check out *this* god and see what he's all about. Maybe confess my sins." He jerks his head toward one of the confessional booths.

"I suspect your confession would take a very long time."

He chuckles. "And yours wouldn't?"

"Not at all." I shouldn't be encouraging him, but I can't help adding, "I just make something up and then confess to lying at the end."

"Simple. Effective." He nods. "I like it."

"Stop talking to me."

"You started it." He crosses his arms and slouches lower as Deacon Mohan opens with announcements. When the worship pastor directs the congregation to stand for the first song, I grab a hymnbook and open it, just to have something to occupy my shaking hands.

As the congregation begins to sing, Heathcliff takes a sideways step toward me. He leans in, as if he's trying to read the words of the hymn, and without thinking, I hold the book closer to him, angling it so he can see.

He reaches for the book casually, sharing the task of holding it open. His big hand spreads across the cover, and the tips of his callused fingers brush against mine.

The touch is like a lighter to gasoline. Heat zaps from my fingertips, flows up my arm, quivers in my chest like a warm, fluttering bird.

Heathcliff is singing, low and deep, gruff and slightly off-key, lyrics about being taken, molded, filled, used...and sure, it's supposed to be about god's spirit or whatever, but damn it if those words don't take on an entirely different meaning with this beautiful man at my side. I can feel my cheeks flaming as I mouth the words I can't manage to sing.

When the song ends, I yank the hymnbook back into my possession. Heathcliff glances down at me, and the corner of his mouth curves up.

The prayer comes next. It's a long one, an endless invocation by one of the older men in the congregation. I'm supposed to stand still, keeping my head bowed and my eyes closed, and I don't know how I'm going to manage that with the churning unrest in my body. I'm desperate for distraction, so halfway through the prayer, I turn my head and sneak a peek at Heathcliff.

He's looking at me. Openly watching me while the rest of the congregation stands with lowered heads. There's a roguish heat in his eyes, a tempting menace in the way he smiles at me. Like a wolf who would devour me whole if it weren't for the rest of the flock standing around us and the watchdogs waiting in the front pew.

He slides his hand to his belt and tugs at the waist of his pants a bit, just enough to tighten the fabric and show me the outline of the thick erection beneath them.

I suck in a tiny breath, face forward, and shut my eyes again.

Heathcliff is a walking blasphemy, and I love that. But I can't really enjoy it because my mind feels like it's splitting open. I'm losing the battle with my secret self. She's compelled to crawl out of my soul, to be heard, to herald the oncoming death of someone in Wicklow. Not even a quickie in the church bathroom would help me now.

I should have told Dad about how I felt. He might have let me stay home from church. Unlikely, though, because I've used that excuse multiple times when it wasn't true, and now I'm the girl who screamed wolf.

Just as I'm making up my mind to slip out during the prayer, it ends, and we're all ordered to sit down. The ushers come forward with silver collection plates, passing them along the rows so people can contribute to the weekly offering.

As Deacon Kitt reads a Scripture passage, the urge to wail out loud swells in me with such violence, I nearly explode. Pressure pounds in my head, a driving pain. I dare not open my mouth to breathe, or a shriek will burst out.

I have to leave. Now.

The ushers retreat, and the congregation rises for another song. Under cover of the movement, I stagger from the pew, lurch to the doors, and haul one open just wide enough for me to slip out. Stars wink in front of my eyes as I hold my breath, one hand clamped tightly over my mouth.

I waited too long.

Fuck my life.

I'm running down the steps, across the parking lot. My temples are tightening, throbbing. Tiny, sharp pains in my eyes tell me the blood vessels are bursting.

Just a little farther.

I crash through the trees, shedding my white sweater on the brambles, tilting and stumbling on the rough ground in my strappy sandals. Tears leak from my eyes in copious streams.

Can't hold it back any longer. Have to let it out, let it out, *let me out—*

I open my mouth, and the monster screams.

4

CATHY

DEATH IS THE GREAT HORROR OF THE WORLD, THE ONE inescapable truth. No matter how much life we experience, how many kisses we give or hugs we receive, no matter how carefully or callously we treat our bodies, no matter how delightful or dour we are, we all end the same way: leaking bowels, stiffening flesh. Blank, jellied eyes. Mouths mouths mouths gaping, sagging, jaws loose and lolling—that's why the undertakers sew them up, little stitches so no one can see. I wish someone would stitch me up— force my jaw shut and run a thread through my lips, heedless of the blood dripping from the holes. Just stitch me up, seal me tight, stop the screaming, the screaming—

I can see the dead man, clearer than I see the trees through which I'm staggering. He's slumped on the floor of his kitchen. It's Mr. O'Brien this time, a hefty guy with a heart problem and a penchant for overindulging in high-cholesterol foods. Even when I don't know the person I'm mourning, their name echoes in my head...sometimes right away, when I first start feeling restless, and sometimes much later.

Adam O'Brien, Adam O'Brien tolls in my mind like a funeral bell. His family has lived in the area for generations. He stayed home from church today. Wasn't feeling well. Now he's dying of a heart attack, and I must mourn him. I must wail for the house of O'Brien, cry for the people he leaves behind.

When I get the first twinges of sadness, the first vision of the face, or the first sound of the name, I'm supposed to go wander the property of the person doomed to die, mourning in advance, warning the family before the actual death—but I can't allow myself to do that. I'd get arrested, locked up in some mental health facility.

If I could warn them, if I could fulfill that part of my role like I'm supposed to, these episodes would be over faster. But since I have to stay far away, the fits last longer, and they're way more violent. I'm constantly pulled toward the person's house or site of death, and I must consciously keep steering myself in another direction or holding myself in one place.

I know where Mr. O'Brien is. I can feel the line connecting me to his body, a burning, poisonous barbwire tightening between us, and as it tightens, the barbs lacerate my heart. A groan quakes through me, bone deep, ravaging my throat, tearing at my lungs.

I *have* to walk that way. I have to. I *need* to. But I *can't*. I can't let anyone see me like this.

Throwing both arms around a tree, I hold on as tight as I can, and I scream against the trunk, the edges of my teeth scraping the bark. I have to try to muffle the sounds. I'm not far enough from the church yet. Thankfully there are a few loud sopranos among the congregation, so I doubt anyone heard me. But I must get control before Pastor Linton starts preaching—or at least get farther away.

My body jerks, pulled toward the dying man. The anguish,

the need to race through the woods and get to his family, to give voice to their sorrow—it's more intense than usual. He has many people who love him. I'm supposed to carry their grief, to make it easier for them to bear the loss and move on.

The spirit of the banshee is a primal instinct, too archaic to understand that things have changed, that I live in Wicklow, South Carolina, that we don't mourn the same way nowadays. We hide our grief in bathrooms or beds, curled up in a ball under the showerhead, or alone in a car while rain pounds the windshield.

Grief is naked, obscene. Grief reminds us of the wretched truth that death is crawling ever nearer to us, grinning with crooked teeth, salivating for us, gibbering with eagerness, yearning to drag us down.

Pain in my hand pulls me out of my clouded swirl of dark thoughts. My nails are clawing through the bark in an effort to keep me in place, and the first nail of my left hand is starting to rip from its bed.

"Fuck!" It's a roar and a scream, an ugly, unearthly bellow. Releasing the tree, I bend double, pressing my hands on either side of my face. Tears drip from my lips and chin—my nose is a mucus-y mess. I curl deeper in on myself, my stomach hardening with the strain as my body readies for another scream.

A deep male voice, tight and concerned: "Earnshaw?"

Oh no. Oh shit… Did he follow me?

"What's wrong?" Heathcliff's boots stop in front of me, and his big hand curls around my shoulder. "Are you in pain? You need me to call 911?"

"No!" I bark, huffing through a spasm of grief. "Noooo…"

The second time it's a wail, a keening note of utter desperation and unspeakable emptiness.

In the brief moments after the wail, I manage words. "You...can't...stop this. I just...have to...endure it. Go, please."

"You need a doctor."

My face crumples, another flood of tears gushing from my eyes. I'm too fragile to lie to him right now. I just need him to understand what he probably suspects anyway. "This isn't medical. It's fucking supernatural. Now go away. I have to move. I have to..."

I force myself to take steps in the opposite direction of the victim, on a trajectory that will take me deeper into the woods. I've mapped the area. I know the best places to go where no one is likely to hear me.

I stagger through the trees, holding each trunk briefly for support, weeping as I go. Time blurs and so do my surroundings as visions of Mr. O'Brien's life fill my head. He killed a man once—a scuffle behind a bar. No one ever knew. He hit his wife one time in anger. She stayed, and he never did it again. His six kids adore him. The second daughter is pregnant—his last thought during the heart attack was that he wouldn't get to see the baby. He won't get to be a grandpa. He and his wife will never take the cruise they were always talking about.

I walk, and I weep, and I watch the memories drifting through my mind like clouds of inky smoke.

Bark under my palms, thorns scratching my legs. I stumble, and my ankle twists. I fumble with my sandals, trying to remove them, and somehow they come off by themselves. Or maybe a rough, warm hand helps with the buckles.

Onward I limp, over crackling brown leaves and mossy stones.

Then there's damp earth, mud. Water rippling around my ankles. My injured foot hurts and I waver, but I'm held upright until I've crossed the stream.

I can't see anymore. That happens sometimes—my eyes go white, irises a milky swirl, veiled by visions. I must turn away from the pull—always turn away. Don't go to the dead man, don't go to the family. Veer in a new direction each time you start to yield. Take the path of greatest pain.

⬦⬦⬦

My lips are cracked. They hurt when I scream. Everything hurts—my ravaged throat, my aching lungs, my bare feet, my ankle, my fingernails.

It's been hours, I think. I can't be sure. Night insects chirp around me, backup singers to my soliloquy of moans and quiet sobs. Cold cracks along my limbs and stabs my fingers to the bone. My body is wrung out—no more moisture for tears.

And still I walk, wheezing the grief of the O'Brien house, bemoaning the theft of possibility and hope. The sudden end of a man so fallible and yet so well loved. He was a jolly man, a big presence, and he leaves behind a hollow no one will ever fill.

I cry for the ones he abandoned, and I cry for *him*, for the soul lingering, unsatisfied, unwilling to accept its fate. He'll let go eventually—they all do—and drift into some afterlife. I don't know where they go. It's my job to stare death in the face, not look beyond it.

"Dead, dead, dead," I whisper. "Dead eyes, dead hands, shrunken lungs. But it's the mouths that are the worst. No more kissing, talking, chewing, breathing, smiling. No more screams.

The silence is so big, it's enormous—it swells until that's all there is: Silence. So much silence. Living things are never really quiet. Bellies burbling, guts churning, blood pumping, hearts thumping, lungs inflating, breath hissing. Death is silence. I fill the silence. I challenge it. But in the end, it always wins. Always."

"You're talking. That must mean you're coming out of it." A low, cautious voice at my side.

I startle and blink. A white, rectangular glow explodes into my sight, and I cringe, hissing, "No, no, no!"

"Sorry." The light angles away from me. "I'm worried you'll cut your feet to pieces. I would have stopped you from walking, but I thought it might make things worse. Can I... Are we done wandering around?"

I know that voice from somewhere, but my brain is still full of murmurs and memories. I can't find the thread that connects the voice to a name. "You shouldn't be here. No one ever walks with me when I mourn."

"This has happened before? Fuck. And your family doesn't follow you to keep you safe?"

"They don't care." I'm still walking but slower now. I blink again, staring at the swath of ground illuminated by the bluish-white light. My sight is back, so I can see the grass and the dead leaves in stark relief, each outlined by a crisp, black shadow. "They wish I would die."

"I'm surprised you haven't. Do you do this often?"

"Yes." Why am I answering this person's questions? Why do I feel as though this gruff voice belongs to someone I can trust?

"You get cut up like this every time?" he asks.

"I heal quicker than most people. No scars." Not visible ones, anyway.

The nauseating urgency in my gut is fading, draining away, leaving me cold and ravaged. Salty blood seams the cracks in my parched lips. I try licking them, but my tongue is thick and dry. "Do you have any water?"

"Shit...no."

"It's fine. I'll just go home."

"In the dark? In this condition? Do you even know where you are?"

"I can sense my home," I say faintly. "I know where to go."

As I turn and take a step, pain spears my ankle. I cry out, grabbing the nearest tree.

"No way am I letting you hobble home on that ankle. I can't believe you walked on it this far."

"Grief suppresses physical pain," I croak, taking another step. My fingers ache with cold. October in South Carolina boasts thirty- or forty-degree temperature differences—eighties by midafternoon, fifties or lower after sundown.

"I've made it back in worse shape than this," I say, more to myself than to my nameless companion, whom I'm fairly sure my brain invented to help me through the trauma of this episode.

Heavy footfalls in the leaves. Sudden heat warms my back, and then a pair of sinewy arms scoops me up, muscles bunching beneath crisp shirtsleeves. The rich scent of sandalwood and amber.

My brows pinch together as I drag his name out of the recesses of my traumatized brain. "Heathcliff."

"Earnshaw," his deep voice replies.

"You *followed* me?" I conjure up scant memories of someone removing my sandals after I twisted my ankle, someone helping me across the stream. "How long was I—"

"Let's see... The service started at eleven, and it's a little after midnight now, so...thirteen hours. Not gonna lie, I'm starving and thirsty myself. I couldn't leave, though. Didn't want to lose track of you."

The bloody remnants of my heart seal themselves back together at those words.

No one has ever come with me or even offered to follow me. After my first couple of episodes, my parents just let me run off and go through the agony, knowing I'd come crawling back eventually, when it was finished. After my episodes, Mom would give me water, aspirin, and food. She'd help me change and clean up. These days, Dad just hands me a water bottle and leaves me to recover on my own.

No one has ever cared enough to go through this hell with me.

If I still had tears, I think I'd cry again.

But even though I'm touched, I'm suspicious, too. Dad says the Lockwoods are bad news—pagans of the old way, through and through. Demon-worshippers. And though my dad has myriad faults, I've never known him to lie about the supernatural world. If he says the Lockwoods are dangerous, they are.

And one of them knows my secret now. He could use it against me. If Heathcliff outs me to the town or to the church, my dad will lose his place as a deacon, and he'll lose his real estate clients. I'd probably have to quit working for Aunt Nellie as well. Right now, she thinks I suffer from migraines and that I'm prone to focal seizures. It's the excuse I've given her for any sudden strangeness or random absences from work. If she knew the real reason, she'd bail on me, like everyone does.

I can't risk Heathcliff telling anyone about this, so I need to tread carefully here. Not easy with my brain fractured by weariness and my body one massive lump of pain.

Heathcliff strides through the woods with me in his arms. With one hand he holds his phone, angled to shed light over the ground so he doesn't trip.

When I'm wandering, I usually move slowly, in circles. Since we're walking in a straight line, it shouldn't take us nearly as long to get home as it did to get out here.

"You want to head slightly more to the right," I tell him.

He scoffs, as if he can hardly believe I'm a supernatural GPS, but he makes the adjustment.

"I'm sorry you had to witness all that," I venture. "I know it's loud and gross." Of *course* the hot guy I hooked up with had to see me when my face was glazed with snot and tears. Because that's just how my life goes.

"It was loud," he admits. "And intense." He strides on for a few minutes before adding, "So you do this often, and you talked about mourning...you said it's supernatural...which means you're a banshee."

He says it so simply. No dramatic shift in tone, no fear.

So I reply just as succinctly. "Yeah."

"How's that work?"

I suck on my cracked lower lip, unsure how to respond. His casual use of the word *banshee* means he's at least somewhat familiar with supernatural ancestry, specifically the kind that has influenced this area for generations. My dad, the deacons, and Pastor Linton are the most recent warriors in a long crusade not just to keep one god buried but to destroy every last vestige of old magic. According to Dad, the Lockwoods have always been on the opposite side of that effort, advocating for a resurgence of ancestral worship and the old ways. It makes sense that Heathcliff would have some knowledge of the topic. But how much does he know? How much can I tell him?

It was a mistake to fuck this guy. He's pretty much stalking me now, showing up at church, following me into the woods. And now he knows my secret.

How am I going to get out of this?

"I'm guessing your dad knows what you are," Heathcliff says matter-of-factly. "But you've managed to keep it hidden from everyone else or explain it away."

He is scarily perceptive. "Aunt Nellie thinks I occasionally have hallucinations or seizures. Between that rumor and my reputation as the congregation's snarky rebel, people interpret my behavior the way they want to—which is usually light-years from the truth."

"So what triggers these bouts of screaming and crying? Death, right? All death or certain ones?"

Maybe it's the powerful flex of his arms around me, the heat of his chest, or the steady way he strides through the chilly darkness. Maybe it's the fact that I always feel fragile and wrung-out after an episode or the relief that I don't have to stagger home alone this time. My hold on the secret relaxes, and I start to speak, slowly and hoarsely through my weary throat.

"Usually I mourn the death of people in established families, folks who have lived in this region a long time. There's a radius to my ability, though I've never been exactly sure of its boundary. But even if I'm in another state, I can be triggered by people in large crowds, especially those with significant Irish ancestry."

I hesitate, struck by the realization that I've never talked about this to anyone. Now that I've confessed a little bit about myself, one of my most traumatic memories is pressing at the back of my tongue like water behind a dam, demanding to be released or I'll crack from the strain of holding it back.

"Not long after my sixteenth birthday, I was super depressed about having to homeschool and everything, so my mom planned a trip to Dollywood—you know, roller coasters and shit. Back then, Mom still wasn't sure about Dad's banshee theory. She thought I was being haunted and maybe if we got far enough away, I'd be all right. But the minute we drove into Pigeon Forge, I started screaming and I couldn't stop. My parents had to sedate me and drive home. Mom had saved up for the trip, and I ruined it all. Dad kept talking about the thousands of dollars they couldn't get back—no refunds for the vacation package."

Heathcliff doesn't respond for a moment. Then, "Could you hold my phone? Shine the light for me? I gotta cross this stream and I don't wanna drop you."

"Let me warm my fingers up for a second." I try blowing on them, but it doesn't help much—so I cautiously slide my hand into the V of Heathcliff's unbuttoned shirt. He's so deliciously big and warm.

"Can we get a drink from the stream?" I ask. "I'm parched."

"You want to risk viruses, parasites, bacteria, be my guest."

"I'm dying here. I need a drink."

"You're not dying. You're way too stubborn for that."

"Don't act like you know me."

"Take the phone."

I snatch it from his hand and angle it low, so he can see his footing. His grip tightens around me as he steps onto one rock, then another. His stride is so long, we're across within seconds.

"My toes are freezing," I whisper.

He puts me down so abruptly I yelp, which hurts my throat. He unlaces and removes his boots, then pulls off his socks. "Put these on."

"I'm not wearing your sweaty, stinky socks."

"Oh, *now* I'm too dirty for you? You know I'd just brushed some dirt off my truck's bumper before I rubbed your clit yesterday."

"You're disgusting."

"You're wearing the socks, Princess." He grabs my foot in his big, tattooed hand and shoves the first sock on. It's slightly damp from his sweat and it smells gross, but it's warm. And I don't have the energy to fight him anyway.

Once the other sock is on, he picks me up again, curling my body against his chest. The fingernail I almost ripped out is hurting worse than everything else, and there's an itchy patch on my leg that's becoming more and more irritating by the minute.

"I think I stepped in poison ivy."

"I tried to steer you around things—thorns, rocks, and such. But I didn't know if it was okay to interfere too much." Heathcliff resumes the trek through the woods, and I force myself to relax, to yield to his rocking gait and lean my aching head against his shoulder.

"It's best to let me do what I need to do," I tell him. "My parents tried locking me up during an episode once and I nearly killed myself trying to get out. Since then I've developed some control over where I go, enough to keep clear of the victims I'm supposed to cry for. The idea is that my screams would serve as a warning to the household where the death is about to happen. In ancient times, people would accept that explanation, but these days, people would call the police if I started wailing outside their house. And if I was proven right about multiple deaths, the cops would think I had something to do with it or they'd put me in a mental health facility and never let me out again."

"You're fucked either way."

"Pretty much."

He's quiet for a moment. It's an oddly comforting kind of silence, the kind that makes me feel acknowledged without a lot of unnecessary words. Like he's really listening, and he gets it.

A few minutes later he says, "So your mom, your dad—they know. But they don't help you?"

"My mom lives overseas now. And my dad—" I hesitate, sucking my lip again. "What do you know about him?"

"I know he's a respected member of your cult," Heathcliff mutters. "That he and his pals hunt down people with supernatural abilities and murder them."

"What?" I rasp. "That's not true. Their job is to keep old magic from manifesting or reviving. But they don't kill people. And the church isn't a cult."

"Whatever you say, Earnshaw." He places emphasis on my family name.

"Your family is the dangerous one, Lockwood."

"Yeah, we're dangerous, too. More so than you realize, I bet. You think you understand everything about this town, about the gods, about supernatural shit, but you don't know half of it."

"So tell me."

"Not tonight."

My throat is too sore to argue with him, so I fall silent. And then I fall asleep.

When I come back to consciousness, Heathcliff's boots are crunching across the gravel of the church parking lot, heading for his truck. A single outdoor light illuminates the front door of the church. Moths flutter around that light—a kind of moth I've never seen before, with big splashes of deep scarlet on their wings. The church looks unfamiliar, dramatic, and dreadful, like someone holding a flashlight under their chin and pulling a wicked face. Its concrete foundation, stained bloody by red Carolina clay, has a wide crack near the east corner.

Heathcliff sets me down, props me against the truck like a doll, and opens the door before picking me up again and putting me on the passenger seat. As he leans in to fix my seat belt, I inhale his scent—the sweat of weariness, and the spicy remnants of the cologne he wore to church. His shaggy hair conceals the side of his face, all except his straight nose, full mouth, determined chin.

He's so close, so ruggedly human, so warm and real and... Fuck it. I grab his jaw, twist his face toward mine, and kiss him. My lips are flaky and cracked, and there's a sourness in my mouth, a metallic hint of blood. He doesn't seem to care. He shoves his hand into my hair, grasps the back of my skull, and kisses me brutally, until I can hardly find room to breathe.

The aching crush of our mouths is messy, and it hurts, and yet the salty, smooth heat of his lips and the wet, warm slide of his tongue in my mouth is the best thing I've ever experienced. It's like he's erasing the clinging film of death from my skin, bringing me back to life. I could swear, I feel the pain in my ankle easing, my irritated skin calming, my fingernail healing.

The seat belt clicks, and he breaks the kiss, backing away and closing the door of the truck. I'm left breathless and chilled, weak and ravenous for more.

I kissed him.

Why did I do that? I touch my sore mouth.

When he swings into the driver's seat, I manage words. "Thank you for everything you did tonight."

"Any decent person would have done the same."

No. They wouldn't. "We can't hang out again."

He laughs a little, hands tightening on the steering wheel. "You think you can fuck me, kiss me, thank me, and then kick me to the curb? It's not gonna be that easy, Princess. I'm in your life now, like it or not, and you're in mine." He starts the engine. "Let's get you home."

Neither of us speak again until we reach my house. I'm not sure how he knows where I live. True, most people in Wicklow know the Earnshaw place...but the Lockwoods don't live within the town limits. Dad says most of them live over in Coosaw, a neighboring town, and they don't come to Wicklow or to my family's house on Wuthering Lane.

Wuthering Lane is a quiet road, with houses spaced far apart, screened from each other by cedars and magnolias. My house is a huge, old, rambling colonial, much larger than anything we could afford if we bought it new nowadays. It's a family place, owned by generations of Earnshaws—a pillared, gabled two-story with dirty white siding, a wraparound porch, and a balcony on the second floor. A semicircle drive curves through the wide lawn, sweeps past the porch, and swerves back to the road.

In the half-circle of turf outlined by the driveway rears a massive live oak, its thick branches arching upward before plunging back down to run low along the ground. Spanish moss drapes every bough, turning the tree into a hulking, gray-bearded monster as the beams of Heathcliff's truck slice across it.

He pulls up, leaves the engine running, and comes around to help me up the walk to the porch. Dad left the two porch lights on, but all the windows in the house are dark. Guess I should be grateful he's not awake to witness Heathcliff Lockwood bringing me home.

I shake free of Heathcliff's hand as I mount the last step to the porch. The imprint of his fingers stays on my skin, searing, tingling.

He surveys the dark house with narrowed eyes. "You need me to come in, help you get settled?"

"My dad would shoot you if he caught you inside."

His mouth twists in a half smile, but the expression vanishes almost instantly as his gaze drops to my feet. "I'll need my socks back."

"Oh. Sure." I pull them off, noting that my sprained ankle looks much less swollen than I thought it would. Feels pretty good, too. I'm healing faster than usual this time.

I ball up the socks and toss them to Heathcliff. He catches them, stuffs them in his pocket. "I carried your shoes along for a while, but then I left 'em behind. You don't need those ankle-breakers anyway."

Something about his statement ticks me off—a possessiveness, an intent to dictate my choices, a hint of *I know what's best for you*. I don't like the vibe, so I snap, "I'll wear whatever shoes I want, thanks."

His dark eyes spark as he catches the belligerence in my tone. "Sure. Fine. Go ahead and break your ankle next time. See if I care."

"No one asked you to care."

"So when you thanked me earlier, that was just performative, huh?"

"Performative?" I raise my eyebrows. "The scruffy delivery guy sure knows some big words."

His jaw tightens. "You be careful, Earnshaw. There are people who would pay a fuck-ton of money to know about this little secret of yours."

I can't read his expression. "Are you... Is that a threat?"

"It's reality."

Okay, here we go. I should have known he didn't do this out of the goodness of his heart. He owns my secret now, which means he owns *me*.

"I don't have much money, so blackmailing me is pointless." My legs wobble, and I grip the porch post to hold myself steady.

"If I wanted money, I'd sell you to the right people and get myself a payday."

"So you want sex, then? And you'll keep my secret in exchange?"

He's glowering, looking absolutely thunderous. "You think I'm that kind of man?"

"I don't know what kind of man you are. I'm grateful that you got me home, but I'm also creeped out that you *stalked* me, first at church and then in the woods. Now you're talking about how dangerous your family is and how you know where to sell me for a 'fuck-ton' of money...and I'm supposed to think what? That you're the good guy?"

"Fuck no. I've never been the good guy, and I don't plan to start now."

"If you're not blackmailing me, why the cryptic warning? You can't just say something like that and not explain."

He fixes me with a defiant glare, then spins on his heel and stalks back to his truck.

I cling to the porch pillar, frowning, trying to figure out why on earth someone would *pay* for me, why anyone would be interested in what I can do beyond medical research or something. Maybe that's what he means. He'd sell me to the government.

It's hard for me to believe that the guy who spent thirteen hours with me in the woods, gave me his socks, and carried me home would sell my secret for personal gain.

But most people are shit, so I guess you never know.

5

HEATHCLIFF

When I get home to the Grange, I gag at the smell the second I walk in the door.

Hindley has passed out in his recliner, his foot resting in a puddle of his own vomit.

"Shit stain," I hiss at him as I walk by. I grab paper towels from the kitchen and clean up the mess. If Hindley knew where I've been...if he knew that I'd found a banshee...

Banshees are like cash cows to necromancers. They predict death, which means if you got a banshee who can give you enough advance warning, you could take her to the person who's supposed to die and use her knowledge to convince them they're in danger. Then you take a down payment, create the matching tattoos, and resurrect the person after they die...which means more money. Buckland told me about a family of necromancers out in California who kept a banshee in their basement and got rich off her. He was always hoping to find one. Never did.

Hindley and the Coosaw Lockwoods would pay a lot for the name of the banshee I just discovered. They'd pay me enough money to leave this place. Flip side of that is, they'd never let me go because they need my abilities. If Hindley ever thought I was really fixing to leave, I'm pretty sure he'd fit me with a shock collar or something...anything to keep me here.

It's all a moot point anyway. I've got no intention of telling anyone Cathy's secret. Not sure why I feel so damn protective of her, but I do. She needs somebody in her corner, watching out for her.

Speaking of watching out for folks, I should check on our unconscious guest. Hindley finally told me the guy's name—Ian Holcum. Not sure if it's his real name, but it'll do.

I flip on the light in the back room and survey the dark-haired man lying motionless on the bed. He's still breathing, which is good, I guess. There's nothing physically wrong with him. I did my work well, and as far I can tell, his soul went back into his body just fine.

But he's still unconscious. It's like he's having trouble re-syncing to mortal life.

He's not consuming anything, and he's not pissing or shitting himself either. He should look shriveled and starved, but he seems perfectly healthy, like he's in a weird kind of stasis. I looked into getting him an IV, but that shit's expensive, and Hindley swore the money wasn't coming out of his share. Maybe it's selfish, but I don't want to pay for it either, especially not when I remember how his soul felt, the wrongness of it.

I lay a hand on his forehead and close my eyes.

I can't heal normal living humans, only those we've just summoned back from death. But Ian's body was rebuilt with my energy and power, so I should be able to figure out what's wrong with him.

Maybe this is happening because he was burned so badly when

we found him. But that shouldn't matter, as long as the tattoo was intact when he died.

"Heathcliff."

I glance up. Hindley's standing in the doorway, looking like death.

"Got a text today," he says. "Everyone's comin' here for Halloween."

Great. The cousins from Coosaw and the rest of the Lockwoods. Hindley treats me like shit, but they're worse. All except Meemaw Lockwood, the ninety-year-old matriarch of the clan. She's actually decent, and we get along. Besides her, the only one I'm actually friendly with is Bean—Benjamin Lockwood. He and his sister, Morgana, have a tattoo shop near Beaufort. Any skilled artist can create the matching tattoos needed for a tether, but Bean and Morgana have a unique talent no other Lockwoods possess—the ability to create ornate, long-lasting tattoos in a fraction of the usual time. It's some mutation of the necromancy gift, and as such, they're considered outsiders. The family uses their skills, and they come to all the holiday gatherings, but they're treated differently.

Halloween is the Coosaw Lockwoods' favorite holiday. They blend it with traditional Samhain festivities, complete with bonfires and weird rituals—and pounds of candy washed down with kegs of beer.

"The rituals might be different this year," Hindley adds. "Salter says there have been...stirrings."

"What the hell is a stirring?"

"Fuck if I know. Has something to do with that goddamn church, the one we can't go near because of the barrier."

The invisible barrier around Wicklow is the reason Hindley sent me to do the delivery to Aunt Nellie's. He can't get through, but I can, since I'm not a Lockwood by blood. The barrier was cast around the same time the Lockwoods' island mansion was spelled, and it surrounds Wicklow and Old Sheldon Church, keeping out the Lockwoods and a few others, like the LeGare and the Byrne families.

Hindley's apparently done talking about stirrings and barriers for now. He jerks his head toward the comatose guy. "He wake up yet?"

"Oh yeah, he did. He woke up, recited a monologue, and bored himself back to sleep."

Hindley gives me a baleful look. "Go ahead, make your jokes. It's your hide if he's not up and conscious by next weekend, you hear me? You better have him awake by then."

"I pinky swear it." I hold up my middle finger.

For a second I think he'll come at me, but then he retches a little and stumbles off toward the bathroom.

I rise, giving Ian Holcum one last look.

Wait a second…

"Hey, Hindley," I call. "Did you flip this guy's pillow?"

"Course I didn't. I'm not a fucking maid," he hollers back.

I could have sworn the open end of the pillowcase was on the left side last time I was in here, and now it's on the right.

But it's been a hell of a long day. I'm probably imagining things.

I head upstairs, take a piss, and throw myself on the bed without bothering to shower. I'm dog-tired, but I can't sink into a good sleep. I keep seeing Cathy Earnshaw, pale and red-eyed, wandering the woods in her little sundress, weeping and moaning and wailing her grief to the skies. I've never seen anything like it. She looked so frail and tragic and beautiful—and fucking strong, too. I could tell it was taking every ounce of her will to control where her wanderings took her, to fight the compulsion of the spirit inside her.

She's a banshee. A real one.

When I was a kid, whenever we hung out with the Coosaw Lockwoods, Meemaw would tell me about creatures and characters from old Irish lore. I ate up those stories: tales of the far darrig, the cunning trickster dressed in red; the fear gorta, phantoms of hunger; the Leannán Sídhe, muses of creative inspiration; and the púca, a shifter capable of taking various animal forms. She told me about the Gancanagh, the handsome Love-Talker, capable of influencing those around him, and Failinis, the gigantic, invincible warrior-dog of kings. My favorites were the abhartach, or vampires, and the banshees.

Meemaw had plenty of tales about all of them. According to her, some of the old gifts still exist, but they fade with each generation or sometimes skip a generation entirely. Which makes a lot of sense, given the decline of the Lockwoods' abilities, but it doesn't explain my extra gifts—the healing, the unnatural strength.

And it doesn't explain the connection I feel to Catherine Earnshaw. There's a wild, whispering energy about her that I recognize—the signature of the Vague, the haunting flavor of Death. Sure, our abilities are two different aspects of the same thing, but it's more than that. It's like I feel an echo of myself in her. Which is damn odd for me because I don't usually connect with women. I could count on my hand the number of women I've fucked, and even though I've always taken my time and learned how to please them, I don't lie awake thinking about them. I don't go online to look up their family connections and their address, and I sure as hell don't visit their church on the off chance of seeing them again.

None of that is stuff I do. Except I did all of it for Cathy.

When I finally fall asleep, my dreams are full of her pitiful, pale face and her anguished voice, weeping and moaning, while her thin, white fingers scratch at my bedroom window, leaving bloody lines on the glass as she whimpers, "Let me in, Heathcliff. Let me in."

6

CATHY

I call in sick Monday and Tuesday, claiming that I have a cold. By Wednesday I'm fully healed, so I show up for my shift as usual.

"Feeling better?" Aunt Nellie asks as I tie my apron.

"Yeah."

"Good. You can work the café."

The "café" is a counter in the back right corner of the store, where we sell coffee, pastries, and prewrapped sandwiches. A side door leads to a covered strip of concrete with a few tables and some colorful chairs. It's open from 8 a.m. to 2 p.m., Monday through Friday. I don't mind playing barista, especially since we keep it simple and the cappuccino machine does most of the work for me.

I've barely stepped behind the café counter when the bell on the side door jangles. I look up just as Edgar Linton walks in.

The morning sun illuminates his wavy, golden hair, and when he smiles at me, my breath catches. He looks fucking angelic. Under his arm he carries a few books, and I glimpse the word *occult* on one of the spines. Not the kind of reading I'd expect a Bible college graduate to be doing.

"Hey, Cathy." He rests a hand on the countertop, drumming his fingers lightly. "I came around earlier this week, but you weren't here. I heard you were sick. You okay?"

"Peachy," I say lightly. "What can I get you?"

"A pumpkin spice latte, please—skim milk. And I wanted to ask if you're free for dinner tonight."

Oh god. "Tonight?"

A soft pink tinges his pale cheeks. "It's just...I know we'll be hanging out at the beach thing this weekend, but I thought it might be nice to catch up before then."

This is a date. Edgar Linton, pastor's son and probable heir to the pulpit of Wicklow Heritage Chapel, is asking me out on a date.

I can't think of a reason to blow him off and I'm taking way too long to answer and... "Um...sure."

"Great!" He brightens. "Moretti's, around seven? Or...what time do you get off?"

"Six or so. We close at five thirty, but I help out with a few things afterward."

"Pick you up at your house, then. Seven o'clock." He turns away, heading for the door.

I clear my throat. "Don't you want your coffee?"

"Oh! Yeah. Yeah, I do." Flushed and laughing, he returns to the counter, and I can't help smiling as I ring him up. He's cute. Why shouldn't I go on a date with him? It's not like I'm dating anyone else, certainly not that grouchy, tattooed Heathcliff with his menacing, mysterious comments.

Once Edgar's coffee is ready, he takes it outside and sits at a table with his books, occasionally glancing at me through the window. Not gonna lie—it feels good to have someone like him notice me. He's so...clean. Such an upstanding Captain America type. Most guys around here are grubbier than Heathcliff and less satisfying in bed—though to be fair, I rarely do it in an actual bed anymore. It feels more transgressive and exciting to do it literally anywhere else.

Eventually Edgar leaves. The lunch rush begins, keeping me too busy to wonder about his motives for asking me out.

Around one thirty, a shiny Rivian pulls into one of the café parking spots, followed by a second car, a BMW M8. Yeah, I notice cars. When you don't have one and you long to travel, they tend to be extra fascinating.

Four of the most beautiful people I've ever seen climb out of those cars and walk toward the café tables. They're eye-catching in a way that goes deeper than surface-level hotness—they all possess an indefinable grace, a cool confidence, as if they're perfectly at ease with themselves in a way most people aren't. I could almost swear they're walking in slow motion, like in movies...but nope, this is real life, and they're sitting down at one of the outdoor tables.

I grab the tablet we sometimes use to take orders outside, and I'm about to go greet them when I see two more cars pulling in— Pastor Linton's Toyota and my dad's Ford. Dad and the pastor head straight for the group of strangers. Like they were expecting them to be there. Like this is some kind of meetup.

What the hell is happening?

I walk to the side door and lean against the wall beside it, right next to the big window. The window isn't sealed well, and if I focus, I should be able to catch a little of the conversation. Pretending to be fiddling with something on the tablet, I concentrate on the voices outside.

"—heard you've been asking questions around here," Pastor Linton is saying. "Thought we might be able to answer them so you can be on your way."

"We also heard you were poking around Old Sheldon Church," Dad puts in.

"Sightseeing," says a light male voice with a hint of a British accent. "That place has quite the history."

"It's an important site, wouldn't you say?" Another man's voice, quieter and sleeker somehow. More dangerous. "We just want to ensure that it's being well maintained. We heard there's a group around here that's in charge of keeping an eye on it."

"That would be us. Our church," says Pastor Linton.

"Ah. Then maybe you can tell me if there have been unexpected disturbances or anything out of the ordinary—"

"For god's sake, Gatsby, just say it." Exasperation bleeds through a third voice, a girl's. "Look, priests, ministers, whatever you are—have you seen any weird supernatural shit? Wolves made out of sticks, clouds of black moths, apparitions, illusions? Signs that the god underneath the church is less than dormant?"

There's a silence so thick, I swear I could cut it in slices.

Then Pastor Linton speaks, his voice so warm and gooey and reassuring it makes me want to puke. "I don't know what you've heard, but everything is quiet and peaceful here."

"Really?" challenges the same girl. "Because when Dorian and I lived in Charleston, it was anything but quiet and peaceful. And we heard a rumor that there had been sightings here, too—maybe even deaths? They might look like animal attacks, but they're not."

In my mind's eye, I see the church lobby—Pastor Linton's

anxious face and the worried, almost haunted expressions of the deacons.

Pastor Linton is lying to these strangers, whoever they are. Something bad *has* happened around here. He just doesn't want to tell them about it.

"We don't associate much with the Charleston branch," says Dad.

Pastor Linton makes a startled, reproachful sound, but Dad continues.

"They already know, Mark. It's pointless to pretend we don't understand what they're talking about. As I was saying...the watchers in Charleston lost their faith. They stopped taking their mission as seriously as they should, and frankly, that's their problem, not ours. But we have things well in hand here. Not that it's any of your business."

A fourth voice speaks, feminine and musical and so entrancing, I instinctively strain to catch every word. "You say it's their problem, but if actual gods start to rise, wouldn't that be everyone's problem?"

"Well, I suppose..." begins Pastor Linton.

"Were you aware that the god Manannán was recently set free?" The girl's voice is softly compelling, slithering through my ears into my brain and coiling there. "Tell me the truth."

I want desperately to answer her, to have the information she needs, but I don't, so I press my lips together and stay put. There's a long pause before Pastor Linton speaks, slowly and reluctantly, as if the words are being forced out of him. "We heard something like that, yes. But there have been no sightings of him, no great works or terrible catastrophes."

"And why do you think that is?" continues the girl in her gentle tones.

"Because the gods need each other," Pastor grits out. "They function as a clan, as a family. No god can attain their true power without the active presence of others in the pantheon and without the faith and worship of human beings."

"Cathy?" Aunt Nellie's raised voice travels across the store, and I startle. I guess I'm done eavesdropping for now.

"Sorry, just…had a problem with the app," I call to her, and I push through the side door into the bright October afternoon.

"What can I get you?" I say breezily to the group.

"Not now, Cathy," Dad snaps.

Pastor Linton notches a finger into his shirt collar, tugging as if it's too tight. He and Dad are the only two standing; the rest are seated, relaxed.

Swiftly, I scan the group, trying to guess whose voices I heard. There's a young woman my age, wearing shorts that show off her long, tattooed legs. Beside her lounges a tall blond man— stunningly pretty, like a twenty on a scale from one to ten. His blue eyes linger on the tattooed girl with such warmth that I instantly know they're together.

Next, there's a man with a serious, handsome face and brown hair. The fourth member of the group is a blond woman who turns to me, smiles, and says, in a light, bright tone, "Cathy."

In her mouth, my name isn't just a word—it's a bell, a clarion call. *Cathy, Cathy, Cathy…* It echoes in my head, shivers in my bones, vibrates my blood louder, louder, until my entire skull is ringing with her voice.

Cathy, Cathy, Cathy…

I drop the tablet and clamp both hands to my head. "Stop," I gasp. "Make it stop!"

"Cathy!" Dad snaps. He hustles in front of me, his bearded bulk serving as a wall between me and the strangers. "Don't lose your shit. Not here," he says, low and furious. "Go pull yourself together. Now."

His voice cracks through the ringing in my head, and it stops. I gasp with relief. "I'm sorry." I pick up the tablet, inwardly groaning at the cracks branching through the glass.

"Oh god, no, don't be sorry," says the blond woman in an entirely different tone. She rises, concern bending her delicate eyebrows. "*I'm* sorry. I thought you were human. I didn't realize my voice would have that effect. What kind of supernatural are you?"

"What are you talking about?" Dad scoffs at her loudly, desperately. "Cathy, go inside."

"What's your gift?" the woman persists.

"Gift?" Pastor Linton's eyes narrow, and he glances at Dad.

My father grips my upper arms so tightly, I wince. "I think you'd all better go now," he declares. "My family owns this business, and we have the right to refuse service to anyone. You aren't welcome here."

The pretty blond man laughs, lazily getting to his feet. "I've been kicked out of shittier places. Come on. We got what we came for." He grabs the hand of the tattooed woman, and she follows him to the BMW.

Past Dad's shoulder, I catch the eye of the blond woman. She's still staring at me, like she sees right down to the screaming, howling, tempest-torn core of my spirit.

"Daisy," says the brown-haired man softly, laying a hand on

her arm. With a final sympathetic glance in my direction, she goes with him to the Rivian, and both cars glide out of the parking lot and disappear down the road.

Dad squeezes my arms until I whimper, then shoves me away. "Get inside, Cathy."

As the side door closes behind me, I hear Pastor Linton say, "Bob, we need to talk."

Shit. He heard what that girl said about my gift. He *knows*. All these years of cleverly hiding the secret, and now...now it's just out. Naked. Exposed. And that can only mean trouble for me.

"Who were those people?" Aunt Nellie calls across the store, handing off a bag to a customer.

"Five-minute break," I gasp in response.

I cut through the storage room and out the back doors of the building. That blond's voice set my skin crawling again, and so soon after my last episode, too. But there's no name or fate or vision attached to the sensation—just a relentless scrabbling and squirming right under my skin, wriggling through my flesh. I hope it subsides. If not, I might have to fuck Edgar Linton on our first date, just to get some relief.

I walk quickly, cutting across the gravel area behind the store, hurrying through the grass into the belt of trees beyond. I'm not sure why trees are such a refuge for me. There's something steady and sheltering about them—something that sings to the core of what I am—the long-lost daughter of a green isle far away, descendant of the wild gods who once walked the world.

Breaking into a half sob, I run until I find a tall maple. I embrace it, press my forehead to it, scrape my bruised arms against its gray bark as if that will relieve my torment.

In the rustling quiet of the woods, someone speaks. "Don't be afraid."

At the words, I yelp and spin around, my back to the tree.

The tall, serious man who drove the Rivian is pacing cautiously toward me, one hand extended. The pale golden light of the autumn afternoon shimmers through the leafless trees, glinting in his brown hair and glancing off a thick silver bracelet on his wrist.

"I'm not going to hurt you," he says quietly. "Daisy asked me to give you her phone number. She would have come to you herself, but she didn't want her voice to affect you again."

I see it now, the slip of folded paper between two of his fingers. "Why does she want me to have her number?"

"Because you're one of us—or something similar. I don't know your situation, but it seems like you could use someone to talk to. If not now, then later. Please take it. Text Daisy anytime." He hesitates, puckering his lips briefly. "I've always had trouble asking for help. I like to do things on my own. But sometimes you need other people around you, people who get what you're going through."

"Like any of you could understand," I whisper. Angry tears pool in my eyes, but I'm not really mad at him, just mad at everything—mad at my curse, at my dad, at the unpredictability of my life.

He shrugs. "Maybe we can't understand. But we can listen. Daisy's a great listener." He smiles, affection in his eyes. He loves her.

For some reason that gives me enough courage to reach out and pluck the paper from between his fingers. "Fine. But you should go. My dad always has a gun in his car, and he'll use it if he sees you out here."

Instead of looking alarmed, the man flashes a grin. His canines are unusually long and sharp. "I'd like to see him try. Listen, if you hear of anything strange going on—monsters in the woods, people being attacked by something mysterious, disturbances at Old Sheldon Church—text or call, would you?"

"So now I'm your informant? I thought you wanted to help me."

"Who said help can't be reciprocal? Take care, Cathy."

"What's your name?" I ask as he's turning away.

He turns back, giving me a smile that warms me right down to my bones. "I'm Jay Gatsby."

Then he's off, running through the forest at a pace that would astonish an Olympic track star.

I'm physically shaken and my legs are wobbling, so after a second, I sit right down in the crunchy fall leaves, trying to understand what just happened.

Best to start with the largest truths, like I'd begin with the biggest pieces when I'm arranging a sales display for the store.

First, there are other supernaturals. I knew that much, though I've never met any. That's the one big truth blaring at the front of my mind right now. *One of us*, Gatsby said. One of *what*, exactly? What is he? And his girlfriend, Daisy—what is she? She's got some kind of voice power, that much is obvious.

Second, whatever the strangers might be, it's clear they're concerned about the integrity of the god's burial site beneath Old Sheldon Church. They're worried something might be happening, and they want to be sure the leadership of Wicklow Heritage Chapel has it under control. Objectively that's a more concerning, more important fact, but I'm still mind-blown that I just met people with supernatural gifts. People like *me*.

Third fact: Pastor Linton, my dad, and the other deacons are hiding something terrible. Pastor lied to the strangers because he thinks the church can handle the situation on our own or because he doesn't want outside interference. Or maybe both.

Fourth, unless my dad can talk his way out of it somehow, Pastor Linton now knows I've got a supernatural ability.

All of these facts, taken together, mean that my life as I know it is over. Not that it was great to begin with, but it's about to get a hell of a lot worse.

I allow myself five minutes. Just five minutes to freak out, to try to cope with what I heard, what just happened, what might happen next. And then I stand up straight, and I do what I've always done—force myself to walk in the direction I need to go, no matter how scary or uncomfortable it may be. I walk straight back to Aunt Nellie's, back to the café counter to clean up and close it down. Dad is gone, and so is Pastor Linton, so at least I'm spared from facing them right away.

As I work, I notice Aunt Nellie watching me, glancing at me now and then—keen looks, like you give a person when you've learned some new piece of information about them that enlightens you about their whole personality. But she doesn't say anything, only smiles brightly at customers and tells me what needs doing in her usual pleasant tones.

I can't be sure she knows anything; maybe it's all in my head. But as I finish out my shift that afternoon, a pit of resentment slowly condenses in my stomach because she has the luxury to pretend the problems in my life don't exist. Like she did when Mom left. Like she did when she dropped by once and found Dad clearly hungover and me with a bruised wrist. Like she has done every time I've had to leave work for "health reasons." She can ignore my pain and go on like everything's fine. And she acts perfectly nice, always, but she never really digs into my life to find out where I hurt. If we get too close to any sensitive topics, she ends the conversation by turning away briskly and throwing me a bright smile.

I've always hated people who can smile, and smile, and be silent, even when you most need them to speak.

But maybe I hate that about her because I do the same thing. I smile and fake it every day of my life, just like I'm doing right now. All the new information racing around in my brain, the new number saved in my phone, and yet I'm working like usual, right up until the store closes. And fuck it, I'm going on my date tonight, as long as Edgar doesn't cancel on me.

When I leave at six and Aunt Nellie says, "Have a good night," I respond just as brightly, "You too!"

And we smile at each other, masks firmly in place. Heaven forbid they should ever slip.

7

CATHY

I CAN SENSE IT THE SECOND I WALK IN THE DOOR.

The roar of football on the TV. The clink of a bottle being set down too close to another. The creak of the old recliner. The smell of greasy fried chicken, of green beans swimming in salty water, of hush puppies and barbecue. The blinds on the narrow window by the front door are closed tight because my dad is a respected man in Wicklow and he can't let anybody know about his secret vice.

He's binge-drinking. Which means it's a good night to be out of the house.

It's not hard to guess what brought this on. The appearance of supernatural strangers in Wicklow shook him up. Not to mention the fact that Pastor Linton now knows there's something supernatural about me. And maybe he's more worried about the god's grave than he let on.

I've always known the god was real, that something slept beneath Old Sheldon Church. I've been told the story ever since I was little, how the gods of Ireland, the Tuatha Dé Danann, fled to this continent, weary from battling with men and their new religions. Eventually most of the Tuatha Dé Danann chose mortality or were forced into sleep beneath the earth.

Years later, when the slumbering Tuatha Dé Danann began to stir again, Protestants and Catholics banded together and built structures of iron and stone over their tombs—military complexes and churches. They appointed some of the faithful to keep watch over those sites throughout future generations.

I knew all of this, even before the manifestation of my banshee side made it impossible to doubt the reality of the supernatural. But hearing strangers talk about it openly today made it twice as real and ten times as frightening. They mentioned an actual god already being raised, walking around free...Mana-something. I'll have to look it up later. One god isn't at full strength without the others, apparently, so as long as our congregation keeps the faith and does our duty, the god under Old Sheldon Church should stay dormant.

I hope Pastor Linton and the deacons have everything under control, but I can't stop remembering the worried looks on their faces last Sunday. I want to ask Dad what made them so scared, but I'm not sure I should.

I venture into the living room doorway to assess his mood. Sometimes, when he's buzzed, he'll tell me things. I have to catch him at the right moment, when he's feeling warm and blurry, before he gets mean and dangerous.

"Hey, Dad," I begin. "I've got a date tonight."

He sits up and turns to look at me, bottle in hand. "Who?"

"Edgar Linton."

"Yeah?" He scratches his chin through his thick beard. "All right."

"Do you think that's okay? I mean, do you think it's a good idea, after what happened today? What Pastor Linton heard from that woman, about me?"

He leans back against the chair. "Won't be a problem. I handled it."

"How?"

"Never you mind. Don't be out too late. And watch your attitude and your mouth when you're with him. He's a good kid. He could sure do better than you."

Right. Because I'm trash. In Dad's mind, my blood is dirty, my body corrupted by a pagan spirit straight out of folklore.

I am my father's greatest shame, living proof of the ancient powers he has devoted himself to suppressing. That's why he hates me. That's why he never follows me into the woods to make sure I'm okay—because he hopes that one of these nights, I won't come back. He wants me to die.

It's a shitty way to live, knowing you're an inconvenience to the man who's supposed to love you.

"And don't drink tonight," Dad says without looking at me. "I don't want you spilling secrets to young Linton, not after I patched things up with his dad. Matter of fact, maybe you shouldn't go after all. It's not like you can really date the boy or marry him. Can't marry nobody, can you?"

My fingers ball into fists. "It's dinner, not even really a date. We're just going to catch up. I'll make sure it doesn't go any further than that."

Dad scoffs and chugs half a beer before replying. "Sure, Cat. I believe you. You're so damn trustworthy."

When he drinks, he allows himself to swear. I don't mind that so much, but when the swearing starts, the yelling and hitting aren't far behind.

I decide to risk a few more questions. "Those people at Aunt Nellie's today—what were they talking about? Are we in danger?"

"No," he barks, too suddenly, too sharply.

So the real answer is yes, then.

"Did someone get hurt?"

He drinks again, exhales a long breath. "Macauley and Quinn went out to do the consecration walk and sprinkle blessed water a few nights ago. They were found with about a thousand sticks stabbed through each of their bodies."

"Sticks?"

"Yes, Cathy, sticks! Like the damn forest itself thought they were pincushions." He gulps from his bottle and crosses himself with a meaty hand.

No way. If that had really happened, I would have seen those deaths. I would have mourned those men. Unless...unless they were hidden from me somehow. Maybe the nature of the deaths made them beyond my ability to perceive. Like their connection to the god messes with my supernatural death radar. A scary thought. We'll have no warning if it happens again.

"You going on that date or what?" says my dad. "Get on upstairs and fix yourself. You still look like shit from your last crying jag."

He's moving into aggressive territory, so I obey quickly.

Once I'm ready, I wait for Edgar on the porch, hoping Dad will think I've already left. Moths jitter and dive around the porch light as I settle onto the swing, careful not to move too much and make the chains squeak. This stretch of Wuthering Lane is usually pitch-dark at night, except when there's a moon. Tonight the pale disc is scarred with thick gray clouds.

I stretch out my legs, pleased that I can't see any trace of the bruises and cuts from my forest wanderings a few nights ago. I'm wearing high-tops, cranberry-colored shorts, and a soft, baggy tan sweater. Nothing that would scandalize the pastor's son too terribly.

Like Dad said, there's no future for me and someone like Edgar, even if I wanted one. But his softness and kindness appeal to me. He's sweet. A good, safe guy. I never feel safe, and I *need* safe right now.

Scratch that—I *did* feel safe recently. Safe enough to fall asleep in the arms of Heathcliff Lockwood.

I shake my head as if the act could dislodge him from my mind. Sure, Heathcliff helped me get home, but then he said all those weird, semi-threatening things. I can't get a read on him at all. All I can do is hope that he won't tell anyone my secret.

When a car finally rolls into our driveway, I force my teeth to release my lower lip. There's blood on it. I gotta quit chewing on myself when I'm anxious. If I'm not biting my nails, I'm gnawing my lip or chomping the inside of my cheek. I probably need therapy or some shit.

I jump off the swing, brace it with my hand so it won't sway and squeak, and then run down the steps to Edgar Linton's Nissan. He hops out of the car and practically trips over his own feet trying to get around to the passenger side and open the door for me. I chuckle and slide in. "Thanks."

"Sure, Cathy."

While we drive, he tells me about his mission work in Zambia, which apparently involved touring orphanages, handing out food and supplies, painting some houses, and then going on a safari and staying in a luxury hotel.

He doesn't ask what I've been up to. I guess he can tell my life has been fairly stagnant—a twenty-two-year-old stuck here in Wicklow, living with Dad and working at Aunt Nellie's. Still, it bothers me that he doesn't ask.

Moretti's doesn't take reservations, but it's the middle of the week, so there are plenty of empty booths. The hostess shows us to one near the bar. As I slide onto the faux-leather bench seat, I eye the shining emerald and amber bottles behind the bar, wondering if I dare order alcohol. Does Edgar drink now? He never used to, but he was underage when we last hung out.

He doesn't reach for the wine list, and when the server comes by, he orders water, so I do, too.

When the server leaves, my gaze flicks to the bar again and immediately fixes on a new arrival who has just settled onto a counter stool—a figure with long, denim-clad legs and a super-hero breadth to his shoulders beneath his red-and-black flannel shirt. His hair is glossy black, slicked back but still voluminous, as if he tried to tame the unruly waves but couldn't quite manage it.

Wait, I know the tattoos on that brown forearm.

Oh, fuck.

Heathcliff is here.

Is he actually stalking me? How else would he end up at Moretti's on the very night of my date with Edgar?

"Cathy?"

I yank my attention back to Edgar. He's looking at me expectantly, like he just said something and wants me to reply.

"Sorry. I zoned out for a minute. Long day. Could you repeat whatever you just said?" I give him my best Cathy Earnshaw smile, the one I've been told gives Natalie Dormer vibes. I wasn't sure who that was until three different men mentioned the resemblance and I finally looked her up, which resulted in me binge-watching *The Tudors*.

The smile seems to work on Edgar. He lights up and leans forward. "I just asked if you'd read any good devotionals lately."

"Oh, um...I'm pretty busy. Not much time for reading."

"Oh. I can recommend a few..." And he begins listing off titles. I nod, pretending to commit them to memory. In reality, everything merges into a saccharine slurry of words like *light*, *water*, *honey*, *daily*, *beautiful*, *wisdom*, and *growth* interspersed with the authors' names.

During Edgar's speech, someone comes up behind Heathcliff and taps his shoulder. Heathcliff turns to greet him—and sees me.

A thrill races over my body as his dark eyes lock with mine.

Then he turns away, casually resuming his position at the bar, only now he's slightly angled toward the newcomer, who settles in beside him and orders a drink.

So Heathcliff isn't here stalking me. He's meeting someone. The guy's wearing a suit and he's got a leather briefcase. Wonder what kind of meeting it is.

Shit, I'm ignoring Edgar again. I smile encouragingly and nod, then quickly adjust my expression to one of sympathy as I tune in and realize he's telling me that one of the devotional authors he mentioned is actually the founder of the group he worked with in Zambia. Something about bringing relief to starving children.

"That's amazing," I murmur, scanning the menu. "Oh, look, they have calzones."

Right after I say it, I realized how callous that sounded. *Poor starving kids—look, calzones! Really, Cathy?*

"Sorry," I gasp. "That was so awful of me."

Edgar's warm blue eyes meet mine, sympathetic and kind. "It's okay. I know you didn't mean it like that. You're a good person, Cathy. You should come with me on a mission trip sometime—as part of the group," he adds quickly.

"Isn't it expensive?"

"You have to raise some of the money, sure, but then sponsors pay the rest."

"Oh, cool. Well...maybe."

"I'll text you the link to apply!" He shifts, reaching for his back pocket, then shakes his head. "I almost forgot—no phones at the table. A personal rule of mine. I'll text it later."

"Wonderful." I hold my smile in place and allow myself a tiny glance at Heathcliff's broad back. I'm weirdly tempted to run over, wrap my arms around his neck, and beg him to carry me out of the restaurant piggyback-style.

What is *wrong* with me?

When the server arrives with bread and butter, Edgar makes several inquiries about the source of the meat and fish, then orders a Caesar salad. He's giving me a look, and I don't know if it means *Don't support unsustainably sourced food, Cathy* or *Order whatever you want, Cathy*, so I opt for the middle ground and order a pepperoni calzone.

Heathcliff is deep in conversation with the businessman at the bar. He hasn't looked over his shoulder once. I mean, I didn't expect him to come over and say hi, but to not even *glance* at me after that first look...

"I'm going to the bathroom." I snatch my napkin out of my lap, pitch it onto the table, and slide out of the booth.

The door to the back hallway is beyond the bar, which means I get to walk right past Heathcliff. I cut as close to him as I dare and give my hips a little extra sway as I head for the restrooms.

The rear hallway is isolated, separate from the kitchen entrance. There are three doors—bathrooms for men, women, and all genders. On the wall hangs a large board with concert posters and service ads pinned to it. The men's bathroom is at the far end of the hall, its sign barely discernible because one of overhead lights is out.

I head into the women's restroom, but I don't really have to pee, so I just run my fingers through my curls for a couple seconds and check my chewed lip in the mirror. Then I head back out into the hallway...just as Heathcliff strides down it.

My heart soars up and lands in my throat, choking off my breath. I shift aside to let him pass, but he grabs my shoulders and shoves me into the single-stall, multigender bathroom. He kicks the door shut and turns the lock.

"What the fuck are you doing?" I whisper-yell at him.

Silently he crowds me back against the wall, plants tattooed hands on either side of my head, and stares me down.

My pulse is rocket fast, and the millions of nerves across my skin are all screaming at once, demanding to touch him or be touched by him.

He leans in, his breath hot against my face. "So that's your type? That soft little preacher boy?"

"Edgar is a gentleman. Something you'll never be."

Heathcliff laughs roughly. "No shit."

"If you've got something to say, say it," I hiss. "Is this some kind of intimidation tactic? You trying to scare me, threaten me?"

The humor leaves his eyes. "You're still worried I'm gonna tell your secret. I won't."

The weight in his tone settles my heart. I'm not sure I should believe him, but I do. "All right." I nod, expecting him to back off.

He doesn't move, and my heart rate ratchets up again. He ducks his head, his lips and nose skimming the waves of my hair. When he speaks, it's low, resonant. "Did you keep that pussy wet for me, Cathy?"

God, yes. "You're such a creep. Let me go."

"You wanna walk out, go. I'm not touching you. Not gonna keep you here."

He might not be touching me, but he's holding me captive with his presence, with the beauty of those magnificent arms, with the surge of his heavy breath under that plaid shirt and the visible swell of his dick against the zipper of his jeans. He's trapping me with his musky, spicy scent and with that sarcastic, seductive mouth.

"I'm not going to fuck you while I'm on a date with Edgar," I whisper savagely.

"Then when?"

"Never."

"Huh. I thought you were the kind of woman who does what she wants."

"I don't *want* to fuck you."

His body surges forward, and I gasp. He's still not touching me but there's scarcely a finger's width between his chest and mine.

His hips sway nearer, the bulge between his legs almost brushing my lower belly. "Liar," he breathes. "You want me so bad, you can hardly think about anything else."

Swallowing hard, I picture Edgar Linton waiting for me at our table, waiting while I yank down my shorts and bend over for Heathcliff, while he pumps that thick cock into me again... Fuck. If I weren't on a date right now...

But I *am* on a date.

I can be catty, selfish, bitter, and judgmental. But I have standards, and also I have willpower, born from years of controlling my banshee side, guiding my own wanderings despite every compulsive instinct.

This is a line I won't cross.

I tip my face up until my lips almost touch Heathcliff's, until his eyes go unfocused with desire and anticipation.

Then I duck under his arm, unlock the door, and leave the bathroom.

I regret the choice instantly. I have to sit across from Edgar, thinking about what Heathcliff and I could have done in that bathroom, enduring the slickness between my thighs, watching Heathcliff stalk back into the main room and resume his conversation with the man at the bar. I should have asked him who the man is. Not that he'd have answered.

Heathcliff doesn't look at me again the whole rest of the time he's there—a kindness, I think. He's respecting my decision. But that doesn't stop me from *wanting* him to look. That doesn't stop me from feeling him there across the room, from regretting every second I'm not back in that bathroom with him, dragging my nails across his strong shoulders.

Heathcliff leaves when Edgar and I are halfway through our meal. With his absence, the restaurant is gutted—no longer a place of cozy warmth, vibrant light, and entrancing smells. It's hollow now—dull carpet, bland food, and the vacant eyes of uninteresting people.

"Enough about me." Edgar's smile blooms again, but his eyes don't have the same purity and sincerity; they're sharper now. "Let's talk about you! My dad mentioned you've had some health struggles?"

Shit. Now I have to perpetuate the lie, talk about the conditions I supposedly have but know very little about. "Um, yeah. Walking seizures. They're also called focal awareness seizures. And I'm bipolar." I know I'm being insensitive to people who live with epilepsy and bipolar disorder by attaching the terms to myself just to cover my ass, but I don't know what else to do, short of blurting out that I'm a banshee who gets uncontrollable fits of grief and has to wander the woods for hours until it stops.

"Is that what happened at church the other day?" Edgar's aqua gaze bores into mine. "Isn't it better to stay around other people if you're going to have a seizure? So they can put something under your head and stuff? Keep you from hurting yourself?"

Yes, Edgar, that would make more sense. "My condition is… unusual. I don't really like talking about it."

"Sure, I understand." His hand slides across the table, covers mine. "But do you talk to *anyone* about it? Maybe it would help to share the burden with someone. I've been told I'm an excellent listener."

Something in his eyes—a keenness, an awareness—

I pull my hand away. "Did Pastor Linton ask you to talk to me about this?"

The answer flickers in his eyes—he's not a good enough liar to hide it, and he has the grace to know that.

Pastor Linton got a pretty strong hint about me from Daisy and her group this afternoon, and I'm guessing whatever Dad said didn't satisfy him. Edgar and his dad had time to talk about it between then and now. I'll bet they decided to turn a simple dinner date into an investigation of my possible supernatural status.

"Dad is concerned about you," Edgar says.

"So he asked you to pry into my life."

"It's not like that, Cathy. I'm here to help. Anything you need, seriously. A listening ear, a ride to your doctor's office. I could even offer you a counseling session. Maybe I can help you find ways to cope, some verses to memorize…"

Is he for real? Acting in the role of counselor or therapist would be totally out of line after he's shown a romantic interest in me. And memorizing *Bible verses* as a palliative for the serious conditions I've mentioned? Really?

This was a mistake.

"I have to go." I grab my purse and scoot out of the booth. "Thanks for dinner."

"Cathy." He jumps up too and clutches my arm. "Cathy, can we just talk about this?"

When his fingers tighten, I jerk away, recoiling with a sharp panic that sends my butt crashing into the table behind me. Silverware rattles, and everyone in the vicinity looks up from their meals.

Edgar pulls his hand back, a shocked look on his face.

Hitching my purse strap higher on my shoulder, I walk out of the restaurant into the night. It's cold, but a few insects still sing among the black trees.

I shouldn't have panicked like that. Edgar isn't Dad. He wasn't going to hurt me. Still, I can't bear the thought of sitting with him a second longer or letting him drive me home. Not that he's running after me to offer.

I march across the parking lot toward the street. Why did I wear shorts in October, at night? I guess I could call an Uber or something, but that's money I can't spare. I'll walk home. It'll take maybe an hour, but I'll get there.

I should have stayed in the restaurant booth and gently redirected Edgar to a safer topic of conversation. By flying off the handle, I just confirmed any suspicions he and his father might have that I'm hiding something.

Heathcliff was wrong about the folks at Wicklow Chapel, though. Even if they discovered what I am, they wouldn't kill me. Kick me and Dad out of the church, maybe. Shun us. Nothing more drastic than that.

They aren't murderers. Of course they're not. I've known them all my life. This is modern-day America. No witch hunts, no burning the devil's children at the stake, no burying me in the earth like the demon. I'm safe. Everything is fine.

If only I could be sure. If only I could have listened in on Pastor Linton's conversation with Edgar. I desperately want to know what they know or what they suspect. I can't shake the memory of what Heathcliff told me—that the people of this town kill supernaturals. That can't be true, or they would have killed the four visitors at Aunt Nellie's. Of course that was a public place, too many witnesses...

I have to stop thinking like this. I'll drive myself insane.

I'm walking quickly just to stay warm, trudging along the edge of the narrow, lightless road. My boots scuff the grass, and chilly air whispers around my legs. The row of trees ends abruptly, revealing a wide, grassy meadow, a dark sea that stretches over low, swelling hills before yielding to forest again.

The primal side of me, the banshee side, loves fields like this almost as much as she loves forests. The urge to run through that meadow hammers against my bones. I wouldn't be roaming in grief this time but in freedom. In some ancient era, an ancestor of mine walked the broad moors with windblown hair, arms lifted to billowing gray skies, laughing in the face of an oncoming storm. I am myself, but I am her, too.

But the world is caged now. Fences along roads, every acre assigned. Every tree has an owner, and the wild places are shrinking.

Impulsively I run down the slope into the ditch beside the road, then up the bank to the wire fence bordering the meadow. I'll climb over it and get into that grass. I'm going to run through it and feel the cold breeze slamming against my cheeks, diving deep into my lungs. There's a tattered moon coming into view overhead, and I want to dance beneath it.

I'm reaching for the wire when light slices the darkness of the road, two beams like pale arrows.

A pickup truck roars past, then slows. Its engine noise fades to a growl, then cuts off as it pulls over.

I hesitate, torn between the impulse to go back to the road like a normal person and resume my walk, or to clamber over the fence and run into the wilderness like a startled deer.

A big, masculine silhouette saunters around the truck. I recognize that walk, the outline of those shoulders.

"Cathy, what the fuck are you doing?" demands Heathcliff.

I vent a hysterical giggle because I asked him that very question not one hour ago. "Are you following me?"

A pause. "Yes."

The admission releases a bit of tension inside me. I'm not imagining it. He likes me. More than likes me. He might be a tad obsessed, and why is that so hot?

"Get in the truck, Cathy."

When I don't answer, he crosses his arms. "Don't make me come down there. Get your ass in the truck *now*. I'm taking you home."

Home. My memory conjures images of Dad's purple, snarling face, his meaty hand crashing against my cheek, his fingers forcing my mouth open, sliding a butcher knife between my teeth. "I don't want to go home."

"Fine. Where do you want to go?"

The words leap out before I can make sense of them. "To Pastor Linton's house."

"Why? So you can make up with your milk-sop date and jump on his limp dick?"

"No." I traverse the ditch and pass Heathcliff, yanking open the passenger door of his truck. "So I can spy on them."

8

HEATHCLIFF

OF ALL THE THINGS I PLANNED TO DO TONIGHT, SLINKING through the trees at the edge of the Lintons' property wasn't one of them. Meeting with a guy about a private business venture I'm starting—sure. Fucking Cathy Earnshaw—if I was lucky enough. But *this*? I got enough shit to deal with. Don't need to add trespassing to the list.

But Cathy seems determined to sneak up to the house. She takes off, out of the trees, running half-bent across the lawn until she's right under the bright rectangle of an open window. Swearing under my breath, I follow her, pressing myself against the siding as well. A few bugs dance over our heads, drawn to the light and warmth, bouncing off the screen. I swat one away and curse. Cathy clamps small fingers over my mouth and I go still, my dick instantly hard.

Does she know what she does to me? I'm furious, raging with lust, but at a word from her, I'd go boneless in a second, just melt into a sacrificial puddle right here at her feet.

Voices drift through the window, growing clearer. A fridge opens.

"I scared her off. I'm not sure she'll give me another chance." That's young Linton. Edgar.

"Is she going to that picnic thing this weekend, on the Fitzpatricks' beach?" That's his dad, the pastor.

"I don't know."

"Text her tomorrow. Apologize for prying and ask her to come on Saturday. We need to understand what's going on. She might be a threat...or she might be able to help."

Cathy's fingers loosen over my mouth. Don't tell me she's buying into this whole "helpful pastor" act. I've seen plenty of holier-than-thou do-gooders in my day. Narcissists, most of 'em, addicted to the hit of self-righteousness they get when they think they're "fixing" someone. They'd never admit it, but they get off on being the leader, the master, the one who's *better*, who's got it together, while the rest of us are red clay to be lifted out of the ground and formed into something useful, into neat red bricks with which they can build their stairway to heaven.

"Those people who came to Aunt Nellie's—any idea what they were?" Edgar asks.

His dad sighs loudly. "One of them has some kind of voice power. The others—I'm not sure, except the brown-haired guy is faster than he should be. The way he moves isn't natural. And did you see his teeth? Like fangs. The girl with the voice had them, too. Abhartach, maybe...vampires."

In the dim light, I exchange startled looks with Cathy.

"Those aren't supposed to exist anymore," Edgar says.

"I don't know, son. I don't have all the answers. And we can't be sure if these folks are trying to resurrect the demon themselves or if they're actually concerned about keeping him quiet."

"But they talked to *our* people, not the Lockwoods. If anyone is working to resurrect the demon, it would be the Lockwoods, right?"

"The Lockwoods and the LeGares try this and that every few years, but those backwoods hicks can never get organized enough to do any real damage. They're a bunch of drunken, inbred blowhards without the intelligence to go head-to-head with us. They've lost the knowledge of their ancestors. To be fair, we've lost a lot of knowledge, too. If there was a way to seal that tomb more effectively, to be *sure* he can't rise..."

"I can do some research," Edgar offers. "I've done plenty over the past four years, but there's always more to learn. If you'd agree to broadening our research beyond Irish folklore, into other cultures—"

"The myths don't mix," the older Linton interrupts.

"There are similarities among myths across many nations," Edgar says. "Mirrored stories with shared elements. Another culture might have helpful information on how to keep a demon buried, how to reinforce the original charms holding him down. If you'd just let me—"

"It's late. Too late to get into all this," his father says firmly. "Go let Judah out, and then get to bed."

In the silence that follows, Cathy's hand drops from my mouth. We're in the shadows, but the light from the window illuminates her features enough for me to see her expression—puzzlement, concern, and a hint of guilt.

She thinks these people might be the good guys. But there's no such thing as good guys—not here and maybe not anywhere. I have to tell her the truth about the leaders of Wicklow Chapel, so she can protect herself. But first, we've got to get out of here. I gesture for her to follow me as I head back across the lawn.

I'm nearly to the trees when a door opens. When I glance back, Cathy is running, fleeing the swath of yellow light. A dog barrels from the doorway where Edgar's slim frame stands silhouetted.

Cathy is racing toward me, her eyes frantic. She makes a leap for me, for the shadow of the forest, but then she screams. The dog's jaws have latched onto her sneaker.

I grab the dog's collar and pull it away, snarling, "Fuck off!" It growls, stiff-legged and threatening, but it seems to recognize I'm willing to do damage if it touches Cathy again.

I scoop her into my arms and run through the woods as fast as I dare. A few minutes of heart-pounding tension, and then we're in the truck, speeding down the road.

"Did the dog get you at all?" I ask.

"Just ruined my shoe, I think. Even if he had, I heal faster than normal people."

"Yeah...why is that, anyway?"

"Well, I'm descended from some old god, right? Some of its regenerative power must still be hanging around in my genes."

"Yeah, I guess." I grip the steering wheel harder. I'm stronger than any human male of my size should be, but I don't have healing powers like she does. My tattoos cover more scars than most people realize.

Cathy's taking off her sweater. Why is she taking off her sweater? Maybe she's hot from running.

I cut another glance at her, liking the way her tank top hugs her breasts. She leans over, unlacing her sneaker, probably to check her ankle and make sure the dog's teeth didn't punch through to her skin. I glance down too, but her ankle is in shadow, and I can't tell if there's any damage. I try to focus on the road, but my gaze is magnetized by the curve of her neck, the little bumps of bone along her spine, the soft tumble of her curly, brown hair.

"Eyes forward, Heathcliff," she snaps, and I whip my attention back to the road just in time to brake and turn for a sharp curve.

"Honestly. Men." She scoffs a little and rolls down the window a crack, angling her face toward the cool air. "So about what we heard back there... Are you Lockwoods trying to raise the god under Old Sheldon Church?"

She says it so matter-of-factly, like every word of that sentence is normal.

No use pretending I haven't heard stories of the god trapped under the church. I'm familiar with the legend, and I've heard the Coosaw Lockwoods talk about stirring him up. Apparently folks have tried, in each generation, but the magical barrier keeps out everyone with a drop of Lockwood blood.

"Are they trying to resurrect the god?" Cathy persists.

"Nope."

"You said the church leaders like Pastor Linton kill supernaturals. But they don't sound like murderers. I think they're decent people. Weirdly religious, sure...but decent. Don't you think so?"

"No."

"Explain." Frustration edges her tone. "You're so cryptic and silent."

"As opposed to Edgar, who talks plenty. About himself."

"At least he has something to say. You're just...a lot of nothing."

"I have things to say. I'm just not sure how to say it in a way you'll believe."

"Try me."

"Fine." I blow out a breath. "You and I live in the same area. Wicklow and Kinsale aren't that many miles apart—two little towns, not much by way of population. But you've never met a Lockwood before me, right? Not from Coosaw or from Kinsale. You and I went to different schools growing up, and we never crossed paths. Doesn't that seem weird to you?"

"I guess...maybe..."

"There's a spell in place. A barrier that keeps Lockwoods from coming into Wicklow. Keeps out a couple other families, too—the LeGares and the Byrnes. They can't get near your chapel or Old Sheldon Church. That's why I took care of the delivery to your aunt's store for my brother, Hindley. He can't physically go there. I couldn't cross the barrier either until I turned twenty-one. Even though I'm adopted, I counted as one of the Lockwoods until I became a legal adult in every sense. Whoever set up that barrier did some high-level magical shit to keep us out."

She nods, seeming to accept what I've told her. "Why, though? I mean...I know the barrier is there to keep your family from resurrecting the god, but why would you even *want* to raise him?"

"Are you kidding? The raising of a god means a power boost for supernaturals, for anyone with inherited gifts, like yours." I delve into memories of Meemaw's stories, uprooting facts I'd nearly forgotten until now. "If you raise one or two gods, they'll eventually fade without the worship of humans and the support of a pantheon. But if you can raise three of them...well, that shit can change the world as we know it."

Cathy pulls on her sweater again and shuts the window. "So the Lockwoods and those other families you mentioned, they want a power boost. Which means they're supernaturals. They have gifts?"

I glance over at her. She's staring at me, her brown eyes wide.

"They are, aren't they?" she breathes. "Heathcliff. Are you... some kind of supernatural?"

"Yeah."

"Oh god." She covers her mouth. "What are you?"

"Can't tell you that, Earnshaw. Family secret."

"But you're adopted."

"They're still my family. We have the same gift." I take a corner faster than I should, and Cathy gasps. "It's safer if you don't know, okay? Not that anywhere is safe around here, especially not for supernaturals. The Wicklow folks come and go through the barrier whenever they want. And they kill off any supernaturals who happen to settle in Wicklow, Kinsale, Coosaw, or anywhere they deem too close for comfort. For the past decade, they've left us alone, mostly. We Lockwoods may fight like dogs among ourselves, but we protect each other against outsiders."

"I still don't believe they're murderers." Her voice trembles a little.

"About four years ago, three young supernaturals moved to Kinsale. Their gifts were all new...a resurgence in their families. Two kelpies and a clurichaun. They were just looking for someone who believed in the old lore and might have information about how to survive in the modern world with those kinds of powers." I pause, thinking of the girl in that trio—sleek black hair and beautiful eyes. I slept with her once. Might have done more if...

I clear my throat. "Yeah, your 'decent people' put together a posse and killed them. None since then...but if I'd called myself a

Lockwood when I walked into your church the other day, I'd have been shot on the steps the second I left the building."

"But you came anyway," Cathy says quietly. "You came to see me."

The gentleness in her tone makes me flinch, slams the gates shut around my heart. I don't do gentle or sweet. I'm fucking toxic and I own up to that. The sooner she realizes it, the better.

"I was curious," I answer in a casual tone. "I did meet another cute girl there, too. Isabella Linton. Nice body. She invited me to some singles thing."

"The beach picnic?" Cathy's voice is cold now.

"Yeah. Might go. See if I can't get the minister's virgin daughter to put out, since you won't."

"Do whatever you want," she says icily. "I'm dating Edgar anyway."

"One date. And you ran away from him tonight—twice."

She bristles. "Just a misunderstanding. I'll fix it. Edgar's nice. He's good for me. Doesn't treat me like a hole to be fucked or a doll to be toted around through the forest."

"Yeah. He just plans to fake apologize so he can take you to the beach and interrogate you some more." Careening into her driveway, I slam the brakes and throw the truck into park. "Next time I see you heading into the woods to do your banshee thing, I won't follow you, not even if you're barefoot and bare-ass naked."

"Nobody asked you to follow me the first time."

"Nope, and I sure as shit won't do it again. Get out of my truck, Earnshaw."

She glances toward the house. One tense, fearful glance. Immediately she shutters the expression, throws me a malicious glare, and hops out of the truck. She eases the door closed instead of slamming it, like I expected. She's scared of something in that house. Doesn't want to make too much noise.

At that realization, every bit of my irritation with her disappears. I'm out of the truck in a blink, striding after her toward the porch. "Earnshaw, stop."

"Go home, Heathcliff."

"I can see you're scared, okay? Hold up! Are you safe here? Do you want—" But I can't invite her home with me. She'd be even less safe at the Grange.

I take the three porch steps in one stride, and when she turns around, I'm right there. She's in my space, I'm in hers, and I can't fucking breathe.

"I said, go home," she hisses. "Leave, before he realizes you're here."

"He?"

The front door opens, and a huge man fills the space. He's got muscle, not just paunch—a real brawler type, even bigger than Hindley. Drunk off his ass, too. And just my luck, he's got a shotgun.

"You Cathy's date?" he slurs. "I thought she was goin' out with that Edgar Linton."

"Oh, um, yeah...Linton's car got a flat, so I brought her home."

"Good Samaritan, eh?" Mr. Earnshaw watches me with narrowed eyes, his thumb stroking the stock of the shotgun. "What's your name, kid? How do you know Edgar?"

I square my shoulders. "I'm Cliff. A friend of his from high school."

"Cliff?" He snorts. "Dumbass name. I got a nose for trouble,

Cliff, and I'm smelling it all over you. So tell you what...why don't you get your ass off my porch before I punch you full of holes?"

"Dad, no!" Cathy steps forward, right into the firing line of the gun. "Cliff is harmless, really. I had such a nice time tonight— don't spoil it."

"Nice time, eh?" Her dad hoists the shotgun again and racks it. "You best git, boy."

Any other time I'd charge him, let him have it, teach him not to frighten his daughter like this. But she's still standing between me and her dad. I can't risk her getting hurt.

"Of course, sir." I hold up both hands and back away, down the steps.

"I don't like you, Cliff," slurs Mr. Earnshaw. "I see you 'round here again, I'll put a bullet in you. Probably more 'n one. I'm friends with the sheriff, see? He'll understand that a man's got a right to defend his land and his daughter's virtue. Get inside, Cathy."

"I'll go in," she says calmly. "After Cliff leaves."

"Hear that, *Cliff*?" barks Earnshaw. "Go on now."

"You have a good night," I say through gritted teeth.

I turn my back to him and force myself to walk to the truck, my spine and shoulders prickling with the awareness that they could get spattered with buckshot any second. It takes everything I've got to climb into my truck, drive away, and leave her there with him.

She has lived with him for years and he hasn't done her permanent harm. She'll be all right. I have to believe she'll be all right.

But this is just one more reason to accelerate the plan I set in motion tonight. I've got to get away from here.

And I'm going to take Cathy with me.

9

CATHY

I HAVEN'T BEEN TO THE BEACH IN AGES. TOO CROWDED, AND there's nowhere to run if I need to mourn, except into the ocean, of course, but families on vacation tend to frown upon girls standing in the waves, screaming and weeping.

This time is going to be different. It's October, not quite as busy along the coast, and the spot where we're gathering is a remote cottage on a large piece of land owned by friends of the Lintons. I think I'll be okay here. I think I can relax and have some fun.

One time, I suggested to Dad that we move far away, to a cabin in the mountains or somewhere I wouldn't ever be triggered. He got mad, told me I didn't understand anything about his responsibility to the church or to Wicklow. When he finally quit ranting and I escaped the room, I decided the mountain cabin plan would never work anyway. I wouldn't want to be trapped there with him.

Trapped... I feel trapped so often, and it's glorious to feel *free* for once. As we crest the dunes and the chilly wind collides with my whole body, I can't hold in my excitement any longer. I drop the towels and the basket I'm carrying for Edgar, leap out of my flip-flops, and run.

It was hot today, and my bare feet fly over sand still warm from the afternoon sun. I race past a stone firepit surrounded by log benches, over the scattered pebbles and chipped shells, onto the smooth, wave-swept sand, into the cold, curling foam of the surf.

A reckless urgency squirms under my skin, and I shuck off my hoodie and my dress as fast as I can, hurling them onto the dry sand. I hesitate for a bare second, glancing at the others along the ridge. They're walking calmly down the path like adults. I've known most of these people all my life, and I've seen them in church countless times, but I wouldn't call any of them friends. They know me, but they don't understand me—never did, even before my curse manifested.

With a rush of manic liberty, I realize that I don't care what any of them think.

Wild and windblown, I laugh at them, and then I turn and wade into the sea.

The water is a frozen shock to my system. My heart rate spikes, my breath catches, and I scream another laugh. The setting sun glitters on the water, paints it rich orange and deep blue, with highlights of pale yellow. I stand upright, toes curling into thick, wet sand, and I run my hand through fringes of foam.

This is glorious. This is everything.

Maybe I should feel bad that I'm not helping everyone set up the food and the fire. But I don't. I wade deeper, relishing the keen slice of cold water around my shins. The wind coils through my hair, tosses it around my shoulders, twirls it into a mess of tangled curls. I wish I were a pirate, standing on the deck of my own ship, headed far, far away from gods and churches and supernatural secrets.

"Cathy!" Linton's voice, thinned by the breeze.

I turn around.

He's on the wet sand, smiling nervously at me.

"It's colder than I thought it would be," he says.

"You never know this time of year," I tell him. "It could be worse. Come on in!"

"And freeze my rear off the rest of the night? No thanks."

I'm about to make a teasing retort when I glimpse a figure behind him, striding forward. Heathcliff's dark eyes hold mine as he pulls off his black T-shirt. He's wearing black swim trunks, too, all his tattoos on full display. The wind ruffles his dark hair as he gives me a villainous smirk.

"I'll take some of that action," he says.

I knew he might be here, half hoped he would be, but he wasn't in the big van that left from church. Come to think of it, neither was Isabella. She must have ridden with Heathcliff in his truck.

The thought makes me unreasonably angry. I give him my most ferocious frown, but that only makes him smile wider.

Edgar stares open-mouthed, like a disapproving fish.

"Your sister invited me." Heathcliff gives Edgar a nod. "I met her right before church last Sunday." He turns toward the firepit and gives Isabella a wave. She waves back with a bright smile.

Well, she's obviously smitten.

Edgar clears his throat. "Cool, so...I'll get the fire going, Cathy. You're going to be freezing after this. Good thing I brought blankets."

He trudges back up the beach, throwing another dour glance at Heathcliff over his shoulder.

"Blankets?" Heathcliff murmurs, looking out over the waves. "Who needs blankets when you have body heat?"

"Stop, you heathen. This is a church get-together for singles, not a frat party."

"Speaking of that—did you do the Greek life thing at college?"

"I went to college online—pretty much the only option for a banshee who might explode into catastrophic grief at any moment."

"I didn't go at all, online or in person. Took a few business classes, though. And I watch a lot of videos, workshops and stuff. You can basically get a free business degree on YouTube if you subscribe to the right channels."

I give him a sidelong look. "You don't seem like the 'start your own business' type."

"Yeah?" He throws me a glare as he wades deeper. "And what is my type, Earnshaw?"

"Deliveries and odd jobs, with a side of beer-drinking and tailgating."

"You got me so wrong, girl." He surges forward, plunges into the waves, and swims away with long, powerful strokes.

I gape at his gleaming, wet back muscles for a moment, and then I follow him in.

We go out until he can barely touch bottom and I'm treading water. The sun is melting into the sea, liquid fire pooling along the horizon. Heathcliff wipes his face with a broad hand and looks at me, his brown eyes honeyed in the golden light, inky lashes beaded with sparkling drops.

He's the most gorgeous thing I've ever seen—and the most dangerous.

"You shouldn't be here." I raise my voice so he can hear me over the rush of the sea.

"You think I'm here for *you*? I'm here for Isabella."

My chest tightens.

Heathcliff moves closer in the waves, his arms sweeping through the water. "I'm going to push that flimsy little dress up around her waist and pull down her panties and thumb her clit the way I did yours. I think she'll whine so prettily for me. Then I'm gonna bend her over, wrap all that blond hair around my hand, and fuck her from behind."

"Good luck with that." I force the words out.

He leans closer. "If I thought you had a problem with it, I wouldn't go there at all."

"Why should I care who you fuck?" I manage. "I'm planning to seduce Edgar. So looks like we're both getting laid tonight."

"Wanna put some money on that?"

"Are you serious?"

"A bet. Who can get a Linton sibling to orgasm first. The stakes...let's say twenty bucks since you're poor."

"You're no Elon Musk yourself," I snap. "And you're on. It'll be a challenge, though. Our 'cult,' as you call it, has one thing in common with literally all the Bible-based religions—purity culture."

"Yeah, but I'll bet Edgar has been inside a girl before. Maybe even a guy." Heathcliff grins. "And Isabella is basically salivating for cock. I can smell her desperation from here."

"You're the worst." I follow his gaze back toward the beach. "But you've got a point. Let's go back. I'm freezing my tits off."

"Can't have that." He swerves, facing the beach again, and we head inland.

Isabella is waiting for us at the edge of the water, skittering backward like a timid bird every time the water glides in and nearly touches her toes. "Here's a towel, Cliff. You must be freezing."

As usual, she ignores me and stands on tiptoe to wrap the towel around Heathcliff's big shoulders. I can't help letting my gaze linger on the tanned expanse of his pectorals, dark, damp hair flecking their contours and the valley between them. Below a prizeworthy set of abs, another swirl of wet, dark hair is plastered to his skin, disappearing below the band of his swim trunks.

Isabella leads him toward the firepit, talking animatedly, while I follow, shivering. When Heathcliff walks past a tote bag of beach towels, he grabs one and flings it over his shoulder without looking back. I catch it, gritting my teeth against the clash of gratitude and anger thrumming in my heart.

I take it back. I *never* wanted him to show up. In fact, he has ruined this for me. I was all set to have a calm, happy, relaxed evening, and then he arrived, with his body and his face and his stupid mouth.

Forget singles night—this feels like high school. Not that I'd know from personal experience, of course—perks of being a lonely, homeschooled banshee. Anyway, a high school party would have beer, and alcohol is notably absent from this gathering. A pity.

Once I'm mostly dry, I put on my dress and hoodie again, and I join the others in a game of beach volleyball, during which Heathcliff seems determined to break either my nose or Edgar's with the damn ball. Maybe his brand of supernatural, whatever it is, possesses an extra dose of strength. Or maybe he's just trying to sabotage my chances of scoring with Edgar tonight.

If this is a game of chicken, he's going to be sorry he started it. I'll fuck Edgar just to prove I can, and if Heathcliff thinks I won't go through with it, he's got a nasty surprise coming.

After the game, there's food—hot dogs and sausages mostly, roasted over the roaring fire. Isabella is vegan, so she brought a fruit salad and some raw veggies. Thomas Chaiya brought egg rolls from his mom's restaurant, which he warms in a pan over the fire. They're a little soggy on the outside and chilly on the inside but they're still damn good.

Our church is disgustingly white and heteronormative, with the exception of a few families. I've wondered before how it makes them feel to be part of this freakish Wicklow community. Why do they even stick around?

But who am I to judge anyone or pretend to understand their situation? If there's one thing that's true about religion everywhere, it's that people keep secrets. At gatherings, they present the side they want everyone to see, and everyone agrees to pretend that those masks are their authentic selves.

I hate the hypocrisy so much.

If I had money, I'd be out of here. If I had literally anything or anyone else besides my dad and a small amount of savings hidden away in an online account he doesn't know about...

"You okay?" Edgar seats himself on the log beside me and offers me a juicy bratwurst in a bun.

It looks and smells amazing, so I take it. "Thanks. I'm fine. Just thinking."

Thinking about running away.

But it's just not feasible. Not alone. Not with this other side of me ready to crawl up my throat at any time. Dad may not provide me with much support, but at least it's something. I wouldn't survive by myself.

After we eat, Edgar gives a short devotional that I think he intends to be super down-to-earth, practical, and inspiring but comes across as kind of fake and insipid. Maybe it's my mood, though, because everyone else nods and hums their agreement. Everyone, that is, except Heathcliff and Isabella, who are sitting on the sand with their backs to a log. I pretend not to notice Heathcliff's hand disappear beneath the blanket they're sharing. Isabella has her knees arched up so I can't see what Heathcliff is doing under there, but I do notice her face growing redder. Or maybe it's just the glow of the fire.

Edgar is finally winding down his little sermon. "How about we take some prayer requests—"

"We need music," I blurt out.

He looks at me, startled. "Okay, I guess we could sing some songs..."

"No, like, *real* music."

"I've got portable speakers and a party playlist," Thomas offers.

I could kiss that boy. "Yes. *Yes,* do it."

The mood of the group changes instantly. Maybe they weren't as into Edgar's pious "singles' night" as they pretended to be. Maybe they were just waiting for somebody to give them a reason to party.

"I don't suppose anybody brought grown-up drinks," says Narinna Madden with a tentative laugh. She's been cozying up to Melanie Dodds ever since we gathered around the bonfire, and I'm starting to wonder if there was something going on under their blanket as well.

Heathcliff rises, letting the blanket slide off his legs. "I didn't know what kind of party this would be," he says, "but I did bring a couple coolers along, just in case, if someone wants to help me get them out of the trunk."

Edgar looks rather crestfallen at the rapid unraveling of his sedate singles' night.

"Come on, Ed," urges Lazar. "We're all over twenty-one."

"Jesus drank," pipes up Melanie.

Edgar's shoulders droop. He's yielding already, soft, weak thing that he is. Not that I want him to resist, but I kind of despise him for how quickly he folds.

"Okay," he says. "Just...everyone drink responsibly, okay? Be sure to put empties in the baskets. We don't want litter on the beach. And let's keep personal boundaries in mind."

"Sure, man." Heathcliff winks at Isabella, who blushes and clutches the blanket closer. He strides off with a few of the others and they return with coolers full of beer. Thomas's speakers are soon flooding the firelit beach with Camila Cabello and Khalid, while the tabs of beer cans creak and hiss, and everyone starts to chatter.

Heathcliff saunters over and opens a beer for me, holding my gaze. Despite the cold, heat creeps along my skin.

"I'm winning that bet," he says, low.

"The fuck you are," I reply under my breath. With my free hand, I unzip my hoodie, showing the low neckline of the sundress beneath. I tug it down a bit farther, smirking as Heathcliff's gaze darts to my cleavage.

"What were you saying about that bet?" I ask sweetly. Then I saunter back to Edgar, bathe him in my signature smile, and hold out the beer. "Want some?"

"I don't usually drink," he replies. "But maybe just a little."

"Okay." I take a swallow, holding the foamy beer in my mouth, and I lean down, pursing my lips. Edgar's blue eyes widen, and he yields, tipping his face up and opening his mouth. I kiss him, parting my lips just enough to let the beer trickle over his tongue. I'm fully conscious that in this position, my ass is pointed straight at Heathcliff and the short dress I'm wearing won't cover any of it. Plus, my "modest one-piece" swimsuit has ridden up, so Heathcliff is getting an eyeful of my ass cheeks.

Smiling at Edgar, I plop myself on the log beside him. He blinks, his lips wet. "You're something else, Cathy. I don't remember you being like this before."

"Maybe you didn't really know me before."

"Should you be drinking, though? With your medical conditions?"

The smile freezes on my face. I have to bite back a nasty retort and formulate one that won't immediately ruin my chances of winning the bet. "You're so sweet to worry about me," I say softly. "It's all right for me to drink a little. But you'll have to help me finish this beer. You can do that for me, can't you, Eddie?"

He swallows hard. "Well, sure."

He's a lightweight, of course, and it doesn't take him long to start feeling the effects. By then, Narinna and Melanie are dancing together, Lazar is dancing with Thomas, and a few others have paired off as well. I can't help smiling about the first two couples. Maybe this group isn't as heteronormative as I thought. And Edgar's not saying anything to discourage them, which is a point in his favor.

Heathcliff and Isabella have been talking in low voices, but as a slow acoustic country song comes on, he lifts her to her feet and pulls her close. She leans against him as they dance, and I start wishing I had a different supernatural power—maybe the ability to make another woman's head explode with a single thought. Could be messy, though.

"Let's dance." I toss the empty can into one of the baskets we brought and grab Edgar's hands, yanking him up.

He wobbles and laughs. "Careful, Cathy."

I press my body against his. "We should hold each other up so we don't fall down."

"Good idea." His arms close around me. I glance sidelong at Heathcliff to make sure he notices. He's watching me over the top of Isabella's head.

We sway like that, eyeing each other while we dance with our respective partners. I let my hand slide to Edgar's ass, but he pulls it back up to his waist.

"Whoa there." He chuckles. "I think this is getting out of hand. We should probably call it a night and head back. Except we've all been drinking, so...who's gonna drive the van?"

"Ugh, the *van*," I murmur, tracing his lips with my finger. "You act like we're a bunch of teens, Eddie, making us ride out here together in a *van*. We're not kids."

"Yeah, I know." His brow furrows. "I just...miss it. The way things were before I went off to college. We used to have such good times."

I don't mention the fact that I was rarely included in those good times. I had to say no so often, they just quit asking me.

"Did you have fun at college?" I say.

"Well, I had some great teachers—"

"No, no. I mean...*fun*." I wiggle my eyebrows at him.

He laughs. "Oh. Um...maybe."

"With girls or guys?"

Alarm flares in his eyes, and his face turns brick red. "Why are you asking me that?"

"It's just a question. I don't care either way. It's all good." I cup his neck, stroking my fingers through the ends of his blond hair.

But Edgar is angry now, and frantic. "This isn't right. None of this is right." He glances around at the others.

Great, I'm definitely losing the bet now. Reluctantly I meet Heathcliff's gaze, and he smirks. Then he cups Isabella's chin, tips her face up, and kisses her. A deep, slow, sensual kiss, with a lot of tongue, while both his big hands squeeze Isabella's ass.

And he's still looking at me.

I'm burning as hotly as if I stepped into the firepit— incandescent with fury, defeat, craving, and a jealousy I can't deny any longer. I have to do something. Stop this...*kill* him...

But Edgar moves before I can. He shoves me away so roughly, I stumble back and sit down hard on the sand. Then he lunges around the firepit toward Heathcliff, roaring, "Get away from my sister!"

Three things flash through my brain.

One, Edgar Linton is an angry drunk. Like Dad.

Two, Heathcliff has broken the kiss with Isabella and he's star-ing at me, concern and anger churning in his dark gaze as I pick myself up off the sand.

Three, everyone else has stopped dancing and drinking, and their attention is fixed on Edgar and Heathcliff.

"I knew you were trouble when you showed up," Edgar snarls

at Heathcliff, and god help me, a Taylor Swift song starts playing in my head. I climb to my feet, smothering a hysterical laugh.

"Eddie, calm down," Isabella says, but Heathcliff cups her shoulders and moves her aside, not roughly but decisively. She's smart enough to stay put.

"You're not here for the right reasons, Cliff." Edgar is white as death now, his hand shaking, the index finger poking Heathcliff in the chest. "You brought beer. You had the nerve to grope my sister. You encouraged everyone to—to act in ways they shouldn't. You're not welcome here anymore, and I suggest you leave."

A slow, wicked grin widens on Heathcliff's face. He speaks to me over Edgar's head. "Cathy, do you want me to leave?"

"Why are you asking her?" Edgar chokes out, furious. "Don't look at her. She's not for you."

"Cathy?" Heathcliff repeats.

I'm torn between the answer that will bring peace and the volatile truth. Of course I choose violence. "I want you to stay."

"Cathy wants me here, *Eddie*," Heathcliff says. "So I'll be staying."

Edgar throws me a look of betrayal and rage before spinning back around to face Heathcliff. "No. You're leaving."

"Make me."

"Oh, I will." Edgar clears his throat. "*We* will. Won't we, guys?" He rakes the group with frantic eyes, searching out Lazar, Thomas, and the other guys.

Thomas nods and Lazar takes a half step forward, which pisses me off. They were all too happy to drink Heathcliff's beer, and now they're ready to kick him out just because Edgar says so?

Fuck that.

"No!" I dart forward, pushing Lazar back. "No. If Edgar wants Cliff to leave, he can make it happen himself. No one else interferes."

Lazar opens his mouth, but I give him my most savage glare. "*No one* interferes. Got it?"

"You can't be serious, Cathy," exclaims Edgar.

Isabella starts to cry—or more accurately, wail. She could rival a banshee, I swear.

"Shut up," Heathcliff and I snap at her at the same time.

"Go on, Edgar." I clench both fists, my heart racing, blood pounding. "You want him to leave...make him leave."

"It's ridiculous," Edgar says breathlessly. "He's like twice my size. If he were a decent man, he'd go of his own accord, but he's clearly not decent. Isabella, you and I are going to have a serious talk later about the kinds of people who are appropriate for church gatherings. And you, Cathy...I don't know what's going on between you and this guy, but I'm disappointed in you. I thought you were better than this."

Heathcliff chuckles. "He's right, Cathy. You *are* better than this. And you deserve better than a milk-blooded coward who can't even—"

Edgar wheels around and smashes his right fist into Heathcliff's face. Then he grunts with pain, shaking his fingers.

Heathcliff staggers back a step. Blood drips from one nostril, a glistening, ruby line over his full lips. He hauls back for a blow that will level Edgar and possibly break his jaw—or his neck. I can sense the power behind that punch, and my whole body vibrates with a sudden, horrible understanding—an overwhelming tidal wave of grief and the devastating urge to scream.

If Heathcliff lands that blow, he will kill Edgar Linton.

"Stop!" I shriek. But it's not just a word, it's a long scream, an air-raid siren of eardrum-shattering, wave-bending power. I feel the concussive force of it ripple through the air. I hear the sudden change in the wave patterns on the beach, the rolling splash as the force of my cry shoves back the tide itself for a second.

Heathcliff freezes. The others in the group cringe, covering their ears.

I clamp a hand over my mouth, choking on another scream. The moment of danger has passed—Edgar isn't going to die now, so I don't have to mourn him, but I'm still being wracked with convulsive waves of grief and confusion. I can't stay here. I need to go.

The act follows the instinct, and I'm running, running out of the firelight, down the dark beach, under the inky sky and the glittering stars. The others call for me a couple times, but their voices fade quickly—I'm not really one of them, and they're more concerned about Edgar and Isabella, more interested in gossiping about what just happened.

I run, run, run. And when I can't hold my mouth shut any longer, I veer into the surf, slogging through waves until the rush of the sea fills my ears, and then I scream. The screams rip from my lungs, retched out in huge spasms that convulse my whole body. They slash my throat raw, scour my tongue, wring tears from my eyes.

The sea takes the tears, the screams, the pain—all of it. Absorbs everything I have to give, until slowly, slowly, I come back into myself.

I'm standing shoulder deep in freezing waves, shivering. I gag out one last sob for what nearly happened to Edgar, to Heathcliff—to us all.

It's over. No one died. I'm okay, and more importantly, so is Heathcliff. I need to calm down, I need to breathe—

The wave comes without warning, huge and black, towering over me. It slams me down like a giant's icy fist, and for a second, I could swear it's even shaped like a fist.

Water glugs in my ears, fills my brain, crushes me down. I flail, struggling for the surface, but it's all dark, and I can't get out, I can't get out—

My face breaks free for a second, and I gasp, gulping air.

Another watery fist rises and smashes over me again, slow and ponderous, forcing me down to the bottom, pinning me to the sand.

This isn't normal. There's something else going on here— something supernatural. In my ears, a voice resonates, and it's unnaturally clear, not distorted by the water at all: "Child of the Morrigan, abomination. Perish."

I thrash, wriggle, and use my scant lungful of air to scream.

The fist disintegrates, and I bob to the surface, desperate for breath.

"Banshee," the voice hisses through foam and darkness. "Enemy of the gods, diviner of death, offspring of Cernunnos, the rejected one. I am the god Manannán. Worship and die."

Manannán.

The god Daisy and Gatsby mentioned, who was raised up recently. God of the sea, apparently.

I have no capacity to process that right now. Scanning the black water, I realize that I'm terrifyingly far from land. I suck in a breath right before another hand-shaped wave sweeps along the surface toward me.

When I go under, I scream again. And once again, the watery hand shatters at the sound.

The god's voice rolls through the deep. "If I were at my full power, I could destroy you easily. But no matter—you will perish soon enough. Your tiny human limbs are no match for my strength. I will keep you here until you drown."

I drag in another breath, ready to shriek through my anguished throat as many times as I have to. I'll fight the water and struggle toward land until my strength gives out. I won't let this fucker take me down easily.

When he submerges me again, I release another shriek. But I'm slower getting back to the surface, and I barely manage a sip of air before the god's hand reforms and shoves me back under.

My lungs are cracking, my chest ready to explode. My heart pounds frantically against my ribs, hammers in my head—

Something brushes against my hip. Then an arm wraps around my back, under my shoulders, hauling me up and dragging me to the surface.

A shiver races through the water, and the voice speaks again, all around us, deep as the ocean, wild as the wind itself: "Son of Juventas." And I could swear it sounds surprised. "Why do you assist this abomination?"

"Fuck off!" roars Heathcliff. Through his bravado, I can hear his terror—I can feel it in the hard tension of his body as he fights to drag us both closer to the beach. "Let her go, you big bastard! You can't have her."

"Do your duty," intones the god. "Destroy the cursed offspring of Death and the Morrigan."

"Eat shit." Heathcliff's muscles surge, and the strength that carried me through the woods for hours now propels us both toward shore. He's clinging to me with ferocious determination, kicking with all his might, and sweeping the sea with one powerful arm.

Strong as he is, I don't think we're going to make it.

Salt water sloshes into my mouth. I choke, gag, fight for control of my traitorous lungs and stomach. I try not to thrash so I won't pull us both under, but it's hard when every cell of my body is screaming with cold and panic.

And then, as quickly as they arose, the icy waves subside, shrinking down to their normal size. After a minute I find the bottom, and we're able to stagger through the surf back to the relative safety of land.

We're so far down the beach that I can't see the glow of the firepit. I wonder if the group heard the god's voice at all or if it was only meant for Heathcliff and me. For now, it doesn't matter.

Both of us collapse on the sand, our faces upturned to the stars.

"I wasn't delirious, right?" I gasp. "That really happened?"

"Yeah." Heathcliff rubs a hand over his face.

"Okay." I haul in a few more jagged breaths, trying to control the shaking of my limbs, the clatter of my teeth. "Okay. We can't lie here. We'll get hypothermia. Gotta move. Got to get up." It's going to hurt. "One, two, three..."

I force myself to roll over onto my belly, and from there, I push up onto hands and knees. I climb to my feet, nearly toppling over again, but I curl my toes into the sand and find my balance somehow.

"Get up," I hiss at Heathcliff.

He groans, but he obeys me, struggling upright as well. "I think we washed up close to where I went in after you. Give me a minute while I look for my phone."

I hug myself miserably, watching as he walks along the sand, then bends to pick something up.

He hurries back, unlocking the phone as he approaches me. "Service sucks around here." He holds it higher. "Okay, I got one bar now. I can call Isabella, tell her where we are."

I hate that he has her number almost as much as I hate the idea of facing the group again. I look back the way we came, at the long, dark stretch of the beach. The wind has picked up, and it feels ten times colder than before. Why did I have to run so far from the fire, from heat and cars and blankets?

"Or we could go there." Heathcliff points to a rooftop jutting above the dunes, its slanted surface gleaming in the faint starlight.

When I don't answer, he sets off, determination in each stride.

I trudge after him. "We can't just break in. It's going to have a security system."

"Not always. Sometimes people put the signs up even if they don't actually have the system. Or they have one but they don't pay the monthly fee and they don't arm it. Especially if they don't use the place a lot. They don't want to bother remembering the code. Come on."

"Do you break into beach houses often?"

"Only when I need to."

We stumble across the tough, windblown grass of the dunes and onto the packed, sandy earth in front of the cottage. It's tiny—one bedroom and a bathroom, if I had to guess. Maybe a kitchenette. There's a sign for Hamblen's Security in the grimy window, but someone has also nailed boards across the front door. Heathcliff's probably right that the security for this place has lapsed. Besides, if an alarm goes off and somebody does come to check it out, we can explain our desperation to get warm. At the very least, they'll give us blankets before they take us to jail.

Heathcliff grips one of the boards and the muscles in his arms tighten as he rips it free. One after another, he tears off the pieces of wood, then gives the door a good kick. There's a snap of rusted metal and a crunch of wood, and the door flies open.

With a grim flourish and a faint smirk, he gestures to the dark opening. "After you, Earnshaw."

Another woman might be squeamish at the thought of stepping into an abandoned cottage that probably hasn't seen pest control in ages. But I'm used to walking barefoot in the bristly undergrowth of Carolina forests, squashing through the marshy landscape of the Lowcountry. During my wanderings, I've stepped on more night-crawling critters than I can count.

Plus, I'm freezing, and I just want to be out of this damn wind. I move past Heathcliff, into the dark.

My foot lands on dusty wood. No sharp nails, no crunch of a cockroach's stiff wings under my toes. I walk farther inside. "Light," I say over my shoulder, and Heathcliff enters behind me, drawing the door shut with a scraping creak and shining his phone around the space.

There's a musty, acrid tang to the air, the sourness of moisture seeping somewhere in the cottage, though the floor I'm walking across feels dry. The phone's pale light passes over a shabby couch, a metal folding table, a big wooden chest that could probably fit a dead body, and, as I suspected, the smallest of kitchenettes.

Nothing here worth stealing, which is probably why the place doesn't actually have an alarm. At least, none that we know of. Someone could still show up, I guess. Funny thing is, I don't much care at the moment. My whole body is trembling uncontrollably, and my head feels weird. Things keep tilting and then righting themselves again. The stark glow of the phone light isn't helping; it makes the shadows jump and dance until my stomach clenches with terror. I can almost imagine a giant fist made of darkness emerging, smashing us both to pulp.

I sway suddenly, careening into Heathcliff.

"Hey." He grips my shoulder with his free hand. "We gotta get you warmed up. Come on, let's see if there's any hot water or electricity in this place."

He hustles me toward the back of the cottage. The first door we open is a closet, full of stale air and dusty blankets and towels. The second leads to a tiny bathroom. Heathcliff turns the squeaky knob, and water spurts out, dark at first, before it runs clear.

"It's not getting any warmer," he says. "But it's not as cold as the ocean. You should rinse that sand off before you wrap up in blankets. I'll hold the light for you."

"Of c-course you will," I manage through my chattering teeth. "You just...want to...see me naked."

"The only thing I'm concerned with right now is getting you warm. We don't know how long this water will last—there's probably not much in the tank, so you get your ass in there right now, you hear me? I won't look. Just hurry because I want a turn when you're done."

"Fine." With trembling fingers, I strip off my hoodie, my dress, and then my swimsuit, which is pretty much congealed to my skin.

I'm coated with sand, and even though the cold shower makes my breath hiss, it *is* warmer than the ocean, and it feels good to rinse the grit away.

When my skin is smooth again, I step out, wet and shivering and naked. There's nothing sexy about it—I feel like a chilled salamander, with my hair plastered to my quivering shoulders.

"Hold the light," says Heathcliff, and I do my best. He shucks off his swim trunks and rinses swiftly, running his hands over his body to clear the grainy sand. I realize I'm watching and I almost look away—but he didn't tell me I couldn't watch. I'm in no state for arousal, but I do like the sight of him. His body is broad, powerful, long-limbed, rippling with muscle. He cups his balls, holding them out of the way while he rinses every crevice.

I glance away then, and if my blood wasn't desperately trying to keep my extremities warm, I'd probably be blushing.

"Come on." He grabs the phone from me, hurries me back into the main room. I'm in a strange headspace now, where the pain of the cold isn't so bad and part of my brain is telling me that's not a good sign.

"Stay with me, okay?" Heathcliff sets the phone on the arm of the couch, rummages in the closet, and gathers up an armful of beach towels and blankets.

I stand where he left me, blinking, feeling oddly hollow inside.

"Hey!" He dumps the blankets on the couch, then wraps one around my shoulders before toweling himself off rapidly. "Don't pass out, okay? Keep talking. Tell me something."

"A god tried to kill me," I murmur.

"Yeah. Yeah he did." He's leading me to the couch.

"Juventas isn't the name of any Irish deity."

"No. No, it isn't." He stretches out his big body, grabs my wrist, and pulls me down on top of him.

I make a small sound of protest.

"Earnshaw, this isn't about sex. You need body heat."

He's right, so I let myself relax against him. He grabs the other towels and blankets, draping them over us both in a big pile. His phone light winks off, burying us in darkness.

The damp hair on his chest tickles my cheek and brushes against my left eyelashes when I blink. He tugs one of the blankets up higher, tucking it around my shoulders and my face.

My left hip is settled against the V of his abdomen, my legs lying between his. I can feel his dick against my thigh, not totally erect but definitely not limp either.

His right arm encircles me, heavy and somehow soothing. Its comforting strength and the weight of the blankets settles me, while the pockets of air around our bodies slowly heat.

After a few minutes, Heathcliff mutters, "How do you feel? I can see if I've got service, try calling 911 if you think you're going into shock."

"No, I'm okay." I rub my chilly nose with my fingers, which are much warmer now.

"Good."

Another stretch of silence.

"You saved me." Words I never thought I'd say in real life. They feel more awkward than I expected—and more necessary. "Thank you."

"Well..." His big chest heaves with a sigh. "You saved me from doing something I'd regret."

I kept him from killing Edgar. "Wonder what they said about us after we left," I murmur.

"I don't give a fuck."

"You really don't, do you?" Dimly I'm aware that my right hand is moving, running along the heated skin over his ribs. "I don't either, most of the time. But the way they look at me at church, like I'm the soiled, stained rag that needs to be washed in the blood of the Lamb—it's tough to handle sometimes. They know I only go to services because of Dad, and they're always trying to 'get through to me.' Like whoever finally forces me to change will get a badge of honor or something."

My hand moves higher, my fingertips gliding over the lower contour of his left pec. So solid. So warm. "They'll probably head back without us. They'll assume I'm riding back with you. Wonder what Edgar will do with my bag. Leave it behind or take it along?"

"My stuff's in my truck," Heathcliff says. His voice sounds thicker and deeper than usual, and as my palm glides higher, over his chest, there's an answering twitch against my thigh. I smirk in the darkness.

"So how was she?" I say softly. "Isabella? How did she taste when you kissed her?"

He sighs again. "What do you want me to say?"

"The truth."

"You don't want to hear the truth. The truth will upset you."

"So she was good then. How about her ass? You seemed to like that a lot."

"Enough, Cathy."

"Too bad you didn't get a chance to taste her pussy."

"Catherine." His voice is a deep warning through gritted teeth.

"What? If you're going to grope and tongue someone, you should be able to talk about it. I just want to know how you'd describe the kiss."

He's silent, while I listen to his heartbeat thumping through his chest. "Not you."

"Hm?"

"The kiss. The way I'd describe it is—not you."

"I don't know what that means."

"Not you," he growls. "Her taste, her smell, the shape of her ass, her flimsy little fingers, her breathy voice, that wispy hair... *not you*. Everything, every day, since I dropped those crates off at your aunt's fucking store—everything is *not you*. That's all I can think about until I see you again, and then...you fill up the world. Everything is you."

It's terrifying to hear those words. Terrifying because there's an echo of that violent truth in my heart and in my mind. I'm convinced I'm wrong, though, because it happened too fast. It's been too easy to fall for him.

But is it really falling, or is it running? Running headlong, arms wide open, eyes wild with joy, wind screaming through my hair? Is it crashing into him, shattering my bones and body against his until we're both broken, until the pieces of us reassemble as one person?

Since I met him, he has simply been *there*. Like he already belongs in my life. We understand each other too well, almost as if I'm him and he is me, and our souls always knew we'd fit together someday.

Or maybe I'm delirious. Drenched in the afterglow of survival, with alcohol still in my blood and the echoes of my screams in my head. Maybe I'm in shock. I doubt it, though, because I'm warm all over now, gloriously flushed under the blankets, bathed in the heat rolling off his bare skin. The long, silky length of his cock lies against my thigh, burning hard. But he doesn't move. Doesn't try to rub against me or get inside me.

He hasn't said a word since *everything is you*.

What does a person even say in response to that?

"Don't do it again," he says suddenly. "Run off like that and almost get yourself killed. Because I'll follow, you know. And we might both end up dead. I can forgive you for causing my death, but I won't forgive you for causing yours."

I smack his chest with my hand. "How was I supposed to know there'd be an actual god out there in the sea? And one with a vendetta against banshees?"

He shifts restlessly. Doesn't answer.

"Once we get back to your truck and have Wi-Fi access again, we need to do some research. I looked up a whole bunch of the gods a few years ago, but I don't remember everything I read. Manannán must be the god of the sea, but I don't know why he hates banshees so much. And what was all that about Cernunnos and the Morrigan?"

Heathcliff exhales sharply through his teeth, the breath accompanied by a sharp bob of his cock against my leg, and I realize that I've been tracing his nipple with my fingernail without thinking about it.

"You keep doing that, and I'm going to come all over us both," he says tightly.

I flick his nipple, then rub my fingertip around it in a slow circle.

A sharp moan cracks from his lips. "Cathy..."

Delight sizzles through me when he uses my first name again.

I adjust my position under the blankets, spreading my thighs so they're splayed across his hips. My torso is aligned with his now, my forearms braced against his chest. The blanket slides down, and he pulls it back up over my shoulders. The blunt head of his dick brushes the lips of my pussy, and I gasp a little. I shift my ass backward, feeling the nudge of his length against me. Then I reach down and circle his shaft with my fingers, dragging the head through my wetness, spreading the slick.

"God, Cathy," he grits out. Under the blankets, his hands find my waist, my sides, sliding up to my breasts. He squeezes them with a groan of satisfaction.

I keep teasing myself with him, rubbing his tip against my folds, against my clit, until he hisses another quick breath and his body tenses like he's about to come.

"Don't," I order him. "Don't you dare. Think about something else—think about dying. Think about the worst moments of your life. I don't care as long as you give me more time with this."

"Okay," he gasps. "Okay." I hear the rustle of his nod in the dark.

I give him a few seconds to control himself. Then I tuck the tip of him inside me and slide all the way down.

I sob when I do it—a sob that's half-moan, half-cry, and all bliss as he fills me up. The angle of my hips is perfect—I'm spread open across him, with my clit exposed and rubbing against his hard lower belly. He keeps this area trimmed, which I like—there's a soft scattering of dark curls across the hard muscle, teasing my sensitive bud as I grind on him.

He's cursing, low and strained, over and over, with his hands clamped on my waist like he wants to move me, but he's holding back.

Leaning forward, propped on his chest, I lift my hips and bob up, then back down. He slides through me, thick and hot and perfect. The blankets are slipping off, and the chilly air hits my shoulders, but I'm still warm enough, and this is more important right now. Fucking him feels essential to myself, to my future wholeness and happiness. I've never wanted someone as ferociously as I want him—whoever and whatever he is. The secrets he's keeping should bother me more, but I'm setting them aside, postponing my theories. All I know is that when I need him, he's there. When I mourned, he followed me, carried me. When I nearly died, he saved me.

One of Heathcliff's hands travels up my bare back, hooks around my neck, pulls my face down to his. We fumble in the dark before we find each other's mouths, and when we do, I want to scream with delight. The kisses are rough, sloppy, punctuated by broken gasps, open-mouthed desperation, frantic bruising force. I fit my lips to the edges of his, begging for his tongue, and he sweeps it inside me, raking across my teeth, lashing the hollows of my mouth. I rock my hips while I kiss him, feeling the soft, wet suction of my body around his cock.

My feelings for the other guys I've slept with were flimsy, like a breeze in the sky, airy and inconsequential, changeful, gone in a breath. What I feel for Heathcliff is like the roots of mighty trees, like bones under flesh, like the bedrock far beneath the ocean floor. It's not only erotic but necessary. I need him deeper inside. I need to feel him wanting me, coming for me. I need to unmake him so I can remake us both.

Most of the time I think of my banshee self as a separate part of me—an inner creature that I keep subdued and dormant—but she's awake in this moment, an active part of this. Heathcliff is getting all of me: the wicked and the untamed.

I stop kissing him, and I focus on taking him deeper, faster. His hands are in my hair, cupping my face, my skull. I'm panting hoarsely against his gritted teeth, fucking myself on him with agonized need. Our groans punctuate each other, primal, violent—I don't know whether we're two animals rutting or two souls blending, but it's primal and it's titanic and god, oh *god*—

I scream, and the banshee screams with me, and the house groans, timbers creaking over our heads, walls shaking, but I can't stop because I'm coming. I'm coming harder than I ever have in my life—waves of scintillating force rocketing through my body. Heathcliff yells out, bucks beneath me—he's soaring too, shuddering, swept up in a hurricane of pleasure so exquisite it's like pain.

Heathcliff's hips surge, his length pulsating inside me, his body shifting against my oversensitive clit. My scream rises to a shrill peak as I burst into bliss a second time, and a window near us cracks. Thankfully it doesn't shatter.

"Oh god," I gasp through my raw throat. I collapse on top of Heathcliff, shaking, and he drags the blankets over us again. His cock is still inside me, still flexing, and his chest buoys me up with every shuddering breath.

I close my eyes and yield to the warmth, to the glowing peace that spreads through my limbs, to the feeling of being held, cherished, and satisfied.

Heathcliff shifts beneath me.

"Did you have to break the window?" he says into my hair with a low chuckle I feel through all my bones.

"Sorry," I whisper with a giggle.

"Damn." A press of his lips into my hair. "If you're warmed up now, we should take some of these blankets and go. I don't trust the structure of this place anymore."

"Yeah, I think you're right."

I'm quiet as we retrieve our swimsuits and shuffle out of the damaged cottage, clad in blankets. The explosive sex we just had worries me. I allowed myself too much freedom, and I can't let loose like that again. I can't be earthquaking houses whenever I fuck Heathcliff.

We pad down the beach in chilly silence, while the wind whips our hair and sneaks under our blankets to thrash our bare legs. By the time we reach the site of the campfire, it's dark and dead. The church group has packed up and headed out.

Our flip-flops are where we left them, so we slip them on and head for Heathcliff's truck, pulled up beside the empty house. My beach bag is lying on the hood. Edgar must have put it there. Maybe he felt bad about how things went down.

I don't bother getting dressed in the extra clothes I brought. I just crawl into the passenger side of Heathcliff's truck with my bag, tuck the blankets around me, buckle in, and wait.

He pulls on a dry T-shirt and gets in, too. Closes the door. Sits there with one palm braced on the wheel, fingers drumming lightly. "Is that going to happen every time? The earthquake thing?"

"I hope not. It hasn't happened before." I swallow, thinking of how I felt my banshee side right there, present with me, taking that moment to the extreme. If I repress her, I should be able to prevent any more glass-cracking orgasmic screams. "I can control it."

"You shouldn't have to."

"I shouldn't have to do a lot of things. But that's life, right? You play the hand you're dealt, even if it's a shitty one." I sneak a sidelong glance at his handsome profile, half-veiled by his shaggy black hair.

"I've never come that hard, or that long, with anyone," he says.

"Same."

He nods once, satisfied. Starts the truck, and we roll out of the driveway, bumping over potholes.

Once we're back on a more traveled road, he says, "Motel? I'll pay. I'm a little tired to drive all the way back."

"I'll have to text my dad." My heart sinks. Dad doesn't care if I'm gone all night on a crying spree, wandering in the forest, but he just might kill me if he knows I stayed overnight with a man. He's sure to give me a backhanded slap or two at the very least.

Digging my hand into my bag, I find my phone and send him a text full of misspellings. Banshe eprsode. Back tomorvo. Hopefully he'll think I'm staggering around, barely able to text him in between wails and sobs. He'll still worry because he knows I was out with the church group, but at least he won't guess the truth. Hopefully Edgar won't tell him anything about tonight's events. I doubt he'd want to admit how completely he lost control of his singles' event.

I stuff the phone back in my bag. "We're good. Motel it is. But no more sex."

"Sleep," Heathcliff agrees. "And then quiet sex in the morning."

I can't help laughing. "Maybe. I think I was just overwrought and tired, and my banshee side was stressed out from nearly dying. Some rest should settle everything down."

"Cool."

He taps his fingers on the wheel, and I study his profile. The god who attacked us had plenty to say, and I know Heathcliff is probably mulling it over. "Juventas" sounds Roman, which would back up Heathcliff's theory that he's got Italian ancestry.

"Sooo...are we going to talk about what that means?" I venture. "You being the 'son of Juventas'?"

"Not tonight."

He doesn't say anything else, so I postpone my curiosity and stare out the window, remembering what it felt like—that concussive supernova between us. It was fucking cosmic, and I don't think it was just because I nearly died. I think it was *him*. Heathcliff. I let myself be whole and wide-open to him like I've never been with anyone else. That was the difference.

And that is the danger.

10

HEATHCLIFF

A SHARP BANG JOLTS ME OUT OF SLEEP. I'M OFF THE BED IN a split second, heart racing, ripping the motel curtains aside.

Not gunfire. Just somebody's beat-up car backfiring. I groan, rubbing my face. The adrenaline has already spread through my body, and I won't be able to go back to sleep.

I turn around, expecting Cathy to blink at me from the bed, maybe laugh at me for being startled.

But she's not in the bed. She's crouched in the corner by the bedside table, naked, her hair wild and her eyes flashing. She's tense, white-faced, like an animal caught in a trap.

This girl knows danger, up close and personal. She's had to defend herself before.

I don't think this part's about the banshee. Maybe it's post-traumatic stress from almost being drowned by a god—or maybe it's something else.

"Just a car backfiring," I say slowly. "It's okay. It ain't gonna hurt you, and neither am I."

She's not quite herself yet, still caught in that space between sleeping and waking. She blinks, hisses a breath through her teeth.

On a hunch, I say, "Your dad's not here. It's just you and me."

Bingo. The panic in her eyes eases immediately, and she rises from the crouch, her slender throat moving as she swallows. "Yeah, I know."

I understand that feeling. The tension of living with someone you can't trust not to hurt you.

I walk around the end of the bed, casual, calm. But I don't touch her. I hold out my hand and let her come to me.

One tentative step, then another...and then she's in my arms, pressing her bare body against mine. "Heathcliff," she whispers, taut and hoarse.

"Yeah." I kiss the top of her head. She feels so delicate and smooth against me, yet there's strength in her too, like she's made of steel cables as well as soft flesh. That's what I love about her— she's wild as the cold wind, sharp as broken shells on the beach, tough as the old Southern oaks. She's like the Spanish moss on the trees—lacy and fragile from a distance but wiry and rough up close.

She sighs against me like I'm a safe place, when I'm anything but.

She's gonna get herself killed someday, for real. She'll wander across a road while she's in banshee mode or her dad will hit her too hard, and I won't be there to stop it.

The idea sends raw panic skating through my chest, knocks my heart into a frantic rhythm.

A world without this girl would be a horrible void. I can't handle thinking on it for too long. So I've got to *do* something about it.

I scoop Cathy up and drop her onto the bed, throwing her

legs apart and diving between them. She squeals and tries to pin her thighs together. "Wait, Heathcliff, wait—I have to pee first!"

"Fine."

But after we've taken turns in the bathroom, she seems jittery, reluctant, so I don't push for sex. She's scared she'll blow apart the motel, and after what I saw last night, I'll admit it could happen. So I suggest we go out to breakfast instead.

This overnight, plus what I have planned for us today, it'll set me back financially. Motels near the coast aren't cheap. But at least it's the off-season, so I got a break on the room rate. Besides, Cathy is worth whatever I have to spend. Whatever I have to do.

I pull the truck into the parking lot of a dingy diner near the motel. Looks like the kind of place that serves a good, hearty Southern breakfast. My kind of food.

"This okay?" I glance at Cathy. She nods. She's wearing the change of clothes from her beach bag—a pair of shorts and a soft gray tank top. No bra, no makeup, and she looks goddamn beautiful, like always. I want to give her everything. All the fancy cosmetics girls like, a big closet full of designer clothes, a car, a house...

I gotta quit thinking like this. Got to follow the plan, take my time. Work my way out from under Hindley's thumb.

Inside the diner, we slide onto the red-leather seats of a booth and scan the menu. Cathy looks like she's starving but she only orders a muffin. She's either trying to save me money or trying to pretend she doesn't need to eat much for some reason. Screw that. I order a bunch of stuff—pancakes, sausages, bacon, eggs, hash browns, more than I can eat. When my food comes, she sneaks envious looks at it until I start piling fried potatoes, eggs, and sausage onto her plate.

"I was trying to save you money," she mumbles, with a cute half smile.

"Who says I'm paying?"

Her mouth and eyes go wide for a second, and I laugh.

"Of course I'm paying. Eat up."

11

CATHY

HEATHCLIFF AND I TALK ALL THROUGH BREAKFAST.
Random stuff. I talk more than him, but I don't think he minds.
He looks perfectly content, gulping black coffee and listening to
me with an intense focus I've never experienced from anyone. It's
like he's trying to learn me. Like he's devouring everything I say.
He's monosyllabic mostly, but I discover that he likes the kind
of reality shows where they forge swords or do glassblowing, or
where people traverse obstacle courses and the winner gets cash.

"Always thought I'd be good at that," he mutters. "Obstacle
courses and shit."

"Are you kidding? You'd be great."

He shrugs, sticking a huge forkful of sausage and eggs into
his mouth. My eyes follow the motion, and I notice something
beneath the swirls of the tattoo on his forearm.

My fingers slide over his wrist, and he freezes.

I was right. There are scars on his skin, here and there. I guess
I was too worked up to notice them last night. My hands were
mostly on his chest anyway, not his arms.

"These scars," I murmur, tracing one with my fingernail.

"From Hindley," he says. "Broken beer bottle."

"Your brother did this?"

He nods. "And his cousins. That's most of the scars, anyway. There's some I don't remember getting and some I don't talk about."

"More secrets."

Slowly he leans back in the booth and pulls his arm away. "Yeah."

He pays the bill, then does something on his phone while I finish my last piece of bacon. When we get back in the truck, he heads down the main street of the little town we're in. Not much of a main street, actually. Shabby, weatherbeaten buildings, all the same shades of gray-streaked white and faded red brick. Dingy shops, mostly closed, in two broken rows under a dull gray sky.

Heathcliff turns down a side street and steers into a narrow parking lot with grass sprouting through broken pavement. There's a smoky glass door with a sign over it.

"Teagan's Tattoo Shop," I read aloud. Then I turn to Heathcliff, my eyebrows raised.

"We're getting matching tattoos," he says.

Of all the things I thought might come out of his mouth, that wasn't in the top one million.

"Matching tattoos," I repeat.

"Yeah." He grins, but it's forced, his movements too casual for the intensity of his eyes. "It's fun, right? Like...romantic shit or whatever."

A dry chuckle bursts from me. "Okay. Sure. I could get a tattoo as long as it's somewhere Dad won't see. But no celebrity faces, or names, or..."

"Nothing like that. I thought maybe…Celtic knot. A hint of your heritage. Those old symbols have power. Might give you some extra control over your inner banshee."

Interesting… I hadn't considered something like that. "And you're getting a matching one because…"

"Like I said."

"Right…romantic shit."

"And I like tattoos." He climbs out of the truck. "Come on, Earnshaw. Get your little ass in there. I know you ain't scared of needles."

"How do you know that?"

He leans back into the truck cab briefly. Meets my eyes. "Because you're not scared of anything."

When he says those words, looking at me like that, I can almost believe him.

Our feet crunch across cracked asphalt littered with pebbles and grit. Heathcliff reaches for the door of the tattoo shop, then hesitates.

"You shouldn't have to do that," he says. "Hide things from your dad. You're an adult."

"Yeah, well…" I run a hand over my face, into my hair. "I'm kinda stuck there. It's the whole 'his house, his rules' deal until I can move out."

"I'd let you stay at my place if I thought it was any safer."

A twinge of pleasure and surprise passes through my heart. "That's sweet."

Heathcliff's jaw is hard. "It won't always be like this for you or for me. I swear it. We'll get free one day, you and I."

"You and I," I whisper. Impulsively I reach up, rising on tiptoe, and wrap my hand around the back of his neck, dragging him down for a kiss.

When his mouth meets mine this time, it's like opening the door to another world, to a future I've never dared to imagine. His lips are hot, faintly rough. He tastes like bacon and coffee and a subtle spice I can never quite identify because it's *him*—it's just *Heathcliff.*

He hums over my tongue, licks softly into the dark heat of my mouth. Seals his lips firmly and tenderly to mine. This isn't hunger—it's a promise.

Does he know what he's promising? Does he understand what a relationship with me would be like? Is this what he really wants, me and my mess?

When I break the kiss, he finds my hand, weaves his thick fingers between mine. "Come on."

A bell chimes as we step inside. Sketched faces leer from the walls. Black-and-white symbols and garishly lettered words are plastered on every available surface. A couple metal chairs with brown-leather padding sit against the collage of tattoo designs. Between them stands a battered wooden end table with a plastic plant on it. There's a tall desk, too, with an acrylic top and several three-ring binders, probably containing more tattoo options. A skinny man in his forties props pointy elbows on the desk. He's got a bristly, reddish mohawk, heavy eyeliner, and a motley of piercings in his ears and face. Tattoos cover both gaunt arms and his skinny throat. A stack of leather bands and silver bracelets encircle each wrist.

"Heath-fuckin-cliff," he says, chomping on a wad of gum that flashes pale between his yellowed teeth. "Good to see you, man. Been a while. This a client?"

"A client?" I frown, glancing at Heathcliff.

"This is Cathy," Heathcliff replies, with a stern look at the man. "She's my—she's with me. Cathy, this is Bean. Benjamin Lockwood."

"At your service." Bean grins, still chewing the gum.

"We're gonna get matching tattoos." Heathcliff's tone deepens with significance, and the man's eyes widen a little.

"Okay, sure. Not a client but matching tattoos. Hindley know about this?"

"Bean," growls Heathcliff. "Enough questions. You owe me one favor without the family knowing, remember? This is it. I'm calling it in. Otherwise I might have to tell your dad or Meemaw about—"

"Okay, okay." Bean lifts both hands in a deprecating gesture. "It's your business. Pick your poison." He shifts the big binders around, then slaps one open against the acrylic countertop. After flipping a few pages, he shoves it forward. "Anything from here or the next three pages."

The glossy two-page spread shows a selection of Celtic knots and similarly complex symbols. How did Bean know what kind of tattoo we were considering?

"You two have a look," Bean says. "I'll go tell Morgana you're coming back in a minute."

The moment he's gone, I turn to Heathcliff. He keeps his eyes down, pretending to study the designs, so I flick his cheek. "Hey. What's going on?"

"We're getting tattoos." He still won't look at me.

"I'm not an idiot. There's something weird going on here. Some Lockwood black magic. Are you trying to kill me? Trap me in some strange Irish marriage bond?"

He glances at me, raising an eyebrow. "You think I'm trying to marry you?"

My cheeks heat. "No, but...what is this?"

"It's protection. For you. Nothing invasive, nothing that will affect your life at all. It's a preventative measure, Cathy. That's it."

"You're being cagey."

He snorts a laugh. "Cagey?"

"Evasive."

"Like I said, it's for your protection. Hopefully you'll never need it. After what happened yesterday...what could still happen..." He grimaces, lowers his voice. "Cathy, there is a fucking *god* swimming around near the Beaufort coastline. There's another god who might not stay buried for long. Things are moving, changing, and it's not good. Just do this, okay? You don't have to believe in it— you just have to endure the pain. You heal quick anyway, so the recovery shouldn't be too bad."

He really believes the tattoo will help protect me. I can see it in his eyes—how badly he wants me to agree to this.

I can't think of a reason why I shouldn't...except the fact that I barely know him and that he's a Lockwood, a member of the family I've been taught to fear. He might have some hideous agenda, and this whole stalking and seduction thing is part of a plan to destroy me.

But in my heart and in my bones, I know that's not true. Heathcliff isn't a good enough actor to fake everything he's shown me of himself. I can still hear him roaring his defiance at Manannán: *Let her go, you big bastard. You can't have her.* My vagina is still tingly and faintly sore from him being inside me. His eyes, his body, and his voice have told me the truth, over and over, since the night he wandered through the woods with me.

He wants me safe. I can trust him with this.

"I can pick any of them?" I ask.

He nods, lips clamped tight.

I choose a design with leaves and lilies woven among the braided lines. "This one."

"Good choice. Bean will do mine, and Morgana will do yours. It'll hurt."

"Pain and I are old friends." I smile up at him.

His gaze warms with tenderness and relief. "Thank you for doing this."

God, are there tears in his eyes? "Like you said, it's fun," I say lightly. "Romantic."

Bean saunters back into the front room. "You bitches ready?"

Heathcliff points out the design I chose, and Bean snaps a photo on his phone. "Come on, then."

The two men vanish into the back, and a moment later a tall woman with hip-length red hair and heavily freckled skin appears. She's wearing a blousy shirt, about twenty beaded necklaces, and a brown wrap skirt. Her feet are bare, and her pale-green eyes are so large, I'm reminded immediately of a gecko.

"I'm Morgana," she says. "You ready?"

"Yes. I chose this one." I show her the design.

"That's a strong one." She nods. "This way. Where do you want it?"

"My hip, I think. How long does it take?"

"How big do you want it?"

I hold my fingers about three inches apart. "Like this?"

"Any normal shop, with a tattoo of this complexity, you'd be looking at three to five hours. But this ain't a normal shop, honey. You'll be out of here in an hour max."

"What makes this place different?"

She stares at me with those pale-green gecko eyes until I think she must have gone into some kind of trance. I have to resist snapping my fingers in front of her face.

"This way," she says abruptly, heading into the other section of the shop.

Once we're settled in a small back room, she doesn't speak to me again beyond basic instructions. The pain sucks, but compared to what I've endured since my banshee side woke up, it's nothing. I busy myself with my phone to keep my mind off the discomfort. Dad hasn't responded to my text. I'm sure he went to church this morning—he never misses. Did he talk to Edgar or Isabella there? Did they mention that after I ran off, "Cliff" went with me? They don't know he's a Lockwood, and neither does Dad, but if he knows a guy was with me, he'll have questions.

I debate texting him to see if Edgar told him anything, but I decide silence is best.

"Done," says Morgana at last.

"You're a Lockwood, too?" I ask as she puts away her tools.

"Yes."

"Cool." I pucker my lips and tug my shorts back up, settling them gingerly into place over the tattoo while I try to come up with a question that won't sound super awkward. *What kind of supernatural is your family? Are you the monsters my dad has always claimed you were? What sort of magic do you practice, if any?*

She hands me a sheet on tattoo aftercare, and I suddenly realize I should tip her. My bag is out in Heathcliff's truck.

"I'll get my purse," I say as we walk back out to the front room.

"I already took care of It." Heathcliff is standing by the counter. "Can I see it?"

I pull down the waistband of my shorts and show him the reddened mark. He lifts his T-shirt and shows me the matching tattoo on his left side, along the slanted V muscle of his abdomen.

"Damn, that's hot," I admit aloud.

Bean chuckles. "All right, you two. Have fun today."

"Remember what I said," Heathcliff replies with a warning look.

Bean holds up a wad of cash between two fingers. "Not a word to Hindley. We swear, don't we, Morgana?"

Morgana drifts vaguely into the back without answering.

Once Heathcliff and I are outside in the parking lot, I touch his arm. "I'll pay you back."

"No."

"Money's tight for both of us. I don't want you to carry that cost yourself. And you paid for the motel—"

"It's fine. I have some money coming in soon."

"The guy you were meeting with at Moretti's?"

He throws me a surprised glance, approval and caution in his eyes. "You're quick."

"I've always had to be. So is that guy a client?"

"Kind of. You could say I'm trying to branch out on my own, get out from under my brother's shadow. Can't make a clean break yet, but I'm working on it."

I think of my own small savings account and the struggle to be less dependent on Dad. "I understand."

"I know you do." He yanks open the truck door for me. "Get in, girl. I need to take you home."

Unease crawls through me as I climb into the truck. When he gets in on his side, I say quietly, "I wish we could just drive. I don't even care where, as long as it's far from here."

"Real freedom takes money."

"That's such bullshit."

He chuckles. "The worst." He punches the button for the stereo, flips through a few channels until he lands on Jackson Dean's "Don't Come Lookin.'"

As we roll out of the parking lot, I reach over and grip his thigh. "Take the long way home?"

"Always."

My hand on his muscular thigh gives me a very naughty idea, especially since he's still wearing his swim trunks from yesterday. He rinsed them out at the hotel last night and let them dry, so they're not sandy, but they still smell like the ocean.

I wait until we're on a long, straight stretch of road, and then I slide my hand up Heathcliff's thigh and settle my palm over the generous bulge between his legs.

He's soft when I touch him, but instantly he jumps a little and says, "Aw, shit." His cock flexes under the shorts, stiffening against the pressure of my hand.

Smirking, I stroke my thumb along the fabric, over the ridge of his length.

"Earnshaw," he says warningly.

"Eyes on the road," I murmur. My fingers work their way into his waistband, tugging down the swim trunks and the bit of netting inside that's supposed to hold his package in place. His length pops free, and I hold the waistband of the swim trunks away from his body, giving his cock space. Slowly I unbuckle my seat belt and lean over. He lifts his right arm and mutters "shit" again as I duck under it.

My lips find the head of his dick, and I tease him with my tongue for a second before taking him into my mouth.

A groan ripples through his body, and the truck swerves slightly.

I pull my mouth off him. "You got this? If you can't handle it, I'll stop. I don't want to die in a car crash with a cock in my mouth."

"I got it, I swear."

"Good." I lick along the veined underside of his dick and swirl my tongue over the tip, tasting the salty sweetness of his precum. Then I run him into my mouth again, deep as I can manage.

"Not gonna lie, Earnshaw," he says thickly. "I've always wanted a girl to do this while I'm driving."

I hum around him and start bobbing my head.

"Fuck," Heathcliff chokes out. "Fuck, fuck—"

He takes a turn, managing it smoothly in spite of the tremors I can feel shuddering through his body.

Drawing back, I leave just the head of his dick in my mouth. There's a spot right beneath it, where it joins to the shaft, that's especially sensitive for most guys, so I let my teeth scrape lightly through that groove before exerting a few pulses of pressure on it with my tongue.

"God, Cathy," gasps Heathcliff, and his cock jumps between my lips. I smile and reward him with several long, firm licks before I swallow him again.

He hisses out a breath as his dick slides into the heat of my mouth and throat. His right hand finds the back of my head, and he pushes down, like he can't help it. I don't mind—I love the loss of his control, his compulsive need to come.

And come he does, bursting with salty heat inside my mouth. His heavy groan reverberates through the truck, and though his steering wobbles a bit, he keeps the truck on the road, as far as I can tell. I take my time swallowing and sucking, so I won't gag and he'll get every last bit of pleasure.

There's a wicked satisfaction in knowing his come is in my belly, his flavor on my tongue. I savor him for another second and then withdraw, carefully pulling his swim trunks back into place over his damp cock. He adjusts himself, still panting.

"Filthy woman," he breathes, with a look of pure sin in my direction.

And then he swerves off the road.

"Oh my god!" I exclaim, bracing myself. "Heathcliff, what are you doing?"

"Off-roading." The truck bumps into a field of brownish grass, over clumps and clods. This field isn't fenced in. It lies open and fallow under the blue autumn sky.

"You're gonna wreck your truck," I say.

"It's Hindley's truck. I don't own a vehicle."

"Oh."

My mental perspective shifts a little, from truck-owning Heathcliff to truck-borrowing Heathcliff. I'm oddly disappointed, possibly because truck-owning Heathcliff represented more possibilities, more freedom, and Heathcliff without a vehicle is stuck here, like I am.

Heathcliff stops the truck. His side is facing the road, while mine faces the field and the trees. He swings out of the driver's door, marches around the front of the truck, and yanks my door open. His big hands close on my wrists and he pulls me out of the passenger seat, onto the grass.

"Heathcliff, what—"

His thick, warm fingers brush my stomach as he undoes the button of my shorts and drags down the zipper. Then he pushes the shorts down to my ankles. I'm not wearing panties, and the kiss of the soft breeze on my pussy makes me shiver with pleasure. The air is golden, the faint bite of last night's chill mingling with the indomitable heat of the Southern sun. The fresh scent of the distant trees and the heavy, damp aroma of the soil fills my nostrils. I think I could breathe this air forever and be perfectly happy.

"Heathcliff," I whisper.

He doesn't answer, just maintains that fierce, purposeful silence while he grabs my waist and lifts my bare ass back onto the passenger seat, taking off my flip-flops, sliding off my shorts, and tossing everything onto his seat. Then he pushes my legs open.

I feel the lips of my sex parting wetly, spreading for him while he braces both palms against my thighs, holding me in place.

Heathcliff goes down to one knee. He looks up at me, and I hold my breath, stunned by how gorgeous he is at this moment, with the sun gilding his black hair and his brown eyes glowing at me like dark embers. He traces his tongue across his full lips.

I think he's asking for permission. Or at least, giving me the chance to say no. Which is wise of him, especially after my banshee got a little too excited last night.

No matter what the risks, no matter what damage I might do, I refuse to give him up. Which means I need to practice self-control, and there's no better time to do that than right now, in the middle of nowhere.

He's still looking at me questioningly—no, wait, his gaze has dipped to my pussy. He's staring at it with a grim-jawed hunger that makes me feel wonderfully wicked.

I reach between my legs and slide one finger through my folds before swirling it over my clit. Then I lean back, bracing myself on both hands, and I give him a smile that's also a challenge.

With a low, eager huff of hot breath, Heathcliff nestles his face into my pussy.

His scruff grazes my inner thigh. It's scratchy, but I don't mind. Weirdly, it's the perfect counterpoint to the slick invasion of his tongue.

His broad lips seal over my sex, and his tongue quivers along the seam of my pussy, a rhythmic licking that sends sheer bliss pulsing through my core. Then his lips close over my clit, suckling that tender bit of me, and I whimper. Can't help it. I plant one bare foot on the dashboard and set the other against the inside of the truck, right where the shoulder belt hangs. In this position I can hold myself steady, even while I'm losing my mind to his thick, warm tongue.

Heathcliff rises and bends over me, eating me out like I'm a feast prepared just for him. Each thorough stroke of his tongue makes me squeal softly, until he takes my clit between his teeth and tugs it gently. Electric thrills jolt through that spot, followed by a surge of pleasure as he lets go and kisses me there instead. Then he's shaking his head, back and forth, back and forth, his tongue and lips rubbing over my clit with just the right rhythm— fuck, fuck. I throw back my head and I come. Somehow I manage not to scream, but frantic breaths burst from my lungs, each one edged with a grateful whimper. As my pussy flutters, spasms, he kisses it deeply, firmly, compressing my clit just right as I shudder and whine for him.

"Heathcliff," I sob. "Heathcliff, Heathcliff." And he grabs me, hauls me against him, kisses my mouth. He shoves one big hand between my legs, cups my pussy, and holds me there, secure and soothing, the tip of his middle finger dipping just slightly into my slippery center.

I wrap both arms around his neck, a convulsive, possessive grip. My kiss turns cruel, my teeth snatching at his lips, his tongue, his jaw. I feel like I could eat him whole, unhinge my jaw and swallow him serpentlike, and that way I could keep him forever.

"Don't you ever fucking do that to anyone else," I hiss in his ear.

His hand leaves my pussy. Grips my throat, right under my jaw, and he kisses me brutally, until my lips are sore and swollen, and yet I'm choking a laugh through the sting of it because he's making me the best kind of promise.

He releases my throat, and without warning, his two central fingers ram deep into my pussy. I gasp, tightening my grip on his neck. He pounds me ruthlessly, those fingers thrusting thick and deep, the heel of his hand hammering against my clit. I'm so wet I'm spraying droplets with each rapid thrust, and normally I might be embarrassed but I'm mindless for him, every inhibition blurred, my body slave to the violent thrusting of his fingers.

I come with a gush of bliss, with a voiceless scream, with a spastic tightening of every muscle in my body. I can't breathe. I bite Heathcliff's shoulder through his T-shirt while my limbs shake and my wetness showers his hand.

When the bliss recedes, I'm limp and soft. The edge of the seat is damp, but Heathcliff produces a roll of paper towels from somewhere and shoves a wad against the cushion to soak up the moisture. He cleans me up, too, wiping carefully between my thighs.

I manage to get my shorts back on, and within minutes we're headed back to the road.

"You gonna tell your brother what we did in his truck?" I ask.

Heathcliff's mouth twists in a wry grin. "Nope. Besides, he's done worse in here."

"Ew." I glance around the discolored interior of the cab with fresh understanding. Not like I've got room to judge, though, after my own contribution to whatever bodily fluids have stained this vehicle. And honestly I've had sex in worse places.

I pull out my phone and my stomach does an unpleasant lurch when I see a text from Dad. You missed church. Again. You better be at prayer meeting tonight.

"Everything okay?" Heathcliff cuts me a sidelong look.

"Yeah." I lean back against my seat with a sigh. "Just...back to reality, that's all."

For some reason, I feel like crying. Not just crying—*weeping*, in the biblical sense. To me, *weeping* represents a more visceral kind of grief, the voicing of an ache that is soul deep. It's the thought of being away from Heathcliff, of not having *this* again—breakfast and conversation, messy sex in an open field, even encounters with strange gods.

"We haven't really talked about the god thing," I venture, attempting to rein in that soul-deep sadness.

"What's there to say?"

"Aren't you curious as to how Manannán was raised? Why he was there?"

"Guess I just kind of accepted it." He glances at me again. "You know something?"

"Not much, but yeah. You overhead some of it when we spied on the Lintons, but I think I should fill you in on the rest." Quickly I tell him about the strangers at Aunt Nellie's, what they said, and what my dad and Pastor Linton told them. "Doesn't that freak you out? Or maybe it doesn't, since your family is all about worshipping the gods and bringing them back."

"Never said *I* want to raise them," he mutters.

"Well...do you?"

"The way I figure, it doesn't much matter who's in charge. Gods, devils, big-talking men with nuclear weapons at their fingertips—doesn't really change how I live my life. I'll keep eating, fucking, shitting, and sleeping all the same. You and me, Cathy, we're at the bottom of the heap, you know? What happens at the top filters down, sure, but it doesn't make a huge difference to people like us."

"The bottom of the heap," I say quietly. "That's how you see me? How you see yourself? Don't you want something more, something better?"

"Sure I do. But I got no ambitions to live in a fancy-ass house and work a corporate job or some shit. Best I hope for is a truck in my own name, food on the table, beer in my hand, and a decent place I can call home."

"And that's all?"

He chuckles. "No. That's not all. There's one more thing I need. Otherwise the rest ain't worth having."

My skin turns hot. I refuse to ask if it's me. If I'm the *one thing*. Because that would be ridiculous. I'm a problem. Having me around would make his life unpredictable, uncomfortable, and depressing.

"I don't let myself think much about what I want," I say. "I don't have a lot of choices. I'm...stuck—stuck with Dad, stuck in Wicklow, stuck with the banshee thing. I used to think a cabin in the mountains would be nice. But that won't ever happen. No use wishing."

Heathcliff is quiet for several minutes. Then he says, "I think you gotta have wishes and plans, even if they look small or dumb to other people. Otherwise you might as well curl up and die right now."

"Is that supposed to be encouraging?"

"It's not about encouragement," he replies. "It's about having a reason to live. And from now on, Earnshaw, you're my fucking reason."

My chest swells tight with a joy that hurts, and my eyes sting. "Fine." I manage to keep my voice steady. "Then you're mine, too."

❖❖❖

His words echo in my head when he drops me off a short distance from my house. I sneak in and shower, but it turns out I didn't have to be sneaky because Dad isn't home. He must have gone to Sunday dinner with someone from church.

I'm not really hungry, so I flop onto my bed and check my email. There's one from Pastor Linton—a church-wide email. Usually I'd delete it immediately, but the subject line catches my attention: "The Power of the Blood." Pastor Linton's emails usually have subject lines like "Weekly Update" or "Church Luncheon Info" or "Prayer Request Chain," stuff like that.

I click on it.

Hallowed Family,

Those who were at morning worship today heard these words spoken aloud, but I write this letter to you now, as an apostle of God, to ensure that you keep this word ever before your eyes. Speak it to your families, guard its message from outsiders, write its truth upon the walls of your heart. Put it on like armor, that you may be ready to stand in the evil day, and having done all, to stand.

Most of us live faithfully from week to week, quiet soldiers of the Lord, never expecting to be called up to active duty. But the time comes when faithfulness alone is not enough, and we must prove our love and loyalty through acts that are not only spiritual but physical. Sacrifice is not solely an Old Testament practice, nor is it limited to the intangibles alone. Our congregation has a deeper experience with that concept than most.

Most of you know the truth of our mission, but for some, faith may have faded and doubt may have crept in. Others may have lingered on the fringes of the church, worshipping with us without being fully attuned to the unique role that Wicklow Heritage Chapel fills in this world.

Now is the time for doubters to believe, for longtime believers to renew their faith, and for those on the fringes of the camp to draw nearer and understand our blessed purpose, a mission unique among God's people.

For generations we have served as the guardians of Old Sheldon Church, which is not only a ruined place of worship but a burial site, the resting place of a pagan monstrosity that some might call a god but that we call by its true name—demon. The demon Cernunnos, bringer of death, enemy of life and righteousness, confined long ago. Our ancestors took up the duty of guarding the demon's burial site and ensuring that he sleeps forever.

We have done our duty well for many years. We sanctify the ground, pray over it, and keep the faith. But there are some, wolves in sheep's clothing, monsters in the guise of humans, who desire to stir up the ancient powers, restore their wicked ways, and bring horrible death upon all the faithful. We have striven to keep them out, even using their own dark magicks against them to build a wall, as Nehemiah did to protect his city from invaders and thieves. This wall, invisible yet effective, has kept us safe for decades. When pagans and those of corrupt blood come too close to our borders, we destroy them before they can conquer us and unleash this unspeakable evil upon the world.

And now, dear brothers and sisters, the painful truth— we are under threat by the forces of darkness. Infection spreads within our town, within the borders of the wall. Evil powers are at work to raise the ancient demon, and our sacred rituals are no longer enough to repress it.

Corruption has wormed its way into our congregation, and yes, into our hearts.

At times such as these, God requires a reconsecration of our souls and bodies. A fresh demonstration of our devotion to His will. Even now, the church leaders are seeking out new paths of faith, discerning new revelations, discovering what kind of sacrifice God may require of us as warriors against the fiends of hell. Until such time as the way is revealed, I beg you to consecrate yourselves and your loved ones. Confess all sin. Chastise yourselves to show true penitence. Undertake days of fasting and nights of prayer, and let no one find rest while we strive and agonize together. This we must do, acting as one. The sin or dissent of a single member of the flock could bring the ruin of us all. So examine your hearts, deprive your bodies, and come together with us tonight as we beseech God for His aid.

Your Assistant Pastor,

Edgar Linton

Stunned, I read the thing twice.

Assistant Pastor Linton? Since when? Since yesterday? What the hell prompted Edgar to send out doomsday emails to the congregation from his dad's email address?

Last night...he must have seen something last night. He heard me scream—everyone did, but I figured they'd chalk it up to the beer and high emotions. Maybe Edgar wasn't as drunk as I thought. Or maybe...maybe when Heathcliff came to look for me, he followed. Maybe he saw something out in the sea—the giant watery fist of a furious sea god. Maybe that's why he and the others packed up and left so fast. Add the sea god and my screams to the encounter with the strangers at Aunt Nellie's, and I guess it could have been enough to flip the switch and send Edgar and his dad into panic mode.

Or maybe something else happened. Something I don't know about. More god-related deaths that I can't perceive. And maybe I can't see them because the thing buried under Old Sheldon Church is the actual god of death, Cernunnos. Cernunnos and the Morrigan—they're the ones who created the banshees, according to Manannán.

Quickly I pull up my phone's browser app and search for Cernunnos. It all fits—the antlers, his connection to nature and the cycle of life and death. I even find one website that claims banshees are the offspring of Cernunnos himself. As his descendant, it makes sense that I'm sensitive to certain deaths. And it also follows that the god of death might be able shield certain killings from my perception if he wanted to. I mean, he's kind of the boss.

But the fact that he's been veiling things from me could mean he's more conscious than we thought. Possibly my dad has realized that as well. He noticed my surprise when I heard about those two deacons being stabbed to death with sticks. He knows I didn't mourn them, that I didn't even realize they had died. And sure, he's been drinking a lot lately, but he can put two and two together.

I feel hollow and shaky inside, like the stabilizing core of my self has been ripped out. Pastor Linton is always the one who sends the church-wide emails. He never lets anyone else do it. What does it mean that Edgar sent the letter this time? And what was all that crap about fasting, deprivation, and confession? And sacrifice? I mean, Wicklow has always been kind of creepy at times, but this is over-the-top. Surely everyone else in the congregation can see that. They can be strict and judgmental, but they're not fanatical like Edgar sounds in the email.

I close my eyes, willing myself to relax, to resist the fear creeping along my spine. There's no need to worry about this. I've seen the congregation get riled up before, begging for a "fresh anointing of the Holy Spirit" or a new revival. It's just people needing a little excitement in their lives. The frenzy always passes pretty quick, and this will, too.

12

HEATHCLIFF

THE MINUTE I STEP INTO THE GRANGE, A BULLET BITES THE wood floor near my feet.

"Fuck!" I shout, leaping back.

Hindley comes down the stairs, twirling his favorite pistol. "You stole my truck."

"Borrowed." He'd be even more pissed if he knew I'd borrowed it the other night, too, for the meeting at Moretti's.

"You missed work."

"So I missed one shift. Big deal." I toss my bag onto the floor and close the door behind me as casually as I can, as if I'm assuming he won't shoot again. "You have three other employees, Hindley. They all know the business better than I do. I'm just the muscle, the guy who lifts stuff."

"Yeah, and we needed your muscle today."

"I'll work a double shift tomorrow." I shuffle past the stairs toward the kitchen. A measured pace, like I'm tired. It's body language I've learned by heart, the recipe for lowering Hindley's boiling point to a simmer.

And it works. I'm rewarded by the click of the safety.

"We ain't done talking about this," Hindley warns, coming down the stairs and following me into the kitchen. "You can't just up and take my truck, you hear? You gotta ask first."

"You said I could use it if I paid the insurance," I point out.

"Still mine though, ain't it? Got my name on the title. You ask me every time you wanna borrow it, you hear? And you don't stay out overnight, ever." His voice is taut, a wobble of fear in the anger.

That quaver helps me understand what's up with him. When I didn't come back last night, he thought I'd left. That I'd gone off on my own.

Which is exactly what I plan to do once I've got enough money saved. But I can't let him know that.

I yank open the fridge, grab two beers, and hand him one. "Hey. You and me, we don't always get along, but you're my brother. Family. This is home. I ain't goin' nowhere."

Hindley takes the bottle, his mouth working under his scruffy beard. "Yeah, well." He clears his throat.

"How's our patient?" I ask.

"Same as ever, I guess. When you gonna get him on his feet?"

"Soon, I hope. I'll go see what I can do."

As I pass Hindley, I keep my shoulders relaxed, my stride easy. He doesn't follow me upstairs.

Again, like I've done a thousand times, I ask myself why I don't grow a damn backbone, face him down, and refuse to put up with his bullying and bullshit anymore. I guess I'm a coward. I don't know how to exist without Hindley, his connections, and this house. I don't have a bank account. Hindley pays me my cut in cash and I keep it hidden in the house. Since I was a stolen kid, I don't have a birth certificate, a Social Security number, or a driver's license. How Buckland Lockwood got me into the Kinsale school system, I'll never know.

Lucky for me, the police are real lax around here. I've never been pulled over, so I've never had to show a license. It's a rural community, and lots of folks don't bring their licenses along when they're driving down the road or into town. If I ever did get pulled over, I could say I forgot mine. Most of the cops know me anyway, since I'm the one who comes to get Hindley if he ever acts up drunk out in public. Whenever he has a run-in with the law, a donation of Lockwood lager to the sheriff's private stash usually smooths everything over.

Yeah, I been too scared to get my own identity, to step outside the boundaries of this family. Hindley's a mess and a mean son of a bitch, but him and the other Lockwoods are all I've had for years.

Except now, there's Cathy.

"Catherine Earnshaw." I whisper her name into the upstairs hallway, like a charm against the dark.

She and I are the same in more ways than I thought at first. The way she is, her situation—I get it. I understand *her*, and she understands me.

I head into our coma patient's room, flip the light switch, and set the beer on the dresser. My back is to the bed, and in the amber glass of the beer bottle, I see something move. Something tall and quick.

I spin around, but there's nobody, just the motionless figure under the sheet. Ian's face is the same as always—placid, healthy, and unconscious.

Unnerved, I scan the room. There's a lot of heavy furniture in here, pieces that wouldn't fit anywhere else in the house, so they found their way into the guest room. My eyes narrow on the wardrobe, and I cross to it with quick strides, yanking the door open.

Nothing.

I'm exhausted. And I had an encounter with an actual god yesterday. This is probably post-traumatic stress, making me see random shit.

I pull the sheet down. Ian is still in the pajamas I dressed him in—an old flannel set of Buckland's. Carefully I check his limbs, his extremities, and yeah, his privates. Still no piss or anything. Still no sign that he needs food or water. His pulse is steady, his breathing is light and regular. He doesn't have a fever. And when I place my hand on his forehead and try to get a read off him, I don't feel anything. Which means no part of him is stuck in the Vague. He's wholly here, just…not here.

Swearing softly, I sink onto the edge of the bed, brace my elbows on my knees, and prop my chin on my hands.

"What's up with you, man?" I say aloud to the unconscious figure. "I need my cut of the payout, okay? I need you to wake the fuck up. I don't know how to fix you."

It's possible Hindley screwed something up on his end of the resurrection. But it's more likely that I failed to repair some vital part of the brain that controls consciousness.

No…that's not it. I've healed my share of corpses. I know exactly what I'm doing, and I always get this sense of completeness when it's done. No way I left anything unfinished.

Unless this guy is supernatural. Hindley mentioned something like that. But he didn't know what kind of supernatural the guy was, so I have no idea how that might affect things.

I partnered in the resurrection of a couple supernaturals back when I was younger, when Buckland was still alive and he was training me. Their resurrections worked the same as any others. If Ian's didn't turn out right, he must be way different than anything I've encountered. And he must not have suspected that a resurrection wouldn't work right for him, or he'd have given us more details ahead of time.

Unless his brand of supernatural is so terrible he thought we wouldn't bring him back. I remember the oily, slithering shape of his soul, the panicked sensation I felt, the wrongness.

I don't feel that wrongness now, or I might be tempted to stick a knife in his heart and be done with the whole mess.

Besides, I need that payout money, for me and for Cathy. Especially since there's no knowing when my own private business venture will bear fruit.

I work over Ian awhile longer, trying everything I can think of. But there's nothing to heal or pull, no wandering spirit to seize and drag back into the body. He's fine. He's just…stagnant. Like a swamp lying perfectly still between cypress trees.

"Whatever is going on with you, I don't know if you deserve it or not," I mutter. "But I'm doing the best I can, man. I got my own shit to deal with." I rub a hand over my face, releasing a deep sigh. "I just found out I got Italian roots. Always suspected, but it's for sure now. I'm descended from Juventas, Roman goddess of life, with some weird connection to Celtic gods like Manannán and I…fuck, I don't know what to make of it. Can't research this stuff online very well, you know?"

I stare at the motionless figure, stroking the stubble along my jaw. "You don't mind if I vent a little, right? I got no one else to talk to, and you can't tell on me anyway."

He lies there, silent and empty, so I keep talking. "My girl, she's a banshee, a herald of death, which is ironic considering what I can do, dragging souls out of the Vague. It's like we're fated or something. Like I've always known her. She's my fucking soul, man, and she's got to realize that it's her and me, it's us against the damn world..."

Tears are forming in my eyes, and I'll be damned if I cry right now. I gotta stop confessing all my crap to this unconscious guy, so I clear my throat and rub my eyes angrily before getting up.

I'm headed out of the room when I see it.

A black feather on the carpet.

I pick it up, peering at it. A single feather, long, glossy, and jet-black.

Ain't no pillows in this house with feathers like that.

It's fucking weird, but it doesn't mean anything. Could have come from anywhere. Hell, I could have tracked it in here.

Just to be sure, I snap my fingers sharply in front of the unconscious man's face. Not a flinch. I flick his cheek, poke his belly, pull a hair from his head. Nothing.

He's not faking unconsciousness, that's for sure. Besides, if he were, he'd have sneaked out long ago, to avoid having to pay us.

When I leave the room, I holler down the stairs at Hindley. "He won't wake up. I tried everything."

Hindley mutters several curses, and a dish smashes.

"Did you wear a black feather boa into Ian's room?" I call.

"No, idiot!" he bellows back.

"Cool down. I don't know your kinks, all right? Just checking because I found a black feather on the carpet."

Hindley doesn't answer, so I head for my room. I got two new tattoos, and they could use some air.

I'm lucky Cathy and I fucked in the dark, so she didn't notice the first one. Not a great idea to go to the beach right after getting a tattoo, of course, but this is no ordinary mark. It links me to my first client that's all mine. I had it done on my ass, just to be sure Hindley won't ever see it, and I didn't go to Bean or Morgana for it, just to be safe. I hired a guy who doesn't work out of a shop—he'll meet anywhere to get the job done. He did mine and my client's tattoos on the same day.

The tattoo is pretty irritated from everything I've done lately. It's swollen and tingling. I'm gonna lock my door and lie naked on the bed awhile, give it some air. Maybe tug one out while I'm enjoying my beer.

I got plenty of fodder for my fantasies, that's for sure, after what Cathy did to me in the truck...and what I did to her.

But I make the mistake of picking up my phone first and checking my texts. Haven't done that since last night. I got an old phone of Hindley's with a cracked screen, and it's slow sometimes, but it works.

The first text makes me sit straight up. It's from the man I met at Moretti's. He's the agent for this rich guy with cancer, Alan Wolcott. Wolcott is in his forties, terminal, on hospice care. Leaving behind a thriving business and a family with kids. He's been shelling out cash right and left, trying all these experimental things to save himself, and none of it has worked.

I found Alan Wolcott on TikTok, did some research on his situation, and messaged him through an anonymous account to offer my services. He was desperate enough to believe me. I kept things anonymous until I was sure he was interested, that he'd keep quiet about me to everyone but his agent. When he sent the agent to Moretti's with the deposit, I knew he was serious. His deposit paid for the hotel and the tattoos for me and Cathy.

Good thing I secured this client when I did because the text I just got confirms that he's already dead. My tattoo didn't even alert me to his passing...or maybe it did. The tingling I felt was probably the tattoo buzzing, but it was so swollen I didn't realize what was going on. Guess I'm gonna have to get used to carrying tether tattoos and paying attention to them.

The agent's text is short, urgent. Wolcott passed. The family will be out of the house for six hours.

There's a second text with an address.

Fuck. The agent texted me three hours ago, which means I got three hours left, and it'll take an hour for me to get to Wolcott's house in Summerville. Hindley's not gonna let me borrow his truck again, that's for damn sure.

I gotta buy my own vehicle. If I can complete this job, I'll be able to afford it... I just need a way to get there.

Stealing a car isn't tough when you know what you're doing. I know a truck stop down the road with parking that backs up to the woods, and the owner keeps his beat-up Chevy out there. No sight lines to it from the windows. It's probably sitting there now. A thirty-minute walk, and I'll be in that car, heading to Summerville.

I jump off the bed, pull my clothes on, and leave the beer on the nightstand. I make it out the side door without attracting Hindley's attention, and I jog up the road. All I gotta do is steal the car, drive to the house, resurrect Wolcott quietly, grab the cash, and drop the car somewhere near the truck stop. I'll wipe it down good to get rid of my prints, and the police will think someone just took it for a joy ride. Hell, it's not a crime if I'm doing it to save a life.

This can work, and if it works, I can do it again. I didn't just sell Wolcott resurrection. I sold him freedom from cancer. The whole package. He'll come back from the dead good as new, ready for another few decades of life.

If there's one prize people will sacrifice anything for, it's life. More days, more hours, more minutes. I can offer them *years*. I can't fix what ails living people, but as I'm bringing them back, I can restore them to perfect physical condition. That's my angle for building my own client list—targeting not just anyone but the really desperate folks. The terminal patients who are right on the edge, looking into that abyss. The ones willing to believe that I can reach beyond death and drag their souls back for another chance at life. I feel guilty sometimes, looking for the folks with no other options, but they're the only ones who won't laugh at what I can do. I'm not hurting them—I'm saving them. Rescuing them from death. And in the meantime, I'm earning the money to rescue the woman I love.

Resurrecting Wolcott is going to take a lot of energy. I'm risking plenty here, hoping I'll have the chance to recover before Hindley needs me to resurrect one of *his* clients. Fortunately for me, the resurrections he does are usually spaced pretty far apart. If he'd take on more people, we'd be a lot richer.

I've asked Hindley a few times if he wants me to try to drum up more business for our necromancy business, but he always refuses. "Can't be too careful," he says. "Stick to folks we know, folks we can trust to stay quiet and pay up. Friends of friends. No strangers. No risks."

Ironic that he's a gambler at heart, yet the area where he won't take risks is the one that could actually make us some money. After all, he's got me, which is an advantage. The Coosaw Lockwoods have all but quit the resurrection business, since it takes three of them to manage a decent pull, and they can't heal the person afterward. Not much point in offering resurrection services if you're just gonna plop the soul back into a ruined body.

I've always had the golden ticket to a better life. I just didn't have the courage to use it until I met Catherine.

Witnessing someone's agony for thirteen hours—it changes you. I watched her suffer and sob, hobbling through the forest on bruised feet. I carried her in my arms—slender and fragile and stronger than I've ever been. Everything shifted, and she was the new sun, me in her orbit. She lit a fire in me and got me going on the plan I've always thought about but never had the courage to try until now.

There's the truck stop ahead, through the trees. If I can pull this off, I'll be back around nightfall, and I can sleep off the post-resurrection lag in my own bed.

13

CATHY

DAD GETS HOME AROUND FOUR O'CLOCK, JUST TWO HOURS before the usual Sunday evening prayer service. I'm sitting at the kitchen table, munching pistachios and scrolling through cottagecore Instagram posts, getting ideas for new displays at Aunt Nellie's.

He heads straight for the coffee maker. Brewing coffee and snacking on pork rinds is his way of coping when he can't be drunk.

"Do I have to go tonight?" I ask. "I got this weird email from Edgar, and it freaked me out. What exactly happened at church today?"

Dad's huge, sloped shoulders stiffen under his suit coat, and instinctively I shrink a little in my chair.

He turns around slowly. He's chewing his lip, his eyes churning with anger and...something else—something frighteningly close to panic. "You gotta be there tonight. They need to see that you're one of us."

"But I'm not."

He slams a palm on the counter so violently that I jump. "Idiot girl. Can't you see I'm trying to protect you? They *know*, Cathy.

Edgar knows. Mark Linton knows. By now the whole church probably knows what you are. Only reason they haven't kicked us out yet is because they need me. There are so few of us left…"

The hollowness in his gaze terrifies me. "So few of the deacons? Did someone else die?"

He wipes a hand across his forehead. "Five more."

My stomach drops. "Did you say *five*?"

"We went out to Old Sheldon Church last night, Cat, and we prayed, sang, dumped gallons of blessed water—even invited a couple priests from Saint Martha's over in Yemassee. I guess the death toll is seven if you count them."

The air around me feels very, very still, incredibly brittle. The hairs on my arms are standing straight up.

I didn't sense any of those deaths. Which means there's no doubt of it now—the god is awake enough to deliberately conceal them from me.

"What happened?" I whisper.

He grabs the bag of coffee from the basket, then sets it down as if it's too heavy to manage. "Don't know if I told you this, but the demon stirred once before, right about the time you were born."

"You told me," I whisper. "You said thick vines like tentacles pushed right out of the ground. Some of them came up right through the trees and made big holes in the trunks, and you and the other church leaders filled the holes with bricks of blessed clay. I've seen those bricked-up places, set right into the tree trunks."

He nods. "We got it under control pretty quick. But I should have known then that something was wrong with you. That you were messed up, diseased. You came out blue and we thought you were gone, but then you screamed—I'll never forget that scream. Just that once, though, and then you were fine. You didn't cry much as a baby. Real quiet. We thought you were just a contented kid. Didn't know you were saving it up for later."

Dad chokes on a laugh, opens the coffee bag, starts scooping. "So last night, the ground was shaking. We could feel it all the way out here, and we knew it was coming from the church. So Pastor Linton, he calls up the two priests and us deacons, and we head over there. Normally it would be enough to sprinkle a little water and pray over the ground, but when we got there, I knew—I *knew* that wasn't going to cut it this time."

I stay perfectly still. It's so strange to hear about the death of people I know without also having the raw, unbearable need to scream my grief for them, for their families.

"So we get to the church, and there's vines, like the day you were born." My father pours in the water, starts the coffee maker. "Thrashing around like big tentacles. And they're huge, three times as tall as me. We started walking, singing, praying. Heffernan went back and got the Wicklow fire truck, and one of the priests blessed the water inside it. But it still wasn't enough." He faces me, lips trembling beneath his thick, wiry beard, his eyes cruel now, merciless. Blaming me with every word.

"Donaghy got it first. A tentacle picked him up and threw him, and these sticks jabbed right up out of the ground as he was falling. Pierced him through in a dozen places. Then it takes Heffernan, then Gainey. Same thing. And we just keep walking, you know, and singing and praying, but the praying's more like screams now, and I'm thinking maybe that's what it wants from us—our screams."

His eyes are bright with hate, but there are tears in them now.

"We kept going. Finally the vines started to calm down, but there was so much blood. Blood everywhere, soaking into the grass. Then it got really quiet, and we all just stood there, staring at the bodies. Gainey, Donaghy, Heffernan, Coffey, and Ward, plus the two priests. I don't remember their names. Pastor knows. He said we should take the bodies, but they were wrapped up tight in vines, and we didn't want to disturb the quiet. So we got into our cars and left them there...in the blood...in the grass."

The coffee maker trickles in the silence, and it sounds thick and dark, like the trickling of blood from the seven dead men.

"Pastor is..." Dad shakes his head. "I guess he's broken. Couldn't preach today, just sat there while Edgar talked to the congregation. Even during Sunday dinner, he was frozen. Didn't say a word. I don't think he showered or anything since Old Sheldon Church—I saw a drop of dried blood on his neck, right above his shirt collar. It's like he's given up. I tried to talk to him, but there was no getting through." He renews his glare at me. "Everything's going to pieces. Headed that way from the day your mama squeezed you out, although I didn't know it then."

I want to say I'm sorry, but it would feel like admitting guilt. So instead I say, "This isn't my fault, any of it. You can't hate me for what's happening."

There's a dull heaviness in his expression now, weariness lining his body.

"I do hate you, kid," he says quietly. "But I'm your dad, so I'll protect you, too. And that means taking you to church tonight. If you stay away, it'll make you look twice as guilty."

I'm still reeling from *I do hate you, kid*. Suspecting how he felt was bad; *knowing* is so much worse. But I manage to ask,

"Will they even let me into the church? Now that they know what I am?"

"They will. Like I said, they need me. So they'll let us in, and we'll show them our loyalty. You're gonna be right up front, and you're gonna pray your lungs out, Cat, or so help me, I'll tan your hide so bad, you'll wish they'd strung you up as the pagan offspring you are."

I'm shaking so hard, I can barely stand. Can barely force my fingers to close around my phone. "Like I said, it's not my fault. I got this from Mom—or from *you*. You've both got Irish in your blood so there's no way to know which of you—"

He lunges, lightning fast for his bulk, and slaps me. One of his lighter blows, but I still taste blood from where my teeth cut my cheek.

"It wasn't me," he growls. "No one in my family ever did what you can do. No one. It was your filthy mother. Had to be. That's why I sent her off, soon as you graduated—couldn't bear to touch her or look at her—"

"Wait," I gasp. "You...you *sent her off*? I thought she left. You *told* me she left!"

He hesitates, nostrils flaring, cheeks crimson. "I didn't give her a choice. I made sure she had no choice but to leave. See, I knew it was her dirty blood that ruined you, so I figured with her gone, maybe I could train you up right. Keep you in church, keep you headed straight. But you had to defy me at every turn, like a true daughter of Babylon."

I swallow hard, retreating slowly out of his reach. "You say you want to protect me, but you're only protecting yourself."

For a second, I think he'll barrel toward me, all fury and fists... but he turns his back, takes the coffeepot out, and grabs a mug from the shelf. "Think what you want. Be ready to leave by five thirty. Wear something decent or I'll rip it off and make you change."

Somehow I manage to navigate the stairs to my room. Somehow my trembling fingers unlock the phone. For a second my fingertips hover over the new name in my contacts—Daisy. But I change my mind and text Heathcliff instead. He gave me his number during the trip back, and I've never needed seven digits more than I do right now.

I can't do this anymore.

A simple message. Too needy, probably. But it's true—I can't anymore. Can't endure my dad's temper, his hatred. Can't keep going to that stifling church and enduring those fake smiles and judgmental gazes.

I cry in the bathroom for a while, then force myself to get ready for church. A knee-length, long-sleeved dress. Plain, close-toed shoes.

At five thirty, Dad bellows up the stairs, and I hurry down to avoid making him angrier.

And still Heathcliff hasn't texted me back.

14

CATHY

IN OCTOBER, NIGHT FALLS EARLY, AND I'VE NEVER HATED that so fiercely as I do tonight. Wicklow Heritage Church stands like a tombstone in the semicircle clearing, the forest rising in a tangle of thatched limbs behind it. In the watery light of the lamps flanking the entrance, the greeters look sallow, sickly. They're dressed in black, and they don't smile as they usually do.

This is no pleasant Sunday morning worship service, where we dress in our best and don our pretty, pious masks. The masks are off now, shredded by the claws of the monster we guard. The darkness can't be denied, and the shadow of death is with us.

I hang behind Dad as we enter the church. The greeters don't say anything as we pass between them; they only stare. The church lobby is crowded with black-clad worshippers, and it feels like a gauntlet of muttering mouths and accusing eyes.

Suddenly Edgar is there, wearing a black suit and a red tie. He grips Dad's hand firmly and gives him a sympathetic smile. "You came. I'm glad." He turns to me, blue eyes gleaming. "Cathy. I thought we could have a private chat, you and I, before the prayer time begins."

"Um..." I scramble for a reason not to, but he's already taking my hand and leading me through the bodies, away from the eyes and the mouths, hustling me into one side of a confessional booth while he takes the other. The booths are soundproof, mostly, and for a moment I'm relieved by the abrupt silencing of the low conversations outside and the absence of all those malevolent eyes.

Slowly I settle onto the narrow bench seat. I'll sit here and deal with Edgar if it means I can hide from the congregation a little longer.

"It's time to come clean, Cathy," says Edgar from the other side of the wooden screen that divides the booth. "You've been lying for so long. Trust me, it will feel amazing to let the deception go."

"I thought you said we were going to chat."

"We can do that, too. In fact, there was something I wanted to tell you, and I hope you'll hear it in the spirit in which it's intended."

It's never good when someone prefaces a speech with those words.

"Leadership is my spiritual gift," says Edgar. "I've led dozens of bible studies and mission teams. I've led prayer groups and class presentations and preaching teams. But last night, on the beach, I lost control. And I've been trying to figure out why."

"Beer," I suggest.

"It was more than that. You see, I can lead groups that include both believers and the lost—as long as the lost are open-minded. As long as they have an interest in the things of God. But there are people who aren't just *lost*, Cathy. They are the damned, the reprobates, like Cliff, the guy Isabella brought along. Elements like that should never be allowed in a gathering of the faithful. They're disruptive, unhinged, and problematic."

"So just because Cliff was there, you couldn't control the event like you planned, and it veered in a different direction. Is that what you're saying?"

"It's a bit more nuanced than that—"

"Honestly, I think it's more primal than that. You were the alpha of the pack until Hea—until *Cliff* showed up, and then he naturally became the alpha. It's basic animal behavior."

Edgar blows out a frustrated breath. "That's a very pagan way of looking at it, Cathy."

"Is it, though?"

"The point is, I've figured out how to rectify that failure in leadership. Eliminate the dissenters, the rebels, the problematic elements, and you're left with a flock that's ready to follow."

That sounds way too much like dictator-speak, but I don't mention it. Best not to antagonize him until I figure out exactly what he wants.

"Let's talk about you," he continues. "About that scream. That's when I figured it out, you know. Dad and I had some pieces of the puzzle, but that was the clue we needed to determine what kind of supernatural you were. A banshee. Your father confirmed it this morning. He told me how it works when he gave me his confession."

"Good. Saves me time." My fingers curl around the edge of the bench seat, white-knuckled, my nails scraping the wood.

"Cathy, I have to ask—do you feel any remorse at all for hiding your nature from us? For being the proverbial wolf in sheep's clothing?"

"Wolf?" I exclaim. "I'm not a predator, Edgar. This isn't something I can prevent or control. The most I can do is choose where I wander, and even that takes a huge effort. But I'm not hurting anyone. I never have."

"Your very existence is a threat to this church and our mission." Edgar's tone is gentle, soothing. "And we have to figure out how to deal with it, especially after the horrible deaths that occurred last night."

"I'm not linked to those deaths in any way." A frustrated panic is rising in me, swirling higher and higher inside my chest, quickening my heartbeat. "Who put you in charge? Seriously, Edgar, you're not my pastor. I'm not even sure your dad is my pastor. You don't call the shots, not here at church and not in my life, okay? You and I have known each other since we were kids. I like you well enough—I went on a date with you, for goodness' sake—but I'll be damned if I'm going to confess anything to you."

I rise from the bench and open the door to my side of the booth, intending to charge right out of the church, no matter what Dad said.

But I stop at the sight of a cluster of women and children moving up the aisle. They're all dressed in black and several of them are sobbing openly.

I hadn't forgotten about the dead men, but I was too worried about myself to really grasp what their loss has done to this church. Five deacons, gone. Whole families shattered in just a few hours. And these people don't even have bodies to bury.

The organ drones mournfully as the families file along the first two rows of pews. The rest of the worshippers fill in the seats behind them. My father stands in the third row, his stern gaze fixed on me. He points to the spot beside him, right at the end of the pew. My seat.

"They're looking for someone to blame." Edgar's voice is low and soft by my ear. "Run out of here now, and they won't believe you had nothing to do with this. Stay, and perhaps I can persuade them you're harmless."

He takes my upper arm. A light hold, not restrictive, so I don't pull away as he guides me up the aisle to the seat Dad has saved for me.

Pastor Linton isn't here, and for some reason that scares me. I never liked him, exactly, but he was familiar, routine, predictable. Edgar is anything but predictable. Last night on the beach did something to him, flipped a switch. Or maybe it tore away his mask, too, and the person he's always been is stepping forward. Maybe the god of death isn't the only dangerous thing being resurrected.

The service begins with hymns. Too many hymns. Then a passage about "weeping, wailing, and gnashing of teeth." I wonder who selected those verses. They seem wildly inappropriate given all the death, and yet their poetry sings to the banshee inside me.

Weeping and wailing and gnashing of teeth...

What does gnashing mean? I think it's grinding...yes, that makes sense...grinding of teeth. I've done that before, in the paroxysms of grief, in my wanderings.

My attention snaps back to the service. Edgar is expressing condolences to the families of the dead. He calls them heroes of the faith. Martyrs.

And then he's looking at me. Talking about me. "...one who lives among us but isn't truly one of us..." And he's telling them what I am. Banshee. He doesn't go into detail, just offers a general explanation. "Supernatural," he calls me, "descended from Cernunnos, the demon beneath." He doesn't say *monster* or *threat*, but I can sense both those words in the rigid stances of the people around me, in the glares thrown my way and the whispers traveling the air beneath the current of Edgar's words...so many useless words.

"Robert Earnshaw has confessed his sin in keeping this secret from us," Edgar says. "He did it out of love, in the hope that faith might purge the evil from his daughter."

Where did Edgar learn to talk like this? I guess this pompous style of speech comes from reading too many old sermons and commentaries from the 1800s. Does he even hear himself? How much he sounds like a cult leader more than his dad ever did?

But he *looks* like an angel, slim and blue-eyed, with that cloud of curly, blond hair, with that delicate, earnest, beautiful face. There's a hectic light in his eyes, a fervent energy in the movements of his slender hands as he reads passages about purging the unworthy and taking the sin offerings "outside the camp," whatever that means.

"Brethren," he continues, lifting both hands. "We must now decide what path to take. Make no mistake—this is not simply a tragedy. This is war. Spiritual warfare, more potent and physical than ever before in our lifetimes. Are we ready for the challenge? Will we stand against this great evil that threatens to rise and consume us all? The demon killed Macauley and Quinn first. Then last night, he came for Coffey and Heffernan. He took Gainey, Donaghy, and Ward, but he will not be satisfied with them. No, he will come for us. For you, and for you." He jabs a long, pale finger at a couple of church members. "He will come for your children. He will come for the elderly. He will come for the *world*. What are you willing to sacrifice to stop him? To keep this ancient horror from rising up once again?"

"We must ask God to defend us," a woman quavers from the pew behind me.

"Yes." Edgar steps around the pulpit and walks to the edge of the platform, lips pursed, nodding thoughtfully. "Yes, we must do that. But God will defend those who fight for Him. There's a time for prayer, my friends, and there's a time for action. Can anyone deny that this is the time for action?"

"We must cast out the evil from among us," someone calls. "Reject the polluted creature! Otherwise God can't bless us!"

"Now, now." Edgar raises a pacifying hand, gives a gentle smile. "I'm not sure calling Cathy Earnshaw a 'polluted creature' is helpful. She is wild, yes...a child of demons and not of God."

"But she is my daughter." My father stands up, his face brick red above the bristling beard. "And she's willing to repent."

"I hope so." Edgar's innocent blue eyes fix on me, his gaze flooded with beneficent concern. "For her sake, I truly hope so."

"This is a matter for the church leadership," Dad continues. "For the pastor and the deacons—"

"Pastor Linton, my father, is in no state to make decisions," Edgar cuts in. "He is grieving the loss of his brothers, his friends, his flock. And as for deacons...we have so few left. I think this question is too big for a few men to answer. We must all come together and find a solution."

Aunt Nellie rises suddenly from her seat. "Bob, have you ever tried curing Cathy?"

My dad stares at her, frowning. "She's a banshee. That's not something anyone can cure."

"But have you ever tried?"

"I... No."

With a triumphant nod, Aunt Nellie turns to face the congregation. "Cathy can come and live with me. We'll see what can be done about her condition. Perhaps the evil spirit can be driven out."

There's a murmur of relieved assent among the church members. Aunt Nellie is well-known and respected. If there's anyone they'll trust with my "rehabilitation," it's her.

I've thought of begging Aunt Nellie to let me live with her— I've even hinted to her about it. But I always got the feeling she wasn't thrilled with the idea of taking me in. And I'm definitely not interested in living with her now, when she's talking about driving an evil out of me.

An impulse I've had since I stepped inside the church is growing stronger. It's not the horrible crawling sensation I get before an episode, but it's almost as urgent. An instinct, a voice in my brain, repeating one word over and over. *Run. Run run run run run...*

But run *where*? Where could I go? Heathcliff said his family is dangerous, too, and besides, I'm not sure where he lives.

Voices surge around me, some in support of Aunt Nellie's plan, others suggesting alternatives. But the voice in my mind cuts through all the noise.

Run run run run run RUN RUN RUN!

I step out of the pew and head down the aisle toward the lobby.

Behind me, the voices rise in pitch and volume, and I quicken my pace. Two ushers get up from the rear pews and step in front of the doors leading to the lobby, blocking my path.

There's a side door. An emergency exit. I take a sharp left and head for it, but three women in black head me off.

Panic sets my nerves on fire. I've always been able to find an exit, an escape route, somewhere to flee. But this time I'm trapped, hemmed in by women I've known all my life—placid-looking Southern ladies who now remind me of harpies, or Fates, or something dreadful out of mythology.

But *I* am something dreadful out of mythology. And I'm not helpless. I've survived this thing inside me, and I can survive them, too.

And what's more...this isn't just "a thing inside me." Sometimes I create that mental separation out of shame or denial...but the banshee isn't some hitchhiker in my body.

I am the banshee, and the banshee is me.

So I let myself be whole, and I release one scream of pure, defiant freedom.

The force of the sound wave throws the three women out of my way. Everyone in the church cringes and crouches down, covering their ears. In that moment of confusion and chaos, I yank open the emergency door and rush out, heedless of the alarm that shrills at my exit.

Cold wind in my face, the scent of damp leaves. There's a concrete step. I jump off it and start running the second I hit grass.

One second, the stretch of grass between me and the forest is clear. The next second, a figure stands between me and the woods. He's tall, with shoulder-length dark hair, sharp features, a chiseled jaw, and a short, neat beard. He reminds me a little of Viggo Mortensen...

His hand lifts. Is that a gun?

Pain explodes through my body, making me jerk and shudder.

Not a gun. Taser.

Fuck.

15

HEATHCLIFF

ROLLING OVER IN THE BED FUCKING HURTS. I HAD TO SPEND a ton of energy repairing Alan Wolcott's body during his resurrection, and I almost didn't have enough strength to wipe my prints off the stolen car and stagger back home. At least the tattoo is fading now, its mission completed. No more irritation from that source.

Groaning, I manage to grasp my phone. Looks like I got a text from Cathy. I can't do this anymore.

She sent it hours ago. Shit.

Can't do what? Can't do *us*? Fuck, I knew I was going too far with the tattoos. I wanted to protect her, but it probably looked real weird and possessive, like some movie boyfriend who turns out to be a stalker. I probably scared her off. Maybe she decided someone like Edgar Linton is better for her. *Fuck* that.

I send her a reply. I'm here. What's up?

That sounds dumb. But I don't have any more words in me.

I try to stay awake. I fight the overwhelming tide of weariness, the heavy ache in my head, the leaden weight of my limbs. Cathy *has* to answer me, has to explain herself. She can't just end it like this. There has to be a reason. Something scared her. Maybe she heard something about me or the Lockwoods, maybe she's stressed out, maybe she went through another one of her mourning episodes and she's saying this because she's tired. Whatever it is, I need to know. So I struggle to maintain consciousness.

But I've drained my energy almost completely, and I have nothing left to draw from. The Vague is in my head, suffocating me, and I need to sleep. I don't have a choice.

I let the phone slip from my fingers onto the mattress, and I drift into darkness.

16

CATHY

Are you really a prisoner if you don't try to get away? If you have nowhere else to go?

Sure, I was taken to Aunt Nellie's against my will, but it's not like I'm locked in or tied up or anything like that. Dad brought over most of my stuff late Sunday night, while I was lying on Aunt Nellie's couch recovering from being tased. I still don't know the guy who tased me, and when I asked, nobody answered.

I've been here three days now. I get up at six, shower, dress, and eat breakfast with Aunt Nellie while she watches Fox News. We drive to the store together, and I do my work like normal—inventory, restocking, arranging displays, helping customers.

There's been no more talk of curing me, no discussion of my unnatural powers or my corrupting influence in Wicklow. Things seem weirdly normal. I guess that should reassure me, but it really doesn't. It feels like the strange, brittle, yellow heat beneath towering, blue thunderheads right before a terrifying storm breaks and skewers the land with lightning.

I have to admit, Aunt Nellie's house feels safer than Dad's. Healthier. She barely eats anything herself because of Edgar's fasting edict, but she lets me make my own meals from the scanty supply of food in the fridge. The sheets in the guest room are clean and soft, and there's no fear of her drinking herself into a blind frenzy and coming after me.

But I don't have my purse anymore. Dad claims he can't find it, so I don't have the debit card hidden in the purse lining. Aunt Nellie took my phone that first night, while I lay on the couch trying to cope with what had just happened.

"You young folks spend too much time in front of screens," she said blithely. "Fear-scrolling or doom-surfing or whatever it is. A detox will do you good. You'll get it back, don't worry."

A phone isn't just entertainment, though. Phones are connection, communication. They're a direct line to support, to awareness, to news stories and information. These days, phones are freedom, even more so than cars. Sure, I use mine mostly to watch stuff and wind down after a long day, but right now I need it so I can contact Heathcliff—or literally anyone who could help me get out of here.

Weirdly, I can remember the number Jay Gatsby gave me—Daisy's number—because I stared at it a bunch of times since that encounter. But Heathcliff's number is too new. I haven't memorized it, so I can't call him, not even from the phone at the store. Every time I get near the phone, Aunt Nellie calls me over to help her with something or picks up the phone herself to make a call. She does it casually, so I can't be sure if it's purposeful. There's no landline at her house, and I know better than to ask to borrow her phone. She'd say no.

If Heathcliff did text me back, he's going to think I'm ghosting him. But he knows where I work. If he wants to see me badly enough, he can come to Aunt Nellie's…*if* he can borrow his brother's truck, that is.

Part of me wants Heathcliff to make the effort to come talk to me. And when he doesn't, I can feel myself sinking inside…sinking so low that I let it all happen. I let Aunt Nellie treat me like a wayward teenager instead of a grown-ass woman. I keep telling myself *It could be worse.* So far, Aunt Nellie's idea of curing me is very mild. I can put up with it a bit longer. She's protecting me from being the congregation's scapegoat, and she's giving me a sense of normalcy, of safety. I can give up a little agency for that… can't I?

But after four days, I'm starting to get a little desperate, way down inside, where it doesn't show.

When we close the store on Thursday evening and hop into Aunt Nellie's car, I ask tentatively, "I was wondering if I could have my phone. I need to text a friend."

"Oh, it's all right. You'll see your friend at church tonight."

"Tonight?"

"Bible study. Everyone will be there. Actually, Pastor Linton has been holding Bible study there every night this week since we're in a time of crisis, but I haven't been able to go because I needed to keep an eye on you, honey." She gives me a warm smile that creases the skin at the corners of her eyes.

"I'm glad to hear Pastor Linton's feeling better."

"Oh, sorry…I should clarify. When I say Pastor Linton, I mean young Edgar. Mark is still at home, struggling with depression, poor man. I hope he comes to Bible study tonight. Faith is the cure for all such ills."

The hell it is, I respond inwardly, but I want my phone, so I bite back the retort. I shouldn't have to beg for my phone. But I have this sense that if I say that aloud, if I demand it, she and I will cross a line from the pleasant coexistence of the last few days into... something else. Something very unpleasant.

"Edgar is such an amazing man, don't you think, Cathy?" Her fingers tighten on the steering wheel. It's dark, but a passing streetlight flashes over her face. Her eyes glint with admiration. "He's like a modern-day apostle, a prophet, sent to help us through this crisis."

"Yes, he's...something special," I mutter. "Anyway...the friend I need to call isn't one of the folks from church."

"Really?" Her voice is warm, soothing. "Well, given the situation, I don't think you need to be associating with folks outside the flock, do you? You need people of faith around you right now."

"I really need to—"

"Cathy." The sharp tone startles me. "This isn't up for discussion."

I grit my teeth and stare ahead at the dark road. Trees arch over it, their limbs dripping Spanish moss. Our headlights turn the gnarled limbs briefly yellow as we drive.

"Have there been any more deaths?" I ask.

She glances sideways at me. "Shouldn't you know that?"

"I can't perceive deaths caused by the god."

Her mouth twitches, like she hates the direct reference to Cernunnos and my powers. "No. There haven't been any more deaths. Edgar, your dad, and some others have been going to Old Sheldon Church after Bible study every night to anoint the earth. Like everyone else in the church, they're fasting. Barely sleeping. Trying to keep us safe."

There's accusation in her tone now—subtle but it's definitely there. I want to address it, but I've got bigger concerns. "Not eating or sleeping? That's not healthy at all. That's why you don't eat with me, right? You're fasting, too?"

"Fasting is an honored practice to draw our minds away from carnal pleasure and center them on the divine," she says.

That doesn't sound like her at all. Sounds like the new version of Edgar.

"But you're eating something, right?" I persist. "The folks at church—they're still feeding their kids and everything?"

"It's up to the parents whether the whole family fasts or not. I'm sure everyone at Wicklow Heritage loves their children and wants to do right by them."

We're pulling into the church parking lot, gravel grinding under the tires. It's hard to find a spot—the place is crowded.

"I hope he's here again tonight," Aunt Nellie mutters.

"Who? Edgar?"

"Bob told me there's been a special speaker at the Bible studies. Edgar speaks first and then this other man. He's an expert in myths and lore, and Edgar says he can help us, teach us how to lock the demon down permanently."

"Is this someone Edgar met at college?"

"I don't know."

"Where did he study?"

"I don't know, Cathy." Aunt Nellie turns off the car and gets out. "Come on. You'll be waiting downstairs in the children's hall during the Bible study."

"Why?" I hop out and slam the car door. "I've been going to church every week for years, and suddenly my pagan vibes are too dangerous to be in the same room with everybody else?"

"This isn't a joke." Aunt Nellie grabs her purse from the back seat, shuts the door, and locks the car. Her face is grim. "You should care about how you affect others, Cathy."

"And you should care about *me*." Impulsively I catch her arm as she's walking past. "But you never have, have you? For years, you've known something was wrong with me. You thought I was sick, mentally and physically, and yet you never asked me for details, never really tried to help or give me any support."

"I gave you a job," she replies, acid searing her tone. "I didn't fire you when you left in the middle of your shift over and over again. I pretended not to know when you followed young men to their cars and went off to fornicate with them."

"You knew about Dad's drinking," I say, breathless and furious. "You must have known. You had to know that he hit me, hurt me, scared me, and you did *nothing*." The last word fractures, split by a sob. "You knew I missed my mom, that I was coming apart, that I was miserable. Did you realize that Dad took my paychecks? I begged you to pay me in cash, and you wouldn't. The only money I could keep for myself was my tips from the café."

"Your dad was entitled to that money. Room and board, honey. The price of being saddled with a creature like you for a lifetime." She's coming unglued now, showing more emotion than I've ever seen from her. "I wish I'd known what you were, what my brother was dealing with all those years. I could have helped him with you, given him some relief. What must he be feeling, knowing he spawned a demon with your corrupted mother—"

I'm bursting, on the verge of exploding—it's either scream at her or slap her, and a scream could cause way more damage. So I slap her face.

"Hey!" someone shouts from across the parking lot, and a couple men start running our way.

I back away from Aunt Nellie, while her gaze burns into mine.

I'm pretty sure I just ruined any chance of getting my phone back, so I speak my mind, even though I'm shaking all over. "I'm not a child. You can't treat me like this—it's not right. I want to leave Wicklow. I want my phone and my purse."

"And where will you go?"

"I'll get an Uber. Go to a shelter until I can get a job. If you care about me at all, you'll let me leave. Let me do this."

"Pastor says you're our responsibility," Aunt Nellie says quietly, soft ice in her tone. "It would be wrong to inflict you and your curse upon anyone else. If you're feeling this way, maybe you shouldn't work at the store anymore. We'll discuss other options."

The two men who saw me slap her come jogging up, and they're joined by a third man and a couple of women, all forming a jagged circle around me. I kick myself inwardly for thinking I could reason with her, for not running when I had the chance. I should have shut the hell up and taken off down the road. But without my phone and card, I'd have even less chance of making it anywhere else.

Aunt Nellie turns deliberately away from me and nods to one of the men. "Put her downstairs."

The two men don't touch me, but there's a clear threat of force if I don't obey. I could try a scream, but it wouldn't knock all of them down, and if I ran, that would incite a full-on chase. They might shoot me with more than a taser this time.

If I let them take me downstairs into the children's hall, maybe I can find a phone and make a call while they're all upstairs for Bible study. I think I remember there being a pale blue phone at the end of the downstairs hallway—the old-fashioned kind of wall phone with a loopy cord.

I relax my stance and let the two men escort me into the church, then down the steps to the children's hall.

"No kids down here tonight?" I ask.

"They're all upstairs. Joining us for the Bible study," replies Mr. Berg. He's on my left. On my right is Mr. Dawson. Mr. Berg's stomach growls loudly as they walk me down the hall.

"Hungry?" I ask sweetly.

He clears his throat. "Deprivation of the body brings strength to the soul. Like Jesus fasting in the desert."

"Except you're not Jesus, so in your case deprivation brings irritability, dizziness, fatigue, tension, and nausea." We're entering the hallway and I spot the phone at the end, like a blue beacon of hope. I keep talking in what I hope is a casual tone. "Eventually your metabolism will slow down, and you'll have trouble regulating your body temperature. Your heart, lungs, and testicles will shrink—"

Mr. Dawson makes a choked sound.

"It's true. I saw it in a documentary. After that you have to worry about organ damage, brain damage—"

"Enough." Mr. Berg opens a green door plastered with images of animals, rainbows, and the Ark. "We'll come get you after the meeting."

I walk inside and flip on the light. The place looks like a storage room. There's a stack of three small desks, their yellow surfaces covered in crayon scrawls. The shelves lining the walls are crowded with paper towels, jugs of finger paint, bottles of cleaning supplies, stacks of colored construction paper, and bins containing glue sticks and crayon boxes.

"Can I color while I wait?" I ask with a saucy smile.

But they're already closing the door. Then a key scrapes and *clicks*.

Oh my god, there's a lock. On the *outside* of the door.

Who puts locks on the doors in a children's Sunday School wing? Maybe that's why they put me in the storage room instead of a classroom—it has a lock on it. Fuck.

There goes my plan to use the phone.

Part of me wants to try smashing through the drywall into the next room so I can escape that way. But they'd hear the noise and come down to investigate.

Another part of me wants to scream at the top of my lungs, over and over, to ruin their little Bible study. But I really don't want to be tased again or tied up.

I sit down cross-legged and try to breathe slowly, to think.

They're not actually hurting me. They just want me quiet so they can deal with the Cernunnos situation in whatever fucked-up way Edgar prescribes.

Is it really that fucked up, though? Maybe I'm the one not taking this situation seriously enough. Seven people died—nine counting the first couple of deaths. Maybe I should be supporting what Edgar is trying to do, instead of resenting their treatment of me. Maybe I'm the problem. Maybe I should apologize and confess...

No. *Fuck!* I'm gaslighting *myself*, doubting everything I know and everything I want. There must be some kind of guilt-inducing aura about this place.

Somewhere above my head, the congregation joins together in a song. I hate to admit it, but the blended voices actually sound kind of pretty.

I've always been *othered* by these people. They're just not hiding it anymore. They've put me in my place...confined me down below, while they, the Chosen, sing hymns up above. As if I'm the demon in Hell, longing for the mystical beauty of heaven.

Except I'm no demon. I'm a woman with an identity they fear, a power they don't understand. Sometimes I confuse myself, and sometimes I wish my life were like theirs... It would be easier. Smoother sailing.

And yet I *don't* want to be like them. I don't. I wouldn't change places with a single one of them.

That realization soars through my heart, and I smile. They can humiliate me, lock me in, take away my connection to the world, but they can't really touch me or change me.

With that settled, I pace the storage closet, scanning the shelves. The doorknob is smooth on the inside, no way to pick the lock even if I knew how. But if I can find a screwdriver, I can take off the whole doorknob. Or maybe I can take the door off its hinges.

I rifle through the bins and stacks of storage supplies. Not a single tool, nothing sturdy enough to give me leverage with the hinges or traction with the screws. Restlessness coils inside me, sending ripples of unease through my body. Right under my skin there's a squirming sensation, and then I gasp and jerk, because it felt as if something slithered up my spine, coiling around the column of my vertebrae.

Oh god.

The name bursts into my mind—Annie-Mae Madden. She's old, mideighties. Fragile. Lying in bed at home while her relatives are at the Bible study upstairs. They think she's sleeping safely, but she's going to get out of bed to use the bathroom in a few minutes—she'll get confused and try to descend the steps alone. I can see it—her frail body bouncing down the stairs like a rag doll, bones snapping like twigs.

This isn't like most of my other episodes. This death is preventable, if only someone gets there in time...within the next half hour. They can still make it; they can save her. Why, *why* didn't someone stay with her? They must have made the decision to leave her alone just ten minutes or so before the Bible study began, which is why this episode is coming on so suddenly, so powerfully.

I can't stop it. I'm moaning aloud already, wracked by the pain of the visions in my head—snatches of her oncoming death.

The people upstairs are singing louder, stamping their feet. It's a repetitive song, a militant song, meant to stir them into a frenzy, and they're all susceptible right now, carried along on this tide of panic together. Little food, barely any sleep, plus the torment of loss, and they have to feel all that grief because I couldn't carry any part of it for them. They're going mad together above, while I go mad below—mad with grief, with the wretched injustice of it all.

As above, so below.

A wail breaks from my throat, blending with the thundering chorus above, with the drumbeat of their marching feet. *Onward Christian soldiers...* I scream, and I howl, a wild warning. "Your grandmother, your mother, she is going to die, and you can save her, you can stop it, hear me, hear me..."

But no one hears. They sing for half an hour. They sing while I drag my nails along the walls and rake the contents of the shelves to the floor, while I claw my face and pull my hair and scream, while I fling my body against the door in a frenzy of desperation because I have to *go*, I have to run, I can't be in here, let me out, *let me out*!

They sing louder while she stumbles shakily from her room and ricochets down the stairs. I shriek at that final crack of her spine, and I crumble, bowed over on the floor, tears glazing my cheeks. Her life's scenes flutter through my mind—school, services, a wedding, lost babies, tarnished dreams—he cheated but she stayed, thought it was her duty and besides she had nothing else, no skills or training, and she stayed, she *fucking* stayed while he did it again and again. He's gone now, and her children and grandchildren are her pride when she can remember their names, but they're upstairs screaming in a religious fervor under the prophetic guidance of one Edgar Linton while she dies alone.

I curl up in the fetal position, hoarse screams tearing from my throat, interspersed with dry, gagging sobs. It's over, and they won't grieve her terribly. She had become a burden, a chore. The grandchildren will miss her because they don't understand how her lingering existence weighed on their parents. The parents will claim to miss her, and sometimes they will, when something reminds them of her—they'll grow misty-eyed and nod and speak a memory of her, but they'll be glad not to have that extra burden.

I can't go where I'm supposed to be. I can't wander through the woods and perform the slow, methodical mourning for this woman. What would usually take hours is condensed into a violent, unbearable cataclysm in my head, a shrieking, howling tempest, a building pressure so intense that I'm convinced I'm going to die. The strain is too great—I'm going to have an aneurysm—something will *break* inside me, liquefy my brain, leave me oozing and mindless on the floor.

The grief cleaves deeper into the red flesh of my heart, blood oozing around the blade. The old woman is me, and I am her—a burden, a concern, a thing of dread to everyone in my life. Even if Heathcliff and I were together, I would eventually become *that* to him—a heavy weight for him to carry.

Maybe it's better if I never see him again.

I can feel something happening in my head, the grief burning through my brain cells like acid. I'm losing pieces that used to be me, and I can only hope they will heal when this is over. Even if I survive, I don't think I'll be myself for a long time.

The urge to escape vaults up my throat like searing bile, and I drag myself up again, a puppet hauled by the strings of a lethal compulsion. I throw myself at the door, shoulders and skull smashing against the unyielding wood over and over. I can't stop it. My voice is gone, but I keep screaming, a wretched rasp from my tortured throat, until my body collapses, battered and quaking.

Never in my life have I needed a savior so badly. And yet he does not come.

17

HEATHCLIFF

I HAVEN'T HEARD FROM CATHY IN DAYS. I TEXTED HER twice, and I even tried calling. I don't usually call people. But she didn't answer the phone or reply to my texts.

Maybe she's rethinking this connection between us. Maybe she's scared because she confided in me but I wouldn't tell her what kind of supernatural I am.

Or maybe that fool Edgar got to her and convinced her that I'm bad news. Which I am. I just thought Cathy might see past that or not mind it.

Maybe she didn't like the fact that I don't own the truck I was driving that day. I guess living with my brother and not having my own transportation are red flags for a woman, especially one like Cathy, who's desperate to escape Wicklow.

Maybe her father is keeping her from contacting me. In that case, I'd best let him have some time to calm down before I go over there. Me showing up might make him act out worse toward her.

Whatever's going on, I can't keep texting and calling like a lovesick idiot. I gotta stay focused on the plan and hope she'll get back to me eventually.

I've got three new tattoos, and a couple of them are terminal clients. One of them's bound to die any day now, which means a payout for me. One step closer to freedom.

My asking price for resurrection isn't as high as Hindley's. He's got contacts who can vouch for him, but since I'm working alone, going after folks with no connection to the supernatural world, my services are untested. No good reviews yet, you might say—although Alan Wolcott was beyond thrilled with his resurrection. In fact, he was so thrilled I had to get out of there quick, before he tried to make me get matching tattoos with his whole family. They weren't around at the time; the agent persuaded them to leave the house for a while, saying he'd oversee the morgue coming to collect the body. I can only imagine how the family reacted, coming home to find Wolcott alive *and* healed.

I never told Wolcott or the agent my real name. Never gave them my address. They could ask around near Moretti's, I guess, throw cash at people in my area and maybe find me. But the folks in the area ain't talkative to out-of-town, big-money types. Pretty much the only places I go are the brewery, the Grange, a gas station, maybe a couple bars. I'm not really a regular anywhere, at least not enough to be recognized. Moretti's isn't a place I usually frequent, what with being in the Wicklow town limits and all.

After I recovered from that resurrection, I took down the account I'd used to contact Wolcott and I started new ones. I figure I'll do the scorched-earth thing after every successful resurrection, so they can't find me again. I'm working out the kinks, finding that sweet spot, where the price is high enough to give my offer some weight but low enough so people aren't too scared to shell out the 30 percent deposit up front.

I've got my own truck now, an old used Ford I bought with cash off a guy who let me keep the plates and didn't ask questions. I didn't ask him where he got it either. I keep it hidden at the back of the Lockwood property, behind an old shed draped in kudzu vines. Hindley never goes back there since there's poison ivy all through that part of the woods. He's probably forgotten that there's also an overgrown dirt track cutting through a tree belt to Gumtree Road.

I don't mind risking poison ivy if it means having my own wheels. I don't dare use the truck often, though. Someone might tell Hindley they saw me in it, and he'd go find it and shoot it full of holes out of spite. Then there would be questions to answer, like where I got the money for it.

My life has always been shit, but it was mostly a relaxed kind of shit. Now it's fucking stressful, with all these secrets and underground deals and the fact that *Cathy hasn't texted me back.*

I want to go over to Aunt Nellie's and see her. But she has ghosted me on purpose, and she's got her reasons. I ain't going over there to beg, no way. I'm waiting until I've got enough money to really offer her something solid, something real. Genuine freedom, not just my broke ass and callused heart.

I gotta wait until I can give her everything.

◆◆◆

I'm fucking exhausted.

Since I've been doing my own resurrections, I've had to spend more time recovering. It's been tough to keep up with work at the brewery and avoid raising Hindley's suspicions while getting the rest I need. I tried energy drinks for a while, but they messed me up bad. At one point I lied to Hindley and told him I had the flu so I could go to bed and recover.

In between work, resurrections, and recovery, I stopped by Cathy's house and Aunt Nellie's store a couple times, just to see if she was there. I was determined not to, but hell...a man's got his limits. The first time—the Tuesday after I resurrected Alan Wolcott—I saw Cathy inside, restocking shelves. She looked fine—cheerful, even. No bruises, no signs of distress. From what I could see, there was no fallout from that night on the beach, no reason why she couldn't call me. She even glanced my way, and I'm pretty sure she saw me through the window. But she turned back around without a second look.

The second time I checked on her was at Aunt Nellie's store around lunchtime. I was hoping to talk to Cathy on her break, but no luck. She must have taken the day off or gone to lunch with someone. Better not have been Edgar Linton.

I'm going out of my mind fretting over why she hasn't contacted me. But I don't wanna push too hard, not until I have everything ready. Not until I can offer her a way out.

I'm still recovering from the last resurrection I did—some college girl who overdosed. Two of her friends were scared for her and paid me to save her if she went too far. They convinced her to get the tattoo design I sent them. Now that she's got a second chance at life, I hope they get her into rehab. They could have checked her into a good one with the money they paid me, but I'm not here to judge how and when folks spend their cash. I'm just here to get the necessary tattoo, collect my fee, and drag the soul out of the Vague.

With all the work I've been doing, my appetite has been fucking ravenous. I've been grabbing a lot of burgers for protein, but

I'm getting sick of them, and the only thing in our fridge right now is soggy chicken fingers and tough old fries. I need something else. Lots of meat, maybe some vegetables for good measure.

"I'm gettin' Brickley's," I yell to Hindley. "Can I take the truck?"

"Long as you bring me back some barbecue," he calls from the couch.

"You got it."

Okay, so maybe I have another reason for going to Brickley's Barbecue. It's past the barrier, well within the limits of Wicklow. Maybe I'm thinking of swinging by Cathy's again.

But I head for the restaurant first. It's one of those greasy spoons that doesn't look like much from the outside, but locals know it's got the best ribs around. The second I walk in, every damn nerve in my body tightens because I recognize the guy sitting alone in one of the cramped booths. Pastor Linton. Cathy's pastor.

I watch him out of the corner of my eye while I order the food. He looks fucking awful. Pale as beach sand, just sitting there, poking at his banana pudding with a plastic fork. Hasn't even touched his pulled pork sandwich, which is a crime. Those sandwiches are damn delicious.

"We're waiting on a fresh batch of macaroni and cheese," says the woman behind the counter. "It'll be about ten minutes."

"Sure thing."

Just as well, 'cause I've got questions inside me that won't quit. I need to find out if Cathy has gotten any blowback from that scream of hers out on the beach. I need to be sure that Edgar hasn't spilled her secret and that the Wicklow Church hasn't done anything to hurt her. The tattoo I share with her tells me she's alive, but there's other kinds of hurt that fanatical folk can cause. Cathy didn't seem to think the congregation would do anything drastic, since she's one of their own and all. Besides, mean as he is, I figure her dad would protect her, even if others turned on her—even if he's been cruel to her himself. Guys like that usually resent any outsiders abusing their family.

But I can't be sure of anything. So while I'm waiting for my food, I saunter over to the booth and slide onto the bench across from Pastor Linton.

He looks up with eyes pink and swollen around the edges.

"Hey there, Pastor." I grab one of his fries and bite it in half. "I'm here for some spiritual edification."

"Oh, um..." He gulps, blinks. "Do I know you?"

"I visited your church once. Sat next to Cathy Earnshaw. How's she doing these days?"

"If you know her, don't you have her number?"

"Sure I do. Weird thing is, she won't text me back. So this is me, as a friend, making sure she's okay." My gaze bores into his. "She *is* okay, isn't she, Pastor? She doesn't have anything to worry about from you or the good folks at Wicklow Heritage, does she?"

His bleary eyes sharpen with awareness. "You know about her. What she is."

That's the confirmation I need. "I do. I also know what your congregation has done to supernaturals in the past."

He frowns. "Who are you again?"

"I'm someone with Cathy's best interest at heart."

"You think I'm not?" His laugh is hoarse, strained. "I've known that girl since she was a baby. Sweet kid, smart as a whip—smarter than her dad ever gave her credit for. I knew she was struggling. I just thought the cause was physical, not...not *this*."

I lean toward him across the table. "You didn't answer my question. Is she safe? From you and your people?"

"Of course she is." His hand curls tight around the plastic fork, and his voice trembles, tears glimmering along his lower eyelids. "I won't deny I've been part of some questionable things in the past, but it's all in the interest of protecting the world from an evil so powerful you can't even imagine it. We've lost good men to that evil lately. But I won't let Cathy become another casualty. Even if she poses some kind of threat, I swear to you before God, we'll handle it differently this time. She's one of ours. One of the family."

I sit back, partially convinced by his vehemence.

Pastor Linton picks up a napkin and presses it to his wet eyes. "When she was younger, I used to imagine her and Edgar getting married. Thought maybe he could her get the help she needs, and maybe she could help him, too. Edgar, he's...well, he has his issues. But I thought if Cathy got her heart right and he got his mind straightened out, they could take over the church. I pictured their kids running around the sanctuary someday." He chokes out another rasping laugh. "Guess God has other plans. Now I think she'd be happiest leaving Wicklow, and perhaps that's best all around."

I almost tell him that I'm working on it. That I'm piling up cash as fast as I can, and that my only fear right now is Cathy saying no when I ask her to come with me. I'd never force the issue—*hell* no. I'll die before I pull her out of this cage just to shove her into another one. But god, I hope she agrees to run when I'm ready to go.

Pastor Linton watches me, gauging my expression. It's his business to read people, and I suppose he's gotten decent at it.

"If Cathy ghosted you, she's probably got a good reason," he says. "Might be too much for her, dealing with all this. We've had deaths in our congregation, frightening occurrences, visitors of the supernatural kind...like yourself, I'm guessing."

I open my mouth to reply, but he holds up his hand. "Don't tell me your name or what you are. It's better if I don't know. All I'm saying is, maybe Cathy needs space and some time to process all of it. Sometimes we gotta let the Lord work. God knows I'm having trouble processing everything myself." His hands start to quiver, and he tucks them under the table to hide the tremor. "I've always been the guide, the shepherd of the flock. And now...I can't shake this terror that I've failed at the one thing I was put on this earth to do. You got any idea how that feels?"

He doesn't sound like the man Cathy and I heard when we eavesdropped under the Lintons' window. That man was firm and confident. Maybe it was a front he was putting on for his son. Maybe the situation has gotten worse since then. Sometimes it's the little things, not the big tragedies, that put a man over the edge.

"I know how it feels to fail, sure," I say. "And to be perfectly fucking honest, that's how I'll feel if any harm comes to Cathy."

The woman at the counter calls, "Order for Heathcliff Lockwood!"

Pastor Linton's eyes widen.

I give him a bitter grin as I rise from the booth. "I guess you know my name now."

"A Lockwood? How are you even here?" His voice is faint, the tone of a man shaken to his core. "Has the barrier failed?"

"Maybe it has, and maybe it hasn't. Just know that I'm looking out for Cathy, whether she wants me to or not. If anyone in your congregation gets out of line, you step in and protect her, got it? And if you see her, tell her to answer her damn messages."

I head over to pick up the two plastic bags of food. On my way out of Brickley's, I cast one more look at Pastor Linton. He's staring at nothing, his eyes full of hollow despair.

Well, damn. Hope I didn't break him.

He's right about one thing. Cathy probably needs time and space to process all the shit that has been thrown her way lately.

So I'll wait. For now.

18

CATHY

"HERE'S YOUR SWEET TEA."

I accept the glass from Aunt Nellie, but it feels too heavy, so I set it down on the nightstand. Leaning over, I sip from the straw.

I've been in her guest room ever since she and Dad found me on the floor of the storage room after the Bible study—a fetal ball in the middle of a rainbow of spilled paint and scattered crayons. Dad helped Aunt Nellie get me home. She cleaned me up like Mom used to do and put me in bed. Even kissed my forehead.

Dad and Aunt Nellie were so kind to me. So gentle. Maybe finding me in that state woke them up, pulled them out of the shared panic of the congregation. And I think Aunt Nellie feels guilty for the incident in the church parking lot. Her actions caused my crisis in the basement, and she knows it. That's got to be why she's being so sweet, so determined to help me. No matter what I am, what Dad has done, or what Aunt Nellie said, the three of us are family. We're all we got.

Too bad it took them a while to realize that because I think I'm broken. Wounded inside, suffering from some kind of PTSD, I'm guessing. I've been feeling wretched for days—over a week, maybe more. This isn't normal for me. Recovery after an episode never takes this long, and I don't usually feel this weak. I can't seem to do more than sip sweet tea and sleep. Occasionally I stagger to the bathroom or eat some crackers, but that's about it. There's a fog in my brain that I can't shake, and I feel hollow inside, like every bit of fire and will has drained right out of me. I guess that's what happens when I'm forbidden from wandering like I'm supposed to. My inner banshee has suffered a deep trauma, and it might take a while to heal. Maybe it will leave me in peace in the meantime. Maybe I can enjoy being taken care of for once. Allow myself to be sick, to be *still*. To let Aunt Nellie play mom. She seems to enjoy it, and to be honest, I do, too.

"It's Saturday night," says Aunt Nellie. "I think you should take a shower and come to church with me tomorrow."

At the mention of the church, the storage room flashes into my brain, and I shudder with terror.

"You can sit with everyone in the service," she says. "Between me and your dad. Might do you some good."

"I don't think I can," I whisper.

"Don't worry, honey." She brushes my hair back from my forehead with a cool hand. "I'll help you."

19

HEATHCLIFF

Enough is enough.

Cathy still hasn't contacted me, but I'm sure as hell not waiting any longer.

I've completed two more resurrections. I've got the truck, and I got me a fake driver's license, one that's good enough to fool all but the most fastidious of cops. There's so much cash stuffed inside my mattress it blows my mind, like why the hell didn't I do this sooner? Guess I just needed somebody besides myself to save.

It's time to get Cathy and leave this place behind. I haven't heard anything about gods or weird deaths from Hindley, but Halloween is in a couple days, which means the whole Coosaw clan is going to descend on the Grange, and that's a paranormal shitstorm I don't want to deal with, besides the fact that more people in the house means more chances of my stash of bills being discovered.

Cathy goes to church with her dad every Sunday, so that's where I'm going this morning. I'll catch her either going in or coming out, and we'll leave. We'll drive to her house, grab a few of her things, and run.

I text her again before I leave, and I keep it generic, in case her dad sees it. Might stop by church.

No response. Not that I was expecting one.

I'm gonna talk to her today, no matter what. If I don't find her at church, I'm going to her house, the store—hell, I'll scour the forest to find her. I'm not giving up unless I hear straight from her mouth that she doesn't want to leave with me.

Hindley's sleeping off an ass-ton of whiskey in his room, so he doesn't notice me carrying a couple bags out the back door and through the trees to my truck. I head inside one more time to check on our Sleeping Beauty in the spare room. Not sure what Hindley's gonna do with him once the Coosaw cousins show up wanting beds and entertainment. They're gonna have all kinds of twisted fun with our comatose buddy.

If I could take Ian with me, I would. But I gotta put me and Cathy first, and there's no way we could lug around some supernatural coma patient. Besides, something about the guy still weirds me out.

"I'm leaving," I tell Ian quietly. "Just wanted to say I'm sorry you're like this. Maybe it's better this way. I got the feeling you weren't a great person. I mean you look decent, but inside...nope. Your soul, man, it's messed up. So yeah...this is probably best for everyone. Maybe you'll pass on quietly one night, if the Coosaw Lockwoods don't kill you first. Or maybe you'll stay like this forever. Who's to say? Anyway, I'm gone, and I'm taking Cathy with me. Good luck."

A muscle in his face twitches.

Frowning, I lean over him. "Hey."

He doesn't respond. His eyes don't move beneath his eyelids, and his breathing remains steady.

If he's waking up, I need to get out of here before he makes any noise. My escape window narrows the longer I hang around here.

I hurry downstairs and out of the house, closing the back door quietly behind me. Then I hop into my truck and check my phone again.

Nothing from Cathy.

The fear that's been dogging me since I last saw her nags at the back of my mind. I've looked for her on socials, but if she had any accounts, they're gone. I haven't set eyes on her in days. What if her dad hurt her? What if the church folks at Wicklow hurt her, despite what that pastor said?

I don't care if she really is ghosting me or not; if anyone has hurt her—if they've so much as touched her or scared her, even a little—I'm going to lose my fucking shit. She doesn't have to be with me, but she deserves to be free.

There's another possibility, of course. She could be wandering around the woods on some crying jag, deep in one of her banshee episodes. Maybe she's had more episodes than usual lately, and that's why she hasn't been in touch. Or...god, what if she had an episode and fell in a hole, broke her leg or something, and she's lying out in the woods waiting for me to come find her? What if she wandered onto the road and got hit by a truck? What if...

The bottom drops out of my world for a second, and my brain screams, *What if she died?* right before I remember the tattoo that links me to her.

If she's dead, I'd know it. But I can't bear to think of her needing me when I'm not there.

Unless my first theory was right and she's done with me. Can't bear to think on that too long either.

I'm driving dangerously fast. I need to slow down. Don't wanna test how genuine my driver's license looks just yet. I got me a Social Security number now, too, all linked up to the license. The guy I bought the identity package from said the SSN was legit, that everything was "clean," so I'd be good to go, whatever that means. He better have been right. I sure paid him enough.

There's a mist hanging over the grass this morning. I pull off the road just before I get to the church and walk through the fog until I'm right at the edge of the trees bordering the church's land. I can see the parking lot pretty clearly, and the entrance to the church. Everything is gray and wet and dripping, and the people entering the church fit the mood 'cause they're all dressed in black.

There's a reddish car pulling up, the dull color of drying blood. It parks, and Cathy's Aunt Nellie gets out.

A couple seconds later, Cathy climbs out of the passenger side.

She's wearing a black dress, long sleeved, high necked. Her brown hair has been combed flat against her skull and woven into a long, tight braid. Not a stray curl. I can only see the side of her face from here, but she looks calm and content. Like this church service is where she wants to be.

Holding a Bible to her chest, she walks sedately at Aunt Nellie's side. She mounts the steps just as Edgar fucking Linton comes through the open double doors. He pauses. Takes her hand in his. Smiles with all his stupid teeth, leans close, and speaks in her ear. She nods and then follows Aunt Nellie into the church.

My hand shoots out and grasps the slender trunk of a sapling near me. I clutch the tree savagely, my chest heaving.

The Cathy I know is wild, mischievous, hungry for sex and

adventure. But in the two weeks since we last spoke, she has changed. They've turned her into one of them.

Here I was, like an idiot, working my ass off, draining myself to the dregs, struggling to make enough money so we could run away together—and all the time she *was* ghosting me on purpose. She was making her choice, and she chose *them*. Him.

I almost leave right that second. But I'm determined to talk to her, to make damn sure this is what she wants, that she's not being forced into this or playing some act—so I stalk through the trees, back and forth, for the next hour and a half, until the churchgoers start filing out of the building and into their cars. It's a slow exodus, since they all seem to want to stop and say goodbye to Edgar Linton, who stands at the door and sheds a benevolent smile over every church member.

Why is he acting like the pastor all of a sudden? And why does everyone seem so fucking obsessed with him? Several of the women actually *kiss* the back of his hand before leaving.

When I glimpse Cathy's pale face in the shadow of the doorway, my stomach flips and my heart starts racing. Shit, I got it bad.

She's smiling at Edgar Linton. Looks a little forced to me, but it's tough to tell at this distance. I'm about to walk out of the shadow of the trees, cross the distance between us, demand some answers from him, from Cathy—but someone else comes out of the church and my lungs seize up with shock and I just stand there, stunned.

It's Ian. The coma guy from the Grange.

But it can't be. I just left him there. He was sleeping. I said goodbye...

And now he's standing at Edgar Linton's side, plain as day,

wearing a suit, shaking hands with the congregation just like a pastor would.

What the actual *fuck* is going on?

Cathy is halfway across the parking lot with her aunt Nellie. If I'm going to talk to her, it's got to be now.

Ian squeezes someone's hand, descends the front steps, and heads around the corner of the church.

I can follow him and see where he's going, or I can run across the parking lot to Cathy.

Cathy is mine and I'm hers. I should go to her. But my brain, my whole body, is yelling an alarm about Ian, and I can't shake the nauseating sense of dread connected with him.

Looks like Cathy's going home with her aunt Nellie. I can find out the address and catch her there later. But if I don't move *now*, I'm losing my chance to figure out what Ian is up to and how he's awake...if it really is him. Maybe he's got a twin.

I jog through the woods, skirting the church property, keeping my eye on Ian.

When he gets to the back of the church, he pauses. No windows back here and nobody around.

Ian shakes himself—a quick shudder—and then he jumps forward. In the middle of that leap, his body fluidly shifts into a new shape—a black stag whose branching antlers look like twin tangles of wicked, gleaming thorns as long as my forearm. The stag bounds into the forest and disappears from sight.

Fuck.

Just...*fuck*.

He's a supernatural, that much is clear. Hindley pretty much said he was, didn't know what kind, but now I do. Shapeshifter. A púca, maybe, from the old stories. Those are rare, but they can shift into all kinds of animals—goats, horses, stags, dogs, crows, cats.

Question is, why has he been pretending to be unconscious this whole time? And why would he show up here, at Wicklow Heritage Chapel? Does he know how dangerous this town is for supernaturals like him?

I can't keep up with a stag, so I head to my truck and drive back to the Grange. My money is in a waterproof gym bag, so after parking the truck in its usual spot, I find a hollow in the ground and stick the bag there, covering it up with a thick layer of leaves and branches. I drag some kudzu vines over the heap for extra camouflage, and then I hoist my duffel bag of clothes and possessions onto my shoulder. No way am I leaving town before I figure out what's going on. If I'm lucky, Hindley will never know I almost left today.

Inside the Grange, I race up to my room and chuck my duffel bag in the closet. I'll unpack later. First I need to check on our coma patient.

I burst into the guest room—and there he is, lying pale and peaceful on the bed.

"No way," I mutter, striding in. I rip back the sheets.

He's wearing the same pajamas he's been in the whole time.

Okay, so as a stag he could head straight for the Grange through the woods, while I had to take the roads. He could have beaten me here and changed real quick.

Swearing under my breath, I search the room for a black suit. Nothing.

"Hey." I smack the side of his face. "Wake up. Game over, okay? I know you're not really unconscious."

His head lolls at the smack, but otherwise he doesn't stir.

And then I lose my temper.

I knock him around a bit, pull his hair, pinch his thigh, yell in his face, drag him off the bed, shake him around. Still nothing. He just hangs there, limp as a rag doll, mouth slack and eyes closed.

"I'm gonna cut your balls off if you don't quit this act," I snap. "I swear it, man. I'm not fucking around." I shove his limp body into a jumble on the bed, then pull my knife from my back pocket and flip out the blade. "Here goes." I poke the tip of the blade against his crotch. "Feel that? I'm not kidding. I'll do it unless you drop this act."

But there's no response. He doesn't flinch, even when I dig the knife into his thigh until a couple red drops bloom through the pajama bottoms.

So...he's not faking. Which makes me feel like an asshole for putting him through all that. But I had to be sure.

There're a few possibilities I can think of. One, the guy has a twin who's a shapeshifter. Two, he's doing that astral-projecting thing I saw in a movie once. Three, he's been waking up sometimes and leaving the house to do things, then returning here to collapse back into his comatose state. Which makes no sense.

None of it makes any sense.

I rearrange the guy on the bed and pull the sheets over him. Then I check the window. It's not made for keeping folks in—easy enough to open and there's no screen. I fetch Hindley's tools and some wood scraps, and I board up the window. There're a couple extra padlocks in the basement, so I fetch one and install it on the guest room door.

Hindley staggers out of his room while I'm testing the

padlock. I'm surprised the noise I've been making didn't rouse him before now. But when he drinks hard and takes drugs on top of that, he sleeps like the dead.

"The fuck you doin'?" he slurs.

"Renovating," I reply.

"You think that's funny? This ain't your house and won't ever be as long as I got somethin' to say about it. I don't care what Dad wanted. It's mine, and—" He breaks off the sentence abruptly, as if he said something he didn't mean to.

"Wait, what does that mean? 'What Dad wanted'?" My heart starts pounding again as the words sink into my brain.

"Never mind," Hindley mutters. "Fuck. I don't care what you're up to. Just give me that key in case I need to check on him."

"You never check on him," I retort, but I hand it over anyway.

Hindley shuffles past me, heading for the stairs and leaving me with my whirling thoughts.

I never did see Buckland's will. Hindley's sleazebag of a lawyer read it aloud, but I never actually *saw* it. The family said Buckland Lockwood left me nothing. Everything went to Hindley. It hurt at the time, but I didn't question it. After all, Hindley was Buckland's son by blood.

Maybe I was wrong to accept it quietly. Too late now, though. If there was an original will that made me the heir to anything, Hindley would have destroyed it long ago. Even he isn't dumb enough to keep a document like that around.

It means something, though—the idea that Buckland might have left me the house or even a share of it. Might have meant more to me years back, when he died. Knowing about the will might have given me a sense of belonging that I've never really had. As it is, I don't feel much more than a flicker of gratitude to the old bastard. I'm out of here soon anyway.

Something crashes downstairs, and Hindley roars several curses. Then he shouts, "Heathcliff, you dickwad, get your ass down here! My right ankle tattoo's buzzin'! Looks like we got a job to do."

20

CATHY

I COLLAPSE ONTO THE SOFA AT AUNT NELLIE'S, TOO exhausted to climb the stairs to my room. Going to church has always been mentally exhausting and emotionally torturous for me, but today it sapped every bit of my physical energy, too.

I blame most of that on Edgar. As Aunt Nellie and I were stepping through the church doors, he greeted us with a beatific smile. "So pleased to have you with us today."

He took my hand, rubbing his thumb over my skin, and leaned close to my ear. "An outburst like last time will not be tolerated. I know who your friend Cliff is now...or should I say Heathcliff Lockwood. A family with the most perverse kind of power. We haven't executed any supernaturals in a while, but I might make an exception, just for him."

My whole body quivered with startled terror, but I couldn't summon the will to do anything but nod meekly. During the service, I considered his words, and I fretted over not knowing *what* kind of supernatural the Lockwoods are. Did Heathcliff ever hint about what powers he has, besides strength? As far as I can recall, Dad never explained the Lockwoods' nature or abilities. He only said they were dangerous, but *how*? What can they do that's so dreadful?

Speaking of dreadful, the congregation looked wretched today—haggard and hungry, thinner than usual. Between them and my racing thoughts, I was so distracted that I barely listened to the sermon. Edgar didn't preach; it was some other guy, an Ian Holcum. Aunt Nellie elbowed me significantly when the man stepped into the pulpit, so I assumed it was Edgar's friend the folk-lore expert. He didn't talk about gods or ancient myths, though. From the scraps I can recall, the message was mostly about the symbolism of blood and sacrifice throughout Scripture. Creepy stuff.

Now that I'm back at Aunt Nellie's and I have time to lie here quietly and think, it seems odd how little of the message I heard. Usually, even if I'm distracted during a sermon, I can remember a few parts word-for-word. But when I think back to this morning's message, it's blurred. I have a vague impression of the topic but nothing distinct. I can't remember a single phrase the man spoke during the forty-five minutes he spent in the pulpit.

I do remember most of the congregation giving me looks of hostility or pity as Aunt Nellie and I made our way out of the sanctuary. But that was to be expected after my last visit.

My body feels tired and weak, like I've just recovered from the flu, but it's like my mind is starting to wake up, burning brighter through the fog that has wreathed my brain since my last debili-tating banshee episode. I've felt so soft and sleepy and passive for days, but I'm starting to regain strength, to remember what I want and what I need to do.

Heathcliff. I need to get in touch with Heathcliff. Except I don't know his number, so I'll call Daisy. Even though we're practically strangers, somehow I know she would help me get away from here.

Aunt Nellie comes over to the couch, carrying a huge glass of sweet tea which she sets on a TV tray beside me. "Drink up. You need to hydrate."

I sip the tea, hoping my obedience will please her enough that she'll grant my request. It's sweeter than usual, with a more intense flavor. "Can I have my phone for a little while?"

"The battery's dead." She purses her lips, considering. "Tell you what. You finish that glass of tea, and I'll charge it for you. You can have it tonight."

"Thank you," I say fervently.

"You're welcome." She strokes my forehead with a cool hand.

"I think I'm getting better," I tell her. "I've never experienced such a bad recovery period after an episode, but it seems to have passed. I think I'll be fine to stay here by myself tomorrow, so you can go back to work." *And I can leave this house.*

"Sarah has been handling everything," she replies. "While you were resting, I popped into the store now and then to check on things and keep up with paperwork and payroll. But I was overdue for some time off anyway."

Her hand continues smoothing stray curls back into the braid she did for me this morning. "If I've been hard on you, it's only because I want what's best. You know that, don't you?"

Best for who? I want to reply, but I restrain myself because I want my damn phone. So instead of answering, I nod. She removes her hand, looking satisfied, and I prop myself up on one elbow so I can drink the sweet tea. I gulp it down so fast Aunt Nellie chuckles.

"I'll go make us a big lunch."

"A big lunch?" I raise my eyebrows. "You're going to eat too?" I've barely seen her eat for days.

"Oh yes." She smiles pleasantly at me—the signature Aunt Nellie smile. "Our time of fasting is over. We understand God's will now, and we know how to seal the demon in his tomb forever. Pastor Linton and the deacons announced it a few days ago, and we've been praying over it as a congregation since then. This morning's message affirmed everything, and I'm ready—*we* are ready to make this sacrifice. So today's meal will be a celebration, and then tonight we will cleanse the world of the god's foul presence."

Well, we had a nice moment before she went all cultish on me again. I hum a sound of noncommittal assent as I focus on draining the last of the sweet tea. Then I lean back on the sofa and relax, waiting for my celebratory meal. I'm so hungry, I feel like my stomach might swallow my insides.

It'll be nice to have something besides crackers. If only I didn't feel...so sleepy... I...can't keep my eyes open...

I blink, trying to clear the film over my eyes. Aunt Nellie has paused in the kitchen doorway and she's looking back at me, but I can't see her expression. My vision is blurring, and my eyelids are so thick, swollen, and heavy, I can't keep them open.

Moments ago I was climbing out of the dreary river of the past week and a half, slogging out of the murk into the bright sunshine, but now I'm sliding backward into the darkness again, my limbs too heavy to fight against the sucking downward pull of the black water.

The realization flickers in my brain like the last spark before a fire dies.

Sweet tea. Aunt Nellie's own special herbal blend.

The nausea, the lack of appetite, the drowsiness, the brain fog...

I wasn't sick or struggling to recover from that traumatic episode. Aunt Nellie has been drugging me.

She's been doing it ever since I collapsed at the church.

I want to yell at her, but I don't have the strength. My lungs are busy hauling slow, shallow breaths through my lungs. My heart beats sluggishly, just enough to keep me alive.

I move my lips a little. Just enough for one breath, one exhaled word.

"Heathcliff."

◆◆◆

I'm distantly conscious of being lifted, stripped, dressed in something filmy. Cold air bathes my skin, then a noise rumbles all around me, fading into the steady hum of a car.

Fragrance wafts into my nose, a fresh scent like lilies by a pond—Aunt Nellie's perfume. The humming and the lilies and the drowsiness are all I know for a long time.

At last, a car door opens and freezing air blasts across my face. The shock is sharp enough to wake me, and I manage to open my eyes.

I still can't move very well. Someone unbuckles me, swings my legs out onto the ground. It's horribly cold, and the frozen breath of the night bites right through whatever I'm wearing.

I'm lifted upright, my arms pulled across the shoulders of two people who brace me from either side, Aunt Nellie and my dad. I recognize his scent, too—Old Spice body spray and citrus detergent.

Unease sifts through my drowsiness, but I can't figure out why.

"Walk, Cathy," Dad says under his breath. "We're not dragging you the whole way. Just...*walk*."

My weary brain tells me I shouldn't upset him, so I try to walk. I force my sluggish feet to move, despite the gnawing sense that something is wrong, so very, very wrong.

"You gave her too much, Nellie," Dad mutters.

"Like you're the expert," she snaps. "Who stepped in to manage this mess? *Me*. Like I did with Mom and Dad. Like I always do."

The venom in their voices helps to clear my mind even more. I lift my head and take in my surroundings. Great, dark trees with hunched shoulders. Grass studded with headstones. Up ahead, brick columns rear out of the earth.

Old Sheldon Church.

I haven't been here since last Easter. It looked different then, gilded by beams of translucent sunshine glancing through spring-green leaves. Now it's jutting bones, the skeleton of a sanctuary twice burned and still standing. Black trees surround it, lifting heavy, naked arms to the chalkboard sky. Mist rises from the ground, birthed by the dramatic drops in temperature so common in the Lowcountry during October.

This isn't right. We shouldn't be here. It's dangerous. Gods and monsters and death...

I want to thrash, to fight, to run, because despite the haze in my head, I can practically taste the threat in the air. But I don't have full control over my body. I can barely walk, and although my thoughts are clarifying, I can't seem to push those thoughts out of my mouth. I can't protest or struggle. So I stumble ahead, buoyed by Dad and Aunt Nellie, watching ethereal wisps of white fog curl from the desolate ground. The mist moves with unnatural purpose, surging and receding like the quickening exhale of some titanic, eldritch thing.

Figures drift through the fog, slow and black clad. Faces I recognize dimly through the gloom and the sleepiness drowning my brain. Some of them have lanterns—actual lanterns with candles in them. I suppose that's more atmospheric for a midnight service such as this.

We're here to consecrate the ground, that much is clear. Whatever ritual they claim to have discovered, it's happening tonight. What I don't understand is why they couldn't leave me home to sleep while they performed it. I'm so tired.

So tired because...I haul the truth out of my drowsy memories...because Aunt Nellie has been drugging me.

A chill traces over my skin, revulsion at her touch. Just moments ago, Dad said, "You gave her too much," so he *knows*. He went along with this scheme of hers to keep me drugged and docile, to control and "cure" the banshee inside me.

Fuck. Fuck me, and fuck them.

The certainty traces through me like a sickening bolt of lightning—that this gathering is somehow about *me*. That I've been tricked, that I've been gullible, that I should have known better, shouldn't have let them lull me into a dazed existence, shouldn't have trusted my own blood, not even for one second, because when did they ever give me a reason to think they truly cared about me? I wanted their love too much. And that was my mistake.

I try to speak, to scream, but the thoughts get distorted on the way to my mouth and they come out as garbled nonsense.

"Hush now," admonishes Aunt Nellie.

Tension stretches between the members of the congregation—taut lines of fear running from person to person as they file slowly from their cars, across the grass, into the columned shadow of the church.

Several of the deacons carry crystal decanters, which I assume are filled with blessed water. Is it really that different from other kinds of water? Does it truly have some kind of power? It must, or the god wouldn't have stayed dormant this long.

No, that's not what's important here. Focus, Cathy. *Focus.*

I struggle against the drugged haze in my brain. What are they doing with me? What the *hell* could they possibly be planning? A baptism, an exorcism...a sacrifice? Aunt Nellie used that word.

No...no, it's not possible, even for them.

But I can't be naive about this, not with all that's been happening. Not with the way they've been treating me for years.

Maybe that's why I believed their gentleness and kindness after that horrible episode at the church—I was so hungry for acceptance. I thought, I hoped, that maybe Dad and Aunt Nellie finally *saw* me, understood me. But it was the worst kind of lie.

I have to get away. I have to *make* my body comply. Sheer fucking force of will... *Come on, Cathy, get it together...*

I go limp and drag my feet, but Dad hauls me up roughly and curses under his breath. Maybe I shouldn't antagonize him, at least until I know what's going on. A few more minutes might give me better control over my limbs. So I walk again, complying for the moment.

I spot one of the trees that has always fascinated me—a crooked, swollen trunk with an eye-shaped split in its side. Within that opening are neat lines of bricks, a bit of wall built within the tree itself. Those bricks cover holes where the limbs of the God Beneath began to emerge on the night of my birth. My dad and the deacons sealed the holes with clay, iron, and salt, and they soaked those trees with blessed water until the god settled again.

We're entering the church now, passing through a brick archway. Dad and Aunt Nellie walk me toward the front, where Edgar Linton and a few of the deacons are standing, illuminated by the glow of several lanterns hung from the arches behind them. Ian Holcum, the guest speaker from this morning, is here, too, his shaggy brown hair casting dramatic shadows onto his hollow cheeks, around his dark eyes. He's wearing a long black coat.

I shouldn't be surprised he's here—after all, he's Edgar's precious "expert" on myth and lore. Still, it's odd. Usually the church is resistant to outsiders, especially when it comes to our private rituals.

We've stopped moving, and so has everyone else. The congregation stands motionless and silent within the walls of Old Sheldon Church, with no ceiling but the night sky.

Edgar steps forward. In the eerie glow of the lanterns, he looks more angelic than ever—that delicate, beautiful face, the golden curls, the fervent blue eyes. He's wearing dark robes I've only seen the deacons wear during special services.

"My father couldn't be here tonight," he says. "What we must do is too painful for him. We agreed that I should lead this consecration service, as it will be my duty and my joy to lead you all through the next few decades as your pastor."

A soft murmur runs through the crowd. Pastor Linton retiring is a shock for everyone, as is Edgar's inheritance of the pastoral role. In some churches, they'd vote in a new pastor or be assigned a minister...but this congregation is anything but normal.

"There will be time for explanations later. For now, let's open the service with a hymn," Edgar continues. "'There Is a Fountain.' You all know the words."

Through the fog and the crooked shadows, voices rise, wavering at first, then finding each other in ethereal harmony. It's hella spooky.

I wouldn't sing with this creepy crowd, even if I could. All I want is to get away, but I'm still having trouble focusing occasionally, and my mouth feels disconnected from my brain. I can only stand on wobbly legs and stare at Edgar, who sings with all the vigor of an old-time revival preacher.

During the second verse, his gaze swerves to me, and another chill rushes over my skin, a tremor so powerful, Aunt Nellie throws me a sidelong glance.

Edgar's eyes burn bright, but they're hollow, too, and remote, like a pair of distant blue stars. I can't help comparing them to Heathcliff's brown eyes, so vivid and warm, full of passion and purpose.

Edgar's gaze moves from my face downward, to my chest. I'm trembling from the cold, my nipples peaked against the frail fabric of the white dress I'm wearing. He takes his time drinking in the sight of me, and all the while, he never stops singing.

Does he know what Aunt Nellie has been doing to me? He must know. My family, the church, everyone has been working against me.

I thought I felt alone and misunderstood before, but that was nothing compared to the loneliness, the panic, and the rage I feel now. I've spent years fighting for some measure of control over my body, my life...and to have it stolen from me slowly, to be so utterly betrayed by the people I've known since I was born—it's agony. It's an unnatural violence I can barely grasp. They're monsters. They're fiends. And I was foolish for letting myself believe they cared, that they were keeping me safe, that they wanted to help me.

I put all my focus, all my energy into mouthing one word. One single word that expresses my defiance, that tells Edgar I know exactly what he is, at his core: *Pervert*.

His eye twitches—he got the message.

By the start of the fourth stanza, I'm beginning to regain some control over my muscles. Another minute, and maybe I can break free. Strike back. Run. Maybe I'll even have the energy to scream, although my banshee still feels shaken, subdued, drowned somewhere deep inside me.

Just as I'm about to make a move, Edgar shifts his attention from me to my dad and nods slightly.

Aunt Nellie wraps her arm around my shoulders just as Dad reaches up and jabs something into my neck. There's a sharp pinch and a quick cold flush of liquid along my vein, spreading rapidly through my neck and shoulder. The sensation trickles over to my spine and drains along it, flooding my limbs with a strange floating, tingling sensation.

I choke a little and stagger.

The needle flashes in my father's hand as he tucks the syringe back into his pocket.

I struggle to yell, to form words, but my vocal cords are paralyzed. It's hard to drag in breaths.

"Shh, honey, shh." Aunt Nellie is holding me still. Keeping me upright.

Shit, this can't be good. *Shit shit shit.* I struggle to force out a scream, a pulse of power, anything—but the stuff in that needle has done its job well and quickly. I can't summon a shriek; I can barely haul air through my heavy lungs, can barely manage to keep my legs from folding beneath me.

The hymn ends, and Edgar speaks again. "You all know why we're here. The demon is stirring and has murdered several of our own. He's killing off his guards, his jailers, we the dedicated few who hold him down and protect the world from destruction. Our hold on him is breaking. If we are to survive, if we are to keep this evil force submerged and protect the world from his dreadful power, we must take drastic measures. We must make painful sacrifices, as our Lord did, as our ancestors have done for generations."

He hesitates, looks back over his shoulder toward the guy in the dark coat.

"The dissonant energy of the demon's awakening brought to us a wise man, someone to help us in our hour of need," Edgar continues. "He understands the lore more deeply than we do, and he knew the ingredient we've been missing, the element used to seal the demon away in the first place and the key to repressing him now. We need someone with powerful supernatural gifts and a blood inheritance directly from the demon himself. By God's grace, we have just such a person among us. In penance for the harm she has done to this community, she has agreed to be our savior. Her blood will saturate the earth and serve as a warning to the demon. Her life will seal him within the tomb forever, and he will rest there in silence. No more deaths among our congregation—no fear of the demon rising and unleashing carnage on this state, this country, this world."

Her blood will saturate the earth... Her life will seal him within the tomb...

The meaning is unmistakable. They're going to fucking kill me. They're going to slash my throat and let me bleed out right here in the hopes that my death will be the magical lock that keeps a god from rising.

I almost laugh. This is the stuff of horror movies—surely Edgar can see that. Surely he can hear how ridiculous and melodramatic he sounds, how foolish this idea is...

Then again, my entire life has been a horror movie. Why should this be any different?

There's a fanatical gleam in Edgar's eyes as his gaze locks with mine again. I struggle to move, to speak, but I can only hang between my aunt and my father, bound by their joint embrace.

"You all know Cathy Earnshaw," says Edgar. "Maybe, like me, you always felt that she was a soul apart, not entirely devoted like the rest of us. There was a good reason for that. She has been unnatural since her birth. She inherited the dark blood of the demon and a wretched gift along with it. That gift rightfully concerned us at first, but now we bless her. We thank her, and we thank God for giving her to us because through her sacrifice, we find safety. We find hope. We rise undismayed to face the future."

You fucking bastard. You absolute fool. You traitor, you asshole... In my mind I reel off every foul name I can think of.

This isn't going to happen. This doesn't happen, not these days. Not *here.*

People can't be this stupid.

But maybe, when you've attended services month after month, when you've been cajoled and conned into trusting every word that falls from another human's lips, you lose the ability to think for yourself. The mind-muscle that can discern truth from bullshit becomes atrophied.

When you're told over and over that wrong is right, that hate is love, that wickedness is holy…when you sit there, week after week, and open your mind to that poison…maybe you begin to believe it.

And what if they're right? What if the stranger in the dark coat knows exactly how to shut the god down for good?

What if this is the only way? What if my death could save lives?

A frantic voice screams in my mind, *I don't care, I don't fucking care! All I care about is me! My life!*

This has got to be a dream, a joke, a hoax. But the second I think those words, my brain reverses course into despair because I can't deny it. It's happening. It's horribly, nightmarishly true.

There must be something I can do…some way I can get out of this…but without the ability to speak, struggle, or scream, I'm helpless.

Shit. Shit shit shit *fuck*.

Dad and Aunt Nellie are pulling me forward. My feet drag and stumble—one of my ankles bends painfully because I can't control my legs.

They release my limp body and step back, leaving me slumped on my knees before Edgar.

My head lolls a bit, but I manage to lift my gaze to his face.

In his eyes gleams the frantic delight of a man who has always envisioned himself as a lord and savior. He's loving this. It's his shining moment, the dramatic pinnacle of his life.

Is it just that he wants to save our congregation and possibly the world? Or is there more to it? Am I imagining the edge of vengeful glee in his gaze? The glitter of jealousy being satisfied?

He hates me because I'm a banshee, yes...and he hates me because I chose Heathcliff.

Oh god—*Heathcliff*. If he ever does come looking for me, he'll find out I'm dead. Or maybe they'll say I ran away, and Heathcliff will wonder why I left him behind.

A tender pain stabs through my heart as I think of the tattoo he paid for. He really thought it would protect me. *Romantic shit*, he said. Sweet man.

Edgar is reciting Scripture now, droning on while I bow at his feet.

I've grieved death dozens of times, loudly, violently. Grieving my own death is a silent trauma. Never have I felt such pure, wretched despair, and it's a keener torture than ever because I can't let it out, can't express its horror with movement or screams.

I will never kiss Heathcliff again. I can't say goodbye or touch him or thank him for turning my painful existence into a thing of beauty, even for a little while.

What must he think of me? After the night we spent, the things we said, the matching tattoos—and then I sent him *one* text before I lost access to my phone. A text that, in chilling retrospect, I realize now sounded suspiciously like a goodbye.

I've already hurt him without meaning to. When he finds out I'm dead, he's going to *break*.

The thought of his pain carves a ravine through my soul, splits me open. Tears slide from my eyes as I stare up at Edgar.

His features tighten, and he lifts his gaze to the congregation. "We won't draw this out any longer," he says. "We'll do it quickly so you can all head home and rest. Let's sing again. Pray these words in song with me: 'Are You Washed in the Blood?'"

His high tenor soars through the ruined church, into the tangled wall of dark boughs beyond.

A shadow moves behind him—Ian Holcum, the stranger who condemned me to death. He has raised the hood of his black coat, and he moves forward with sinuous purpose, a serpent bent on striking. He steps swiftly behind me, with his back to the congregation. I feel his fingers sliding into my hair, knotting there, pulling my head back to expose my throat.

A red flash sears my vision—terror burning through my mind. I'm going to die. Edgar isn't going to do it himself; he's letting this man perform the sacrifice. And I can't stop it. No force of my will can fend it off. It's happening now.

No no no—

I thrust all my energy into my arms, but I can only manage a limp, ineffectual brush of my fingers against the man's wrists. The drug made me helpless, and all I can do is scream inside my head, shrieking mutely against the vivid, intimate reality of my own death.

I'm engulfed by my killer's ominous presence as he bows over me, his broad back shielding the audience from what he's about to do.

His hand appears in front of my face. Slender masculine fingers wrapped around a knife, an ancient-looking silver weapon with runes on it. My brain fixates on the thumbnail—pale pink, well-manicured. A flex of his thin wrist and the knife dips out of my sight.

Fire burns across my throat. Panic—hot liquid spilling out of me, spilling down my esophagus. Flames roaring through my neck, my head, lungs spasming, heart flying into an arrhythmic panic, throbbing loud, loud, louder, then stuttering as I choke, gargle, collapse to the ground.

I can smell the wet grass, the stony earth. A wisp of fog breathes wetly against my cheek. The voices falter, but they keep singing, slow and determined. *Are you washed in the blood...*

I think I hear a sob... I think it's my dad.

I can heal faster than humans, and for half a second, I claw at that hope. But it's a false one. I don't heal fast enough to stop my life from leaking out.

Images flash through my mind—not pictures from my life but from the lives of all the people I've mourned. Because that has been my existence, bemoaning the absence of others. I've never had the chance to truly *live* myself. My life has always been about everyone else. And now it's over. I'm done.

The injustice of that hurts worse than my family's betrayal.

Something tingles on my hip, barely noticeable amid the pain and the quivering spasms of my dying brain.

And then a shift—the world slants, tipping me off its edge, out of my empty body.

A sickening drop into the dark.

I am floating, voiceless and sightless, in the great Nothing beyond the border of life.

I know that I *am*. I know that Heathcliff *is*, that he exists still, somewhere, forever beyond my bodiless reach. And that knowledge is agony worse than the bite of any blade.

21

HEATHCLIFF

I RISE FROM THE FLOOR, MY KNEES WET WITH BLOOD AND my hands trembling.

"Rockford was a longtime client of yours, wasn't he?" I ask Hindley. "You guys were friends?"

Hindley doesn't answer. Instead he walks over to the bar cart and grabs a decanter of whiskey, yanks out the stopper, and pours himself a glass.

"Never mind," I mutter. "Just thought you might have some idea who would murder him."

Except murder is too tame a word. This guy was butchered.

When Hindley and I got here, to a suburb just outside Augusta, Georgia, we had to force our way into the house. No one had found the body yet. The stench was goddamn awful, and there were actual chunks of him missing. This guy's gonna have to rip out his carpet, throw out his furniture, and repaint his walls when he comes to, which should happen in just a few minutes.

I haven't had such a tough job resurrecting someone since Ian.

Ian, the shapeshifter, the trickster. Found dead on Lockwood island, inside that revenant mansion, why, why? I'm missing something. Can't quite grasp it.

The carpet squelches under my boot as I step backward, reeling from a sudden wave of weakness. At the same moment my eyes land on a small glob of squishy red flesh, just beneath the edge of the sofa.

Aw, fuck—

I run for the kitchen and vomit into the sink. My whole body is shaking, worn-out from pouring so much energy from myself into this guy just to bring him back. I'm gonna need a couple days to recover from this one.

Turning on the faucet, I rinse the sick down the drain. I wash my hands, my face, my goddamn neck and arms, every bit of exposed skin. I want a shower, but I gotta watch the guy and make sure he wakes up okay.

I stagger back to the living room and drop into a chair. Hindley passes me a glass of whiskey and I drink. I need it.

The guy on the floor starts to stir. He's still slick with his own blood, but he's alive. He's moving, sitting up, wiping gore out of his eyes, staring around like he can't believe the mess. Spatters of his blood decorate the coffee table, the couch, the drapes.

I raise the bottle to him. "You'll have a hell of a cleaning bill," I say. "But you're alive. Best money you ever spent, huh?"

"Shit," he exclaims. "I remember...some guys came to the door, just barged in and attacked me. God, it hurt."

I lean forward in the chair, offering my whiskey glass to him. He accepts it and drinks gratefully.

A wave of weakness rushes over me, turning my limbs watery.

I'm gonna need an ass-ton of food after that resurrection, and there's no way I can eat until I get out of this house.

"We should go," I tell Hindley. "I need to eat."

"Wait, you're just gonna leave?" exclaims Rockford. "What about the mess? What about the guys who killed me? What if they come back? I'm gonna need another tattoo."

"Naw, man," I tell him. "It's a one-time thing. Can't happen again."

"So if I die next time, I just stay dead?" Rockford's voice rises an octave, his eyes bugging out.

"Most people do," I respond dryly. That's just like humans—ungrateful bastards, all of us. This guy's got himself another shot at life, and now he's bitching about being mortal? He's lucky I've got no energy right now, or I'd give him a good right hook to the jaw to remind him to be thankful. Gratitude, man. It ain't that hard.

I'm about to rise from the chair and insist Hindley drive me to a diner when I feel a buzzing burn along the left side of my abdomen.

I yank up the hem of my T-shirt, even though I already know which tattoo it is. *Who* it is.

It's Cathy.

It's *Cathy*.

I keep saying it in my head, trying to grasp it.

Cathy's tattoo is buzzing, burning.

That means...

That means Cathy...my Cathy... She's...

I'm out of the chair in half a second, my fist crashing into Hindley's face. His nose cracks and he chokes, dazed. I grab a fist-ful of his shirt, holding him still while I jam my fingers into his pocket and grab his keys. Didn't have time to ask nicely for them. He'd have said no anyway.

Out the door I charge, into his truck. I roar out of the driveway and careen onto the road.

A wave of dizziness hits me, and I retch. My stomach is hollow, my body empty, my energy reserves bone-dry.

The timing is too fucking perfect. Somebody planned this. Someone wanted me down for the count, didn't want me to resurrect her.

Who, though? Her dad? That snivelly Linton kid? But they don't know what I am, what I can do. Somebody *knew*, and they had Rockford butchered on purpose, to keep me from bringing Cathy back. Maybe that Ian bastard. I still don't know what his deal is.

I can sense which direction I need to go to find her, sort of like she can tell where the people are that she's supposed to mourn. It's a bone-deep instinct, passed down through generations.

Her body is somewhere to the southeast, about two hours away.

A raw sob cracks through my throat.

Cathy.

"Don't leave me." My voice grates through my clenched teeth. "Don't you fucking leave me. You stay close, baby. Don't go so deep into the Vague that I can't find you."

My trembling fingers can barely grip the wheel. Much as I hate it, I've got to eat, or I'll pass out before I get there.

Twenty minutes later, I'm speeding down a dark lane. I barely remember pulling up at the first open drive-thru I found and demanding half a dozen burgers and the biggest Coke they had, but somehow I've got the protein and the sugar, and I'm fueling up while driving as fast as I dare.

I have to get there quick, before she drifts too far. The longer I wait, the deeper into the dark she'll go. It usually takes about seventy-two hours before a soul is beyond reach, and seventy-two hours isn't enough to regain all my energy, not after what I just did for Rockford. If I wait and try to gain some of it back before I rez Cathy, she could be too far away in the Vague. Or her murderer might move her body somewhere else or worse—cut her apart and take the pieces to different locations.

Whoever arranged this knows me. Knows what I can do. Understood how to drain me to the dregs so I couldn't interfere with whatever scheme they got going on.

Cathy.

Drops start spattering my windshield. I peer through the slashing wipers and the hammering rain. The road is dark and wet now, black and shimmery as the Vague. I've always wondered where the souls go after their time in that limbo is done. Do they just vanish into the depths of Nothing, or is there a destination?

I finish the burgers and gulp down the soda. Then I turn on the radio and sync up my recovery playlist, ignoring the missed calls and texts from Hindley. I got a bunch of songs whose rhythm seems to scratch the itch just right after a tough resurrection. If I were a scientist, I'd probably look into it more, figure out how the sound waves resonate with my necromancer energy, but as it is, I wouldn't know where to start, and I don't care to explain it. I crank up Nirvana's "Come As You Are" and lean harder on the gas.

By the time I reach the end of the playlist, I'm almost there.

The road to Old Sheldon Church is like a tunnel to hell. The trees hunch over it, their gnarled branches meeting at the peak like snakes planning to swallow each other. Their trunks are yellowed in the beams of my headlights. Rain pelts through the boughs, slicking the black pavement.

Before I reach the church, I pull to the side, onto gravel, and throw the truck in park.

Whoever planned this knew I might come for Cathy. Which means this could be a trap.

I'm the guy who always took it on the chin and didn't fight back, who toughed it out because he couldn't see any hope. But Cathy changed me into someone willing to fight, not just for her but for myself. I don't like hurting or killing people...but by god, if anyone tries to stop me from getting to her, I'll drop them on the spot.

I leave the truck, easing the door shut instead of slamming it. I keep to the darkest shadows of the trees, my steps muffled by the pouring rain and wet grass. The trees are mostly bare by now, but it's the South, and the undergrowth is still leafy, so I've got some cover. Unfortunately, that also means I'm noisier, so I try to time my movements with the biggest gusts of wind and sweeping rain.

As I get closer to the church, a figure moves in the darkness ahead. He's hiding in the shadows, too, but he's got his back to me, far as I can tell. Waiting.

A twig crunches nearby, and I almost leap into action—but I hold myself still.

It's another man, approaching the first. "Hell of a day," he mutters. "First that guy in Augusta, now this watchdog shit? I'm soaked, man."

"Hey, I don't mind the rain. We all needed a shower after that job," chuckles the first man. "Never seen so much blood shoot out of one guy."

These guys came from a murder in Augusta, where Rockford lives. And now they're here, watching the graveyard where Cathy's body lies? It can't be a coincidence. I'd bet my dick they killed Rockford. Which means whatever I do to them is justified.

A vicious, glorious rage swells inside me. I've never had the chance to test my strength on someone who really deserved the pain. These guards are a fucking gift, just the outlet I need.

The burgers I ate renewed my strength but not my necromancer energy. Lucky for me, beating up some assholes doesn't require necromancer shit. Even if I'm dizzier and weaker than usual, I should be a match for these bastards.

"I'm going to check the road," says one of the men. "If nothing happens in another hour, I say we leave."

"I'll back you up on that, but Aaron's a stickler. He'll want all four of us to stay the full eight hours we were paid for."

"Aaron," the first man scoffs derisively. He walks off toward the road.

As soon as he's far enough away, I leap forward, clamp my hand over the second man's mouth, and drag him backward, against my chest. When his hand moves, mine darts to his hip faster and seizes the gun he was going for. I throw it with all my might into the bushes, still gripping his face so tightly I can feel his teeth through his cheeks. He's trying to scream through my palm, so I wrap my other arm around his throat and squeeze.

His hands are flailing, elbows jabbing, trying everything he can to damage me. I'm unmovable. A fucking rock.

Within three minutes of losing his air supply, he softens and goes lax. I wait another count of ten to be sure he's really gone.

The first guy is coming back. He sees me there in the shadows and apparently thinks I'm his buddy because he says, "Saw a truck parked a ways down the road. Think we should check it out?"

I greet him with a thunderous punch to the face. It's a weaker blow than I could usually manage, but it does the trick. Throws him off-kilter long enough for me to punch him again. But my foot slips on the slick grass, and I go down to one knee.

He pulls a gun. Desperately, I grab his wrist, wrenching, twisting—he drops the gun with a shout of pain, and I use his arm to pull myself up. A blow to his stomach and he doubles, but then he's back up and smashing a fist against my cheekbone. I grab his shoulder, sidestep, use it for leverage while I stomp on the back of his calf at an angle, right below the knee. Saw the move on TV, and it fucking works—there's a crack of bone, a sharp give of the leg. He screams in agony. When he goes down, I kick his head as hard as I can for good measure, and judging by the resulting crunch, he won't be getting up again.

Tremors run through my body, and I brace myself against a tree.

I killed both of them.

It's for Cathy. For Cathy, I'd do anything. Carve out my heart. Soak my damn soul in blood—

A gunshot rings out, and I crouch, hunkering behind the tree. The last two guys must have heard their buddy scream. They know I'm here.

Waves of drowsiness and weakness are rolling over me. My body telling me it's about time to get some rest. But I gotta finish this. I've got to get her back.

I left my phone in the truck, so I don't have any light, but I root around in the grass where I think the second gun fell. My fingers brush wet metal, and I pick up the weapon, checking to make sure the safety's off.

For once, I'm grateful to Hindley. His constant need to compete with me for Buckland's approval drove both of us to be better marksmen. Since I never go hunting, I thought those hours of target practice in all weather conditions were wasted, but it looks like I'm about to reap the reward.

I do a sidelong half crawl, half crouch through the bushes, quiet as I can, until I've gained some distance from the two bodies. I'm right on the edge of the graveyard now; I can see the dark pillars of Old Sheldon Church.

Something moves near one of the arches.

I squint through the rain, silently cursing the low visibility.

There it is again. Someone peeking out from his cover, growing bolder with every passing second.

I aim for the edge of that arch, and I wait.

When he appears again, I pull the trigger.

Head shot. His neck jerks, and he falls backward.

Swiftly I move through the trees, bent over, grateful for a rustling gust of wind that covers my steps.

A few minutes pass—and then a figure goes streaking past my hiding spot, running full tilt for the road. The fourth guard. He knows his buddies are gone, and he's done playing watchdog. He's hightailing it outta here, to wherever they parked their vehicle.

But I can't let him leave. He might call whoever set this up and warn them that I'm here for Cathy.

I try to run after him, but my balance is shit, so I plant my feet, narrow my eyes, and shoot twice. Three times. Four, and he falls, right at the edge of the road.

My heart is pounding and my lungs feel thick. Breathing heavily, I walk up to the wounded guy, grab his arms, and drag him into some bushes. Then I crouch and rub the gun around in some wet leaves and dirt to get rid of any fingerprints.

The guy I shot is moaning, fumbling for his pocket. Probably try to get his phone.

I could just take the phone, smash it on the road, then knock him out. Or I could hold his head just right and snap his neck.

This guy participated in Rockford's murder. He's been hired by whoever killed Cathy. Which means he's guilty as sin.

I kneel. Brace his skull between my hands. Look down into his eyes.

"Where is she?" I demand through the cold rain streaming down my face.

"She?" He coughs, spits blood.

"Don't play dumb. The woman who was killed tonight. The one whose body you were sent here to guard. Where the fuck is she? Tell me, and I'll let you live."

"The crypt." He lifts a shaking finger and points. "The big one, on the right. Please..."

One, two, three...*snap*.

I bow over him for a second, a silent confession of what I've done. Owning it.

Then I drag myself upright again and stumble toward the crypt. It's an old one, a huge rectangular stone box with a cracked slab of stone as the lid.

There's a smear of blood glistening on the underside of the granite edge, where the rain can't reach.

Cathy.

She's in there. My girl is in there, and I have to get her out.

I ram both palms against the stone cover of the crypt and shove.

My boots slip on the muddy ground, and I nearly fall. I take a second to find my footing, renew my grip, and brace myself.

Then I roar, my whole body straining with effort, and the stone grinds grudgingly across the mouth of the crypt, inch by inch, until it tips and slides to the ground with a dull boom. Rain shatters into the tomb.

There she is. There she fucking is. They *left her* here—they left her in the dark, in this grave.

Hoarse sobs crack from my lungs as I reach in and drag her out. She's already soaked to the skin, her white dress a transparent film over her body. She's thinner than the last time I saw her—frail and brittle in my arms. Her head lolls back on her delicate neck, exposing the ugly wound across her throat. She's bloodlessly white, her eyes closed, her lungs still, and her heart silent.

"Damn it, Cathy," I whisper. I gather her into my lap, sink my fingers into her wet, dark hair, and pull her head against my shoulder.

I need to resurrect her here. That's one of the rules—the corpse must be kept as close to the location of death as possible. Otherwise, it's almost impossible to find the soul.

Blinking through the rain, I scan our gloomy surroundings. I don't see anyone else watching, but that's not to say someone won't show up, especially if the gunshots were overheard and reported.

I'll be in a sort of trance during the resurrection. I won't be able to respond to any danger around us, and I won't know how much damage I'm doing to myself until the job is done.

I'm weak. Drained low. I probably won't survive this. Thing is, I don't much care, as long as Cathy lives.

There's no way around it—I gotta do this now.

I lay Cathy down in the grass and adjust her limbs so she looks like she's resting. Lifting my right wrist, I bite down until blood oozes from the torn skin. With my fingertips I paint the blood over the tattoo on the left side of my abdomen. Then, with a silent apology, I pull up the filmy skirt of her dress and paint more of my blood over the tattoo on her hip.

The rain is still coming down, but the blood soaks into the tattoos faster than the drops can wash it away. Cathy's tattoo lights up, a red glow seeping through every inked line. Mine comes to life too, red and raging.

Kneeling beside her, I slam one palm over my tattoo and the other over hers. I scan the church grounds one more time, peering through gray rain at the gravestones, the brick pillars, the trees. There's no sign of anyone.

Good enough. Let's do this.

Shoulders bent, head bowed, blood still running warm from my wrist, I press harder against both our tattoos, and I close my eyes.

"Mors aperit ianuam."

My mind slips into the Vague, punching through the veil between life and death, pressing deeper. The dark shimmers here—a sort of black iridescence, a lightless rainbow. Like being inside a prism of smoked glass or the most twisted mirror maze, where you can actually walk upside down or phase *through* the mirrors. That's the best I've ever been able to describe it. A necromancer like me can walk, or imagine that he's walking, across the slanted panes of glass, tilting with the angles of the maze.

I visualize the line that connects me to Cathy, and it appears in my hand. Ahead of me, it seems to bend jaggedly upward, then disappear into a glassy surface.

It hasn't been long. Couple hours. She can't have gone far.

"Cathy!" I shout into the Vague. My voice has some traveling power here, but it's a matter of luck whether it bounces off the correct surfaces and heads in the right direction.

My shout comes back to me in a mocking whisper right by my shoulder. *"Cathy."*

As I climb toward the spot where the line bends, I see something shift in one of the iridescent panes to my right. It's quick, but I catch a glimpse. Faceless, slick as oil, with spindly legs and arms. A sluagh, a creature that preys on the souls of the dead—or the living.

Shit, I've barely stepped into the Vague and there's already a sluagh on my tail.

I climb, planting my bare feet carefully on the tilted glass, following the line. "Cathy!"

"*I can be Cathy,*" echoes the faceless figure behind me. *"I can be Cathy, Cathy, Cathy."*

It repeats her name over and over, a dirge from its mouthless, oval head.

Ignoring it, I reach forward, sliding my palm across cold glass until it gives and I can press through. Instantly I flip to the other side, emerging like a monster through a mirror.

But the sluagh is already there, crouched in front of me, head cocked. *"Cathy. I can be Cathy."*

"You're not her," I growl. I run past it, along a helix-shaped corridor where the floor eventually becomes the left wall and the left wall turns into the ceiling. Parts of the corridor are transparent; others are glossy black. I bruise myself against them more than once, but I keep going because I can feel heat traveling along the line now. I'm getting closer to her, to Cathy's live, fresh soul.

"Warmer," hisses the sluagh. *"Warmer, warmer."* It somersaults in front of me and makes a grab for my face, but I swat it away and keep going. These things only have power if you give it to them. The more annoyed with it I get, the more solid it becomes— and if I start hitting it, the sluagh will return the aggression with interest.

The Vague quakes—or maybe the tremor isn't from the Vague but from the living world. Possibly thunder. While my spirit is hunting in the Vague, my physical body is still kneeling in the graveyard, being drenched by a freezing October rain, while I try to bring my dead girlfriend back.

No, not girlfriend. She's more than that. She's my actual life, my fucking soul. I can't live without my soul.

Faster, I follow the line, hand over hand. It's getting hot now, starting to glow red.

I risk one more bellow into the shimmering, shifting kaleidoscope of the Vague. "Cathy!"

"Cathycathycathycathycathy," pants the sluagh.

But from somewhere ahead, and down, and to the right, I hear a reply. A real reply, in a familiar voice, half-amazed, half-doubtful. "Heathcliff?"

I step forward and nearly tumble off the edge of what I thought was glass but is really a downward slope studded with tiny, iridescent crystals. Cautiously, I slide down it. Some of the crystals shatter as I go, releasing a tinkling, chiming sound into the stagnant air.

My spiritual self is wearing the same clothes as my real body, and normally sharp pieces of crystal would tear up a pair of jeans... but they're perfectly fine because this place has no logic. No physics. I've long since quit trying to figure it out, and now I just go along with the weirdness. I keep sliding, one hand on the line and the other on the slope, until my feet hit a cold, smooth surface. A wall of glass, thicker this time, and darker.

The line is red-hot now. It leads right through the smoky wall. I peer through. "Cathy?"

A small, white hand slams against the glass, and I jump. Cathy's face is a milky blur, her hair a murky cloud. "Heathcliff?" Her voice is muffled, like it's coming from underwater. "Let me in!"

"Hang on!" I shout. I can feel my heartbeat racing higher—the heart I've left behind in my real body. The fast pulse—that's okay. It's when my heart slows down that we have a problem.

I scan the wall, moving a little farther to the right until the dark tint of the glass fades and I can see through it better.

Cathy isn't in the mirror maze, where the souls usually stay for the first twenty-four hours or so after death. She's floating in a vast chasm, her hair streaming and her pale body wreathed in smoke.

It looks like the wall separating us ends farther on, so I climb over giant wedges of glass, heading for the place where it melts into air. Cathy does the same, and the glowing line that connects us follows, seeming to phase through the glass. But when we get to that empty space and reach for each other's hands, the transparent wall materializes between us again, solid and impenetrable.

Whoever set this up did something to keep me from getting to her. A spell or a curse most likely. I've never met a supernatural who can actually cast spells or curses—Meemaw says that gift died out decades ago. People who swear they can do it are just fooling themselves or others. But this sure looks like a curse. I've heard about something like it before, with one of Hindley's clients. Real classy woman, lived in this big house full of artifacts. Someone broke in and killed her before she made it to her safe room. Stole a rare talisman, she told us after she woke up. She was fucking hard to resurrect. Hindley said he found her deep in the Vague, in a glass box covered with runes, with something called an "impossible riddle" etched on it. He read it aloud to her, and she solved it within minutes. Apparently the intruders had wedged a curse totem into her throat to make sure she'd stay dead. But even in death, she was too smart for them.

I don't know why Cathy is behind this wall, but it's gonna make it that much tougher for me to bring her back.

"I'll get you, I promise," I call to her. "Just give me a second to think."

In the case of the woman in the box, a necromancer had to come for her, but she also had to do part of the work. She had to save herself through something she possessed—her cleverness.

Cathy is smart, but she's got another gift, too. Her nature as a banshee: a scream that can shatter glass.

She's floating a little farther away now, her eyes mournful, her voice soft and faint. "Heathcliff? Why won't you let me in?"

"You're drifting, Cathy. Come on, baby, focus on me. Here, see my hand?" I press it to the wall between us.

She blinks and reaches out, laying her palm against the thick glass, opposite mine.

I plead with her, my voice a hoarse echo. "Cathy, I want to save you, but you have to save yourself first. You have to scream."

"Scream?" She shakes her head slowly. "That's not me anymore. I don't wail for death. I swim in death. Death is a part of me, as it always was—as it is. As it ever shall be."

She's going vague on me way faster than souls usually do. I've got to connect her back to her humanity, to the emotions that link her to life.

"Cathy, I need you to think, to focus. Look at me. You remember the first time we fucked?"

A spark ignites in her eyes—the ghost of a smile plays across her mouth. "Yes."

"Good. Think about that. Think about how I stalked you afterward. That made you mad, right? Pissed you off. Remember how that felt?"

"Yes." Her eyes are a shade brighter now, clearer.

"Yeah. You were mad at me. I saw that fire in you from day one. Don't tell me that fire's gone out 'cause of some little thing called death? You're still Catherine fucking Earnshaw. You're that bitch."

She narrows her eyes at the word *bitch*, so I say it again. "You're the bitch who loves life...really loves it...but you barely had a chance to enjoy it. You didn't get to travel, to dine at fancy-ass restaurants, to see the wonders of the world. You didn't get to leave Wicklow with me. How does that make you feel?"

Her small fists clench. "Angry."

"That's right. You get fucking angry." I ram my fist against the glass. "Because you don't belong here, Cathy Earnshaw. You belong in the living world with me. You are a banshee. You announce death, you scream for it, but you do not fucking *yield* to it, do you understand me?"

"Do not go gentle into that good night," she says.

"What?"

"It's a poem. Dylan Thomas. I memorized it because I liked it so much and because it was short. 'Do not go gentle into that good night, Old age should burn and rave at close of day—rage, rage against the dying of the light.'" Her voice rises, stronger, shriller. "Wild women 'who caught and sang the sun in flight, and learned, too late, they grieved it on its way, do not go gentle into that good night!'"

I'm beside myself, my chest swelling with her rage, with my love, my fists beating on the glass. The sluagh who followed me has been joined by several more, but they don't speak. They cluster in silence, watching without eyes, listening without ears.

"I am a wild woman," Cathy says, eyes flaming, her hair billowing around her. "I sang under the sun, I grieved under the moon, and I refuse—I *refuse* to go gently into the dark!"

And she screams.

She screams with such power, I slam both hands over my ears, as if it would make a difference, as if the earth-shattering power of her scream could reach right into the living world and burst both my eardrums. Maybe it could.

The sluaghs flee, shrieking, into the maze. Cathy's voice shrills higher, louder, filling the entirety of the Vague. The thick glass of the wall between us splits, forked cracks spreading wide before it explodes in fireworks of colored glass.

The bits of glass freeze in midair, and Cathy passes through them, untouched by a single shard.

I reach for her, pull her in. Clasp her. Mine, in my arms. My heartbeat stutters, and at first I think it's joy, but then I realize we're out of time. My body is failing, and I must get her back to hers.

As I turn to follow the line back to its source, a heavy, booming thunder reverberates through the maze. It's as deep as the void in which Cathy was floating, immense as a mountain. It's the rumble of something awakened.

Everything trembles.

This isn't thunder from the living world. This is happening in the Vague.

Cathy's clutching me, her arms wound around my neck. I'm facing the chasm, where something is shifting in the dark. Something so huge, the sight of it nearly shuts down my brain.

Antlers. Antlers branching out as wide as the entire length of a mountain range. Rising higher.

I don't want to see the head they're attached to, so I turn, with Cathy in my arms, and I run.

Boom. Another reverberation through the Vague. *Boom. Boom.* The slow pounding of my heart when it should be fast. Fuck—I'm not going to make it.

I'm stumbling along faceted boulders, sliding down slopes and then somehow sliding *up*. Clawing my way through shivering ropes of crystal. Climbing, running, while the maze shakes and mirrors shatter intermittently around us.

Cathy's soul weighs next to nothing. If she were corporeal, there's no way I could make it back. But I'm almost at the root of the line, where it disappears into a mirror that isn't a mirror, because through it I can see my corporeal self, kneeling in the dreary graveyard with my palms on the matching tattoos.

My spirit is slowing, shuddering. Each step more sluggish than the last.

Just a little farther...

But my feet are rooted, my mind paralyzed. Buckland warned me about this. He saw it happen once—a Lockwood overextended herself, and she died along with the soul she was supposed to save.

"Heathcliff." Cathy pats my face frantically. "Heathcliff." Her voice shrills suddenly, the frenzy of pure terror. "Heathcliff, behind you!"

Her shriek stirs me, propels me forward again. I don't look back to see what she sees. I only stumble forward.

As I take the final step toward the mirror, a hideous sense of *wrongness* floods my consciousness. There's a drag on our spirit forms, a sodden weight that shouldn't be there. Like something trying to pull us back.

Lunging forward, I leap through the mirror. And as I do, I realize that the dragging force isn't trying to keep us in the Vague—it's trying to come along.

With a lurch, I tumble back into myself, and I drop Cathy's soul into her body.

Air like knives, sharp with cold, stabbing my skin. But the rain has stopped.

Mud cakes my knees, layered over Rockford's blood. I'm

shivering, weakness hollowing out my limbs. I'm unnaturally strong, but two resurrections in a row has destroyed me.

At least the dragging weight on my spirit is gone. Maybe I imagined it. And if not, I'm too exhausted to worry about what it was, or what it means.

My overtaxed body pitches forward, nearly collapsing on top of Cathy—but I manage to haul myself upright, keeping my palms on both tattoos. I have to heal that slash across Cathy's throat. A small wound, thankfully—it closes in a few seconds, taking the last wisp of my energy.

Cathy's lashes blink apart, and she stares up at me wonderingly. "Heathcliff?"

"Princess," I rasp.

"You brought me back." She sits up, touching her throat. "You...fixed me. You're a..."

"Necromancer." The word feels heavy on my tongue.

"Thank fuck," she breathes, and I can't help smiling. "They sacrificed me, Heathcliff," she exclaims, betrayal and fear in her eyes. "They took away my phone and poisoned me, and then the church sacrificed me so my blood would seal the god away forever."

"That doesn't make sense," I mutter. "Sacrifice always strengthens the gods. If the Lockwoods ever got through the barrier, that's where they planned to start—lots of blood sacrifices."

"Well...that's what Edgar said. That my death would lock the god away for good. It was horrible." She blinks, gives a broken sob, and brushes away the tears flooding her eyes. But more tears are spilling out, and she sobs again. "I'm—I'm so upset about it, but it's not just that. It's...something else... Oh god, it's...god, I keep hearing your name in my head, and it makes me want to cry..." Her gaze flashes up to mine, realization fracturing her eyes. "Heathcliff Lockwood, you fucking idiot. You're dying."

"I'm not."

"Don't lie to me," she says savagely. "I'm a banshee. I *know*. How could you do this to yourself? How *could* you? I hate you! I fucking hate you!"

She grips the slick fabric of my shirt, hauls me close, claws me to herself. Her thin fingers arch against my back, nails digging into my flesh as if she could keep me here by sheer force of will. We're shivering, dripping, wrapped together in a mess of slick, cold limbs and chattering teeth.

I want to kiss her, but my body is too heavy for me to hold up anymore. I'm sinking, slipping from her arms, collapsing to the ground beside her.

"You moron," she gasps between sobs. "You wretched, wretched man. You killed yourself saving me. Don't you realize how fucking stupid that is?"

"I'm so...fucking...stupid," I agree. My eyes are closing. I wish they wouldn't. I want to see her. "You'll be all right," I manage.

"I will *not*. Don't you do this, Heathcliff. Don't you give me everything like some—damn—movie—hero!" She's pounding my chest in sync with her words. "I won't let you." Her voice cracks. "I fucking love you."

At first I think those words will be the last thing I hear. But as my mind dissolves, I hear one more sound.

A wild, primal wail of grief soaring from Cathy's throat into the night.

22

CATHY

I SCREAM.

I scream until the trees around the clearing groan with the force of my voice. I scream until Old Sheldon Church quakes. I howl my grief to the sky like some monster of the old world, like a demented herald of death.

I can't stop shrieking, crying, sobbing. Can't save him. I know he's still breathing, but he's slipping away so fast. I'll feel it when he goes.

I'm already getting flashes of his life...the scenes, the names, and the emotions, all in one overwhelming torrent. His adoptive father, Buckland, grinning and ruffling his hair. Fights with his brother, Hindley, and some Lockwood cousins. When they were younger, the cousins teamed up with Hindley to torture Heathcliff, yet as adults, Hindley expected Heathcliff to take his side in disputes. And through it all, Heathcliff rarely used his supernatural strength. Rough as he seems, he's gentle at heart. Not a fighter unless he has to be. Unless something he values deeply is at stake. I see him fighting four men in the graveyard so he could reach my body. Killing every one of them.

More flashes of his life, each one a split second, but they're all imprinted in glaring high-definition in my brain. Resurrections that caused him horrible agony because he had to complete them in tandem with Hindley. Resurrections he completed in secret, so he could earn the money to take me away from here. One resurrection that disturbed him deeply—a body burnt beyond recognition—and I don't see the face because the memories move on, to a day decades ago when a very small Heathcliff resurrected a dog that had been smashed by a car. I see Buckland Lockwood approaching him, bending down: "Come with me." And Heathcliff did. Back still further—glimpses of a past his conscious mind doesn't remember. A woman stirring sauce. Several men clustered together, voices raised in argument. A dim, shabby room, where Heathcliff lay on a thin blanket while a woman cradled his head in her lap, singing softly in Italian. Her name floats just out of my reach. Heathcliff doesn't know it, not even in the distant recesses of his mind—she was simply *Mamma* to him.

A long, keening sob issues from my throat as I bow over him. My fingers flutter over his mouth, trying to feel his breath.

I've grieved so many times, as deeply as if the grief were mine. But this grief has sharper edges. It lacerates my heart and lungs with every inhale, every sob.

Suddenly a jolt of energy passes through me, running over my skin, lifting every hair to stand on end. Something tremors in my soul—a new presence. Like a weighty hand laid over my bleeding heart.

As if pulled by a puppet string, my head lifts. And I look up, up, and up—to It.

Its towering form is made of vines, grass, slender branches, and moss. Skinny legs, like a deer, but three times taller. From its mossy shoulders rears a thick, flexible neck. There's no head, only antlers, huge and ponderous, constructed of sticks, branching out impossibly far on either side.

In the center of the Thing's neck, the twigs and moss and vines withdraw, rearranging, folding themselves backward and inward to create an aperture like a mouth. Inside, enmeshed twigs line the hollow like netting. Something about the texture makes me sick. My whole body shakes with the need to recoil from the Thing, and yet in my bones, I feel my connection to it.

"I can save him," says the Thing. Its voice is a horrible, grating, breathy sound, cold air pushed through the web of sticks that form its vocal cords.

I can save him.

The urgency to mourn Heathcliff recedes a little. My banshee self senses the potential change in his future, and the grief is paused for a moment.

I find my voice, croaking out the essential words. No pleading, no questions, just the basics. This is not a gift but a bargain. "What do you want in exchange?"

"For centuries, I lay asleep," the Thing grates out. "Generations of unease and torment. Shunned by my fellow gods and by humans alike. You are of my blood. You know the hunger when you are alone, the pain of being the enemy of all."

The Thing—no, not just any *thing*; it's Cernunnos in some form—steps forward with one long leg. "Your blood loosened the bonds of my spirit, and your scream in my domain did the rest. I have returned, but my body has not. I require a flesh form. Yours will do." The weight on my heart intensifies, as if the invisible hand is squeezing. "Accept, and I will spare you and the son of Juventas. Deny me, and I will let him die and destroy you as well. I have touched your soul already when you fled my realm. It will be easy to end you or to slip inside you. Make your choice."

Oh god…this is bad. I can't consider this option, not even for a moment. It's fucking *possession*, by an ancient god no less, not something any sane person would agree to. To have my body overtaken, shared with some eldritch being who could have any number of malevolent plans and motives… It's irrational to say the least.

But maybe I'm not rational when it comes to Heathcliff. Maybe I'm recklessly, ruthlessly devoted to him, so much so that I'll do anything to make sure he survives. He went into the darkness and dragged me out, knowing he might die in the process. And I won't let him sacrifice himself like this—I won't. I refuse.

My existence is already difficult enough. If I allow him to die for me, it will be unbearable. I will wake up every day thinking about him, and I'll dream of him all night long. I'll live in a perpetual state of agonized mourning, until the day I finally die again.

He wouldn't accept the misery of losing me, and yet he would put *me* through the pain of existing without him? No. *No, Heathcliff*.

He contributes something to the world. He saves people, rescues souls. And what do I do? I howl and scream about death. I can't even fulfill my true purpose as a banshee. I'm practically useless. If either of us deserves to live, it's him. Kind, strong, tender, protective, wonderful *him*.

My decision is made. But I need to do the smart thing and ask a couple of questions, just so I know what to expect.

"Will I be conscious?" I ask. "Will I be myself? Otherwise, letting you possess me would be as bad as dying."

The Thing shifts its weight, its body creaking. "You will have both thought and sensation. And until our bond is complete, you may retain full control of the body. You will have stamina and strength beyond normal humans. Choose quickly. Three more breaths, and he is gone."

I don't have any more time to think about what I'm agreeing to. As far as I'm concerned, it's done.

"Yes," I gasp. "I consent. Do it. Save him, and take me."

The tall creature shudders, and its form disintegrates. As the sticks fall apart and tumble to the ground, a thick, white mist surges from the center of the Thing and rushes toward me. It plunges straight between my parted lips, rocketing down my throat.

I can feel its presence instantly, like pale threads curling around my mind and heart, coiling along my spine, creeping through my bloodstream, settling against my bones.

The urge to mourn is entirely gone, and in its place is a beguiling sensation of warmth and strength. The exact opposite of what I'd expect from the god of death.

I rise smoothly to my feet, marveling at the healthy flush of my skin, despite the deprivation of the past week and a half. I've stopped shivering, and I barely feel the cold, even though some of the grass nearby is tipped with frost.

Heathcliff's chest jerks as he inhales sharply. He coughs, mumbles something. He's still unconscious, but he's all right. He'll recover.

And I feel amazing...for now. No amount of comfort can make me forget what the god said: *Until our bond is complete, you may retain full control of the body.*

Until then.

I'll be damned if I give anything full control of me without a fight. I've spent my whole life developing the strength of will to subvert the banshee's instinct, to control where I go and when. I can handle this—at least until I get some help.

I don't know how long it's been since Heathcliff killed those four men, but cops could arrive any minute. Heathcliff and I need to get away from here and find somewhere safe where he can recover and I can figure out what to do next.

I stare down at Heathcliff, chewing my lip. My muscles feel full and tight, packed with strength like the god promised. Tentatively, I lean down and slide my arms under Heathcliff's body.

He's shockingly easy to lift, so I shift him into a bridal carry and head toward the road, frosty grass crunching lightly beneath my bare feet. We probably look ridiculous—a slim girl like me carrying a tall, muscled guy like him.

Hindley's truck is a ways down the road, skewed onto the gravel. I lay Heathcliff down for a second while I open the passenger side door. Then I check his pockets. The keys are there, but no phone, so I poke my head into the truck and find his phone sitting in the cupholder.

A sudden ripple of energy passes through my body, and there's a tightening sensation around my spine and lungs. I freeze for a second and focus on breathing steadily. The feeling of the god's presence inside me has intensified a fraction.

I don't know how much time I've got.

Quickly, I turn on Heathcliff's phone. He's got it set to unlock with his face, so I hold it in front of him and it lets me in.

I know Daisy's number by heart. I enter it quickly, press the green phone symbol, and wait.

Fuck, it's like four in the morning. She's not going to answer…

"Hello?" Her voice is unmistakable, smooth and clear and musical.

"Daisy." My voice cracks, so I swallow and try again. "It's Cathy Earnshaw, from Wicklow. The—the girl who had a weird reaction to your voice."

"Oh! Oh my god, I'm so glad you called! You sound scared—don't be scared, okay? I'll be careful about the tone I use."

"That's the least of my worries right now. I was sacrificed to the god last night."

"You *what*?"

"The church at Wicklow. They sacrificed me to Cernunnos. And Heathcliff—he's my… He's… Well, I love him, and he brought me back. He's a necromancer. And then he almost died, but Cernunnos said he could save him, so I made a bargain and Heathcliff's okay, but I think the god is inside me—I *know* he's inside me. He's taking over slowly, and I don't know what to do. Oh, and I'm a banshee."

"Oh. Oh god, that's a new one." Daisy's voice sounds a little breathless but firm. "Okay, we're coming to help you. We're leaving right now."

A man speaks, his voice like warm velvet. "Cathy, this is Jay Gatsby. Where are you right now?"

"I'm near Old Sheldon Church."

"You need to find somewhere safe to go. Somewhere no one will think to look for you. Do you know a place like that?"

My brain races through the options. I can't go to Aunt Nellie's,

Dad's, or the store. I don't trust the Lockwoods, so I couldn't go there even if I knew where Heathcliff lives.

There's one place where no one will be in the wee hours of a Monday morning. The very last place where I would willingly go.

Wicklow Heritage Chapel.

Yes. There's eager assent from the god inside me, a nudge toward that choice. The faint, heated glee of impending vengeance. Cernunnos wants to go there, and not for any good reason.

In the end, I'm not sure who decides—me or him.

"Wicklow Heritage Chapel," I tell Gatsby. "Meet me there."

"On our way," he replies.

"Cathy." It's Daisy's voice again. "You can do this. We'll get there as fast as we can, but until we do, I want you to know that you're going to be all right. You're smart, and you're strong, and you've got this."

"Thanks," I whisper. "Hurry."

I end the call, tuck Heathcliff's phone back into the cupholder, and lift him into the car. Once I've got all his limbs arranged and his seat belt on, I slam the door, hop into the driver's side, and start the engine.

Thank god Dad taught me to drive both manual and stickshift. I'm not very good, since he rarely lets me drive his car, but I can manage.

I've got this.

I put the truck in gear and press the gas pedal, angling the vehicle onto the empty road. There's a flare of interest in my mind, fascination with the truck and the way I'm driving it. I can feel the god's intensity as he drinks in the information.

"They didn't have cars back when you were awake," I comment aloud.

No, he responds.

It's so weird to have another voice in my head besides my regular thought-voice. He's not raspy now; his voice is rich, deep, and dark. Like the most bitter chocolate, melted.

Part of me is revolted and terrified, doesn't want to acknowledge him at all in case it speeds up the formation of our "bond." But another, sneakier part of me wants to engage, to learn about him, because information is power, and I need every bit of power I can get.

"Were you aware of cars or anything else where you were... beneath?" I ask.

Somewhat. I had some knowledge of your machines, your language, your attire. Many people visited my resting place, and I gleaned from them in the moments when I was most lucid.

"People coming to take Instagram photos with Old Sheldon Church," I say dryly.

Instagram? I've heard that word, but I don't understand it.

"Think of it as a series of beautiful moments, some captured naturally and some created, like art."

Your kind can manipulate time?

"No. Moments captured as images. Sometimes the images move, and sometimes there's music—"

Music? His interest perks immediately.

"You like music?"

Yes. I did not get to hear much of it Below. Only the hymns that hurt me or the scraps of other melodies.

"Music has changed quite a bit from when you walked the world." I reach for the radio and turn it on. Looks like the radio unit was a custom install, probably an upgrade Hindley added.

It must be synced to Heathcliff's phone because the readout says "Recovery Playlist." I skip through a couple songs until I see Blue Oyster Cult's name pop up, and I pause to listen. When "(Don't Fear) The Reaper" starts playing, I crank that shit up and press harder on the gas, sailing along the road away from Old Sheldon Church.

My heart swells with a kind of raw, bitter triumph, and I feel my face stretching in a smile that would probably look terrifying to anyone else. Blood is dried on my neck and shoulder, and I'm wearing the thin, bloodstained gown from last night, and I've got an eldritch god riding in my rib cage—but I'm here. I'm alive, and Heathcliff is alive, and we have friends who are coming to help us.

Daisy was right. I've got this.

Cernunnos's presence inside me surges, tightens against my bones. Something about the rhythm or the resonance is making him stronger. Which is not what I want right now, so I turn the radio off and grip the steering wheel again.

A few seconds later, my hand moves toward the radio's power button and punches it, turning the music back on.

Fuck.

I did not do that. The god did.

I'm terrified. The terror hovers at the edges of my thoughts, a gibbering, shrieking, incapacitating fear that will grip my mind if I let it and send me right over the edge into madness. And then it will be easy for Cernunnos to take over.

I can't give in to that fear, that hollow horror. If I think too deeply about what has happened to me in the last twenty-four hours, I'll break. I need another emotion—rage, dark humor, sheer fucking stubbornness.

I can do that. I can be obstinate and sarcastic and angry. I will fill myself up with all those emotions until there is no room for fear.

Apparently my first battle of wills with Cernunnos is going to be about music. Fine by me.

I shut the music off. And this time, when the god tries to control my arm and play it again, I resist. I fight the impulse, just like I've fought my banshee instincts since I was sixteen.

Cernunnos pushes back, and I have to grip the steering wheel tightly to avoid reaching for the radio, but I manage to hold him at bay. Eventually the pressure of his will eases, and I feel a trickle of wry amusement in my mind. He's letting me have my way—for now.

I've been so intent on fighting him that I didn't pay enough attention to the road. I think I've gone past a turn I was supposed to take. The question is, should I do a U-turn, or can I cut over to Chapel Road from the next street?

From the passenger seat, Heathcliff mumbles, "Take a left on Azalea."

"Heathcliff!" I scream his name, accidentally swerving the truck.

"Easy, Cathy!" he exclaims. "Shit!"

It worked, it actually worked, and he's *here*, he's back with me. Even in my joy and relief, I still feel the horror of his impending death and what I did to prevent it.

But all I say is, "You're awake, thank god."

"Want to tell me why I'm awake?"

I swallow and shrug. "I guess you weren't as far gone as you thought."

"Catherine. Don't lie to me. I know exactly how far gone I was. And even if I managed not to die, I'd be comatose for a lot longer than—" He leans over to check the dashboard clock. "Half an hour. I'd be in recovery for hours, if not days, but I feel totally fine. You hiding some kind of healing power you haven't told me about?"

"Yeah, let's talk about hiding powers from each other," I say. "You didn't think it might be a good idea to tell me you're a fucking necromancer?"

"You didn't need to know."

"The tattoos had something to do with it, didn't they? Matching tattoos, for 'protection,' you said."

"You're smart," he replies. "I love that about you. But I'm smart too, Princess, and I know you're trying to distract me. Answer the question: How am I alive?"

Again the tightening sensation grips my insides, and I shiver. "I can't tell you. Not yet. Not until we get where we're going."

"Which is?"

"Wicklow Heritage Chapel."

"Oh, hell no," Heathcliff says.

"It's fine. No one will be there this early on a Monday morning. We just need to lay low there until Daisy and Gatsby arrive— you know, those people I told you about, who visited Aunt Nellie's store asking about buried gods. I called them, and they're coming to help me with...um—" I break off the sentence, biting my lip hard. Now that Heathcliff's awake, it's somehow harder to stay strong and fend off the panic. When I'm alone, I can handle pain. I can deal with huge, excruciating emotions. But when he's there, asking about me in that rough, low voice of his, I just want to throw myself against his chest and hide my face until everything is over.

He is your weakness, comments the god.

"Shut up," I say aloud.

"I didn't say anything," Heathcliff answers. "Cathy, pull over and talk to me."

"No." I grip the steering wheel tighter. "Just guide me to the church, okay? Once we're inside, I'll explain everything, I promise."

"And you're sure no one will be there?"

"I'm sure. There's no prayer, Bible study, or confession time on Mondays. And Pastor Linton always did his sermon preparation at home, where his books are. Pretty sure Edgar will do the same."

Edgar's name triggers an image in my mind—the broken silhouette of the church, golden lanterns, the dark forest, and Edgar, with his halo of blond hair, euphoric and fervent, standing over me and eloquently condemning me to death.

My fingers turn lax, slipping from the wheel.

But before the truck can swerve, a steadying impulse rises inside me, strength coursing along my arms to my fingers.

We will have revenge on them all. Cernunnos's deep voice echoes in my mind. *Until then, hold true.*

I hate that flow of unnatural strength. Over the past several years, I've fought to keep my entire life from being swallowed by my banshee nature. I managed to work around it, live with it, even exert some measure of control over it. I won't give that up for an existence as the sidecar passenger to an ancient deity.

"I don't want your help," I seethe.

"Cathy." Heathcliff's large, warm hand slides over my right

one, and instantly my body relaxes. His strength is wholesome, honest, and true.

I glance at him, my eyes filling with tears, and he looks back at me, his handsome face taut with concern. I don't know if I can bear confessing to him that he might lose me again.

"Let's just get to the church," I whisper. "And then I'll tell you everything."

23

HEATHCLIFF

IT'S NOT HARD TO BREAK INTO WICKLOW HERITAGE CHAPEL.
The locks are a joke against my strength—and Cathy's, apparently.
She turns on the lights but adjusts them to the lowest setting, so
the place is gloomy. She's light-sensitive sometimes, I've noticed.

We sit on the back pew where we sat that first Sunday. Cathy's
pretty face is salt white, her brown hair creating a cloud of wild
curls as it dries. She's fidgeting with the hem of the flimsy, white
dress. The bloodstain along the neck and shoulder is freaking me
out even worse than the Rockford murder scene.

She tells me everything.

When she's done, I don't move or speak. I'm processing.
Might take a while.

I would believe her anyway, but the fact that I'm sitting here,
feeling rested and whole when I should be dead or worse, is more
than enough proof. Supernatural intervention is the only way to
explain it. The god brought me back—in exchange for crawling
inside Cathy's body.

A haze of red rage burns behind my eyes, and I'm breathing
fast even though I'm trying to stay calm.

"Cathy," I begin, trying to keep my voice calm, "what you did—"

"I didn't have a choice," she interjects.

"You called me an idiot for saving you," I point out. "All I gave up was my life. You're giving up your will, Cathy, signing up for god knows what...literally."

"That's not funny." But there's a hysterical glimmer of amusement in her eyes, and her mouth twitches.

"Let's lay this all out." I clear my throat and poke the cushioned seat of the pew for emphasis like I'm showing her parts of a blueprint. "The cult thought sacrificing you would keep the god down forever, which is bogus because any Lockwood knows that blood *resurrects* things. But the Wicklow congregation believed what some shady stranger told them. I don't think you ever mentioned his name..."

"Ian Holcum," Cathy says.

My body erupts into goose bumps.

Ian Holcum, the coma guy from the Lockwood mansion. He's been sound asleep at the Grange, but he has also been up and about, the sneaky bastard. He's been coming into Wicklow and talking to the members of the church, brainwashing them to do what he wants. He's been listening when I thought he was asleep. That's how he knew all about my powers and how I need to recover afterward. That's how he knew about my connection with Cathy.

"Heathcliff, what is it?" Cathy's slim fingers slide over mine.

"I know the fucker."

She gapes. "How?"

Quickly I explain. "I swear he's been truly unconscious most of the times when I checked on him. I knew something was off about him, but I didn't think he was a threat—at least, not like this."

"It doesn't make sense," she says. "How could he get in and out of the house without you or Hindley seeing him? How did you never notice he was gone?"

I pinch the bridge of my nose. My body may be strong as ever, but my brain isn't working as fast as I'd like. "Hindley never checked on him...not that I saw, anyway," I say slowly. "It was mostly me, and I checked maybe once a day, usually in the late afternoon or early morning. And there were a few days I didn't look in his room at all, when I was extra tired after a resurrection. When Hindley and I aren't at the brewery, we're in the living room or in our own rooms. He could have slipped past us either way. Besides, there's a window in that guest room. I boarded it up yesterday, but maybe he's been climbing out..." My voice drops as I remember the black feather I found. "Motherfucker. I saw him shift into a stag once. I'll bet he can shift into a bird, too. A crow, most likely. Could've flown right out."

"Heathcliff." Cathy's forehead wrinkles with concern, like she's doubting my sanity. "People can't turn into crows."

"There are supernaturals who can shapeshift. Like the púca."

"Pooka? Sounds made up."

"Yeah. But then again, you're asking me to believe that while we were in the Vague, a god decided to grab hold and ride out with us for some reason."

Cathy cocks her head for a second, her eyes distant, like she's listening to something. "Cernunnos says the sacrifice was meant to raise him. But he didn't rise right away because there was deeper spellwork in place to suppress him...more than was laid on the graves of most other gods. The other Tuatha Dé Danann laid those bonds upon him because they hated him."

"Can I join their club?" I growl. "And tell him to stop fucking talking. You and I are having a conversation."

"He knows things that could help us understand this. Maybe he knows about the púca thingie—"

"Cathy!" I grab her hands. "We'll talk about folklore later. Right now, we gotta face the facts, baby, because it's looking like I brought a homicidal púca back from death and you gave your body to an eldritch god, so we're both seriously fucked, okay?"

"But Gatsby and Daisy—"

"They sound great, but what do we know about them? What can they do about this? They're more than three hours away, longer with traffic. How far gone are you going to be by then?"

"I don't know," she says quietly.

"Well, you fight it," I grit out. "You fight that bastard, and meanwhile, I'll..." I rise from the pew, fists clenched. "I'll do *something*. I'll figure something out."

Cathy rises, too, a wistful smile on her face. "I *am* fighting. And I won't stop. But there's nothing you can do to fix this. You've already given me everything."

She slips her arms around my waist and moves close, leaning her head on my chest. I wrap her up and hold her tight. There's more strength in her grip than I expected—the god's strength.

I have her here with me. But she's still not free, and it's my fault. My throat tightens, tears stinging my eyes. I refuse to let those tears out, though. Last thing she needs is me losing my shit.

"Dry clothes," I say abruptly.

Cathy leans back and quirks an eyebrow at me.

"We're both covered in mud and blood. There's gotta be something else around here—a giveaway bin of clothes, maybe some choir robes. I'll check, and you can go get cleaned up."

Cathy looks down at herself. "Yes. I'm definitely on board with that."

I decide to go through a door to the left of the pulpit platform and snoop around. There're a couple narrow rooms back there, on each side of the baptistry, and sure enough, one of them has a bunch of the choir robes I saw people wearing when I visited. They're a weird plum color, and the buttons only go down to the waist, but I'd rather Gatsby and the others see Cathy in that than the transparent tissue of a dress she's wearing. Plus she'll be warmer, drier, and more comfortable.

After grabbing two choir robes that look about the right size for us, I head to the women's restroom in the lobby.

I don't know what I expected to see, but it sure wasn't a nude Cathy standing in front of the sink, wiping dried blood off her neck with a wet paper towel.

"The rain didn't wash it all off." There's a tremor in her voice, tragedy in her eyes. It's starting to really register—what those bastards did to her. Her town, her church. Her own family. She's hurting. But at the same time, she's so goddamn beautiful—the curve of her spine flowing into the roundness of her ass cheeks, the slope of her stomach down to her pussy, her long legs.

Shit, I'm being an asshole. An *asshole*.

I will not get a fucking hard-on. *This is not the time, Heathcliff, you selfish bastard. Not the time.*

"Here." I hold out the choir robe stiffly.

She gives me a pitiful little frown. "I could use a hug."

If she hugs me, she'll feel how hard I am. She'll know what a horny ass I can be at the worst times. "No hugs."

"Okay." She sighs, turns toward me, and lifts her arms, gathering her hair up, twisting it, then letting it fall down her back. Which leaves her tits on full display.

Jaw clenched, I look away.

"If you won't give me a hug," Cathy says softly, moving nearer, "will you give me something else?"

"Clothes." I wave the choir robe a little, still looking away from her.

"Heathcliff." She's in front of me now, gathering the damp, grimy fabric of my T-shirt in her hands. "Heathcliff, I don't know if I'm going to be myself a day from now, let alone an hour from now. I have this feeling, this itching in my bones, this crawling sensation under my skin—it's the banshee, Heathcliff."

"A death prediction?"

"I can't be sure, but I feel unsettled. Like the god is rearranging my insides, and it's uncomfortable." Her palms stroke my pectorals. "My dad and Aunt Nellie—they *killed* me, by intent if not with their own hands. And there's a god in my head, and the banshee squirming under my skin." Her whole body gives a violent shudder. "I'm brimming with horror and unease and wretchedness, Heathcliff, and I need to feel something *else*. Something good."

I bite back a groan as my dick jumps, pressing against my pants. "What about *him*? Cernunnos? If we do this, he's going to watch."

Cathy's slender fingers cup the back of my neck, and she gives me a fierce, reckless look. "Let him watch. We'll pretend he doesn't exist."

Her face quivers right after she says it, and I suspect Cernunnos said something to her. But the next second, she tightens her grip on my neck, her expression resolute. "Come on, Heathcliff," she urges. And then, with a sudden, malevolent smile, "Haven't you ever wanted to fuck a girl in a church sanctuary?"

She's for real about this. Utterly serious. This is what she wants, what she *needs*, just like she needed me the day I delivered the beer to her aunt Nellie's store.

I kiss her lightly on the mouth, then set my cheek against hers and feel her tremble with anticipation at my low voice in her ear. "As a matter of fact, I have had a fantasy or two of that nature. Let me get myself cleaned up real quick, and then we'll see what we can do to defile this place."

24

CATHY

I SIT ON THE EDGE OF THE COUNTER IN THE WOMEN'S BATH-room and wait while Heathcliff pees, strips, and washes up. I'm swinging my legs, trying to dispel some of my nervous energy, while wetness squishes from my pussy onto the counter. I'm getting more desperate by the second, which means somebody's going to die soon. Today or tomorrow, I think, and it feels like more than one person, but I can't be sure. It's like the future isn't settled yet.

My fingernails drum rapidly against the faux marble surface, and I squirm, pressing my legs together. My back arches at the familiar, uncomfortable sensation of many-legged things slithering up my spine. I don't think Cernunnos likes the feeling; he keeps sending tight, anxious pulses of energy through my bones, like he's trying to counter the banshee effect.

When I was trying to convince Heathcliff to fuck me, Cernunnos reacted with interest. *What you feel, I will feel. I hope he's a skilled lover.*

Since then he has been silent, neither approving nor disapproving. I try not to think about the fact that in doing this, we're essentially engaging in a weird spiritual threesome.

Nope, not going to think about it. I'm going to think about Heathcliff, who is standing next to me wiping himself down with paper towels.

Fully naked, Heathcliff is a glorious sight. The cheekbones of a prince. Thick, sensual lips. Brown skin laced with tattoos, muscle and sinew packing every inch of his body.

He pitches the paper towels in the trash, picks me up, and shoulders his way out of the women's bathroom, heading straight for the sanctuary.

With me in his arms he strides down the center aisle, toward the pulpit, toward the great, ancient tapestry looming over us from its place on the wall. The dimmed lights and crimson carpet give the room a red-gold cast, gleaming off the wooden pews, shining in the droplets clinging to Heathcliff's damp black hair.

He sets me down on the platform's edge, with my back against the front of the pulpit and my feet on the steps. When he moves back and takes a moment to just look at me, I feel like an entirely different kind of sacrifice...something beautiful and precious. A grateful sob hitches in my throat, and I reach for him because I can't bear his body being separate from mine any longer. I need him inside me, deep and firm and warm—I need his strength countering the unfamiliar power flowing through my limbs. I need him to make me believe that I'm still *myself*.

Heathcliff drops to his knees. Crawls up the steps and pushes my legs apart like he did in the truck. Then he buries his beautiful mouth and his thick, warm tongue in my pussy.

It's instant relief, and it's exquisite torture. Everything else is wiped from my mind as Heathcliff coaxes my clit to a frenzy of need, licking it delicately, then plucking it with his teeth, then stroking my folds with long sweeps of his tongue.

My hands reach above my head, fumbling for something to hold on to, and they find the edges of the thick wooden cross nailed to the front of the pulpit. I dig my nails into it, gripping it for leverage. Heathcliff lifts his head, his lips and jaw damp from my wetness. He grins. "God, you look beautiful right now. Can I try something?"

I'm not sure what he has in mind, but I'm in a wild mood, so I nod.

Rising quickly, he runs up onto the platform, out of my line of sight. I wait, my pussy quivering, every puff of air against it feeling like a cold gust of wind. I need him to kiss me there, devour me, swallow me and claim me before the god can.

Heathcliff returns with one of the gold cords they use to tie back the curtains for the baptistry. Bundling my wrists together in one hand, he pins them against the decorative cross, wraps the gold cord across them, and then winds the cord around the pulpit and knots it before kneeling in his place again.

I'm bound to the pulpit, staring out at the wooden pews, the dull white walls, and the ceiling beams of the sanctuary. I never see the church from this angle—no one does. The pastor is always standing on the platform, higher than everyone else, while the people are below, gazing upward. I'm hovering between the two, suspended in the heated haze of lust, with my hands tied to the cross and my legs splayed in the most profligate way. There's a god in my head and a beautiful man kneeling between my thighs, and I am suspended between both of them. I need Heathcliff to touch me, to tether me, to ground me.

I lurch toward him, but the cord keeps my hands in place above my head.

"That's it," Heathcliff says, gazing at me. "I wish I could take a photo of you like this. You look like a goddamn saint. The profane kind."

"Gloriously profane." I smile at him, and he gives me one of his warm grins, the kind that's usually tinged with sardonic humor—but this time I sense the pain at the edges.

"Be still for me, Cathy," Heathcliff murmurs, lowering his face to my sex.

I understand now why he bound me. With my arms tethered like this, I'm even more at his mercy, and everything is heightened. Each heated puff of his breath, the sliver of space between his mouth and my clit—it's intense, exquisite, overwhelming.

Heathcliff seems intent on making this the best orgasm I've ever had. He's building toward it carefully, adding the restraints, teasing me with his breath, torturing me with tiny flicks of his tongue.

"God, just...*please*," I whimper.

He releases a shuddering breath, as if he's exhaling the last of his restraint. Then I squeal breathlessly as he tucks both hands under me, lifts my ass several inches off the platform, and sinks his face into my pussy again with a contented rumble of pleasure.

My entire existence narrows to the space between my legs where he's doing the Lord's work, creating a storm of explosive sensation. My eyes roll back and I arch in his hands, my head tilting back against the pulpit. "Ah...ah...Heathcliff...oh shit..."

Inside me, the god is writhing, climbing, urging, almost pleading. He wants to come—to connect—as badly as I do. I ignore him as best I can and give myself over to Heathcliff, who is humming between my thighs now, causing a delicious vibration while his tongue drives through my folds, over and over, lashing my clit with every pass.

With a wriggle and sharp scream, I come. My body jerks and my thighs shake, but Heathcliff holds me, steadies me, soothes me with his mouth.

There's a jolt of bright energy in my mind during the orgasm—the deity inside me sharing the effect of Heathcliff's clever tongue. It's almost like having sex in public while someone else jerks off to the sight of me and my partner. I've had sex in a bunch of places, and though I've never been caught, I've always liked knowing it could happen. This is next-level naughty and erotic, not to mention weird and terrifying, but I refuse to let myself think too hard about the god's presence and what it's stealing from me. Nothing exists except me and Heathcliff. Right here. Right now.

"Untie me," I gasp, wrenching against the cord. "Untie me, I need to touch you, I need—"

He obeys immediately, setting my ass down and loosening the knot. I tackle him onto the platform, flinging myself on top of him and smothering his startled exclamation with my mouth.

"Kiss me like I'm dying," I whisper.

"Fuck, Cathy, don't say that." His hands tighten on my body with possessive force, almost enough to bruise. But I want his bruises. I want his fingerprints on my bones, his breath in my throat, his blood under my nails.

"Tear me apart." My voice is harsh, wretched. "Fuck me until I beg for mercy, please, please... I need this. I'm strong now, like you. I can take it."

I finish the plea with a crush of my mouth against his, and I bite his lower lip until I taste blood.

He responds with a great surge of his muscles, heaving himself up and rolling us both over. He's ruthless when he shoves inside me, not giving me a second's warning or a moment to adjust.

Yes, yes—this is the brutality I crave. I want to be fucked out of myself, out of this nightmare.

His body hangs low and heavy over mine, a wall of muscle that could crush me if he let it. He braces one forearm right above my head. His profile hovers above my face, his rough breath gusting across my lips.

"Catherine." His voice is sharp, commanding. "I'm not just your escape from the things you find uncomfortable. I'll be that for you, but I am *more*."

"Not just more," I grit out, tears leaking from the corners of my eyes. "You are everything."

His eyes flame at the echo of what he once told me. A darkly triumphant grin and then he's kissing me, kissing my forehead, cheeks, and mouth while he thrusts inside me. I wrap my legs around him, locking my ankles above the curves of his muscular ass, and I give myself to the ecstasy, to the surge of his skin and the flow of his strength, to the hot brush of his lips and the scent of his sweat.

My fingers find the edges of his biceps, the beads of his nipples, the slanted muscles above his hips, the expanse of his back. All of his rough The silken heat of his skin is mine, and the soft curls of hair coating his chest, and his thick, strong fingers with their calluses—they are mine. The glossy black tangle of his hair is mine. His dark-lashed eyes are mine, and his tongue teasing the inside of my mouth is mine. All of him is mine, no matter what happens.

Death couldn't keep us apart, and nothing else will either.

"I'm going to love you after I'm dead," I pant in his ear, my voice shaken by his fierce thrusts. "Promise you'll do the same."

"Easiest thing I've ever promised."

I nod, letting my eyes drift shut as bliss swells warm between my legs. "Harder. Faster."

With a low growl of determination, he quickens his rhythm. "Cathy...god, Cathy, I—"

A heavy groan rolls from him, and I feel goose bumps break out all over his body as he comes, but I barely notice because he's still going, still pumping, and I'm clutching him frantically, nails sunk into his back as the swelling pleasure crests suddenly—a cord snapped, a wave of bliss released.

I want to scream, but I fight it with all the force of my will. The last thing we need is a banshee scream echoing through the woods beyond the church and calling attention to our presence.

So I bite Heathcliff again—his neck, his shoulder—not hard enough to draw blood, but he'll have marks for days. My marks.

The orgasm is slowing, and my eyes fly open, meeting his in startled amazement as I realize we're pulsing in sync, our bodies joined in perfect rhythm. I've never experienced that with anyone before, and it's euphoric on another level. Like we're connecting soul to soul.

Of course we are. Because his soul and mine were cut from the same shimmering fabric, hewn from the same rock, dipped from the same pool. Wherever souls come from, we share the same source. I am Heathcliff, and he is me. Anger and arguments, terror and tragedy, chaos and pain—none of that will ever change what we are to each other.

Heathcliff is looking down at me with a torment of wonder and love in his brown eyes. I lift a trembling hand to touch his cheek.

And then a shout startles us both. "Hey! What the hell do you think you're doing?"

I turn my head, and so does Heathcliff.

Edgar Linton stands at the entrance to the sanctuary, carrying a stack of books. He reaches for the dimmer switch on the wall and turns up the lights, flooding our faces and bodies with the bright glow.

His books avalanche to the floor and he nearly falls over, catching himself on a pew just in time. "Cathy?" His voice wavers. "Is that you? But you're...supposed to be—"

I look up at Heathcliff, a hysterical giggle bubbling out of me. He chuckles too and tilts his forehead against mine. He rocks his hips, his ass clenching as he drives deep one last time. His breath huffs against my cheek. "You feel like heaven."

"I'm calling 911," falters Edgar.

"Go ahead." Heathcliff shifts back, his big body moving away from mine. His cock slips out of me, and I cup myself instinctively, needing pressure to replace the thick wholeness of him.

Naked, Heathcliff saunters down the steps toward Edgar. "Go ahead," he repeats. "Call the cops. Tell them how you murdered an innocent young woman and raised a god."

"Raised a—what are you talking about?" Edgar retreats a step as Heathcliff paces toward him. "We performed a ritual to seal the demon away. To keep him suppressed forever, so your kind can't raise him. My father says you Lockwoods have been a plague on this town for years, always trying to cause trouble. Well, now we've won. It's over. Except..." His eyes flick back to me. "How... how did she..."

"I resurrected her. Because I fucking love her."

"But you couldn't have brought her back," Edgar protests. "You were away, you were...busy, and there were men to watch—"

He doesn't get a chance to finish the sentence. Heathcliff's hand clamps around Edgar's neck, lifting him right off his feet and shoving him against the nearest wall.

I leap off the platform and run toward them. The banshee inside me is restless, ready to scream, but I think Cernunnos is throwing off my perceptions. I can't tell if Edgar's death is imminent or not.

"I don't usually use my full strength on people," Heathcliff growls. "But I used it on those watchdogs you mentioned, and I've got a mind to use it on you now."

"Heathcliff," I say warningly.

"Cathy," he replies through gritted teeth. "Don't ask me to spare your murderer. How can I?"

"He may have agreed to it, but he isn't the one who held the knife," I say. "And we need answers. About Ian Holcum. Would you please loosen up before you crush his vocal cords?"

"Fine." Heathcliff eases off on the pressure and allows Edgar's feet to touch the floor. "Answer her questions, limp dick, or else."

Edgar's gaze twitches to me—and unfortunately for him, his eyes flick down to my naked body.

Heathcliff catches the glance and smashes a fist into Edgar's face. He pulled his punch, thank goodness, or I'm pretty sure

Edgar's delicate facial bones would have all been smashed. As it is, he seems to have escaped with a bloody nose and some sore teeth. He chokes and drools blood.

"I'm going to put some clothes on," I tell Heathcliff. "We both should. Then we can question him."

"Question me?" sputters Edgar through the blood streaming from his nose. "I'm not your prisoner. I'm the pastor of this church, and..."

Heathcliff cups one big hand over Edgar's mouth. "Go on and change, Cathy. I'll take his phone and make sure he's not going anywhere."

⬦⬦⬦

We must form a strange scene, the three of us on the church platform. Heathcliff and I are dressed in choir robes, facing a bloodied Edgar whom we bound to a folding chair with some duct tape Heathcliff found in a closet.

I don't know what Heathcliff said to Edgar while I was cleaning up and getting dressed, but it worked, at least temporarily. Edgar speaks slowly, his bluster gone. "I met Ian Holcum at a coffee shop. He saw the books I was reading, about the occult and Irish folklore, and he came over to chat. Said he'd spent years studying all the lore. He told me he had a master's in folklore studies and a PhD in Religion, Psychology, and Culture from Vanderbilt. We got to talking, and I felt like I could trust him."

"Why?" asks Heathcliff.

"I...don't know. Whenever we talked, I got this feeling that he knew what we were dealing with, really understood it, you know? I felt like he cared about me. Like we could be friends...brothers.

He called me 'brother' all the time. And he said I was special. That I might be a prophet, sent to keep down the old gods and prepare the way for the Second Coming of Christ."

"He talked you into *killing someone*," Heathcliff points out.

Edgar's forehead furrows. "To keep the demon from rising—"

"No. The opposite. He's a *god*, not a demon, and he rose already. He's awake."

Edgar's eyes widen. "What? Where?"

"He's..." Heathcliff clears his throat. "Inside Cathy."

"*Inside* her?"

"His spirit. Yes."

Gancanagh, says Cernunnos suddenly in my head.

"Gancanagh?" I repeat aloud. "What is that?"

Heathcliff twists around, staring at me with alarm. "What did you say?"

"It's not me saying it, it's *him*, Cernunnos. He just said 'gancanagh' out of the blue. What does that mean?"

"Love-talker," say Heathcliff and Edgar at the same time. And then Heathcliff says, "Oh shit," and Edgar's expression shifts to one of realization and horror.

"Gancanagh," Heathcliff says, rising. "That's what Ian is. The Love-Talker who can convince people to do his will. And he's a púca, too, a shifter. Some kind of hybrid of the two. Shit, I gotta call Meemaw."

"Meemaw?" I ask.

"Yeah, she's one of the Coosaw Lockwoods, the family expert on all the old stories. I'll get my phone from the truck and call outside—her hearing is uncanny for a ninety-year-old lady, and if she hears anyone she doesn't recognize in the background, she won't talk to me."

He jogs out of the sanctuary, and I pace in circles around Edgar's chair, wishing I had my phone to look stuff up.

The sex calmed my restlessness a bit, but the discomfort is starting to resurface. Other than the word gancanagh, Cernunnos has been quiet, but it's not the reassuring kind of quiet. It's the busy kind of quiet accompanied by weird pulses of energy throughout my body and vibrations in my bones. I get the feeling that he's learning me, adjusting, settling in...maybe even *changing* me, deep inside, where I can't see or stop it.

"Where did you go?" Edgar asks.

I pause and frown at him. He's looking at me with desperate curiosity.

"When you died," he clarifies. "Where did you go? Did you see anything?"

"You mean heaven or hell?"

He nods, fear and eagerness warring in his eyes.

"I didn't see either of those places," I say slowly. "I don't know if they exist. I was in a great void, right on the edge of this maze of crystals or mirrors... It went on forever, as high and as low as I could see, and just as far in both directions. Maybe beyond the part I saw, there's more to it. Some final resting place. But no...I didn't see heaven or hell."

Edgar's face crumples for a second, then hardens. "I don't believe you. You're lying just to upset me because you're angry. And you have every right to be angry, but lying to someone about the afterlife is...well, it's beneath you, Cathy. Although after what I saw you two doing on this platform, maybe nothing is beneath you."

I'm about to tell him that he's fucking *right* I'm angry, and several other things, but suddenly I'm turning away from him. Descending the steps, heading down the aisle.

Why am I going this way? What's happening right now? When did I make the very mature decision to end the conversation with Edgar and leave him to wallow in his crisis of faith?

I didn't make any such decision. Nor do I understand why I'm walking down the aisle with such purpose, as if...

Oh shit.

I'm not in control of this. Someone else is steering me. It's like being in the driver's seat of a car, but your passenger has reached over and grabbed the wheel.

Frantically, I struggle against the pressure of the god's will. But he has grown stronger.

Relent, child, he says. *I let you have your moment with the boy. Now you must yield, while I reshape your flesh to suit my needs and wishes.*

"No!" I grab one of the pews, halting my progress along the aisle. I cling there, straining against the urge to stand up and walk out of the church. "Why do you want to leave?" I pant. "I thought you wanted revenge on the congregation who held you down for so long."

I do.

"Well, this is the best place to get that revenge." Sweat breaks out on my forehead, and a hollow chill traces along my spine and legs. "We'll get Edgar to call everyone here for a meeting, and then you can...reveal yourself."

The pressure eases a bit. *How will he summon them?*

"He can call, text, email—lots of options."

Explain.

He's not pushing anymore, so I sit down on the pew and start explaining modern technology aloud to the god in my head, while Edgar Linton watches me from his chair.

25

HEATHCLIFF

I'm not worried about leaving Cathy alone with Edgar Linton. Even if she wasn't currently possessed by a god and gifted with extra strength, she'd be more than a match for that sap on her worst day. And I taped him up good. He's not getting out of that chair.

It crosses my mind that maybe I should worry about Cernunnos hurting Edgar. But Cathy seems to be in control for now. If anything did happen to Edgar, I sure wouldn't cry. But it would be another mess to clean up, and I'm fucking tired of those.

Outside, it's pale and misty. Early morning. The damp, cool air feels good on my face, against my bare legs.

Everything's soaked from the rain. The eaves of the church drip slowly and the gravel in the parking lot gleams black. Before coming outside, I grabbed my boots from the women's bathroom and put them on, but they're soaked too, and coated with mud. They squish as I walk.

Yanking open the door of Hindley's truck, I pluck my phone from the cupholder and call up the Coosaw Lockwoods.

Meemaw will answer the phone. She'll be sitting in the den,

in the old brown recliner. On the folding table beside her, there's always a glass of sweet tea, the TV remote, the cordless phone, and a heavy crystal ashtray with a cigarette propped on the edge. She has smoked a pack a day for years, but no lung cancer. That resilience and her unusually sensitive hearing are extra gifts, along with her necromancy skills.

Other than me, she's the most powerful necromancer in the clan. But she hasn't resurrected anyone since she was about sixty-five years old. Said it was getting harder and harder to find the way back out of the Vague.

During one Thanksgiving at the Coosaw Lockwoods' place, when I was about nine, she grabbed the front of my shirt and pulled me close with a gnarled hand, her smoke-bitter breath in my face. "You listen up, boy. I got my sons all here, my daughters-in-law, my grandchildren, my nieces and nephews, and a couple great-grandchildren, too. All my blood. And none of them—not one"—she poked my chest for emphasis—"have a fraction of the power you got. And you got an extra gift, too, like me. You got that strength. You hide it, but I see it." Her dry, wrinkled fingertips drifted along my cheek as she muttered confidentially, "That's why you're my favorite. You may not be blood, but you're more like me than any of 'em."

After that, I loved her, no matter how many times she cuffed my ears or swore at me. I don't call her often, but I'm always relieved when she answers. *Still alive.*

She answers this morning, with her usual croaky rebuke. "Heathcliff. You ain't called me in a coon's age."

"Sorry, Meemaw."

"Damn right you're sorry. You're interruptin' my show."

"Sorry," I repeat. "I got a couple questions, Meemaw. Ain't nobody else got answers but you."

"That so?" She clears her throat. "Well, go on then."

"Have you ever heard of someone getting rezzed and then not waking up?"

"Sure. That's what happens when someone's been rezzed before, and then they get another tattoo to be rezzed again."

"I thought no one could be rezzed more than once."

"They *shouldn't*," she says. "Never said they *couldn't*. You rez someone a second time, and they can't quite grasp life again. They liable to never wake up at all...or if they do, it'll be for short periods of time. They'll be up and about awhile, and then they start feeling strange, and they go unconscious again."

That explains why Ian always came back to the Grange after his excursions.

"You rez somebody twice?" Meemaw asks.

"Yeah. Me and Hindley. I don't think Hindley knew he'd been rezzed before."

"That Hindley. Got dirt for brains and beer for blood. But at least he's still practicing. Most everyone else had to quit. Just couldn't manage a decent rez no more. Not like in my day. When I was young, I was making money—ooh, you shoulda seen it! That's how we got this house, this land. And now all these relatives just keep sucking away what I saved up, sucking it dry. They don't wanna work. Nobody wants to work these days."

I'm not getting into that conversation with her, so I pivot to my next question. "Meemaw, I remember you told me once about the Gancanagh."

"The Love-Talker," she says quietly. "The ruiner of

women—and men, too. He's got the gift of persuasion. Can't make you do anything right away or control you, exactly—it ain't so obvious as that. He works on you awhile. Makes you believe things are your ideas when they're his. Softens you up so everything he tells you seems true, plain as day."

"Sounds like you knew one."

She doesn't answer right away. Probably taking a pull of her cigarette.

"That was long ago, when I lived in N'Orleans for a while. I knew this man—gentle, quiet, always at the edges of parties. He was handsome, kinder than most. He asked me a lot of questions about my family, my ancestry. And I told him everything. Not because I was young or stupid, mind you, but because he *persuaded* me. Later I realized he had his hooks into a whole lot of people, and he pulled the strings. A puppeteer, he was. Master of marionettes. Gancanagh and dúbailte, like us—double-gifted."

"Are you sure he was Gancanagh?"

"Some things get blurry when you're old, Heathcliff, but others become clearer than ever. I know what he was." There's a clink of glass through the phone, a slurp of liquid. "There's patterns, if you want to see 'em. Like what I seen over the past couple years. I been gettin' more phone calls like yours, sometimes from people I ain't spoken to in decades. Calls about new supernaturals poppin' up. Gifts we thought was lost for good, comin' back to light. New generations growing stronger, instead of the gifts fading like they used to…"

My attention strays from her words, veers to Ian. The Gancanagh who brainwashed a whole church congregation and instigated Cathy's murder. Everything fits now. The times when he'd leave the Grange and come back. Double-gifted, with the power to shapeshift. He's fucking dangerous, and he's out there somewhere—or he's lying in bed at the Grange right now, asleep. Which means he's vulnerable.

"Meemaw, I gotta go. I need to call Hindley."

"I gotta go, too. We're all leaving soon, heading up your way."

"Why?"

"It's Halloween, dumbass," she snaps. "You got cotton in your head? Samhain rituals tonight."

"Right." *Fuck.* "See you soon."

She mutters something and ends the call.

Shit...the Coosaw Lockwoods are coming up to Kinsale, and my girlfriend is possessed by the god they've been wanting to raise, there's a Gancanagh-púca hybrid running around, and I've got the leader of the Wicklow congregation duct-taped to a chair. Plus there's a handful of unknown supernaturals on their way from Asheville.

Perfect. Just fucking perfect.

I call Hindley next. I already saw a bunch of missed calls and enraged texts from him, so I'm more or less prepared for the storm of profanity he unleashes the moment he answers my call.

"Shut up!" I bellow. "I'll let you knock my lights out next time we see each other if you'll just shut up and listen! You're in danger!"

Hindley holds his tongue for a second, long enough for me to say, "I talked to Meemaw about Ian. I can't explain right now, but, Hindley, he's been getting up and sneaking out. He's fucking dangerous. I need you to go into that room right now, and if he's asleep, you gotta chain him to the bed, duct tape him, whatever. He can shapeshift, so maybe use iron or blessed water if you got any—"

"Why the fuck would I have iron shackles and blessed water? That's Wicklow anti-pagan shit."

I ball my hand up into a fist and set it to my forehead, breathing through the frustration. "Whatever you got that can limit someone's powers, use it. Lock him down until I can get there, or until the Coosaw folks get there. Shouldn't take 'em long, they're leaving soon."

"I know. I was supposed to be back here in plenty of time to get the place ready, but since *someone* lost his shit, punched me out, and stole my truck, I had to Uber back to the Grange. Do you know how much Ubers cost? Too fucking much, that's what. I swear, Heathcliff, when I get my hands on you—"

"Hindley! Go to the fucking guest room and see if he's there!" I yell. "And watch out, because if he knows you're onto him, he might kill you."

"You'd probably buy him a drink if he did," Hindley snarls. His voice changes a little, like he's moving, and I hear the squeak of stairs, the rattle of the padlock I placed on the guest room door.

I hold my breath, waiting. "Is he there?"

"Hold your horses."

A long pause, and then Hindley says, "He's here in bed, like always."

"Lock him down," I urge. "Tie him up, chain him, hold him at gunpoint—just don't let him leave the house."

"You're talkin' crazy," Hindley replies. "Where you getting this idea that he's been waking up and wandering around?"

"I'll explain later. Right now, you just need to restrain him, you hear me?"

No answer. I look at my phone and see that the call has

ended. Either he hung up on me, or…something else happened. Something worse.

Crap.

I stride back across the parking lot and take all the steps in one bound. After setting my phone on a console table in the church lobby, I head into the sanctuary. "Cathy, I've got some answers."

At first I don't see her. I only see Edgar Linton, his face ashen and his eyes bulging. He jerks his head toward the pews on my left.

About halfway up the aisle, something's hunkered down between two pews. Something wreathed in twining black shadows that leak from it like ink into water. Some of the shadows flow along the tops of the pews, while others creep like tentacles along the floor, out into the aisle, where they join together in a shifting pool.

The shape hunched between the pews has shoulders and a head…and antlers. Antlers with thin, needlelike prongs that are still growing, still forking into new spines of slender, gleaming black.

I'm locked in place. My chest feels heavy, lungs fighting to haul in breath.

I don't want to walk up that aisle and look at the thing between the pews. I already know what it is. If I don't look, I don't have to believe it.

But love—love is a monster, a sick compulsion, a ferocious loyalty that won't let me back down. It drags me forward, foot by foot, until I'm nearly standing in the pooled shadows. I force myself to rotate to the left. To look down between the pews, into the swirling darkness. At the horned thing.

"Cathy," I croak.

She turns. Her face is still hers—pretty features, that sly pouty mouth, big eyes looking up innocently at me. "Heathcliff." The voice is hers, too. But there are naked brown vines twining around her throat, crawling along her temples, slithering into her hair. The choir robe she wore has been shredded. Vines and shadows encircle her body instead, gaps of bone-white skin showing between them. The antlers spring from her curly brown hair, forming a delicate, lethal crown.

Her voice is light, unworried. "I was just explaining modern technology to Cernunnos. He doesn't quite understand it yet, but we're getting there."

The god is messing with her mind somehow. She has no idea what's happening to her.

"Cathy." I move closer, daring to shuffle through the shadows. They shift and swirl around my feet. My voice breaks. "Baby, he's distracting you. Changing you."

"Changing me?" She frowns, lifting her hand, and I almost gag. Where her slim fingers used to be, five impossibly long claws twitch and gleam. They're black and spiny like the antlers. Around her arm writhes a complex network of tiny vines in a pattern like Celtic knotwork.

I was outside maybe twenty minutes. And in that time, the god accomplished all this. If I hadn't come back when I did, he might have swallowed her entirely.

Through the horror and the bile in my throat, I choke out words. "Cathy, you have to fight it. Fight *him*."

Pain quivers across her features. "We were getting along. He doesn't seem cruel."

"That's what he wants you to think." I reach for her face, trying not to flinch at the chill brush of the shadows and the rough texture of the vines against my knuckles. "See the truth, Cathy. You always do."

Her brows bend, and she grimaces, like she's straining to lift a heavy weight. Alarm wakes in her eyes, and they widen, flooding with shocked terror. "Heathcliff...Heathcliff, what's happening to me? Oh god...help me, Heathcliff..."

"I will," I gasp. "I will. I'll help you. Can you stand up?"

She shifts and tries to stand upright. Her body unfolds, then stretches, higher, higher. She's towering over me, eight feet tall at least, shrouded in vines and shadows. I glimpse *pieces* of her here and there—legs, shoulder, breast—but they're not where they should be, not her normal proportions. Her hair is longer, too, tumbling in a rich brown cascade and merging into the twisting shadows. She is horrific and beautiful. A nightmarish goddess.

Edgar Linton screams. A howl, a shriek of terror, but there's a note of grief in there, too.

I hate him for grieving her. He has no right when he consented to her death the first time. I'm the one with the right to grieve. I'm the one she saved by turning herself over to this monster.

My whole body is hollow, shaking. Even my reserves of strength aren't enough to bolster me in this moment.

"You—" I almost gag, but I resist the impulse. "You have to keep fighting, Cathy."

She looks down at me, remote, despairing. "It's too late."

"It's not," I grit out. "It's not. Use your banshee. You've got power, Cathy, you're stronger than anyone else I know."

"I can't scream," she whispers. "He's in my throat, in my mind.

I am silenced, Heathcliff, I am stolen. But even if all of me disappears, I will still—"

Her mouth stops moving midsentence, and her eyes fix on something in the distance. And then it's like all of her personality drains out of those eyes until they're blank and glassy. Void of her fire, her passion.

That blankness guts me. I want this to be a nightmare. *I have to wake up.*

Cathy blinks. Swivels her gaze down to meet mine...but there is something else looking out of those eyes at me, and another voice issues from her lips. "A valiant effort but ultimately pointless. To regain my power, I require full control of this body. But do not fear, boy. I will ensure she is comfortable. I find her pleasant company. She and I will commune together often within ourself. She will not be alone...but she will be mine alone."

Tentacles of shadow thrash outward from the god, accompanied by a blast of icy wind. I'm thrown backward, through the doors of the sanctuary into the lobby. My spine slams against the floor, the impact paralyzing my lungs.

As I flip over, struggling to breathe, the doors of the sanctuary slam shut, blocking my view of the god.

Get up, Heathcliff, get up, get up!

I climb to my feet, but my stomach lurches. I stagger outside onto the church's narrow porch, crashing against the railing and vomiting over it.

Dimly I register Hindley's truck, Edgar's car...and two more vehicles. They must have just pulled in.

I try to calculate how long it's been since Cathy called Daisy. I was still unconscious at the time, so I can't be sure...but it's been a few hours, I think. Possibly enough time for Daisy and her group to get here. Either it's them, or it's someone from the congregation. At this point, I'd welcome anybody, whether they're here to help or to fight. I could use some support or something to punch.

I wipe my mouth on the sleeve of my choir robe and wait, gripping the railing. It's wet, and the peeling paint is rough against my palms.

The driver's side door of the BMW opens, and a long-legged blond man gets out. He's well over six feet and skinny, like some kind of male model. The bones of his face look especially crushable. He reminds me of Edgar Linton—except more vivid. More intense and alive somehow.

He saunters toward me, hands tucked into the pockets of his slacks. Looking me up and down, he smirks. "Aren't you a little old to be a choirboy? Or is this just a bold fashion choice?"

"Dorian, stop." A tattooed girl with pink-and-black hair runs up behind him, grabbing his arm. "Sorry," she says to me. "He's still learning to be *nice*."

"I can be nice," Dorian mutters. He reaches into an inner pocket of his jacket and pulls out a flask, like guys in old movies carry. Unscrewing the lid, he holds it out to me. "You look like you need this."

If there's alcohol in there, then *hell yes* I need it. I descend a couple of steps so I can grab it from him.

"See?" Dorian shoots the girl a saucy look. "I'm helping the traumatized choirboy."

I relish the burn of the drink. Rum, I'd guess, but a fancier kind than I've ever sampled. Rich and syrupy, with a hell of a kick.

Four more people have climbed out of the other car and

crossed the parking lot. One of the guys is as tall as Dorian but broader. He mounts the lowest steps and reaches out to shake my hand. There's a casual dominance about his stance that tells me he's the boss of the group—and the boss of this whole church and everything in it for as long as he wants to be. Maybe it's stupid to feel instantly relieved, but I am. I may have walked beyond death, but I'm out of my depth here. This guy looks like he's met with a lot of shit during his life and shoveled his way out of it every time.

"Jay Gatsby," he says. "You must be Heathcliff. We came as fast as we could."

Mechanically I shake his hand, then take another swig before handing the flask back to Dorian. My voice is a haunted rasp. "I think you're too late."

I hate the words even as they come out. Feels like I'm giving up on Cathy. I want to fight for her, and I will. I'm just not sure how these strangers can help me.

Two more men stand just behind Gatsby. A redhead with an upturned, freckled nose. A Korean guy with a shock of black hair. But it's the young woman moving quietly into place beside Gatsby who catches my eye.

Her golden hair shines faintly in the morning light, and there's a silken grace in the way she moves, but it chills me too, like my body recognizes her as a predator. "Where is Cathy?" She keeps her tone light, but there's a honeyed warmth underneath it. Like if you could *hear* rum, that's what it would sound like.

"She's in the church," I tell them. "That thing inside her, the god—it's changing her. Breaking her." I fight the impulse to vomit again.

Gatsby reaches for Daisy's hand, then glances back at the two guys. "Fangs out, boys. Baz, you hang back a little. Dorian, try not to make it angry."

"Don't pretend like you've faced a god before," Dorian retorts. "Of the six of us, Baz is the only person who has actually spoken to one."

Gatsby ignores him and turns back to me. "Show us where she is. We'll go in, take stock of things, and devise a plan. Baz, you have your supplies?"

The girl with the pink-and-black hair pats a leather satchel she's carrying. "Got 'em."

That sounds promising. Sounds like hope, like a fighting chance. And even if there ain't a snowflake's chance in hell of saving my girl, I will die trying to finally get her that freedom she's wanted for so long.

Clenching my fists, I lead the way into the lobby. "I know I said you're too late," I mutter to Gatsby, "but I appreciate you coming here so fast."

"We were speeding," he says casually. "We were stopped a couple times, but Daisy talked the cops out of giving us tickets." He nods to the blond.

I meet her eyes. "What are you exactly?"

"A blend of merrow and Leannán Sídhe," she says. "And most recently, a vampire. I can persuade humans, to a certain extent, and when it comes to my fellow vampires like Gatsby, Nick, and Cody, I can force them to do whatever I want. My voice compels them."

Vampires. Abhartach, from the old legends. But Meemaw told me they had died out. I have about a million questions, but most of them will need to wait until I get Cathy back. One question, though, seems important enough to ask now. "Would your voice work on me?"

"I'm not sure. I haven't tried it on many other kinds of supernaturals." She glances at Gatsby. "We've learned a lot since I became a vampire, and we've gained even more insight since Dorian and Baz found us. My voice is more effective on Dorian than Baz, but both of them seem more susceptible that regular humans."

"What matters most right now is figuring out how she affects Cathy," Gatsby interjects. "When we first met Cathy and Daisy said her name, Cathy had a strong reaction."

"And I wasn't even using my compulsive voice," Daisy adds. "She reacted to a completely different tone. It seemed to cause her pain."

The black-haired guy, Cody, is leaning against the wall, inspecting a set of claws that definitely weren't there a second ago. His canines have elongated, too. "The real question is, how will Daisy's voice affect a god?"

I grip the handles of the sanctuary doors with both hands. "Let's find out."

26

HEATHCLIFF

THE DOORS RESIST WHEN I TRY TO OPEN THEM. I PLANT MY feet and I pull, straining.

Gatsby steps forward to help, but I grit out, "No!" This is something I need to do.

I haul on the doors with all my might.

Inside me there's a wall, like a dam, one I've been building all my life to hold back the full force of my strength, so I wouldn't cause irreparable damage to the things and people around me. Without warning, that dam bursts—explodes like the glass Cathy shattered in the Vague—and a new surge of power gushes into my body. My muscles swell larger than ever before, my heart pumps faster, and a rush of hot blood through my veins gives me fresh energy.

With a violent heave, I wrench the sanctuary doors open. They rip free of their hinges with a groaning crack, and I stand there, holding the two heavy oak doors in my hands as easily as if they're a couple of beer bottles.

"Damn, choirboy," Dorian says appreciatively.

I set the doors against the wall, taking my time about it while the others file into the sanctuary. I'm being a coward, hanging back like this, but I can hardly bear to see the god and what he has done to Cathy.

When I'm done with the doors, I follow the group. They've halted just inside the sanctuary, and they're all staring up at the god.

He's even taller now. His antlers divide into dozens of branches, the tips of them grazing the ceiling. His face is Cathy's, but his body is masculine in shape—a titanic figure formed of solidified shadow, grayish brown in color and ridged in texture like the bark of a tree. More vines and shadows have emerged from the central column of his body, like secondary limbs undulating and stretching outward. His clawed fingers are each as long as my arm.

When he speaks, his voice is deep as the bones of the earth. It's monumental. "Have you come to worship me?"

Gatsby glances at Daisy, a question in his eyes. At her nod, he steps forward. "The body you're using isn't yours. It belongs to a friend of ours, and we would like her back."

"You're barely friends," responds the god. "Acquaintances, perhaps. Don't try to fool me, little abhartach. I know the mind of my host. You have come to worship Cernunnos, god of death, though you may not yet realize it."

"Worship?" Cody hisses through his fangs. "I worship no one."

"What is fear but a futile resistance to the impulse of worship?" The god moves closer, stalking slowly on massive legs. "Yield to that natural impulse, and your fear will diminish. Worship, and I will grant you power."

He's stalking nearer, taking step after step on his long legs, shadows flowing off him like water.

"Every one of you trembles at the idea of death, and that fear has driven you to become greater," he intones. "You are so terrified at the idea of your lives ending that you have done wicked and wonderful things. You have surpassed the state of normal human existence. And yet you still fear the end. You fear being cut off long before your natural span of years. You fear the decline into old age that brings about a slower demise. No matter how the end comes, you will always fear it. You will always fear *me*. And this one." Cernunnos bends, grazing Dorian's jaw with pointed claws. "This one fears me the most."

Dorian grins, defiant. "You can't kill me."

"It's not your own death you fear," replies Cernunnos. "Perhaps once, but no longer. You fear the death of another. You dread it with all your heart, soul, and mind. The terror of that impending loss consumes you. Every second you want to scream at your loved one to protect herself. To become abhartach, like them." He gestures to the four vampires.

"Dorian, is that true?" Baz steps forward, frowning. "I mean, I know you want me to do the whole vampire thing, but I thought we agreed there was no rush."

Dorian's blue eyes dart to each of us, as if he's looking for someone to help him. But I'm out. I can't handle anything beyond my own raw, throat-searing terror for Cathy. I wish they'd all shut up so we can get on with this and get that fucker out of her body, if that will even help. The way Cernunnos has changed her... I don't see how it could be reversible. And if it's not...if she doesn't survive, I can't either.

"No rush?" Dorian stares at Baz, his words tight and clipped. "No rush with people getting killed in car crashes every day, contracting cancer, choking to death on a morsel of food? With ancient deities and monsters stalking the coastline? Yeah, Baz, I think you need to become a vampire and soon. Like yesterday."

Cernunnos cocks his head—Cathy's head—and stares at Baz with those cold, calculating eyes. "Baz's fear is less than yours. She accepts life and death as they are, and celebrates both in her art."

"What are you, a mind reader?" I choke out. "Let's cut the crap. I want you out of my girlfriend right the fuck now, and I want you to put her back like she was."

Baz pushes her way in front of Dorian, looking up at the god. She's so small compared to him, and her voice is a little breathless but strong. "I can make you a body," she offers. "I need to connect with you a bit, and then I should be able to draw the form you used to take among humans—or close enough. I've done it before. I'm not of your bloodline, so I'm not positive it will work, but we can try it."

"Why would I want another body when I have this one to build upon? And the little banshee is so intriguing. I don't think I'll give her up." Cernunnos smiles too widely, and the corners of Cathy's mouth split a little. Blood trickles down her chin.

I want to scream. To roar. To beat my fists against him, but he is also Cathy, and I can't bear the thought of hurting her more.

Gatsby steps forward with a smile of his own, wide and charming. His canines glint. "You seem to think you have a choice in this, Cernunnos. You do not. You will be leaving the girl's body, with or without your consent."

A deep chuckle grates from Cernunnos, through Cathy's throat. "You think you can force a god to obey you?"

Gatsby looks him dead in the eyes. "Not me. But the two women you see here, Baz and Daisy—they can. And from what

I've seen, the woman you're holding hostage has a formidable will of her own. I wouldn't count her out just yet."

Fuck, I like this guy. The confidence in his tone gives me hope.

And then Daisy begins to speak. Her voice is pitched much higher than when she spoke to me outside. It's light, bright, and soft, like spring air. "Cathy. Cathy." She's trying a slightly different tone each time. "Cathy, if you can hear this, show me a sign."

A shudder passes over the god's form, and my stomach flips.

That was Cathy. She responded.

"Cathy, I need you to fight," Daisy continues in the same tone. "Resist him. Take back control of your mind, your voice, and your body, and expel him. You may have descended from his bloodline, but your power doesn't come solely from him. During the drive here, Nick did some research, and he discovered something else about the source of the banshees—another reason Cernunnos was hated by his fellow gods."

Cernunnos is seething, growling through Cathy's mouth, shadows churning restlessly around his body. Without warning, one of his extra limbs rockets toward Daisy, extruding long fingers as it reaches for her throat.

Daisy leaps aside with catlike grace, her blond hair swinging in a golden arc. But another limb is driving toward her from the side, and more are rising, a forest of arms and sharp-nailed hands racing to rip her apart.

Gatsby springs forward, snarling, seizing one of the arms and raking his teeth along it. Oily shadows spill from the cut like blood, and the arm dissolves within a few seconds.

"Baz, start drawing," shouts Gatsby. "The rest of us need to protect her and Daisy!"

I don't need to be asked twice. Judging by the way that first arm dissolved, the extra limbs of the god aren't connected to Cathy, so I can tear them apart without hurting her. That's all I need to know. I grip one of the arms headed for Daisy, and with a powerful twist, I snap it clean off.

Daisy steps onto one of the pews, her eyes bright, fixed on Cathy's pale face. "Hear me," she continues, her voice soft and bright and sinuous all at once. "The gods hated Cernunnos because he seduced the one being none of them could have. The Morrigan, Mistress Fate herself. She was the one woman who did not fear him, the only one with the power over death—the will to control it. You have her courage in your very soul. You are a descendant of Fate herself, and I command you, in the name of the Morrigan, to fight."

I hope it's working. I got no time to glance at Cathy's face because the god is thrashing, sending out a hurricane of arms and vines and shadows. He's mostly attacking Daisy, trying to make her stop talking. Cody, Nick, and Gatsby seem to have Daisy's defense well in hand, so I pull back to the rear of the sanctuary, where Baz is sitting against the wall, drawing rapidly on a tablet with a stylus. Dorian is there, too. He doesn't strike me as much of a fighter, but he has produced a pair of knives from somewhere and he's poised to protect her.

The god doesn't seem to be paying Baz as much attention. He thinks Daisy is the main threat. I don't understand Baz's power, but something tells me it's gonna be the key to getting Cathy back, so I take up a position next to Dorian. Every time a vine skates her way, aiming to slither around her throat, I grab it and pull it tight while Dorian slashes it in two. A couple ridged arms shoot along the floor toward Baz and then rise, their knifelike claws aiming for her chest, but I grab one, pivot, and seize the other, smashing them together until they explode in a slurry of shadows. Dorian leaps lightly onto another incoming limb, bearing it to the ground and whipping a blade through it.

Baz doesn't look up. Doesn't speak to either of us, just keeps drawing, her stylus flying over the screen. Sometimes she tips her head as if listening. Dimly I register Cernunnos shouting above Daisy's voice, trying to drown her out.

Suddenly, a fierce wind howls through the church, blasting toward Baz. It hits Dorian first, sending him flying through the sanctuary entrance. His body crashes into something in the lobby, and I could swear I hear bones crack.

Fuck. He's down for the count.

The wind is tinted with shadows, and I can see it rising, curling, doubling up for another attack. As it condenses and rushes toward us again, I throw myself in front of Baz, blocking the oncoming gust with my back. I slam my palms against the wall, bowed over her, fighting to resist the pressure of that wall of wind.

I glance down at Baz's face as she sits curled up in the shelter of my arms. She's pale under her tan, and tears are racing down her cheeks. But she doesn't take her eyes from the tablet.

"Don't stop," I shout over the roar of the wind. "Keep going. I've got you."

It's on me to protect her, since Dorian's probably out cold—

But Dorian leaps through the sanctuary doors at that moment, his shirt tattered and streaming from his body, his blond hair torn by the wind. He glances over and sees me hunched over Baz, shielding her from the ongoing force of the gale. The ferocity in his eyes surprises me—but what shocks me even more is that he's not bruised, bloody, or damaged at all. He's lost his knives, but he pulls another from somewhere, gives me a nod, and dives into the thrashing storm of tentacle-limbs again.

I don't know how long this will go on. But I have to believe that we're not doing this alone. Somewhere in that fucking mess of eldritch magic and flailing limbs and vampire teeth, Cathy is fighting, too.

27

CATHY

I'M BURIED INSIDE MY OWN MIND. I CAN SEE THROUGH MY own eyes but distantly, not directly. As if the picture of what's happening outside is being broadcast to my consciousness.

I have no arms or hands. No legs. No tongue or teeth or lungs.

I am bodiless again. This is another kind of death, more dreadful than any of the deaths I've felt before because this life was mine. For years I battled for autonomy, for power over my limbs and lungs, and to have them stolen like this is a travesty. The death god's large, cold hands have closed over mine on the steering wheel, and he's *inside* me, a violation I can hardly bear, even as he tries to numb me into acceptance. There's no physical agony, but I know that he's plucking at my nerves like puppet strings, rearranging my skeleton, unstitching my flesh. No amount of weeping could relieve this sense of loss.

I did it for Heathcliff. And I would do it again a thousand times over. But inside, in the muted hush of my own consciousness, I am mourning.

Daisy and Gatsby are here, with their friends. I know this, and I can hear everything they say, but my thoughts are dim and clouded, muffled as if Cernunnos laid a thick, heavy layer of cotton over my mind. He doesn't want to talk to me or bother with me right now. I'm supposed to sit quietly in the back seat until he's ready to notice me again.

My will is a flicker somewhere deep in my soul. Suffocated, nearly snuffed out, just like at Aunt Nellie's house. I want to coax it out again, to feed it into a wild bonfire, but I'm weighed down, wilted. Everything is fuzzy and nebulous, and I'm only sinking further into the stifling stillness.

Why do they stifle me over and over?

Cathy. A voice pierces the cottony depths like a golden blade, clearer than the other mumbling voices from outside. They're foggy and distant because I'm not in control of my ears—but this one is sharp and bright as a dagger.

I know that tone. I recognize the way it echoes painfully in my mind. It's Daisy.

I hate the sensation of her voice—it grates against my nerves, nails on a chalkboard. But I welcome it, too, because it's like a hot knife slicing through a thick sheet of ice, breaking it up. The jarring force of her tone knocks me out of sync with Cernunnos, and for a second, I can control the body we share—a response to the keen clarity of Daisy's voice.

My body responds with a compulsive shudder.

My body. *Mine.*

Cernunnos seizes control again, but I can still hear Daisy. She's telling me about Cernunnos, about his past. My bloodline does not belong only to him, to a male who would crush and confine me, but to the one goddess he could never tame. The Morrigan.

Cathy. Daisy's voice reverberates through my darkness. *You are a daughter of Fate herself, and I command you, in the name of the Morrigan, to fight.*

Cernunnos addresses me then, sharply, a disembodied voice in my consciousness. "We had a deal, child. Your lover's restoration in exchange for my residence in this body. A bargain with one of the Tuatha Dé Danann is not easily broken."

Terror turns me cold. "If I break the bargain, will Heathcliff die?"

"He has been restored, and that cannot be undone. But I can always kill him again, in some new way. And I will as a penalty for your faithlessness."

"They're making you another body," I reply. "You heard what they said. You can see Baz's mind—is she telling the truth? Can she craft you a new form?"

He hesitates. "I cannot see everything in their minds—only their attitude toward me and the nature of their abilities. Baz's gift is unfamiliar. I cannot discern its limits, and I will not trust it. I prefer the flesh and blood I now possess—bones I can build upon, blood I can use to fuel my greater form."

Cathy, you will fight. I demand it, Daisy says.

Like oxygen fed to a flame, the words strengthen the flicker of willpower I have left, and it rises higher, brighter.

"My blood. My bones," I tell Cernunnos. "I am not your fuel or your amusement."

"And I am your god, not some market vendor with whom you can bargain. Sit quietly while I get rid of these complications." His consciousness veers away from mine, roaring outward in a great pulse of wind.

Cathy, Daisy persists. *Your will is more powerful than you know. Baz is drawing the god's portrait. Once the portrait is complete, it should leave her tablet and appear in physical form. Cernunnos has already absorbed your blood through the sacrifice, so this plan should work. Baz did it once before with Manannán, but she's not descended from Cernunnos, so she can't complete the process alone. You have to push Cernunnos out, press him to enter his new form. I can help you. Together, we will overcome him.*

Her words are interspersed by loud protests from Cernunnos. He's shouting over her, over the wind, his voice swirling both inside my head and throughout the church. "She's lying. The bitch is lying... There is no such magic. Your human technology and your science do not work with the old gifts. They are not compatible. It's not possible."

Through the layers Cernunnos has wrapped around my mind, I can see what he's doing to Gatsby and the others. He's hurling pulses of crushing wind at them, whipping them with vines, thrashing with ponderous limbs, and stabbing with spear-like claws. But I also see a hazy glow around the women. Baz and Daisy each form their own locus of power, while the men defend them.

My vision becomes clearer, as if I'm stepping nearer to a window. I'm closer to seeing properly through my own eyes.

Enough, says Daisy. *Cathy, it's enough. All of it. Time to rise up.*

"Enough," I echo, and suddenly I feel my lungs again, my throat, my lips. My mouth is bleeding at the corners, and the pain is so sharp that I almost retreat. It's comfortable inside Cernunnos. My senses were dulled, and I felt the loss of control, but there was no physical pain. And I have suffered so much pain in my life—the physical pain of exposure, wounds to my body as I wandered...the lashing of branches and the tearing of thorns. Rocks bruising my feet. My father's drunken blows. The inner torment of grief upon grief, cracking me open, spilling my blood and tears for people I didn't even know.

I don't want to endure all that again.

"It's too much for you to handle," Cernunnos says softly. Outside, in the church, he's still roaring at the others, demanding their worship, but he's in here, too, speaking to me intimately, quietly. "Let me be your safety. I will filter the world for you. You will have all the pleasant sensations and none of the terrible ones. No more tears, or screams, or wandering. No more sharing grief that isn't yours. You will teach me all the ways of the world, and as a part of myself, you will never die. You will experience wonders with me, and you will never need to weep again."

It's tempting. More tempting than I want to admit.

Some people might agree to that life, to the absence of pain. I wouldn't blame them. Not one bit.

But I have always pushed against the boundaries that were set for me, even when it hurt. And since I met Heathcliff, I have fully come to life. Staying blanketed and protected inside Cernunnos would mean giving up all freedom—giving up the beautiful anguish of being human, the aching joy of experiencing the world with Heathcliff. Whatever pain I have to endure, no existence could be satisfying without *him*.

"My life has been wretched at times," I say. "But it's mine, and I'll be damned if I let you have it."

I feel the surge of Cernunnos's anger. But I'm awake again. I'm not a cringing little soul in the back of his mind or a drugged sleeper in Aunt Nellie's guest room. No matter how much it hurts, I won't dull this pain. I will take it like a woman, like a fucking goddess, and I'll get past it, like I always have. Maybe I'll die doing it—maybe the pieces of me are separated beyond repair—but death is better than prison. All I care about is Heathcliff, *alive*... and myself, mistress of my own fate.

I swallowed a god, and I can spit him back out.

My consciousness expands, and I find my eyes, my mouth, my voice. Two words. "I'm ready."

Daisy hears me, and she smiles, showing her fangs.

Above the wind, above the thunder of Cernunnos's protests, above Heathcliff's roar of defiance and the snarling of the vampires, I hear Daisy's voice, clear as a bell. "Baz, time to sign off!"

"Got it!" Baz shouts back without looking up from her tablet.

"I have died a hundred deaths before this one." My voice is mine, but it's blended with Cernunnos's deep tones as he fights for control. "I know you, and I do not fear you. This is my body, not yours. My will, not yours. I no longer consent to your presence here."

Cernunnos hisses, our shared body rising taller, shadows condensing into a dozen more arms, antlers expanding. But I can feel something else now—another will, separate from mine or his, tugging at him. Drawing out his spirit.

The god panics. Wrenches control back from me, bellows, "No!" and sends everything he's got toward Baz in one destructive maelstrom.

Gatsby takes a clawed fist straight to the gut. It punches right through him, then yanks back, leaving a gaping hole in his stomach.

He chokes and staggers, collapsing into the aisle.

Daisy screams and falls to her knees beside him. She rips at her own wrist, then shoves her bloodied arm desperately against his mouth.

Vines coil around the other two vampires, binding them together. They're lifted higher, higher, while the vines constrict their bodies.

I know what's going to happen, but I can't stop it.

For a moment the two men struggle pointlessly in midair—and then the red-haired one yields, relaxing his body. He leans in and kisses the other man, fangs and all.

"Don't give up, Nick," shouts the black-haired one, still writhing and bucking—but the redhead gasps brokenly, "Cody. Cody, it's all right."

Then something snaps inside him, and his eyes go vacant, startled. Cody gives a yell of anguish, but his cry is choked off by another snap as his own spine breaks.

Cernunnos isn't satisfied. He smashes them against the pews over and over. Wood splinters, more bones crack, and there's a wet sound of flesh being pounded into pulp.

Heathcliff yells, charges toward me, toward Cernunnos. I can see the god reaching four clawed hands, can feel his intent to shred Heathcliff's flesh from his bones. And I can't stop it in time.

But Dorian gets there first. Throws himself in front of Heathcliff.

All the claws of those four arms sink into Dorian's body. His face goes perfectly still, and in that instant, he looks innocently, pitifully young. Blood trickles from his mouth.

Heathcliff seizes two of the god-arms, rips them in half before they can whip outward and tear Dorian apart. With a scream of defiance, I struggle to control the other two limbs, but they're not part of me. They're shadow-limbs of Cernunnos, and I'm not fully in control of him yet.

Blood jets across the pews as the other two arms jerk out of Dorian's body, slashing him in the process. He falls out of my sight line, shrouded in shadows.

Heathcliff is left standing, his hands and robes dripping red. He is Baz's last defense.

She hasn't taken her eyes from her drawing, but her shoulders are shaking, and a broken sob echoes through the church, which has fallen suddenly, strangely quiet.

"It's over," says Cernunnos aloud. Wings of shadow expand from his shoulders and curve along the sides of the church, blotting out the light from the narrow windows, covering the lamps. The only illumination streams in pale, translucent rays from the doorway of the sanctuary, lancing around Heathcliff and turning him into a dark silhouette.

"You tried to expel me, Catherine," Cernunnos says in a voice like black ice. "I consider our bargain broken, and for that, your lover will die."

Countless hands rise from the floor of the church. They rise on long arms veined with ridges, studded with thorns and blinking eyes. Heathcliff makes a sound I've never heard from him—the desperate growl of a cornered animal. And though there's a way of escape right behind him, he will not run. He will not leave me.

He loves me like no one ever has, and I hate that he is standing alone in this. I hate that I'm not quite strong enough to save him.

But before the hands can seize Heathcliff, Daisy rises from her knees, her eyes shot through with white, pale claws extruding from her fingers, her yellow hair stained crimson at the tips. Her voice vibrates against my consciousness, but she isn't speaking to me now. She's speaking to the god—to Death himself.

"You," she says, low and lethal. "You will leave this girl's body, and you will go into the new one Baz has created for you. This is the will of the Leannán Sídhe and our sister, the banshee. In this world, *we* are the new gods. And you are nothing."

Her power slams against Cernunnos, penetrates his spirit. At the same moment, Baz yells out, and I feel her power too, yanking Cernunnos free, snapping the tethers he formed within me.

A defiant scream builds inside me, roars up my throat, tears across my tongue, and sears the air of the church. It rises to an ear-splitting, keening shriek that bursts every window in the building into splinters, and on the crest of that shriek, the god's spirit is ejected violently from my body.

Baz leaps up, holding out the tablet, the portrait she made. The image on the screen is draining away, and as it leaves the screen, it begins to take shape in the far aisle, by the north wall of the church. The figure is a tall, slim man with handsome features and short, wavy black hair. But as the right side of his face is form-ing, Baz takes her stylus and rakes it viciously across the screen several times.

There's a rush of wind and smoke as the god is sucked into his new body—a body perfectly formed, except for the right side of his face, which is striated with red wounds.

Cernunnos stares at himself, seeming disoriented. Before he can recover, Daisy moves inhumanly fast, takes his face between her hands, and looks into his eyes, speaking quickly, quietly, intensely.

She keeps talking, on and on, but I have no idea what she's

saying because I'm...sinking. Shrinking. All the pieces that were Cernunnos and not me are dissipating into smoke and vanishing into the sunlight that floods the church.

My body is wrong. Parts of me were severed by the god's magic, yet they're still linked together by tenuous, straining threads. And as the magic recedes, the pieces of me are snapping back into place, reconnecting. Arranging themselves like they're supposed to be, until I'm standing in the center aisle, my right size and shape.

But I'm not quite right after all, because a second later, I fall backward. Agony lacerates my flesh like whips of fire. When I manage to raise my head and look down at myself, I nearly vomit.

I've been put back together, and I'm alive—but there are angry red seams along the edges of the chunks that had to be reattached. I look like a jigsaw puzzle, like a patchwork quilt, like a rag doll. Like something horrible that shouldn't exist.

The agony is fading, and the redness is calming as well...but the scars are still there, ridged and unmistakable.

The scars shouldn't bother me. I'm *alive*. That's all I should care about. Alive and whole and myself. Most of the people who came to help me might be dead, and I'm sad about my fucking *skin*? What the hell is wrong with me? At least I'm not in chunks all over the sanctuary. At least I'm breathing. At least my heart is beating...

Tears spill over, and I choke out a sob.

Heathcliff rushes to me, claws me against himself. "Cathy. Cathy, Cathy, Cathy." He's sobbing, too, horrible heavy sobs jerked straight out of his heart. He's kissing me, kissing all over my wet face. Feeling my body, pressing its new seams. "You're all right. You're okay."

"But...them." I point to the slumped figure of Gatsby. To Dorian's body. To the place where I saw the other two vampires fall.

"Shit," he says. "I've got to... I'll be right back."

I nod. "Try to help them."

He goes to Dorian first. Gets there a second before Baz does.

Dorian's not a vampire like the others. I don't know what he is, but there's no way he could have survived that—

He sits up. Fucking sits up, covered in blood, and he's gory but he looks...whole.

"Well, shit," says Heathcliff blankly.

"Thank goddess." Baz runs her fingers through Dorian's hair, strokes his cheek. Then she glances over at me. "Girl, we gotta get you some clothes. Here." She pulls off her jacket and tosses it to me. I drape it along the front of my body and hold it in place with both arms.

"Nick and Cody," Dorian says, his voice threaded with worry.

"They'll need blood," says Baz. "So will Gatsby, if he's...if he isn't..." She lowers her voice to a whisper. "I think that punch took out a couple major organs. Might take him a while to heal. He'll need more blood than the others."

"Happy to donate." Dorian climbs to his feet and walks over to Gatsby. He sits cross-legged on the floor, pulls Gatsby's head into his lap, and rakes his arm along the vampire's fangs, opening a shallow cut. "Drink up, you self-righteous bastard. Can't have you dying on us, can we?"

From behind me, on the church platform, a shaky voice says, "Can someone cut me loose?"

I twist around, still holding the jacket in place. "Oh shit... Edgar." I totally forgot he was there.

"Who's that?" Baz asks. Quickly I explain Edgar's role in everything, and she gives him a stern look.

"Maybe he's not completely useless," she mutters. "Heathcliff, help me get him over to the boys. They could use some blood."

"What?" exclaims Edgar. He's trembling, and there's a wet spot on his pants where he must have pissed himself. "Nobody's taking my blood. Haven't I been through enough?"

Heathcliff strides up onto the platform, grabs the roll of duct tape from the floor where he left it, and rips off a piece. He places it firmly across Edgar's mouth. "Asshole. Least you can do is help the people who had to fix the problem you caused."

I lean against the end of a pew, too tired to do anything but watch as Heathcliff carries Edgar to where Nick and Cody fell. He and Baz hunker down over the bodies. I can't see what they're doing, but after a few minutes, I hear slurping sounds and Edgar's muffled screams.

"We don't want him dead," Baz says to Heathcliff. "We'll have to stop them in a few minutes and find another source. Dorian can give a lot, but too much puts him out of commission for a while. We need somebody else. Human, not vampire."

"I can do it," Heathcliff offers, but I can tell he's reluctant. Honestly I don't blame him...but I don't think we have much choice.

Then an idea pops into my head. It's vengeful and wicked, but after what I've endured, I don't fucking care. "Edgar's phone," I murmur. "Should be on the pulpit. Text Robert Earnshaw from Edgar's phone and ask him to come to the church. Ask him to bring Nellie Earnshaw, too. Tell them it's an emergency."

28

HEATHCLIFF

CATHY'S DAD AND AUNT SHOW UP ABOUT FIFTEEN MINUTES later. Doesn't take me more than a few seconds to get Mr. Earnshaw under control and tape his wrists, mouth, and ankles. Then I pick him up like he weighs nothing, even though he's about the same size as Hindley, and I carry him over to Nick, the redheaded vampire, while Dorian and Baz subdue Aunt Nellie. We tape their mouths so they can't scream, and when I feel a twinge of pity, I picture them standing there, watching Cathy's throat being cut. Fixes my guilt right up.

It's funny how quick you can get used to things during a crisis. After watching Cathy get dismembered by a god and reassembled afterward, seeing Nick's freckled face pressed into the crook of Mr. Earnshaw's neck, sucking his blood, doesn't seem so shocking. But it's still strange as hell watching the vampires' wounds closing and their shattered bones clicking back into place as they drink.

Cathy doesn't explain anything to either her aunt or her dad. She's wearing a pair of faded, stretchy leggings and an over-sized T-shirt that Baz found downstairs in some donation bin. She stands there, arms folded, watching her relatives struggle while the vampires drink. I notice her fingertips fumbling along the seams of her new scars. They don't bother me a bit, but they seem to make her self-conscious, and I hate that. She's been so strong.

While I hold Mr. Earnshaw still for Nick, I glance over at Daisy. She's been locked in a low, one-sided conversation with Cernunnos's new form for a long while now.

"Think she's okay?" I ask Baz.

She shrugs. "Dorian and I haven't been part of this group very long. I don't know everything about Daisy's powers. But I do know she once got deep inside the head of this older vampire—really messed him up. Made him pretty much catatonic. He's still locked up in Gatsby's dungeon, and he's got just enough brain function to take care of himself, nothing more. Maybe that's what she's doing to Cernunnos. Locking him down."

"Can she do that to a god?"

"I guess we'll see. Maybe she wants to be really sure he's contained, and that's why she's taking so long. I hope it works."

"I'll drink to that." Cody lifts his head from Aunt Nellie's neck, smiles, then takes another long pull at her vein. He licks the wound afterward.

"They lick it to heal the punctures," Baz explains. "Their saliva has some healing properties. Can't heal deep injuries, though...or scars."

She says "scars" quietly, but Cathy still flinches and tightens her arms around herself. After a second she walks away, up the aisle. She turns left when she reaches the platform and disappears through the door that leads to the back room.

"You good?" I ask Nick, and he nods. He's a skinny guy, but

now that he's had some blood, his vampire strength is returning. He can handle Mr. Earnshaw.

I jump up and head to the back room. At first I don't see Cathy at all. Then I locate her, wedged into a corner beside a rack of hymnals, curled into a ball, sobbing.

"Cathy." I kneel down and keep my voice as gentle as I can. "Can I help? Is it okay if I touch you?"

"God, always," she chokes out, and she lunges into my arms.

I hold her head close to my chest with one hand and wrap my other arm around her while she cries. I'm wearing cast-off clothes now, too—gray sweatpants and a T-shirt that hugs me way too tight and has a big wet spot from Cathy's tears. But she's here with me, and that's all that matters.

I duck my head and inhale against her tangled brown hair. She smells like midnight, the winter kind where you walk out under the stars and the cold is so sharp it stings, but the air is fresh, too, so you can't help inhaling again. It's the smell of darkness, and cold, and death. Beyond that, she smells a little bit like the soap from dispensers in the woman's bathroom. There's a bitter coppery smell, too. And then, underneath it all, as I nuzzle deeper into her hair, she smells like Cathy. Honey and magnolias, green leaves and wild summer.

"Are you *smelling* me?" she asks.

"You bet your ass I am. You smell sexy as hell."

She mumbles something, and all I catch is the word *scars*.

"I got scars, too," I tell her quietly. "Yours just mean you were strong enough. Not even a god could keep you down."

She hiccups a laugh. "But they look awful."

"Nah. They're badass. But hey, if you ever want to cover them up, I know a few good tattoo artists."

She lifts her head, brightening. "Tattoos. I could be good with that."

"Yeah? Okay then. We'll get it done. On second thought, though, maybe we shouldn't do it around here. Maybe we wait until we get wherever we're going? If you still want to leave Wicklow, that is."

"Leave Wicklow? Fuck yes." She brushes her brown curls out of her eyes. "We're not just leaving Wicklow—we're gonna leave the damn state, maybe even the damn country."

"That can be endgame, but we'll need passports first. Maybe we can stay with this bunch"—I jerk my head in the direction of the sanctuary—"until we get the passports, and then we hightail it down to Mexico."

Cathy winces, shakes her head. "I was thinking Canada. Less humidity, no swampy areas or roaches like in South Carolina. Cold weather, big open spaces. Huge stretches of forest where no one lives. If I'm far enough from people, I won't have to mourn anyone. We can travel a bit, too, north to the tundra, west to the plains—anywhere we have room to roam."

"You and me living in a cabin, middle of nowhere," I muse. "I like it. Maybe I'll start my own brewery. Small at first, see where it goes."

Cathy's eyes light up. "I'll help with the marketing. Take pictures, set up the website, create an Instagram account—"

"Make a business out of it. Hell yeah. And I can do some resurrections on the side to fund the startup costs. Already got a chunk of change waiting for us on Hindley's property. Speaking of which...aw, fuck."

Hindley. I haven't thought about him since our phone call

got cut off. I have no idea whether he's dead or alive. And no idea where Ian Holcum went. He could still be passed out, or he could be out walking around, itching to cause more trouble.

"If you can manage it, we need to go. That sick-ass jerkwad who set this whole thing up is still unaccounted for, and that makes me nervous."

"Same." She shudders a little.

We get up, hand in hand, and walk out into the sanctuary. I pause by the platform, taking stock of the group. Dorian is lounging with his legs kicked over a pew while Baz feeds Gatsby a little of her blood. Cody's got a hand wrapped around the back of Nick's neck and they're talking quietly, foreheads pressed together. Aunt Nellie, Edgar, and Mr. Earnshaw are duct-taped at the mouths, wrists, and ankles, lying on padded pews since they're done serving as blood bags. And Daisy…she's still holding Cernunnos's face, eye-locked with him, murmuring words none of us can hear.

I'm opening my mouth to get everyone's attention, to explain about Ian—when the motherfucker himself strides into the church.

Dorian scrambles upright.

"The fuck?" he gasps. "Lloyd-Henry?"

"Lloyd-what?" I exclaim. "He's Ian Holcum, a Gancanagh and a shapeshifter, and he's the one responsible for all this."

Ian's gaze fixes on me, and he lifts his eyebrows. "You figured it out. Well done. I'll admit, I underestimated you. Hindley told me you weren't very clever—'dumb as balls,' isn't that how you put it?" He glances over his right shoulder just as Hindley steps in beside him, holding his favorite shotgun.

"That's right." Hindley spits on the sanctuary threshold. "Dumb as fuckin' balls."

"Such a delicate turn of phrase." Ian—or Lloyd or whoever he is—chuckles.

Gatsby climbs to his feet. There's no hole through his middle now, but from the back I can see his spine and a lot of red muscle. He's nowhere near fully healed.

"Lloyd-Henry Woodson," he says quietly. "So this is your doing."

Lloyd-Henry raises a cautionary hand. "Now before you start getting all riled up, I didn't come here to fight. Baz understands, don't you, love? Yes, she knows I don't enjoy violence or confrontations. I'm simply here to collect Cernunnos. I assume that's him?" He points to the tall, dark-haired man. Daisy has finally stopped speaking to him, and Cernunnos stares around vacantly, confused.

"Well now, that's not very nice." Lloyd clicks his tongue. "Daisy, Daisy, what have you done to him, you interfering little cunt?"

Gatsby lurches forward, but he wobbles and Baz has to steady him.

"Nasty wound there, Jay," Lloyd says. "Might want to wait a bit before you try to defend your lady's honor."

"We welcomed you as a friend when you visited us in Asheville." Gatsby's tone is low and menacing. "I showed you— fuck, I showed you *everything*."

"Not at first." Lloyd gives him a tight smile. "I had to work on you awhile, longer than I expected, because of *her*." He nods to Daisy. "Her voice doesn't work on me, and I can't seem to influence her—due to the similarities in our powers, I assume. Her resistance delayed me, and things in Charleston did not go smoothly because of it."

"Because I shot you," Dorian puts in. "Did that fucking house resurrect you?"

"No, that was my good friend Hindley. The entire Lockwood clan have been my friends and allies for a long time. Well, except for you, Heathcliff. Couldn't trust you, as an outsider. And the old lady had to be kept out of the loop—she knew too much about me due to our past encounters."

He's talking about Meemaw. He must be the Gancanagh she knew back in New Orleans.

My brain is racing to catch up, trying to adjust, trying not to be *dumb as balls* about this, but I've had a shitty day, and I'm hella tired. I'm furious with this Lloyd guy, but I can't seem to solidify my whirling thoughts into any kind of purpose or plan.

Cathy's fingers tighten around mine, and she whispers, "He's the one who killed me."

Hot, choking anger fills my chest.

Lloyd slit Cathy's throat. That plain fact is the motivation I need to meet Hindley's gaze, to speak out. "You knew who he was all along? You knew when we resurrected him?"

"Sure did." Hindley leers. "We go way back. Bunch of the cousins and uncles and such know him, too. Like he said, we had to keep it quiet around Meemaw. She wouldn't have wanted us working with him. Too dangerous, she'd say. But he said our abilities would be stronger once the god was raised. Strong as they used to be in the old days. And he promised not to use his powers on us."

"You believed him?" I scoff.

"I ain't done none of this under anybody's sway," Hindley says. "It's all me. My choice."

"Of course it is," Lloyd echoes.

"Damn straight." Hindley spits again. "Anyway, when we rezzed him, I knew he was gonna be in and out of consciousness for a while. But it was hella funny pestering you about wakin' him up, watchin' you nosing around, trying to take care of him. He had to sleep a lot, sure, but he was up and about more than you ever knew. Sometimes it was a damn hassle keeping you occupied until he could get back to bed for his rest. But hey, it worked. The god was raised and by the same fuckers who wanted to keep him down. That's what you call irony, ain't it? Barrier's down now, so I just walked right into Wicklow. The Coosaw Lockwoods'll be along soon, too. We're gonna have us a Samhain bonfire, burn this old place to the ground."

Edgar Linton makes a panicked sound. He's still lying in the pew where Baz put him after his "blood donation."

Lloyd speaks up before Hindley can continue. "The fate of this church doesn't concern me. All that concerns me is *him*. Send the god over to me, Daisy. Quietly now, there's a good girl."

From my angle, I can't see much of Daisy's face. But I hear the savage hiss she makes, and I see her body tense, claws twitching as if she's about to pounce.

"I wouldn't do that," Lloyd advises. He speaks sidelong to Hindley. "Point that shotgun at the tattooed girl. She's fully human. Would die in a second. Dorian, you make a move to shield her and Hindley will shoot. At least some of that buckshot will find its mark in her pretty little body."

Dorian freezes in the act of moving toward Baz. Cody shifts restlessly, like he's thinking about intervening, but Nick holds him back.

I feel fucking useless. I'm too far away. Can't stop Hindley or Ian.

"Give him what he wants, Daisy," Gatsby says. "You've done all you can, sweetheart."

Daisy's head whips toward him, and another growl ripples from her throat.

"Gatsby," Nick says quietly. "Her bracelet. Orange. She gave you too much blood."

I don't know what bracelet he's talking about, but Nick's words seem to alarm Gatsby.

"Daisy can't listen to you right now, Lloyd," he says. "I need to go to her, to persuade her to hand over the god. You claim you don't want violence—let me reason with her and prevent more bloodshed. I won't make a false move, I swear."

Lloyd surveys Daisy, then nods.

Quickly, Gatsby crosses over to Daisy, drawing her into his arms. She jerks against his hold, hissing again.

"Drink from me," he says quickly. "Drink from me, sweetheart. Just for a minute, and then we'll get you some human blood."

"Jay," Cody protests. "You don't have any to spare."

"When she gets like this, she has to be fed," Gatsby snaps. "Or...you know what happens."

"Interesting." Lloyd taps his chin, watching Daisy with renewed interest. "Not like other girls, is she? A bit more feral than your usual vampire once her blood supply gets low enough? Better hold her tight, Gatsby—she looks positively rabid."

"I can hold her." Gatsby's voice tightens with strain as Daisy begins to struggle in his arms. "You'll have to come get Cernunnos. I don't think he's able to walk there on his own."

"Because she fucking ruined him." Lloyd's voice rises sharply. He takes a deep breath and closes his eyes for a second. "I swear,

Daisy, I'll have your little blond head one of these days. If you weren't immune to me, I'd eat your soul, slowly, over several years. That's another part of the Gancanagh lore, one people don't like to talk about—the way we swallow souls gradually. I'm a bit of a gourmet in that department. That's how I met you, Dorian. You were so beautiful. I desperately wanted to taste your soul…but as it happened, your soul was safe from me, trapped in that fascinating portrait. I assume, since you're here, that you have a new portrait now. Anyway…as for the soul-eating process, it usually takes several months. I like to savor each bite, and my victims never realize what's happening until it's done. But for you, Daisy, I'd slow the process down even further. Keep you in a cage, make it really torturous." He sighs. "That will have to wait, I suppose. Nicky, be a dear and bring me my broken god."

Nick glances at Gatsby, who nods.

Sighing again, Lloyd adds, "Just *once* I'd like for this process to go smoothly. Is that too much to ask for? Well, as they say, third time's the charm."

Nick propels Cernunnos toward Lloyd, past the muzzle of Hindley's shotgun. In that second, Dorian leaps in front of Baz, shielding her with his body.

Lloyd clucks rebukingly. "Dorian, my love, I warned you not to do that. Now I'll have to choose someone to shoot as punishment." He scans the church, and his eyes land on me. "Let's take out Dumb-As-Balls over there. Shoot him now."

Hindley aims the shotgun at me. I pin Cathy to my back, holding her there with my strength in case she tries to save me.

Across the church, Hindley's eyes lock with mine. He's a good shot. No chance of him missing.

"Let Daisy at him," hisses Cody. "We can take them out, all of us."

But Gatsby says nothing, and without his word, nobody moves.

Hindley licks his lips. Renews his grip on the shotgun.

"Do it," says Lloyd.

"He's my fuckin' brother."

Now you say it? I want to yell. *After all this, now you fucking say it?*

"He's not even your blood," sneers Lloyd.

Hindley clears his throat. "Ain't always about blood."

"Yes, it is. It is *always* about blood."

But Hindley's shaking his head. "You take Kare-noon-us there and git going. He's what you want. I'll hold 'em here until you're gone."

Lloyd gives him the coldest stare I've ever seen, and suddenly I remember what his soul felt like as it slid back into his body. A slimy, clawed thing, hateful and vicious and determined to hang on to life with its teeth.

Without another word, Lloyd turns and walks out of the church, leading the docile Cernunnos with him.

"Are we just going to let him go?" Cody asks.

"For now," says Gatsby.

"For good." Nick retreats to Cody's side again. "We got our vacation coming up, remember? Just you and me. We deserve it. Ever since we met it's been nothing but danger and drama."

Cody looks over at Nick, speaking in his soft British accent. "I know. But I also know what happens when you run from someone like Lloyd-Henry Woodson. Maybe he doesn't hurt you anymore, not directly, but he'll hurt others, won't he? In this case, maybe thousands of others. We have to go after him."

"None of you's goin' anywhere," says Hindley. "You're all staying here until the Coosaw Lockwoods arrive. Then we'll see." He swings the gun around, raking his sight line across everyone in the church—and as the gun swerves away from me, Cody pounces.

He's on Hindley in a second, ignoring the spatter of shot through his body as the gun booms. Then Hindley's down, the gun knocked out of his hand, and Cody is crouching over him with gleaming eyes. The vampire looks up at Daisy, who is still struggling in Gatsby's arms, and he says, "Come on, Coffee Beans. Drink your fill. Sorry if he tastes like asshole."

Gatsby releases Daisy, and she's off like a shot, crashing to her knees beside Hindley and sinking her fangs deep into his neck while Cody keeps his arms pinned.

"Looks like she doesn't mind the flavor of asshole," Baz comments.

"Neither do I," Dorian says with a suggestive grin, and Nick howls with laughter. It's the reckless, hysterical kind of laughter that comes after a crisis. And I can't help chuckling myself.

29

CATHY

WITH HINDLEY UNDER CONTROL AND DAISY OCCUPIED, Heathcliff and I can finally move down the aisle and rejoin the others. I'm a little pissed at him for holding me behind his back like that, but I guess it was his turn to protect me. Not gonna lie, it feels good to have someone take care of me for once. Doesn't mean I can't handle things myself most of the time—but sometimes, I really can't. Sometimes, he gets to be my defender, and that's okay. That's what partners do.

I've never had a partner before. It's fucking amazing.

Once Daisy has drunk enough of Hindley's blood, she becomes herself again. "Sorry for the...you know," she murmurs, wiping her bloody mouth on the back of her hand.

We all mumble that it's fine. But if Gatsby hadn't been there, I'm not sure it would have been fine at all.

None of us want to stay in that church and wait for the Lockwood gang to show up, so Nick and Cody tape Hindley's wrists and ankles, and Dorian gives Edgar Linton a knife so he can saw through the duct tape for Aunt Nellie and my dad after we leave. That way they won't be at the mercy of the Coosaw

Lockwoods, who according to Heathcliff will probably arrive drunk off their asses and ready to burn buildings, with or without people inside them. It's Samhain, after all.

As we're walking out of the church, Heathcliff mutters, "You go ahead. I got something to say to Hindley."

I nod and move on, though I'm curious about what he'll say. His brother fooled him for weeks—longer, really. He hurt Heathcliff his entire life. Even if he wasn't willing to kill him there at the end, those wounds don't go away. It cuts deep when family treats you like that.

For my part, I've got nothing to say to Dad or Aunt Nellie. I don't plan to speak another word to them ever again. I died right in front of them at the ritual, and now they are dead to me. I don't need closure, nor do I owe them that gift. My heart has already written "the end" under their part of my story.

Walking out of Wicklow Heritage Chapel *alive* without a ride-along god in my head feels like a miracle. I gulp lungfuls of October air, and in the sunlight, I look down at my fingers. They're wreathed with tiny scars, much paler and less noticeable than the big ones on my limbs and torso. But they're *my* fingers. Not the god's.

I am not his. I am my own.

A shiver skates over my body, raising goose bumps.

"You okay?" Baz squeezes my shoulders lightly. "Dumb question, right?"

"Maybe."

"It's okay to be messed up inside, especially by stuff like this." She traces the toe of her boot through the gravel. "It sticks with you. You'll need to talk about it. Lucky for people like us, with the supernatural sort of trauma, there's a counselor at Gatsby's. You two should come to Asheville. Hang out for a while, until you're feeling more…settled…about everything."

It's exactly the invitation I was hoping for. "Yeah, I'd like that."

"Cool."

She and I stand there while Gatsby, Daisy, Nick, and Cody climb into the Rivian. Dorian is holding the passenger door of the BMW for her.

"He's such an old-fashioned gentleman in some ways," she says, humor in her voice. "And in other ways, he's so *not*."

I laugh quietly. It feels good, the humor, the almost-girl-talk, the we-could-be-friends vibe.

"Wanna ride with us?" Baz asks as Heathcliff comes bounding down the steps. His tanned face is flushed, his eyes bright with emotion he's trying to suppress.

"What do you think?" I ask him. "Should we ride with them?"

"I'll drive Hindley's truck." He holds up a wallet and his phone. "Forgot I left my phone in the lobby. And I grabbed my wallet out of those pants I left in the bathroom, so I have my driver's license with me." His gaze latches on to the truck, and a sudden shadow passes over his face. "You know what, never mind. I don't want to drive that piece of shit anymore. I got my own truck, if y'all can drive us to pick it up."

"Sure," says Baz. "Hop in."

We climb into the back of Dorian's car, and Heathcliff directs him where to go.

I can't describe the relief as both cars turn out of the church parking lot, onto the open road. About three minutes later, we pass two weathered pickups and an SUV full of people hollering and whooping out the windows, openly waving beer bottles around. Heathcliff hunches down in the back seat.

"Coosaw Lockwoods?" I ask, and he nods.

"Don't worry, choirboy. Windows are tinted," Dorian says.

"Good to know, ass-licker," Heathcliff retorts.

"Ass-licker." Dorian cocks his head, pondering. "I like it. It's got that ring of truth to it, eh, Baz?"

Baz snickers and puts her hand over his mouth. "Hush, you."

"Fuck, I need to get *drunk* after all this," says Dorian through her fingers.

"Not while you're driving." She withdraws her hand and settles back in her seat.

"Fine. When we get home?"

"I'll pour you a drink myself."

"And then you'll tell me you've decided to become a vampire."

Baz looks over at him sharply. "After what happened with Daisy? Dorian, you saw how she got."

"Not every vampire is like that."

"Exactly. Some are gluttons, and some are ferals, like her."

"She's not totally feral. Only when she gets low," Dorian counters. "And most of the vampires are perfectly normal. Ask Gatsby. He can tell you the percentage—"

"I'm not interested in percentages. I was into the idea at first, but I've had time to think since then, Dorian, and I'm just not sure. I need you to quit asking. If and when I decide I want to do it, I'll tell you. Until then, don't mention it again."

He inhales slowly through his nose and blows out the breath. "All right. I won't."

I exchange glances with Heathcliff. It feels good, somehow,

watching another couple fight. Feels weirdly normal, even though the topic of their conversation is anything but normal.

My fingers crawl across the seat between us, and his fingers curl between mine, thick and warm. A silent *I love you*.

We stop by the Grange, where Heathcliff has lived since he was a child. I barely catch a glimpse of the house because Heathcliff directs us to the back of the property. Dorian grumbles about the rough lane we have to take, but at its end, a truck sits half-hidden under some low-hanging trees.

"Yours?" I exclaim.

"Mine," Heathcliff says proudly. "Earned by dragging souls out of the Vague. Come on." He hops out, then leans back in to speak to Dorian. "We'll grab my money, then follow you."

"Grab your money?" Dorian lifts an eyebrow in the rearview mirror.

"Yeah. Got it buried right over there." Heathcliff jogs off and starts moving aside some undergrowth.

"He's got money *buried*," Dorian says in a dramatic undertone to Baz. "I think I'll call him 'pirate' instead of 'choirboy.'"

"He would make a really hot pirate," Baz replies.

I expect Dorian to have some jealous retort, but he only says "Right?" with unmistakable enthusiasm.

I like these two. I liked them at first because they came to help us, and I like them more now that I've seen a glimpse of their chaotic, affectionate relationship.

As I move to get out of the car, Baz says, "Hey, Cathy, you got a phone?"

"I had one. It was taken. Heathcliff has one."

"Well, here." She twists around, grabs my hand, and produces a pen from her bag. She writes ten digits across my scarred skin. "That's my number. You can put it in Heathcliff's phone. That way if we get separated, we can meet up again, and you won't get lost."

"If you do get lost, just head to Asheville and ask around for Jay Gatsby," Dorian advises. "That's what we did."

"We were traumatized, too," Baz adds. "We left behind a mess sort of like this one."

"It's a victory as long as you walk away alive." Dorian turns his head and gives me a smile—a warm, genuine, beautiful smile. "Travel safe, little banshee. See you on the other side."

30

CATHY

Six months later

HEATHCLIFF TURNS THE TRUCK OFF THE MAIN ROAD, ONTO a narrower lane that tilts uphill. My stomach is full of butterflies, and I'm drinking in the scenery—pale birches, thick evergreens, slopes coated with scruffy blueberry bushes.

After a short climb through forested land, we break out of the trees onto a broad, flat hill. And there it is—a cabin, a huge barn, and a sprawl of rolling hills under a bright blue sky.

Tears spring to my eyes immediately, which surprises me a bit. I guess when the heart is full, the emotion has to spill over somehow, and for me, tears are the most familiar outlet.

I'm opening the door before Heathcliff has fully parked, and he yells out, alarmed, as I dive out and race across the grass to the lip of the hill, where it starts sloping down again. I spread my arms to the April wind, and it dries my tears, leaving only faint traces of salt and a sense of reckless joy.

Heathcliff turns off the truck, slams the door, and jogs up beside me. "Hell of a view, ain't it? Gatsby says the cabin's furnished and stocked—Daisy's goodbye gift to us. Electricity should be all hooked up, and I got all the info for taking care of the well and the septic system—"

I grab the paper-stuffed binder he's holding and drop it into the grass. Then I seize his hands and dance him around, through the wind, under the blue sky. "It's ours, Heathcliff! It's all ours!"

"Yeah, yeah," he drawls, but he's grinning. "How do you think two Southerners gonna fit in up here with the Canadians?"

"Just fine!" I shout. "We're gonna fit in just fine, and who cares if we don't, anyway? Not fitting in up here is a hell of a lot better than not fitting in with the folks of Wicklow or the damn Lockwoods, wouldn't you say?"

"You got that right."

I sober a little, catching the tinge of bitterness in his tone. "You heard from Hindley at all?"

"Nope. Don't want to."

"What did you say to him that day when you stayed behind? I never did ask." Truthfully, it seemed like too sensitive a subject. But we have some distance from it now, both physical and emotional.

Heathcliff sighs. "Told him he was a mean son of a bitch, a loser, and an all-around dickwad. And..." He grimaces. "Told him I loved him anyway."

"Oh god. What did he say?"

"Well, when I yanked the tape off his mouth, he spat in my face and called me something I ain't gonna repeat, as it was god-damn homophobic." He shakes his head. "Typical Hindley."

"Well, he can't bother us now. No one can, except Gatsby and the others, if they need us."

"Doesn't look like they will. It's been quiet for half a year. No sign of Manannán or Cernunnos."

"Except those two weird hurricanes," I remind him. "And the floods that came out of nowhere, remember?"

"No one died, though. Coulda been climate change or some shit."

"Could have been." I doubt it, but I understand why Heathcliff is so determined to believe that the two gods aren't going to be a problem—that Manannán is helpless without a pantheon and worshippers and that Cernunnos is still trapped in his own mind, his powers chained by Daisy's voice.

Maybe Heathcliff is right. Maybe we'll never have to deal with them again. But he told me what Meemaw Lockwood said about dormant powers awakening and lost magic resurfacing. That's not something we can brush off like it's nothing.

Or maybe we *can*. Maybe we can leave all of that in the hands of Gatsby, Daisy, and their group. Maybe Heathcliff and I, the necromancer and the banshee, really can escape it all and live out our days in this stunning landscape, with a cute little town just half an hour away and a highway that could take us anywhere. Thanks to Gatsby's advice, our business plan is solid, and we've always got Heathcliff's necromancy talent in our back pocket if we need extra money.

More than all of that, we've got each other. Which is more than I ever hoped to have.

Heathcliff moves nearer, aligning his broad body with mine, cupping my face in his big hands. "You look sad now. I didn't mean to bring you down."

"Are you kidding?" I capture his hands and pop up on tiptoe

to kiss him. "This is the best day of my life. Ain't nothin' gonna bring me down for long." I twirl, dragging him with me.

"Get outta here with that Southern drawl, girl," he says. "We gotta learn to say 'eh' and 'aboot' and 'God save the queen' and shit."

"Plenty of time for that later. Why don't you take me inside and I'll make a few new sounds for you. I hear there's a really comfy couch."

Heathcliff crouches, wraps both arms around my thighs, and lifts me right off the ground while I squeal in mock protest. His strength returned to its usual levels shortly after the battle with the god, but the inner reserves are more accessible to him now—like a temporary bonus he can tap into as needed. Not gonna lie, it makes me feel safer.

He carries me into the cabin, and sure enough, it's outfitted with sturdy, cozy furniture, all thanks to Daisy—though I'm guessing Nick helped her get the vibes right. The aesthetic pleases my heart deeply, and I can't wait to add my own personal touches.

Heathcliff dumps me onto the big, cushy sofa and starts taking off my boots.

"Do you ever think about asking Gatsby if you could be a vampire?" I say, lifting my hips so he can get my shorts and panties off.

"Sometimes." He pulls off his T-shirt. "Not sure how well I'd take to that life."

"Me neither. Although Baz seems to be adjusting well. It's been a few months, and she's not a feral or a glutton, so at least there's that." I remove my tank top, exposing my breasts, and Heathcliff's jaw tenses, his eyes glinting with appreciation. He's got his boots, socks, and jeans off now—just the boxers left.

"She just needed Dorian to quit pushing for it," he says.

"I guess Dorian is used to getting everything he wants. He had to learn to shut up and listen to his partner."

"Uh-huh. Enough about them." He chucks away the boxers, sits down on the couch by my thigh, and leans over me, gathering one of my breasts in his hand and kissing the nipple. "Goddamn, you're gorgeous."

I don't question him this time, and there's only a tiny hesitation in my mind before I believe it. Ever since I got my scars, Heathcliff has done everything he can to show me I'm beautiful to him, both in spite of and *because* of what happened to me. I did get a few tattoos to cover the scars on my arms and legs, but I didn't cover the ones on my torso. Sometimes, when we're having sex, Heathcliff kisses those ridged seams where I was put back together. Kisses them gratefully, reverently. It heals me every time.

He grasps my chin in his hand and kisses me deep, his tongue twining hot with mine. My legs part for him as he settles between them, as he reaches down and nudges the tip of his cock inside me. He pushes in, and my eyes roll back, my body arching eagerly to take all of him.

"This is a good fucking couch," he whispers. "But you know what would be even better?"

"Hm?"

With a great surge of his muscles, he rises off the couch, lifting me with him, keeping my body close to his and his cock still inside me while he walks outside, carrying me into the sweeping landscape of green forest and open sky. He stands there naked under the blue arch of the heavens, his hands cupping my ass, and he starts moving me up and down. The sheer power of him is so fucking hot. I'm dripping, helplessly needy, while he works me on his dick.

With my arms pinned tight around his neck, ankles locked just above his ass, I let him use me, let the pleasure build, let the ecstasy of this moment roll through me from head to toe. The banshee in me loves this, sex in the open air—hell, *all* of me loves this. Loves his firm chest, dusted with dark hair, pressing against my soft breasts, loves the swell of his biceps as he lifts me, loves the dramatic planes of his handsome face, the black, wind-tossed waves of his hair. And his deep brown eyes, locked with mine.

He smiles, dark and glorious and wickedly happy, and I come, throwing my head back with a gleeful scream that echoes over the open land. He comes inside me, feet braced, holding us both steady.

Afterward, we walk naked together in the grass, under that peaceful sky, while tiny white butterflies stir and flutter at our steps. The world can be vicious, but this place breathes hope. And I think, as I walk the curve of the hill, that when my time comes and I meet death again, I can go quietly, having once been given a moment like this.

BONUS FEATURES

You are cordially invited to step into the
world of *Ruthless Devotion*, containing
exclusive bonus content including:

Heathcliff and Cathy's Playlist

A bonus scene of the 1800s Heathcliff and Cathy

An extended excerpt from *Cruel Angel,* the
story of *The Phantom of the Opera*'s passionate
triad: Phantom, Christine, and Raoul.

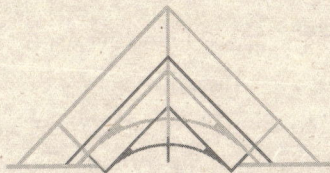

HEATHCLIFF & CATHY'S PLAYLIST

"Still Alive"—Demi Lovato

"Don't Come Lookin'"—Jackson Dean

"Howl"—Florence + The Machine

"Bones"—MS MR

"Bang"—Armchair Cynics

"Hey Boots"—Merci Raines

"Hayloft"—Mother Mother

"Ghost"—Natasha Blume

"Holly Holy"—Neil Diamond

"Ghost of You"—Mimi Webb

"Don Abandons Alice"—John Murphy

"Six Feet Under"—Billie Eilish

"The Magic"—Lola Blanc

"Running Up That Hill (A Deal with God) (cover)"—Kurt
   Hugo Schneider & Madilyn Bailey

"Tattoo" (cover)—Corvyx , Primo the Alien

"Come As You Are"—Nirvana

"(Don't Fear) The Reaper"—Blue Oyster Cult

"But Daddy I Love Him"—Taylor Swift

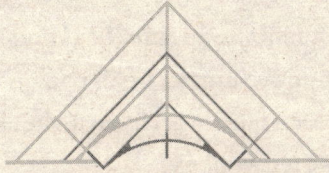

BONUS SCENE

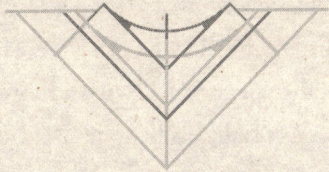

A HOUSE ON THE YORKSHIRE MOORS

The Late 1700s

AS HOUSES GO, WUTHERING HEIGHTS IS A DESOLATE ONE.
I have always felt more at home outside its walls than within
them—one of my many oddities, which my brother Hindley is
anxious to correct. He says I will never find anyone to marry me
unless I curb my boisterous spirit. I tell him I'm glad of my odd
nature, that I never wish to marry. Such speeches vex Hindley terribly, and I enjoy watching him fume and fester.

Lately I have to be more careful how I bait him, though,
because when Hindley is furious at me, he often turns his anger
on Heathcliff, our adoptive brother.

Not really my brother, I remind myself every time my gaze is
drawn by the breadth of Heathcliff's shoulders, the packed muscles
of his chest, or the surging of his biceps as he labors around the house

and the yard. I say it under my breath when I notice the length of his strong legs and the powerful grace of his body as he pitches hay for the livestock. I repeat it quietly as I listen to the cadence of his deep voice as he soothes a restive horse.

Heathcliff is not my brother.

Since Hindley returned with his new wife, Frances, he treats Heathcliff worse than ever—worse than a servant. He still cuffs and kicks Heathcliff like he did when they were boys, even though Heathcliff is the taller of the two, with a more powerful build. Yet Heathcliff does not fight back, no matter how badly Hindley berates or abuses him.

Every day, Heathcliff and Hindley circle each other in a terrible dance. Hindley knows that without Heathcliff's strength, his quiet intelligence, and his uncompensated service, Wuthering Heights would quickly fall into disrepair. Heathcliff knows that if he goes too far and indulges in an overt act of rebellion or vengeful violence, he will be turned out of the house.

Hindley's vanity is a balloon, stretched taut, filled with hot air, easy to puncture. Heathcliff's pride is like the dark rocks in the soil beneath the moors…patient, solid, and unshakable.

Heathcliff is waiting. And in all our conversations about this and that, about the world and its vagaries, I have never asked him what he is waiting for. I'm half-afraid of the answer.

I'm waiting, too. Waiting for something wonderful to happen. Waiting for the gray, windswept skies to realize I belong up there, with them, and to grant me the wings of a reckless bird so I can leave the moors and sail on the breeze to mystical, faraway lands. Waiting for a faerie ring to transport me somewhere tragically beautiful. Waiting for a great cataclysm to crack open my monotonous world.

But I do not have Heathcliff's patience. If no cataclysm arrives soon, I shall have to invent one.

Today, I'm pondering what sort of cataclysm I might like the best. I rather favor the idea of an earthquake that splits apart continents, creating new boundaries and channels. Something to carve apart the bones of the world and end the old wars.

"What if an earthquake split Wuthering Heights right down the middle?" I say, only half-conscious that I'm speaking aloud.

"Good gracious, what a terrible idea!" exclaims Nelly, our housekeeper. "I declare, Miss Cathy, you are a shock to the nerves. Go and find something to do, there's a good girl. Perhaps a little embroidery…" Her voices fades at the expression on my face. "No embroidery, then. A short ride, perhaps?"

"I ride every damn day," I reply, just to watch her eyes flare wide and her lips tighten.

"You really must stop using such language, Miss Cathy. It's the influence of that rogue Heathcliff." She clucks her tongue. "Don't be gone long, now. Edgar and Isabella Linton are coming to lunch, and you'll need to be clean, tidy, and well-dressed by the time they arrive."

"Why are they coming?" I pout, flicking a spoon on the table, sending little blobs of breakfast porridge across the wooden surface. "I don't want to entertain them. They're both so dull."

"But Edgar Linton is rather handsome, don't you think? He would make a fine husband."

I roll my eyes. "He's pretty as a porcelain doll, and he looks as though he would break if handled too roughly. I want a husband who appreciates a little rough handling."

"Miss Cathy!" gasps Nelly. "Enough of that talk. It's indecent. Take a quick ride, and then I'll help you bathe and dress. Go on, off with you. I have work to finish."

As a child, I would have taken a selfish delight in continuing to distract her. I spent my younger years annoying everyone in the house and being a veritable plague among the poor servants, charming and irritating them by turns, always interfering with their tasks.

As a young woman of marriageable age, I am expected to behave differently now. When I torment the servants, it's no longer out of peevish boredom but more out of sheer, panicked desperation—the kind of despair that drives one to yearn for a disaster, to ache for a violent rending of the world. The despair of an animal trapped in a cage.

When Nelly shoos me away again, I wander outside reluctantly. Much as I love to ride, the glorious wind and speed never lasts long enough, and in the end I must always return to Wuthering Heights. During a ride, my heart is temporarily lightened, only to be crushed between ponderous stone walls again. The dread of returning home steals much of the joy from the brief escape. If only I could find a new diversion, a new adventure to ease my mind.

As I approach the stables, I spot Heathcliff standing by the pump, shirtless, dousing himself in water until his brown skin gleams and his shaggy, black hair glitters. I have no idea why he is washing up in the yard at this time of day, but I thank God and all the angels for the sight.

Or perhaps I should thank the Devil because the thoughts in my head are anything but holy.

I slow my steps, wanting to enjoy the view for as long as I can before Heathcliff notices me—which he does almost instantly. Sometimes I swear our two minds are linked. The way we can sense each other's presence is uncanny.

He cups more water in his hands and splashes it onto his neck and chest, while I swallow a lump of need in my throat. I remember a time, just a few years ago, when he was a gawky boy who preferred being dirty. When did that dark-eyed boy turn into a strapping man with an affinity for cleanliness?

Heathcliff shakes back his wet hair and swipes the water from his face. Droplets cling to the dark scruff cloaking his jaw. The glistening sheen of water on his chest is mesmerizing—I cannot rip my gaze away from the contoured muscles.

"Going for a ride?" he asks. "Shall I saddle your horse?"

For a second I forget what words are and how to form them. Only when Heathcliff's full lips quirk upward at the corners and his eyes turn warmly bright do I clear my throat and say, "Ride... yes, I am going for a ride. Saddle my horse. And...come with me." The last three words escape me in an impetuous rush.

He sobers, glancing toward the house. "The last time we rode together—"

"Hindley was furious, I know. But he is off to London with his wife today. And if Joseph or Nelly sees us, I can persuade them not to tell him. I have my ways."

"Of course you do." He laughs a little, shaking his head and snatching his shirt from a nearby post. "Wait here, my lady, and I'll fetch the horses."

I'm too excited to let him do all the work himself, so I follow him into the stable and assist with the horses while discussing all the routes we might take on our ride. I was a fool not to seek him out earlier this morning, and I chafe at the lost hours. Then again, Hindley's trip to London was unexpected, so I had no chance to scheme any sort of lengthy outing—which was no doubt my brother's plan all along. I'm sure he also orchestrated the Lintons' visit to prevent me from spending time with Heathcliff.

And now, I'm faced with a dilemma. Heathcliff and I could take a short ride and be back in time to prepare for Edgar and Isabella's visit—and perhaps manage to conceal the whole thing from Hindley. Or I could defy Hindley outright, skip the lunch with the Lintons, and spend the entire day on the moors in the company of my best friend.

I know which one I prefer, but I fear the consequences for Heathcliff if I defy my brother and spurn the Lintons.

"You've been chattering like a magpie, and now you're quiet," Heathcliff comments as we ride down the lane to the gate.

"I'm thinking," I reply.

"Of course. But you usually think aloud."

"A lady should keep some thoughts private."

He chuckles, then swings down to open the gate. He lets me through first, then leads out Hindley's horse—a fine, sensitive animal who seems to bear far more affection for Heathcliff than for his actual master. It's a risk, taking Hindley's horse. Heathcliff has been beaten for far less.

When Heathcliff has closed the gate and mounted again, we continue down the lane, keeping our horses at a walk. I steal glances at him now and then. He's wearing an old greatcoat of my father's, and despite it being worn in places and too tight in the shoulders, Heathcliff cuts a fine figure in it.

"I'm very curious about these private thoughts of yours," he persists. "What indelicate ideas are racing around inside that pretty head?"

"I never said they were *indelicate*," I protest, while heat floods my cheeks and a burst of glittering excitement sparkles in my chest, like a sudden splash of water from the pump.

Heathcliff and I have been inseparable for years, ever since my father found him starving in the streets of London and brought him here to live with us. Yet in all that time, Heathcliff has never once complimented my looks. He has quietly praised my riding skills, laughed at my wit, and admired my aim with a slingshot, but he has never called me "pretty," until now.

He has watched me, though. Sometimes I catch him staring at me with the heat of a midwinter bonfire in his eyes, a hungry blaze so intense that I fear I might burst into flame from sheer proximity to it.

He's looking at me that way now, with a ravenous heat barely concealed beneath a veil of merriment.

"If I ever did have indelicate thoughts, you are the last person I would tell," I say saucily.

Rather than being piqued, he gives me a triumphant smile, as if he has secured a prize. "You tell me everything else that enters your mind. Why should those thoughts be the exception? Unless... could these indelicate thoughts be...about *me*?"

"Of course not," I gasp, too quickly, too breathlessly.

He grins wider, and my heart flutters into a frenzy. I cannot sit still, cannot sustain the sedate walking pace of the horses, so I urge my mare into a sudden gallop and tear away from Heathcliff.

He follows, keeping pace just behind me at first, then bringing his horse abreast of mine once we're out on the moors. We follow the routes we know, where the ground is good for the horses. They seem to relish the run as much as we enjoy the ride, but at last we pull them to a halt at the crest of a hill to let them breathe.

The wilderness stretches before us, a sweeping expanse of low swells and rocky outcroppings; green grass and gray, jutting stone; misty, purple heather and smoky-blue sky. The wind blows past my cheeks, tossing my curly hair into a hopeless tangle, whipping fresh blood into my face, filling my lungs with freedom. Each breath I take feels like laughter.

"Where shall we go?" I ask Heathcliff.

"Wherever you need to go," he replies. There's a weight to his words, a significance that makes me turn and look at him. It's there again, in his eyes—the torches of a thousand dark nights, the heat of unspoken promises, of heavy breath against warm skin.

I have touched him a million times, in so many different ways. Pinches and smacks when we were petulant children fighting over nonsense. Hands gripped to pull each other over stiles or onto rocks. Fingers squeezed under tables when my father was drunk and brawling through the rooms of Wuthering Heights, hunting for someone on whom to focus his anger.

I've brushed Heathcliff's hair back from his forehead when he was sick. Squeezed his shoulder to warn him not to further antagonize Hindley. And I pushed Heathcliff once, not long ago—shoved both hands against his broad chest during an argument, after he called me "haughty and headstrong." I've been called much worse by my own blood-kin, but from him, the words rang true, and they stung.

He let me shove him, though his fingers flexed at his sides as though he longed to lay hands on me in return. I lay awake that night, wondering exactly what he would have done to me if he hadn't managed to hold himself back. There was something wild and tender in his gaze during that argument, and the same violent affection shines in his eyes now, as he sits on his horse beside me.

I know him so well, and yet I hardly dare to interpret that look. I can scarcely admit what I want it to mean or to confess to myself why I'm mentally running through a list of places we might visit that could provide us with some privacy.

"The ruins of that little church in the hollow," I say at last. "The one with the huge gravestone broken in three pieces."

Part of the stone church is intact, and in the shade and shelter of a secluded corner is a bed of rich, thick grass on which two people might recline in comfort and do certain indelicate things without being seen.

I know how men and women lie together. Years ago, I witnessed a drunken tryst of my father's from a hiding place I dared not leave, and once I heard a few women gossiping in the village about various tawdry affairs. I listened to them for as long as I could before Nelly hurried me away. Since then, I have also discovered a few books with naughty sketches which Hindley keeps hidden in the library. I thought about showing one to Heathcliff, but the mere thought of seeing those images while in his company made me blush furiously and set my pulse racing so fast, I thought I might faint.

"The church in the hollow, then." Heathcliff does not comment any further on my choice. After all, the ruined church is a place we have visited often since we were children. He has no reason to suspect that I might have ulterior motives for selecting it as our destination.

After a short ride to the church, we tie the horses in the shade of a tree not far away, so they can graze while we...explore.

I very much want to explore Heathcliff, if only he will let me.

My breathing feels thick and slow, punctuated by my rapid heartbeat. Thrills ripple through my lower belly and a feathery sensation wakens between my legs, in places I've only tended when I'm alone. I've managed to achieve a climax twice, with difficulty and persistence, while picturing a certain dark-eyed man with tousled, black hair and broad shoulders.

Now that we are here, I feel incredibly foolish. We used to come to this place to practice with our slingshots, and we played among these gravestones. It feels almost sacrilegious that today I am considering a very different kind of play—a game I've never tried, one that could lead to ruined reputations for both of us.

I am not even sure where to begin or how to ask Heathcliff if he wants me. Perhaps I have been reading his expressions all wrong, seeing only what I wished to see. Perhaps I am a fool.

"I do not think I will be back in time for lunch with the Lintons," I say suddenly.

Heathcliff's shoulders stiffen. "Edgar is coming to lunch?"

"Yes. And Isabella. But I will not be there, and that will cause a great deal of trouble with Hindley."

"And with Edgar, I imagine," Heathcliff says dryly. "He fancies you."

"I cannot think *why*." Frustration leaks into my tone. "I have never encouraged him in the least."

"He cannot help it." Heathcliff's words are curiously taut, as if he is repressing a great tide between his clenched teeth.

"Yes, well…he is rich and handsome," I muse, kicking a tuft of heather. "A good match, I suppose."

"Oh yes, very rich and handsome." Heathcliff's tone darkens. "He and his sister are both beautiful, wealthy, and well-educated, with excellent prospects. The perfect family."

I glance sharply at him, narrowing my eyes. "You think Isabella is beautiful?"

"Of course."

I stare at him for one incensed moment. Then I march away through the thick grass between the tombstones.

Heathcliff scoffs. "Does the truth offend you so deeply?"

"Not at all. Perhaps we should go home now and dress you up in some old finery of my father's. You can come to lunch and court the beautiful Isabella. Maybe she will marry you. Picture it—me with Edgar and you with Isabella. What a happy group we will be!"

"I'd sooner marry a turtledove than Isabella Linton," he growls. "She is a soft, fragile creature with no mettle and no backbone. I like a woman with fire in her belly and a razor for a tongue."

I've reached the edge of the ruins. As I'm stepping inside the broken remnants of the stone church, Heathcliff darts past me, whipping around to face me and block my progress. I hate how handsome he looks in that greatcoat and how my knees tremble at the aching fury in his eyes.

"Catherine," he says, and the word jolts through my chest like the purple lightning that pierces the heart of the moors on stormy nights. In his mouth, my name sounds like an immortal curse, like a violent blessing.

"Tell me," he manages through gritted teeth. "Tell me you are joking. Tell me you do not plan to marry Edgar Linton."

"I will do what I must," I say icily, attempting to move past him, but he slams a palm against the broken wall and bars my way again.

"We would be apart, Cathy." His chest heaves beneath the coat. "Edgar would separate us for good. I could not bear it. Could you?"

The wind off the moors rushes through the ruins at that moment, swirling around both of us, carrying the sweet, spicy scent of the grasses and the freshness of the wild.

A hot, fierce joy surges through my soul at the look in Heathcliff's eyes. I have my answer without ever asking the question.

"That is why you stay, isn't it?" I say softly, but I know he hears me despite the wind. "That is why you endure Hindley's abuse, why you debase yourself and perform all the menial tasks he gives you when you are capable of so much more. You do it so you can remain here, with me."

His eyes shine with ruthless devotion. "Why else?"

Perhaps I rise to meet him or he bends to meet me, or the universe curls inward to push us together—all I know is that his lips are finally touching mine, burning with all the feverish need I have sensed from him through these past months.

Our souls have been knitted together since we were young, but this passion is new, potent, and as terrifying as it is exhilarating. Heathcliff wraps me up in his great arms with a groan of relieved delight, sinking deeper into the kiss. I'm transported, whirling through scintillating realms of sensation, immolated by the rush of his hands as he gropes along my body, devouring every part of me like a man starved for touch.

I curve my body against his, crush myself to him as if I could blend our two selves into one. I press him backward, and he lets me move us toward the shaded corner of the ruins. At my breathless instruction, he removes the greatcoat and spreads it there, over the grass.

Seating myself on the coat, I stare up at him, feeling small and melted and wild with joy all at once. He's advancing, looming over me, huge and beautiful...and I think I might shatter into brilliant fragments if he touches me again, so I gasp out, "Take off your clothes," in a voice as commanding as I can manage.

Heathcliff hesitates, then obeys me, divesting himself of his damp shirt first, then everything else. His body is a work of art, crafted by years of hard labor, scarred by Hindley's cruelty. Between his thighs is the proof of his primal craving for me—a part of male anatomy that I've never seen up close or touched. I rise on my knees, curious and eager, and I reach for him.

But he steps back.

"I will not fuck you simply because you crave something new." His voice hitches in his throat, deep and ragged. "I will not be a toy for you to play with, Cathy."

He knows me too well and yet not well enough.

Rising to my feet, I lunge for him, hooking both hands around the back of his neck and pulling him close. My mouth closes over his and I bite his lip hard, a vicious pinch that makes him snarl in response.

"How dare you?" I hiss. "When have you *ever* been a plaything to me? You are more than brother, more than blood, more than life. You are part of my soul, the truest piece of myself. Stop talking nonsense, Heathcliff, and consume me. Burn me to ashes, inhale me, suck me into your lungs. I will be your breath and your torment forever."

At my words, he is unleashed. He tears the clothes from my body with large, shaking hands, every desperate movement clarifying how long and how deeply he has craved this. I let him dismantle me down to my skin, and when he stands there, stunned, taking in the sight of me, I draw him close again, aligning my body with his. The wind tears at our hair and swirls around us like an eldritch force winding us together, binding our bones in a fated circle of immortal lust.

Heathcliff lowers me down to the coat. His lips wander the plush softness of each breast, each tight nipple, the tender flatness of my stomach, the hollows of my hip bones. He releases a warm breath through the soft curls between my legs, then licks me.

I writhe at the explosion of delicate sensations. Never have I felt anything so delightfully wet and supple as his tongue teasing every secret part of me. It feels filthy, and wonderful, and deliciously wicked.

He's uncertain at first, eager but untrained, like I am. I direct him with a few gasped words, and we learn together.

Heathcliff seems to relish the taste of me, the avid swirls of his tongue dispelling any of my lingering doubts or insecurities. His tongue glides through my folds, then laps at my sensitive peak with a quick, torturous rhythm until I am quivering on the brink of a cataclysm—and then, only then, does he spread my legs apart, take himself in hand, and guide his length into my opening.

It hurts, and I tighten involuntarily. Heathcliff stops, strokes his hand along my side, and runs his thumb over my breast. The caress soothes me, and I let out a long breath, blinking away the tears. He waits until I nod, then eases in deeper.

A shuddering groan rolls from his throat, and his eyes close with utter bliss. Seeing him react that way to the sensation of being inside me is the best balm I could ask for. My muscles relax, my thighs turn liquid, and the tightening sweetness at my core returns. I reach for Heathcliff, twine my arms around his neck, pull him closer, deeper.

"Never let me go," I whisper fiercely. "Hold me, take me. Be *in* me, *with* me. We are the same, you and me. Don't leave me, *ever*. Promise you won't."

"I swear it, my darling," Heathcliff murmurs between bruising kisses. "We will never be apart, not in this life or the next."

"Swear it with your body," I plead, and with another moan, he begins to roll his hips...long, slow thrusts into my slick center. With each surging thrust, the sweet tension builds higher, higher. I strain for the great cataclysm; I pray for it aloud, with Heathcliff's name punctuating my gasps. And at last, with a violent explosion of pure, bright bliss, my world cracks apart, rivers of ecstasy flowing through new chasms.

The rending of my body is more beautiful than I could have imagined because Heathcliff caused the exquisite ruin. He chokes out a ravaged cry, a groan of wild pleasure, and he holds me tight while he comes undone, while his body pulses into mine. A shiver of bliss runs over his skin.

Even when he slips out of me, we remain tangled together, broken and healing, naked on my father's greatcoat in the ruins of the church.

For a long time, we make only the smallest of movements—a hand drifting to a new contour of warm flesh, lips pressing a tender place for the first time, bodies shifting to a slightly different angle.

But after a while, a tender desperation swells inside me, filling me up until I *have* to speak. I must let him know how deeply I felt this interlude between us—how vital our connection has always been to me.

"Years ago, I dreamed that I went to heaven," I whisper, twisting my fingers through locks of Heathcliff's dark hair. "I hated it there, and I begged to leave. I sobbed and pleaded until the angels threw me back down to earth. I went to find you, but you were gone—you had died, too, and gone below, to hell."

He hums a low assent, as if to confirm hell as his final destination.

"I couldn't exist on earth without you," I whisper, curling my fingers more tightly into his hair until I know it must hurt him, but he doesn't flinch. "So I summoned the Devil and told him I would commit my soul to hell if only it could exist beside yours. He agreed. And in that fiery torment, we were the happiest we'd ever been."

Heathcliff turns his face up to mine and kisses me. In the warm crush of our lips, there is relief, solace, escape. But like my flights on horseback, it is only temporary. We cannot stay here forever— eventually, we will have to return to Wuthering Heights.

"If Hindley finds out what we have done, he will kill you," I whisper.

"Let him try," Heathcliff mutters darkly.

"No, Heathcliff." I sit up, panic icing my bones. "He will shoot you for defiling me. Even if I enjoyed being defiled..."

He smirks, his gaze heating again, his mouth seeking mine.

I push him back gently. "You must be serious now, Heathcliff. Promise that if he kills you, you will haunt me. I could not bear to exist in a huge, hollow world without you in it. Haunt me, or I swear I will kill myself and join you in whatever fate follows this life."

"Much as I love the thought of haunting you, love, I have a better idea," he replies. "A less lethal one, perhaps. I have been taking money from Hindley for years now, a little at a time. He robbed me of the inheritance your father wanted me to receive, so this is fair recompense. We can take the money and the horses and go far away, somewhere they cannot find us."

The idea makes my heart bolt like a restive colt. "How will we get the money? We cannot go back to the house."

Heathcliff gives me a grin of malevolent satisfaction. "It so happens that I hid the money in this very place. We spent so many happy hours here as children, it felt appropriate. I have a small chest buried beneath one of the three slabs of the broken gravestone."

"Truly?" I exclaim. "You brilliant bastard."

He whistles low. "Such a naughty tongue for a well-bred lady."

"I have never been well-bred," I reply. "Perhaps I can feign good breeding as we travel, if needed, but in private, when it is just us two, I will show you how naughty my tongue can be." Interest lights his eyes, and I smile. "We have a little time before we begin our great adventure. Perhaps I should offer you a demonstration now?"

Heathcliff doesn't respond, but his body answers for him. His eyes widen as I settle into a new position, open my mouth, and slide him inside, over the slippery surface of my wicked tongue.

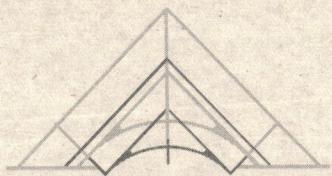

CRUEL ANGEL

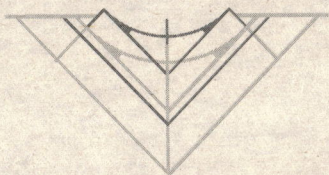

PLEASE ENJOY THIS SNEAK PEEK
COMING SOON!

1

THE GOD-RAISER

"IT'S LLOYD-HENRY, RIGHT? OR DO YOU PREFER LLOYD?" The therapist welcomes me with a smile.

"Lloyd is fine." I'd prefer my true name, but no one has spoken it aloud in centuries.

"Come on in. I'm Dr. Jekyll." His voice is low, soothing. Designed to put people at ease, to lower their resistance.

I know that sort of voice all too well. If I had enough time with this doctor, I could charm him into doing anything I wanted. And I won't lie—it's tempting.

But I'm not here to exercise my powers today. I'm here because I could use some fucking therapy. I've tried almost everything else to cope with what's happening to me.

This is my final stop before I go to *them*. This man is my last chance. The best in the business of healing minds...or at least the best in Nashville, Tennessee, where fate has led me. No, "led" is too gentle a word—I was discarded here. Cast away like a piece of garbage.

"Have a seat wherever you're comfortable." Dr. Jekyll glances down at his clipboard as I drop into an armchair. "You mentioned you're feeling a lot of stress from work? Do you want to maybe talk about that a little bit?"

"Sure."

"Okay. Tell me about what you do."

"I manage a lot of projects, a lot of people." I prop my ankle on my knee and try to look relaxed. "Lately I've been letting things slip. I've been…failing."

The word tastes bitter in my mouth, but it's time to say it.

"Failing." The doctor leans back in his desk chair, tapping his chin with the end of his pen. "That's a strong word. What's an instance where you believe you failed?"

What would he say if I told him the truth? That I've been working tirelessly for decades—no, centuries—to become Earth's ruler and protector, the balm for all its ills? I have allies throughout the world, research in progress to find a cure for that greatest of evils—death. Vampirism, soul-infused portraits, necromancy, the return of the gods—each strategy was one piece in a plan, a gear in a great machine that should still function, even if one part is fractured.

And yet somehow, each piece has managed to contort itself into an unrecognizable, unusable shape. The vampire factions turned on each other, then rebelled against me. The first god I raised didn't possess any power; he needed more of his fellow gods at his side before he could do anything useful. Raising the second god proved disappointing, to say the least.

Oh, and I've died twice—once quite recently. *Let's talk about that, Doctor.* Let's explore how it feels to be shot in the head and ejected from my body into the afterworld, where I waited in the dark until a necromancer dragged me back into my body again.

It took me weeks to recover, and yet I still managed to keep my plans in motion. I summoned a second god, who was ruined by the interference of the vampires. He's practically useless to me.

I'm on the verge of giving up. I'm so fucking tired. Coming back from death the second time wasn't good for me, and I'm terrified that I'm...unraveling. My insides feel different, ill-fitting. Sometimes they *writhe*. I can see the bubbling and surging of my essence under my skin, and when that happens I'm compelled to take a different form—raven, wolf, crow, stag, anything but a human shape. I'm less and less comfortable as a man, and the only time I can find any peace is in beast form.

Maybe I've been alive too long.

Dr. Jekyll's calm voice penetrates the churning cloud of my thoughts. "It's all right if you can't think of a specific instance right now."

"I think I'm trying to do too much," I reply. "I've always preferred to set things in motion and let others do the work while I observe them and nudge them in the right direction as needed— but lately that hasn't been working out for me. It's so hard to find good, hardworking, self-motivated people."

"So you feel you've been counting on people who aren't reliable. They've broken your trust."

"Yes."

"Typically we can't control how other people act." Dr. Jekyll gives me a sympathetic smile. "They may hurt us or disappoint us, and there's not much we can do about it. What we can work on is our reaction...how we respond. And that's where stress management comes in. Let's talk about some ways you can cope with the pressure you're feeling. Have you tried meditation?"

I stare at him. "Meditation?"

"Sure. Meditation and mindfulness can be very helpful tools to—"

"I don't want to fucking meditate."

Dr. Jekyll's eyes widen slightly at my tone. "Well, there are other techniques, but let me explain what I mean by meditation. There's so much misinformation out there…"

He continues, but I'm barely listening. I'm staring at my hand, where my veins are arching up like inchworms, stretching the skin. All through my arm I can feel that writhing, squirming sensation, the contortion of a soul that doesn't belong in this body, in this world.

"You seem very agitated," Dr. Jekyll says, interrupting my thoughts. "Do you want to talk about someone who betrayed you?"

Betrayal…

Dorian…I betrayed Dorian…

For the greater good, for a larger cause…

Something twists violently in my chest, and I gasp.

"This was a mistake." I rise from the couch.

"Lloyd, let's talk just a little longer," pleads the doctor.

"Do you see this?" I hold out my hand, where the veins and tendons are knotting and coiling under the skin. My very bones ache until I can hardly stand upright.

"Good god," mutters Dr. Jekyll. "What is that?"

"You can see it?" I confirm. "I haven't lost my mind?"

"I can see it, and I think you need a different kind of doctor," he falters.

"Usually I have more time between episodes." I pull my hand

close to my chest. In a moment the small bones will begin to disconnect from each other, and I will have to transform or watch my body disassemble itself. "It's happening at shorter and shorter intervals now. Do you think meditation will help, Doctor?" I laugh, shrill and wild.

The doctor rolls backward in his chair, putting distance between us. "What's happening to you?"

"I'm *shifting*, motherfucker. I'm a Gancanagh and a púca, a bastard hybrid of two ancient races, a survivor. I came to Nashville because there are other shifters here, and I thought perhaps I could ingratiate myself to them, but I've been sick, as you can see, and I haven't had the *time*." My spine rolls involuntarily, and I grit my teeth, forcing out my next words. "They're a close-knit group, not easy to penetrate. But I may have to go to them and beg them to help me, to cure me. I thought I would try this first—mind over matter, you know."

"That's not really a thing," murmurs the doctor.

"I should have known this wouldn't work. You humans pretend to know the mind, but the chasms in your knowledge are vast, and you are confidently wrong about so many things—aagghh!" I grimace as my shoulder pops. "Open that window, will you?"

"Look, I'm not just a therapist," says Dr. Jekyll. "I was premed and bio-chem once, before...well, that's not important. Maybe I can take a blood sample, figure something out to help you—"

"The window," I gasp.

He hurries over to it, but the latch barely budges. "It's an old building," he apologizes. "We never open the windows because there aren't any screens—"

"Hurry!" I roar.

He wrenches one last time and manages to shove the window wide, just as I lurch forward and transform into a raven. I soar past him, cawing with the sheer relief of being out of that body.

Maybe I had it wrong. Maybe I was never meant to save the world from itself. Maybe I should leave humanity behind and become a beast or a bird forever.

If that is my path, I will first have to make some arrangements for Cernunnos, my useless, pathetic, lost puppy of a god, before I disappear. And perhaps I will go to the Shifter Collective in Nashville, just once, to ask for their help. Imprisonment or death at their hands can't be worse than my current torturous existence.

I wheel in the sky, cawing again for the benefit of Dr. Jekyll, who is gaping at me from the window far below. Perhaps I'll give him a vial of my blood before I take beast form forever. He can amuse himself studying it.

Higher I rise, into the crisp air of the September sky. I've seen beautiful cities, but this one is unmatched for its mystical energies. I sense the power of the ancients everywhere, traces of the muses, the Leannan Sídhe, lingering in the blood of everyday citizens. A resurgence is occurring, new powers unfurling and old ones awakening.

But for once, my heart doesn't thrill at the thought of being a part of it all. For once, I'm not energized by the possibility of the future but exhausted.

After millennia, I believe I have finally grown old.

2

THE PHANTOM

IN THE CITY OF MUSIC, I AM HAUNTED BY THE CRIES OF THE dead.

The souls of deceased humans usually find their way into the afterworld, but occasionally some are misdirected, left behind as unsettled echoes, doomed to rove the world, out of sync with life.

The lost spirits can sense my former status as lord of phantoms, god of the afterworld, but many of them don't understand that I no longer have the power to grant them safe passage. I cannot guide them or give them rest. My lack of response infuriates them, so I have become a locus for their anger, the eye of a howling hurricane of wretched souls. I rarely know a moment's peace.

I've been abandoned by my summoner, the one who raised me from my cursed sleep. He is a hybrid creature, a blend of shape-shifting púca and wicked Gancanagh, love-talker and soul-eater. I was his goal, his hope, the next step in his complex plan...and yet he was foiled in his purpose, cheated when his enemies trapped me in this form. I'm not the powerful ally he wanted. With my memories blurred and my powers reduced to a mere flicker of the inferno they once were, I'm useless to him. Useless to everyone.

The feeling of being unwanted and outcast is familiar to me. I was always hated by the other gods, most of whom still sleep, bound to earth and darkness.

One of the gods is awake, though. I can sense him distantly, can feel the incessant dirge of his wrathful mourning for the glory that once belonged to the Tuatha Dé Danann. He feels me too, and he despises my existence. I try to shut him out of my consciousness, like I do with the ghosts.

Left alone in this subterranean lair while my summoner pursues his goals elsewhere, I wait and I wander, empty of purpose, tortured by voices. I meander through dripping tunnels and forgotten halls, aching and angry.

"Stay here," my summoner told me before he left. "Stay away from humans at all costs. If you must go out, stay in the shadows and wear this." He handed me a white mask, designed to cover every feature except my mouth and jaw. "You're disgusting without it."

I could not answer him. For weeks after being trapped in this form, I could barely move, and I had trouble speaking my thoughts. The blond vampire who locked down my powers possessed a compulsive voice, a mental control I've never seen, not even in the days of old. A magical mutation of sorts. I still hear her voice in my head sometimes, a low, sinuous threat, a golden chain, deceptively beautiful and horribly irresistible.

Thanks to the echoes of her voice, the sneering rebuke of my summoner, the distant roar of the sea god, and the cries of the merciless dead, I am going mad.

The only time I feel the slightest relief is when I listen to music. In my subterranean dwelling I have a radio—my summoner called it an antique—and I listen to it with the volume turned all the way up, to drown out the wails of the ghosts. There is something called a record player as well, and a few boxes of records my summoner purchased from a shop somewhere in the city. He said they were cheap, that no one wanted them anymore. I cannot fathom such disregard for music.

Music is a mercy. It tears my emotions out of my chest and lets them soar in midair, exposed and soothed at the same time.

I began with the radio and the records, but they did not provide enough variety for my voracious appetite. Before my summoner abandoned me, he left me a few treasures to ensure my survival—a laptop, a phone, and a plastic rectangle called a debit card, apparently connected to a vast supply of human currency. The laptop sits on a desk, plugged into a yellowed socket in a wall of bare brick. Through it, I have discovered a world full of music... and other possibilities. I can purchase food and clothing for this body, and I can have them delivered to the old service door at the end of the canal.

With the laptop, I can investigate any subject as deeply as I desire. I can access a vast library of music composed within the past several decades. Most of my days are spent devouring music, studying its structure, reveling in its ascendancy beyond scientific rules into a realm of creative magic.

And yet, despite having all this at my fingertips, I feel empty, haunted, hollow. There is an aching void inside me, as deep as the chasm in which I dwelled for centuries. I am always searching for new music, for a song that will perfectly express everything I feel...and for the perfect voice that will serve as the balm to my wretched soul.

ACKNOWLEDGMENTS

Thank you to my wonderful agent, Eva Scalzo, who is always there to answer my questions, talk me down when I panic, and look out for my best interest. I am so grateful for this partnership.

Thank you to Mary Altman and the Sourcebooks Casablanca team for all their work on the Gilded Monsters series so far, and thank you to my fellow authors from Sourcebooks and Bloom for their kindness and friendship.

Thanks especially to my husband and kids for understanding that they live with a writer and for accommodating all my quirkiness and my moments of creative frenzy. You're my best and most beloved people.

And last but not least, thank you to the beautiful readers who have made this series possible. Without you, this book would not exist.

ABOUT THE AUTHOR

Rebecca Kenney writes spicy contemporary and fantasy romance about sassy, strong women and hot guys with tragic backstories. She is the author of the Wicked Darlings series (spicy Fae retellings of the Nutcracker, Wonderland, and Oz), the Dark Rulers series (standalone fantasy romances in a shared world), and the For the Love of the Villain series. Rebecca is represented by Eva Scalzo of Speilburg Literary. She lives in upstate South Carolina with her handsome, blue-eyed husband and two smart, energetic kids. For updates and information about upcoming novels, follow her on:

Instagram: @rebeccafkenneybooks
TikTok: @rebeccafkenney